Acknowledgments

There are two people that I would like to thank specifically above all others. They are my two girls. They are beautiful sisters. They are my mother, Sandra Jones and my aunt, Barbara McDaniel.

Without Aunt Barbara's initial impetus and prodding I never would have sat down and typed even one word of this novel. She was the initial inspiration. She helped me learn how to sit down and dedicate myself to my craft. She saw that I had the ability and the desire to write something when I didn't even know it myself. She has been a tireless editor and my biggest critic. I rarely liked or agreed with her about anything and I know that she didn't like a lot of what I did, but she made me fight for my ideas and thus inversely she made me believe in my story even more. She was no push over and in the end, even when it wasn't the story that she had envisioned initially, she still remained a strident, if not a begrudging, supporter of my endeavor. So for good or bad, she is responsible for this book, even if she didn't write it herself. Thanks Aunt Barbara. You are my rock.

My mother, Sandra Jones, was equally instrumental because like any mother she was proud of her little boy and encouraged me all along the way. But she was more than just a proud mom. She was the person that I went to when I got stuck on dozens of occasions. She helped me break my mental log jams. She could always figure out what to do next. She was also my daily sounding board. She was the one that sat at my dining table every night and listened to me read my daily drafts and rewrites over and over again ad nausea. No matter how many times I read them to her she always listened with the greatest enthusiasm. And I think she has read the book more times as I have. Thanks Mom for being my number one fan.

I would also like to thank all of my friends who indulged me and acted as my survey readers. Dr. Nick Bellos, Barbara Copeland, Joel Flores, James Helwig, Bob Hogue, Onice McClain, Greg Neiberding, David & Suzanne Palmlund and Todd & B.C. Talbott.

Everyone's criticism and feedback was immensely helpful. Thank you all for taking the time out of your busy schedules to help a newbie with his first novel.

And thanks to my best and most faithful friend, Butch, who loyally sat by my side every day and every night as I wrote this until he passed away at the ripe old age of sixteen. I miss you, my old friend.

Homages and Disclaimer

All characters are fictional. Resemblance to anyone alive or dead is purely coincidental. However, some character names are real and are intended only as an homage to my friends so that they can see their names in print. They are not meant to represent nor be the person in this novel. This novel is a complete work of fiction that I created from my own imagination, however, some of the events depicted in this novel are based upon or are drawn from my own life experiences in prison and in life.

The Monkey Trap

by

S. Hark Phillips

Prologue

Chapter 1

Bentley Braxton III laid on the yacht naked and erect.

Everyone was naked. Girls were all over the boat. Some were laying. Some were sitting. And the one sitting on top of him right now was doing a reverse cowgirl while two other hookers fed coke up her nose and played with her enormous breasts.

Her breasts were real. Real expensive, that is.

She loved to brag about her size forty, triple L's. Each breast was only a few teaspoons shy of a gallon. Together they were seven thousand c.c.'s of nippled peccadillos and over twenty one pounds of freakish fun.
Yes, Bentley loved these little get-a-ways to South Beach. It was so different from his straight-laced and buttoned up conservative life in Dallas. This was the only time that he was able to be the total deviant that he like to be. He could do whatever and whoever he wanted here. They didn't know him and he didn't want to know them. It was perfect.

Waterbags finally stopped grinding on him and stood up with help of her two admirers. Bentley looked down at the now empty bowl of cocaine. Only an hour ago it had been overflowing with pure Peruvian flake.

'Two thousand dollars sure doesn't go as far as it used to,' thought Bentley.

"I really had a great time." said Waterbags as she sat down beside him. *"By the way, my name is Debbie."*

Bentley stared at her for a moment with contempt for ruining a perfectly good hump.

"Honey, if I had wanted to know your name, then I wouldn't have fucked you."

And with that he grabbed the empty bowl and walked away.
*****

The week in Miami had gone by in flash. The debauchery was non-stop. He was such a different person on cocaine. He was no longer Dr. Do-Right. He was King Dong. It was truly as if he was the modern day incarnation of the old Dr. Jekyll and Mr. Hyde. Cocaine was his transformative elixir.

He loved these trips because he got to feel so free and so powerful. It was the complete opposite of how he felt in his everyday life. He wasn't going to lie to himself. The sex was great. The sex is what he lived for on these little trips.

'Damn that Debbie for ruining his last night.' he thought.

The yacht had docked yesterday morning and he had used the entire day to sleep and sober up. Now it was time to make the deal, pay the piper and get the hell out of Dodge.

"Hola, El doctors!" Said Carlito as he came on board. *"I just love this big fucking boat. You doctors really got it good."*

Pleasantries were exchanged as Carlito's men searched the boat from top to bottom. A nod from one of them gave Carlito the all clear sign.

"It's so good to see you again, doctors." said Carlito with a big toothy grin.

Bentley heard the engines rev up and he felt the boat slip its moorings. They were moving and Bentley felt his heart rate rise with anxiety. They were headed out to sea with a drug dealer and thirty thousand dollars in cash.

'What the hell was he doing?' asked a sober Bentley to himself. His buddies, Malcolm and Perry, seemed oddly at complete ease as they face into the wind and sip on their cold beers.

Bentley knew that Carlito and his muscle thugs could easily toss them over board and take the money. And the boat, for that matter. No doubt that it would be a good days profit for them. It was insane to go out to sea with no protection or any way to defend themselves. The only thing Bentley had in his luggage was some floss and a dental probe.

'Maybe he could scare them with a dental appointment.' Thought Bentley sarcastically to himself.

Bentley was nervous.
*****

The ride had been long with lots zigging and zagging. His buddies, Malcolm and Perry, were on their third and fourth beers, respectively. Carlito was very cautious and he wanted make sure that they weren't being followed. Once satisfied, the boat's engines powered down and the anchor was dropped. The ocean chop swayed the big cabin cruiser gently up and down with each seductive swell. Bentley looked out over the moving expanse of the sea. The water was an ominous and murky green. There was no doubt that they were now in some very deep water.

Bentley looked around. Land wasn't visible in any direction. He was more than a little scared at this point. This is exactly how people were killed in the movies.

"Gentlemen, let's take care of business." Carlito pulled out a brick shaped kilo of cocaine and laid it on the table as he addressed the three doctors.

"I will show you mine and you can show me yours."

Everyone's eyes widened and half of the room did an involuntary sniff at the site of so much cocaine. Bentley felt his stomach begin to itch.

"Okay," said Malcolm as he threw out an envelope with ten thousand dollars in it.

Carlito handed it to one of his associates that proceeded to count it. Carlito received an affirmative nod.

Bentley produced and passed a similar envelope to Carlito. Once again, another nod from his associate.

Finally, Carlito looked to Perry expectantly.

"Ummm...you see it is like this." said Perry sheepishly. *"I don't have it right this minute, but you know I am good for it."*

Carlito polite disposition changed dramatically in a millisecond as he turned to his associate.

"Ernesto, do I look like his wife?" asked Carlito sarcastically as he stood up.

"No, boss." replied Ernesto

.

Carlito turned to Perry. *"Do I look like your bitch-ass wife?"*

Perry was visibly shaking.

"N-n-no." He stammered.

"Really?" Carlito stepped up and was now right up in Perry's face.

"Because I just assumed that I must look like your wife since you are trying to fuck me." Spittle splattered out of Carlito's mouth and onto Perry's face as he screamed.

"I promise you that I will get you your money." Perry cried.

Carlito leaned back in mock disbelief to look at Perry crying.

"Can you believe this, Ernesto?" Said Carlito. *"Now this faggot bitch wants a pity fuck."*

"No, boss, I can't believe it." replied Ernesto in bored monotone.

"Ernesto, what do I do when people try to fuck me?" asked Carlito loudly as he began to circle around Perry.

"You fuck them, boss." responded Ernesto calmly.

"Please!" begged Perry. *"I thought that we had a deal to....."*

Before Perry could finish his sentence, Carlito grabbed a foot-long fish hook sitting on the rear deck. Bentley and Malcolm could only watch in horror as Carlito swung the heavy hand held hook high over his head. Bringing it down with all his strength. Anger shot from his eyes as the hook was buried deep into the top of Perry's head.

Blood spewed up out of Perry like a gushing oil well. Shooting up several feet before it reached its apex; showering everyone in blood. Splattered pieces of slimy gray matter speckled Bentley's shirt.

Bentley saw Perry's eyes cross inward and roll up into his head. His mouth was agape, but not a single sound could be heard from it. Carlito gritted his teeth and bared down even harder with the hook. Driving it deep into Perry's skull and him down to his knees.

A sick crunching could be heard as Perry's skull was being pried apart by the heartless drug dealer.

"How that's feel, puta?" screamed Carlito. *"Is it in deep enough for you?"*

Carlito buried the hook as far it would go and then lifted up and back on the wooden handle. A loud pop followed by a sucking sound came as Perry's cranium gave way and cracked completely open. The giant hook had effectively severed Perry's brain right down the middle. Both bloody and wrinkled hemispheres of Perry's brain fell to the varnished teak deck.

Hot spew erupted from Bentley as he wretched violently and uncontrollably. Perry's body lay twitching as dark blood flowed copiously out of his head and drained into the deck grooves; channeling it to the side wells and out into the quenchless sea.

Attracted by sudden fresh blood in the water, sharks circled the boat wildly.

Carlito raised the large hook and used it to impale the Perry's ribs cage. He dragged the still convulsing corpse to the rear deck well and opened the railing.

Bentley watched in horror as he dangled Perry's body over the side.

"C'mon, mi amigos." hollered Carlito out to the sea. *"I have comida especial for you."*

Carlito turned his head and shouted to Bentley and Malcolm.

"Watch this, el doctors. It is my favorite part."

Almost on cue a large bull shark's head raised up out of the water and bit into Perry right leg. The whole body shook as the shark sawed and gnawed on it with three rows of razor like teeth. Before he could chew through it, two more sharks emerged to grab onto Perry's other appendages.

It was clear that Carlito was struggling to keep from being pulled into the feeding frenzy. He held onto the hook as long as he could, but it was clear that the three man-eaters were not going to let their lunch go.

Carlito released the hook and the three predators were immediately joined by half a dozen more sharks of all sizes. A wild feeding frenzy erupted in the water as each beast fought for its pound of flesh. Within twenty seconds there was no evidence that Perry ever existed, except for the occasional dorsal fin that still searched the bloody water for another meaty morsel.

Carlito picked up a nearby towel next to the railing as he turned to face Bentley and Malcolm.

"It seems that you two gentlemen are now ten thousand dollars short."
*****

Prologue
Chapter 2

Bentley was almost home. He couldn't wait to see Large Marge. She was big and she was would be lit up when he got there.

Large Marge was the new Margaret Hunt Hill suspension bridge leading into downtown. Margaret had been the daughter of the famous H.L Hunt, who had at one time, been the richest man in America. She was now dead, but she was still a very permanent fixture over the Trinity River.

The road was quiet.

'Almost eerie'. He thought.

After midnight and cars on this stretch of highway were far and few between.

Bentley pressed the pedal to the metal of his Porsche 911 and the yellow glowing lights of the highway slid by quickly on the hot night. He was sober. Once he left Miami, and started driving on the highway, guilt and regret had taken his mind captive. Sure, Perry was a prick, but Bentley didn't want to see him dead.

But the reality was that Perry was extremely dead and Bentley was very much alive.

'Shouldn't I be happy about that?' Bentley questioned himself repeatedly.
He knew what he was doing was illegal and immoral, but he couldn't help himself.

The real truth was that he didn't like himself very much. Sure, he had lots of money and a fair amount of notoriety, but he wasn't a happy person.
'Never had been, really.' he told himself.

Even as a child he had been unhappy. Nowadays he had a million dollar smile on the outside, but he was a miserable man on the inside. His heart was empty. This was his lot in life.

Successful, but lonely.

He could walk into a room and know a hundred people that adored him, but he didn't feel the love of a single person. He liked them all, but he couldn't find anyone that he could connect with. There had only been one person like that in his life and she was gone forever.

So he filled his nights with vapid women with no ambition beyond the next bump of coke. Waterbags had been 'jonesing' for another bump of cocaine so desperately that she begged him and Malcolm to both titty fuck her simultaneously. Bentley had stood over her head so that he was able to tea bag her in the face with each stroke between her boobs. He felt ashamed of his depraved behavior.

'Was this all he had to look forward to in life?' The question droned on inside of his head for the hours between Pensacola and   New Orleans.

'Life sucked,' said Bentley out loud, 'and it only seemed to be getting worse.

First he witnessed Perry being turned into fish bait and then he had to give that psycho Carlito his Rolex watch. The Oyster Perpetual Datejust Special Edition watch had been a graduation present from Boyce when he passed the boards to get his license. It had cost over twenty seven thousand dollars. That watch and his racing yellow Turbo 911 Porsche with a British right hand drive were his most cherished possessions in the world. Both had been gifts from his older brother.

Carlito had made it clear that neither Malcolm nor he would ever make it back to shore alive unless he got paid Perry's portion right then and there somehow.

The watch had been the only thing of value that Bentley had on him. And it had been the only thing that saved his and Malcolm's lives.
Carlos was going to take the watch or Bentley's life in lieu of the ten thousand dollars. And the way Bentley saw it, Carlos would get the watch either way. So Bentley handed it over willingly.

Afterwards, he went below deck to change his soiled shorts before they arrived back at the marina.
*****

Porsche's were fantastic automobiles, but being on the road steadily for four hundred miles was tough on anyone's butt, including Bentley's, no matter how plush the seats were. The Waffle House parking lot was filled with semi's and big dually trucks covered in mud from the southern Louisiana Bayou country.

"What's it going to be today, mistah?" asked the young waitress.

She didn't look more than seventeen years old, but what she did look like was a pregnant woman with a baby bump as large as a beach ball. It was still riding high. Black stick-on letters spelled out "Earline" crookedly on her name tag.

13

"What's good here?" asked Bentley.

"Everything, but the food." said an exhausted Earline as she blew a piece of hair out of her eyes. Her hands and her order pad rested on her extended belly. *"Look, I'm sorry, mistah. I can see that you ain't from 'round here. I have been here for since six a.m. yesterday morning. I am pulling a double because the other waitress, Shelly, didn't show up and I need money in the worst way. Truth is, anything off the grill is good, but stay away from the egg salad. It'll kill ya."*

"Six o'clock yesterday morning!" exclaimed Bentley out loud. *"Are you crazy? You should be home resting in bed. You look like you are about to drop any minute."*

"Mistah, I can't afford to rest." stated Earline matter-of-factly. *"And I got nine other tables and two dozen coffee cups to fill and two other kids at home waiting for me. Would you like me to come back in a few minutes?"*

"No, I am ready." said Bentley as he ordered the trucker's special.
*****

"He's sitting in the Waffle House eating." said the man sitting in the camo SUV. *"He is talking to some waitress right now, but he is alone. Tell everyone to relax for a bit and we should be there in a couple of hours. I will call to tell when and where to pull him over."*

The man was dressed in a plaid flannel shirt stained with remnants of coffee and fast food. It had been a long drive from Florida and he was glad for the stop.

"Look, I gotta go piss like a racehorse. And don't worry, I ain't gonna loose him. I put that little thingy under his car just in case. Now let me go before I piss all over myself."

The man ran into Waffle House and made a bee line to the men's room as fast as he could.

The Monkey Trap

*****

Earline was a sweet girl who had fallen in love a little too easily and way too quickly. Bentley had been able to chat with her intermittently as she made several rounds to fill his coffee cup. He watched her with fascination as she meandered and squeezed through the restaurant's patrons. She had to twist awkwardly in order not to bump into everyone with her belly. He noticed that after she filled the coffee cups of the table by the front door that she dropped something on the floor as she cleared the man's plate.

'It was probably just some dirty napkins' thought Bentley. He knew that she was in no condition to bend over and pick them up. As she walked away the man sitting in the booth bent over and picked them up for her. When the man from the SUV emerged from the restroom there was a commotion going on with the manager and a pregnant waitress.

"I don't know where I lost the money, Mr. Lipton. I had it a minute ago, but now it's not in my apron." exclaimed Earline tearfully as she continued to search every pocket.

The whole restaurant could see and hear the exchange. Bentley knew now that it hadn't been napkins that dropped on the floor.

"Earline, you know that you are responsible for all of the money for all of the tables on your shift." said Mr. Lipton scoldingly. *"So if you can't find your bank, then I am going to have to let you go."*

"Please, Mr. Lipton." cried a hysterical Earline. *"I got two babies at home and this job is all I got to support them. Their daddy took off and I am having to do it all by myself. Please, Mister Lipton, please don't fire me."*

It broke Bentley's heart to hear Earline's pitiful pleas to keep her crappy and thankless job. He couldn't believe that the person sitting by the door wasn't saying anything.

Bentley got up out of his booth and walked over to the man sitting by the

15

door.

"Excuse me, but I think you have the waitresses money, so why don't you give it back to her."

The entire restaurant became quite as all eyes were riveted on Bentley and the man by the door. The place was silent. There were no forks scraping on plates and no spoons clanking in coffee cups.

"I don't know what you are talking about, Mister." said the man looking around sheepishly at all of the eyes focused on him.

The manager immediately came over. *"Is that true, sir? Do you have Earline's money?"*

"I don't have anyone's fuckin' money. This is my money." said the man defensively. *"I came in with it"*

Bentley was turning red with rage.

"That's not true. I saw her drop it and I saw you pick it up."

"Prove it, city boy." said the man as he stood up and got into Bentley's face.

He was a big man and looked like he was used to fighting and that he enjoyed it.

Bentley was scared, but he wasn't going to run. Earline needed him.

"Umm, sir." said the manager meekly *"I am going to have to ask you to leave, please."*

The big man glared at the manager for a few long seconds.

"Fine. I was finished anyway." He said as he reached into the booth to retrieve his 'gimme hat'.

As the front door closed a sigh of relief went through the restaurant and people continued on eating and talking.

"Thank you, mistah" said Earline as she ran up to Bentley. *"I appreciate you saying something and standing up to that guy."*

"Well, I am sure that your boss here will understand and that everything will be alright now." replied Bentley.

"Oh yes sir." chimed Lipton *"I certainly do, but unfortunately Earline is still responsible for her bank and company policy is that unless she covers all of the money that she lost, then I have to let her go."*

Earline broke down and began to sob. *"But there is no way that I can cover it Mr. Lipton. There was over four hundred dollars in it and I have only made about thirty bucks on tip*s."

"Well, then I am sorry, Earline." said Lipton *"but I have to fire you."*

"WHAT!" Bentley was outraged. He had listened to the exchange and was dumbfounded by the manager's heartlessness. He couldn't just stand there and do nothing.

"Earline" said Bentley handing her his credit card, *"before you leave can I get my bill?"*

The crying little pregnant waitress took the card and went to the back and returned with a credit card slip for him to sign.

Bentley sat down. He signed the little white slip, then returned it to her hand. *"You go tell that jerk to wait on his own tables. You go see those babies and get off your feet."*

Earline looked back at him perplexed through her tear filled eyes.

As she looked at the charge slip she couldn't believe her eyes.

"Are you serious? This is real?" Asked Earline.

Bentley only said one word. *"Yes."*

And with that she grabbed a hold of his neck and squeezed it as hard as she could. *"Nobody has ever done anything like this for me, mistah."*

"What is going on out there?" shouted Mr. Lipton from grill.

"Look y'all, this man," said Earline as she wiped the tears from her eyes to look at Bentley, *"this kind and wonderful man, just left me a tip that is big enough to cover all of my tickets and more."*

Tears reappeared in her eyes as she waved the credit card slip in the air. *"He gave me a thousand dollars!"*
*****

Bentley felt like a new man. Helping that girl gave him an indescribable feeling of goodness. After she had shouted out what the tip had been and how he had helped her, everyone in the place began to pull money out of their pockets and purses to give her. Several had even left money under his windshield wipers along with notes thanking him for being such a good and caring person who had restored their faith in mankind.
Some had even called him a hero and a saint.

'Those are some big shoes to fill', thought Bentley.

He knew he wasn't no hero, but he did feel better about himself. Better than he had in a very long time.

The little yellow sports car was racing home with renewed enthusiasm now. The time alone was good for him. It allowed him to think about his life and what he had been doing with it.

He realized that the money he gave to Earline had changed her life for the better, but as the hours on the road made him reflect on his life, he realized that it had changed his life for the better too. When he got to home to Dallas, he was going to flush all the cocaine down the toilet. He was turning his life around. He was going to be a new man. A better man. A decent man.

And he was going to call his brother, Boyce, just to tell him how much he loved him.

'That ought to shock the hell out of him.' thought Bentley.

He reached over and turned on the radio. Stevie Wonder wailed soulfully through the ten speakers, and the haunting instruments combined with his smooth lyrics, enhanced the blissful reverie that Bentley was feeling as his beautiful Porsche skimmed above the pavement with its motor purring sweetly.

Everything finally felt right to Bentley.

'Was this what happiness felt like?' he wondered.

He was on cloud nine and nothing was going to change that tonight.

A cacophony of sirens exploded in the night air. Flashing red and blue lights blinded Bentley. They simply appeared out of thin air. He looked down at the speedometer. The speed was set on seventy-three miles per hour. The speed limit was seventy.

He quickly counted at least five or six squad cars immediately around him and noticed two more up ahead blocking the road. An army of vehicles that had descended upon him from all around.

"What the hell is going on?" Bentley asked himself. *"How did they just appear out of thin air?"*

His heart rate was probably over two hundred and it felt like it was going to jump out of his chest. Panic set in immediately. He knew what he was carrying in the car would land him jail, if they found it. Thank goodness, that it was hidden. Nobody could find it just by looking. The thing he worried about was dogs. Dogs were different kettle of fish.

He had been busted before and had gone through rehab a couple of times. It was all bullshit and it didn't work, but it did satisfy the courts. However, this time he was carrying a lot more cocaine than he ever had before.
Police cars were moving in towards him.

'What am I going to do?' Bentley asked himself. For a split second it crossed his mind to try and out run the police, but no matter how fast any car in the world was, it couldn't ever beat the radio. Plus, he had seen enough car chases on the show COPS to know that they never ended well for the runner. After all, he wasn't O.J. Simpson.

He had a police car on each side of him and several more behind him. There was nowhere for him to turn.

'What the hell was he going to do?' His brain screamed.

He was trapped. Bentley saw the figures up ahead throw spike strips out across the road.

He stomped on the brake. Tires squealed and smoked. The smell of burning rubber assaulted Bentley's nose as the luxury sports car left long black stripes on the smooth gray concrete. With the right hand drive, Bentley instinctively veered the Porsche in that direction. The police car next to him swerved into the breakdown lane to avoid getting side swiped by the Porsche. Sparks arced skyward as the patrol car over compensated and rammed into the metal side barriers. Bentley watched in horror as it flipped over the silver guard rail and down the steep grass embankment. Pieces of flying metal and flinging lights could be seen going in every direction under the sodium vapor lights of the highway. What was left of the patrol car tumbled past the perimeter of the highway lights into the dark oblivion of the night.

Fear was now a tangible taste that was bitter and palpable in Bentley's mouth.

A night in the county jail was now inevitable and certain.

The streaking yellow blur of the Italian sports car drifted to a "J" stop. Bentley was snapped back against the car's racing headrest and he was now facing the headlights of the pursuing patrol cars.

"Get your mother fuckin' hands on the wheel and don't you fuckin' move a muscle." screamed a very angry voice from the behind the flashing lights.

Bentley froze.

Uniformed officers moved in with guns drawn.

This was it? This was what he feared and dreaded the most in life. He prayed fervently that they didn't have dogs.

Bentley stiffened his arms onto the small steering wheel. White knuckles held it tight as his head dropped to his chest in defeat.

Screaming cops could be heard shouting a multitude of conflicting orders. Doc sat in his seat completely still until the first pair of hands grabbed him and pulled him out onto the pavement. Doc showed no resistance, but that fact was of no consequence to the cops who were speeding their asses off from the adrenaline that coursed through their bodies like pure heroine.

Bentley felt himself being pulled and pushed in every direction as more and more hands, knees and feet where used to drive him into the pavement.
A small pebble on the concrete felt like a huge shard of glass being gouged into his cheek as the knee on his neck drove his face further into the side of the highway.

"Get this mother fucker under submission and in handcuffs now." Came

the command from the Sheriff in the big Stetson hat standing over him. Bentley screamed out as his arms were being pulled unnaturally backwards. He felt like his shoulders were about to be separated from their sockets.

"You're hurting me, damn it." Hollered Bentley.

"Stop resisting." said the officer whose knee was on Bentley's neck.

"I am not resisting." screamed Bentley into the street as tears of pain filled his eyes.

The final cuff was snapped onto Bentley left wrist and he was jerked up roughly.
"You had better toughen up, Princess, because where you're going you are going be someone's new punk." said the Sheriff as the fat officer stuffed Bentley into the police car.

"Deputy Jones, if you would be so kind, please go get the dope out of the car, so we can all get out of here." said the Sheriff as he looked over and winked at the young Hispanic girl sitting in vehicle. *"Some of us have better things to do tonight."*
*****

Bentley sat in the back of the police cruiser.

He watched out the rear glass of the patrol car as the uniforms swarmed his precious Porsche. They had found it.

It was as if they went right to it.

But as the lights and the outside excitement swirled on all around him, he began to get light headed. He felt a strange sensation.

Time and movement both seemed to slow. The sounds of the police officers and noise just faded away. All he could he could hear was Patsy Cline. The tinkling of piano keys could be heard in his ears. This couldn't be real.

Patsy Cline was singing "Crazy".

It was all too surreal.   This couldn't really be happening.

It felt like a dream.

'Yes, that was it.' Dr. Bentley Braxton told himself.   'It had to be a dream.'
"...Wondering, what in the world did I doooo.......Ooooh, Crazy......"

The Monkey Trap

Chapter 1

Dr. Bentley Braxton, III was laid out on the steel slab completely dead, except for the fact that he was still breathing oxygen.

His eyes were closed, but he couldn't sleep. The light was on. It was *always* on. It never went off. It just got a little dimmer or a little brighter. He just wished someone would cut it off for a little bit. He needed some sleep. The deprivation of sleep was like he had heard about in POW camps. His thoughts drifted into a dreary gray haze, matching the steel furniture and dull gray walls. The same guard was coming around for the ninth time to wake everyone up for another head count. The constant noise and cold were utilized to torture.

"What time was it?" Bentley asked himself for the hundredth time.

He never knew what time it was. There were no clocks. Time stood still here. But that was the point, wasn't it? He was supposed to be alone with his thoughts. He was supposed to contemplate everything he had done. He was supposed to think about everything he had lost. He wished that he could look at his Rolex just one more time, but his watch was like his life. Gone. Stolen from him. All that remained was a feeling of emptiness and isolation.

So cold here.

He just wanted to know what time it was, 'Damn it!'

He lay there a broken suggestion of a man in threadbare, over used, oversized boxers shivering, chattering and freezing in the dim dankness.

He could hear toilets flushing somewhere close. The sound of rushing water made him colder and even more miserable. He was rubbing his arms more furiously than ever. He pulled his arms inside his thin cotton t-shirt hoping that it would give him just another single degree of warmth.

He wanted to cry, but he couldn't let them see his weakness. He would be eaten alive by the others. They would jump on him and devour him like wolves. They were like a wild pack. They were just waiting to see who was weak so that they could feed on another carcass. He would show them he had fortitude and that they could pull all the 'scared straight' shit they wanted to. He would not break.

'What time is it?'

'It's got to be time to eat. It's been forever since dinner.' The food had been horrible, but right now he would eat anything. What did he have to eat last night? He couldn't remember. How long had it been? What time do they get to eat? Where was the food, 'damn it?'

They were really playing with him now. They wanted him to think that this was all real, didn't they? Well, he would show them. He could stand whatever they threw at him.

KLA-chang clank-ity. Ka-BANG!

The sudden sound shook him violently awake. His cerebral fog was brutally displaced by the shuddering vibration of metal.

"Pack your shit, Doc. You're on the chain."

He jumped up and slid on the ridiculous brown plastic slides that had been issued him. Some sick bastard had molded a weave design into the top of them for the illusion of a Mexican huarache sandal, as if this were some sick ass vacation. From down the run, he could hear, *"Roll the doors"*.

Gears begin to turn, and the door slowly grates open. He followed

25

several others along the blue line. *"Everyone on the wall. Turn and face it."*

Okay, this is different. They have never done this before. These guys look serious. They don't look like they are going to rehab. They look like real criminals.

"Alright girls, drop you panties and grab your cheeks"

He barely has to move his small hips to have the dingy boxers and his dignity fall to the floor all by themselves in a dirty crumpled pile. He bends slightly forward with his delicate manicured hands grasping his smooth buttocks for the inspector to walk by and half-heartedly glance into the most embarrassing aspect of a man's pride. He swallows hard because he can feel the hard lump building in his throat.

"Now turn around and lift your nuts."

He wasn't going to cry, but he could feel the watery glaze beginning to form over his eyes.

"Open your mouth and run your fingers through your hair."

Opening his mouth helped stave off the watery onslaught. He had to hold it together. It wouldn't be much longer until they revealed that this was a warning of what might happen to him and that it wasn't real. 'It couldn't be real.'

"And now, lift your feet."

This was the most elaborate charade ever done to scare him. They were really putting on a dog and pony show this time. 'This rehab must think I am a novice at this. They really want me to believe that I am going to prison. I have to hand it to them they sure make it look real.'

"Okay, Doc, meet your new sweetheart. This here is Farmer. Now go ahead and slip into these chains so that you two can get real close on the ride." The sadistic moron moved along laughing under his breath at his own cleverness.

Chapter 2

'Okay, they are really taking this to the extreme now.'

Farmer was 6'2" and over 250 pounds of pure ebony thug. Central casting would love this guy with his prison tear tattoo that was raised from Keloid scarring under his right eye and his straight razor faded haircut. He even had a geometric style design shaved into the sides. He was one scary mother.

As they were shackled together Doc trembled a bit, but he couldn't help notice how good this monster smelled. He exuded the aroma of lilacs. He had seen other blacks using the flowery scented pomade, but this was the first time he had really noticed how deliciously fragrant it was. He had heard the blacks in his cell say to one another,

"Man, this nigga smell good."

Now he comprehended what was meant because the sweet tang of Farmer's essence was a pleasant momentary distraction. Doc breathed in gulps to relieve himself of the constant smell of nasty ass, which he had been exposed to for the past month.

A jab in the back brought him back to the reality of his situation. *"Grab your bag and get on the bird."*

Doc couldn't understand why they called these buses Blue Birds when they were all painted white. It was just another jailhouse idiom that baffled him.

They were the oddest couple in the chain gang. Colossus Farmer and Lilliputian Doc finagled themselves up the narrow steps and twisted, pulled and pushed each other onto the bus. The inside was partitioned into sections of meshed grating, heavily rusted orange by decades of neglect. Even the windows had been grated over. Nothing, including fresh air, was getting in or out of this bus. It stunk of sweat and fear. Being dragged down the grimy aisle like a potato sack, Doc knocked over the piss pot causing all the men to wretch as putrid stench spilled out into the bus. Inmates cursed at him and made very disparaging remarks about his Caucasian heritage and very low intelligence.

"Ignert white boy mutha-fucka!"

He and Farmer trudged on in tandem to their seats in the back of the bus.

The bus lurched forward throwing them into the cracked plastic seats. Doc was squished into the window by his new found partner, who wasn't too inclined to give him any more room. He stared out the tiny holes in the grates for almost an hour in total silence with his shackled hand in the obese thug's lap.

Seeing other handcuffed pairs talking, Doc decided to break the ice with his new buddy.

"They sure are making this drama realistic, aren't they? I've never ridden this long before to get to a Rehab? Where are we going?" Doc asks.

Farmer turned his head and just looked at Doc for what seemed like an eternity. Finally, Farmer smiled, and Doc was taken aback by a toothy full arch of ten diamond studded teeth from ear to chocolate ear. These diamonds resembled emerald cut Chiclets trimmed in gold window pane. Having seen all kinds of dental work for over twelve years, Doc's immediate thought was, *"Huh, 'San Francisco' dentistry, no doubt."*

"Rehab?" Farmer says incredulously,*" We ain't goin' to no mutha-fuckin' rehab. This bus be goin' to Huntsville, and it's fixin' to get really real up in here, my nigga!"*

Chapter 3

Doc just stared at him in stunned silence.

'Oh my god! It's real. They really are sending me to prison. This can't be happening.' He had been in trouble and arrested before, but always sent to rehab. Sure, they threatened to send him to prison, but he didn't think they could really do it. He was a doctor for Christ's sake. He wasn't some ghetto kid robbing convenience stores to buy a dime of crack rock on the street corner. They couldn't do this to him. He was white and from a rich family.

'They love me. Why don't they do something? Why don't they have a new lawyer working to get me out?'

'Oh Lord, how did it come to this?' Bentley asked himself.

Snapshots of his life reeled though his mind with no particular sequence or apparent reason.

His brother, Boyce, was standing before their father while little Bentley stood half hidden behind a chair. His father's voice was harsh. Boyce was defending Bentley.

"It's only a broken glass." screamed Boyce to his father. *"It can be replaced. He can't."*

Then suddenly their father thumped Boyce with his huge knuckle. An instant goose egg lump arose right in the middle of his forehead, but Boyce didn't cry. Boyce never cried.

Young Bentley cried. A fleeting picture of tiny Bentley wrapped in a blanket being carried in the arms of his mother and slipping out of her grasp to the hard ground crying. Then in a snap Bentley curled up in a ball alone in the middle of a large bed crying because of pain - a headache? No, a toothache? His chest hurt too. Suddenly a frightening shadowy figure behind the curtains in bed room. Fear. Crying. Chest pain.

He saw himself and his mom pouring over a catalog together. She was sitting in her favorite rocker and he was perched on the arm of the old chair with her. He could hear her voice, *"Just put a mark by anything that you would like for Christmas, Honey"*

Then it was Christmas morning in front of a roaring fireplace and beneath a giant Christmas tree decorated with silver tinsel and old shiny ornaments. He was ten years old and every gift he had marked had been under the tree, including the yellow three speed bike with the banana seat and the wheelie bar.

Suddenly, the dusk of a summer day was settling, and the last tiny remnants of the sun were still barely visible on the horizon. He and Sandy were locked in a warm embrace. There was nothing sensual about the embrace. It was all a feeling of comfort, security and a love transcendent of anything sexual. Her hair smelled of light vanilla, almond, a field of flowers. Her softness was ethereal.

Then all went black.

Doc realized that he had drifted off, but he held that last moment with Sandy for just a fleeting second. He felt warm for the first time in weeks. His heart no longer hurt.

Chapter 4

Doctor Bentley B. Braxton, III didn't have a worry in the world. He was riding high. High as a kite, in fact, in his brand new yellow Porsche 911. He was almost home free. Twenty more minutes and he would be pulling into his five car garage. It had been a good trip. He had partied all weekend with his old buddy from dental school and it had been a non-stop frenzy of cold booze, hard drugs, fast boats and even faster women. The cocaine was everywhere. It was just sitting around in bowls like nuts at a cocktail party. This was the good life and he was one of the beautiful people.

In his mind, he kicked over the traces of his disciplined life. When growing up he convinced himself that he could transform himself to anyone that he wanted to be. A dozen years of his life had been devoted to just that single purpose. For long hours and endless days he had applied himself to his career. He had taken a leap of faith into the unknown, blindly on advice of an acquaintance, when he located his posh boutique office in a new suburban development that quickly became ensconced with young and affluent entrepreneurs and techies who wanted, and could definitely afford, his new upscale cosmetic services, which went far beyond just necessity. As he made them more beautiful and successful, he too was catapulted to the pinnacle of his profession. His stature in the conservative community broadened and expanded exponentially despite his deliberate and very conspicuously low profile. He had his glorious and very public persona that everyone adored, but he also had a very private life that fulfilled his hedonistic cravings and satisfied his most base desires. When he was high, everyone wanted to be with him and paid endless attention. He adored those epic feelings of affection that enveloped him. Simply put. He was loved and was unequivocally addicted to the emotional elixir that he had found in this harmless white powder that he imported.

He made this trip every six months and each time was better than the last. He and his buddy Malcolm in South Beach would split a kilo of pure Peruvian Flake. The rush was nothing like the 'bar coke' that they sold in Dallas. That stuff just stopped up his nose, but one blast of Flake made him feel like he was going Mach 5 with his hair on fire.

What a difference this stuff was to the amphetamines and barbiturates that were the standard issue with his little black bag in dental school. That had seemed like perfect unguent for all his woes back then. He could do anything when he was high. He could study for hours on end and ace every test he took. He could party all night long and have sex for hours on end. It was the perfect drug. It made him feel like a God. It had always treated him well.

But if it had treated him so well, then how did he get here? How did he get on this damn bus?

The lump returned to his throat, and it hurt so bad it felt as if it was going to burst. In that unguarded moment, a tear welled up and escaped from one eye, but nothing escaped Farmer's attention.

Farmer quickly looked around the bus and then back to him.

"Man, you better hold that shit in. You need to check yourself. Don't be

letting any of these mutha-fuckas see you weak."

Eyes from around the bus were already starting to glance at Doc. Whispers could be heard from various twosomes. And then it came. The first attack.

"Aaaah! What we got here? I think we got us a little bitch who's crying. Do you need something to suck on like a little baby? Huh? I got something for you to suck on boy." Laughter erupted.

Farmer whispered to Doc. *"You gotta suck it up, man."*

Doc couldn't help himself. The tears came rolling down his face. The pack of convict carnivores could be heard. *"I'll make him my bitch." "Fucking pussy." "Kick his ass." "What he needs is this big black dick."*

Farmer reached over with his handcuffed arm and grabbed Doc's shoulder. 'Oh my god,' Doc thought, 'he is going to execute me right here. I am going to be killed before I even get to the prison. Maybe it would be better that way. It would be quicker and more merciful, that's for sure.'

Farmers grip was firm and forceful as he shoved Doc's head down in between the seats.

"Shut the fuck up. My man's sick." Farmer yelled.

The other convicts didn't believe it for a minute, but they accepted it because it came from Farmer. And they were not about to go head to head against him all by themselves.

The bus jerked to a halt.

They had arrived.

*****

The bus had come to a halt at the three story guard tower. The transport guard got out and secured his shotgun and his sidearm into a lock box. Doc had thought that it was so peculiar that he sent the key up to the guard in the tower on a pulley rope that reminded him of his childhood days in his summer tree house. Apparently, even guards weren't allowed to carry firearms inside the prison for fear that they would be over powered and killed by an inmate. Once disarmed the outer gate was opened by hand and the white bus entered the prison. Doc watched as the gate was closed and locked behind them with the silhouette of the tower guard cradling his rifle. It was still surreal to him.

Deliberately Farmer waited until last to get up. Doc used the extra time to pull himself together. His eyes were puffy red. Farmer didn't talk much, but then he didn't really have to because his actions had said enough. Doc didn't know how to express his gratitude, but he would find a way. Somehow, he vowed to himself, he would find a way. If he lived long enough.

"Get your candy asses off my bus", screamed the driver.

Doc nearly jumped out of his seat, but Farmer eased up like he hadn't even heard the guy. They were herded like cattle at a meat market into a large holding cell. When their names were called the handcuffs were removed, and one by one they were put into another holding cell where they sat for hours. Doc was separated from Farmer and put into a different holding cell. Guys were sitting almost on top of each other. Some were laid out prone, sleeping on the floor trying to pass the tediousness of waiting. Most used rolls of toilet paper as pillows and pulled their arms inside their jumpers to try and stay warm. Inmates would just casually step over them to relieve themselves in the stainless steel toilet. The boredom got to some of the guys and the silence was just too awkward for them to bear. There was always one guy who just couldn't stand the silence. He would just start talking to someone, who would then become object of his attention, but the entire holding cell was trapped by his never ending spew of verbal diarrhea.

*****

Doc was grateful when an inmate announced that they could come out of the holding cell five at a time to get haircuts. Everyone rushed the gate to be in the first group to get out. Doc didn't make it until the sixth group.

People in Doc's circle of friends rarely admitted to their vanity, but it was obvious to others instantly. Even Doc's choice of where he cut his hair in Dallas exemplified his inherent snobbery. It was a deliberately plain no-frills looking barbershop that catered to the societal elite men of the city.   Power moguls, visiting Hollywood celebrities, current mayors and governors along with a former President were its daily clientele.

His pampered visits always concluded with an essential manicure, since dentistry was a dangerous profession, according to Doc.   A torn cuticle could allow a fatal infection, such as one of the 4Hs - Herpes, Hepatitis, HIV or Heart.

His manicurist was a legend in her own time. She freely admitted to practicing quackery as she dispensed home spun psychology and sealed minor cuts with five second nail glue, a practice that would later become the norm in America's operating rooms. After 30 years of buffing nails and telling hilarious off color jokes to the 'good ol' boys', she was a permanent fixture and was definitely Doc's favorite stop in the shop.

When it was time to go, Fred the shine man gingerly slipped on Doc's freshly polished Gucci loafers and dusted his shoulders non-stop until the requisite tip was put into his KIWI stained palm with a hearty handshake.

He sat down in the plain cafeteria style chair while another inmate proceeded to sheer every single hair off his head. They called it a Buzz because all you heard was the buzz of clippers in your ears as you watched all your hair fall to the floor. Doc looked at himself in the polished metal mirror that was riveted to the wall. He was horrified. He had never seen himself look worse. It looked so hideous.

He had always worn his hair on the longish side to the consternation of his freshman professor who never missed an opportunity to say "get a haircut". He looked like one of those hideous mug shots that they flash up on TV news. He felt like Sampson from the Bible. With the loss of his hair, he began to feel like his soul had been weakened. Now he looked like all the others. He looked like a criminal.

Chapter 5

An older guard appeared with a clipboard. *"When your name is called, get on the yellow line, strip down and wait in line"*

Doc was near the front this time since they seemed to be going alphabetically. He felt vulnerable standing there naked. He stood there shifting from foot to foot covering his genitals with his hands clasped together in front of him nonchalantly. Guys, who had been there before, casually stood around displaying their manhood as a subtle method of intimidation to the smaller guys. That went double for Farmer. The man was a physical monster in every way. He had always heard the stories about black guys but he had never witnessed it firsthand like this. There was that one cadaver in his gross anatomy lab that everyone sneaked around to snicker about. The freshman marveled at the dead man's Johnson that reached to his knees even in the limp and flaccid state of death, but the consensus was that surely it must have been mutated by disease. Doc moved from window to window to receive his clothes piece meal until he had two of everything.

Running water could be heard as he neared the last window to receive a postage stamp size green chip of prison made soap intended for a single use. Clothes were sitting in piles all over as guys were grouped around the carousel of shower heads that filled the gray cement room. Drainage sloughs and the floor were littered with green and blue discarded mushes that used to be soap. Doc noticed that the old guys, who had been in prison before, were all wearing their slides or even their newly issued canvas slip-ons in the shower while the newbies stood barefooted. They would have to learn the hard way about communal living and showering. Prison was a pietrie dish of germs and bacteria waiting for their next victim. Doc slipped his slides on and stepped under the stinging spray of water. Doc felt intimidated by all of these massive thugs around him and that intimidation was only doubled standing there naked in the shower with ice water bombarding him like a fire hose. Doc was a little guy of five feet seven and weighed only 140 lbs. wet, which is exactly what he was right now. He soaped up, rinsed off and got out as fast as he could.

*****

"Bentley B. Braxton," someone called, but to Doc's surprise this time it was a female voice. She was a homely corn fed country gal with unadorned hair and unskilled make-up. She wore run of the mill discount clothing from one of the large box stores and attempted to disguise her emerging muffin top. He followed her to a desk scattered with a dozen photos of children in various states of costuming. From the number of pictures, Doc got the impression that she must have been exceptionally proud of a teenage boy in his football uniform. He sat there as she typed in all his vital information. When everything was finished, she took his photo and printed up his Inmate I.D. Card. He was now inmate #690479. He wanted to cry. He had never been a crier, but in these endless hours of humiliation, tears were assaulting. He was really in prison. They had stripped him of his clothes, his hair, his dignity and now his identity. His hope was replaced by an empty futility that surpassed any understanding. Going forward felt heavy. Someone called, but to Doc's surprise this time it was he was just another faceless blob.

He was just another number.

Chapter 6

Prison was laid out as a single concrete hall one half mile long with cell blocks and departments on each side. Doc was issued the standard baby blue vinyl covered mattress, a single woolen blanket and two thin worn out sheets with small slits cut all along the sides of them. The mattress was bigger than he and very heavy as he trudged slowly down the hall. He arrived at his cell block exhausted and almost totally spent. The door was electronically opened by the picket boss. Doc was told by the guard working the run to wait in the day room.

"You're going to have to wait until the next in and out." *S*he said slamming the metal door closed behind Doc.

What the hell was an in and out, he wondered? As he sat down he saw everyone stop what they were doing to look at him and to whisper to one another. Doc felt extremely self-conscious and very nervous.

"In and out!" came a curdling scream.

Everyone jumped up and rushed the door and headed up the stairs and down the run. *"Doors!"*

Click, Click, Click. Click. Click. Click…….

Electronic clicks could be heard in tandem going from one door to the next, and when it got to the end, all the doors opened at once. Everyone who was standing in front of their cells entered them and disappeared. The run was instantly empty except for Doc who struggled to push his stuff in the cell as fast as he could.

"Coming back with the 'Out' in 2 minutes", the guard yelled at the top of her piercing voice.

Both bunks were empty, so Doc threw his stuff on the lower one because he had heard from the talker in the holding cell how hard they were to come by. He had barely gotten his mattress on the bunk when he heard, *"Doors"*.

He was startled when someone stuck their head in the open door and said, *"Aren't you coming? C'mon. You have to go to the day room."*

Doc started to ask why, but the guy just grabbed him by the arm and said, *"Hurry, before the doors close."*

Doc figured it must be chow time. He didn't know what time it was and all he had eaten was a smashed up dry bologna sandwich in one of the holding cells, so he was hungry and grateful to the young guy for letting him know not to miss it.

It must be chow time because everyone seemed to be coming out of their cells. He fell into the crowd and followed them down the stairs to the day room. The noise was deafening almost. The room was packed with convicts, but when Doc entered it went silent. Dead silent.

Every eye was upon him.

A white guy wearing a wife beater under shirt and with tattoos covering his arms and neck approached Doc. *"Okay, don't you worry. This guy looks tough, but he don't have much wind in him."* And just as quickly he moved around behind Doc.

'Worry? Worry about what?' Doc thought. *'What does he mean by 'wind'?'* He opened his mouth to ask, but just then a little black pigmy emerged from the throng of inmates. He was as shorter than Doc and that's where the similarity ended.

This guy was a fire plug with a long sloping forehead, dull expressionless eyes and the most humongous lips Doc had ever seen. He looked like one of those miniature African carvings come to life.

At that instant, the realization hit Doc like a ton of bricks. He was supposed to fight this guy. Now it made sense as to why every inmate in the cell block was here. They were here to watch him get murdered by this pituitary deficient mongoloid. And afterward, they would go eat some tamale casserole like nothing ever happened. It would just be another day in prison. No big deal. Except that it was a big deal to Doc because he would be the dead one.

"If you go down on the ground, remember to protect your head. Get into a ball and cover you face." Came the voice behind him. *"You don't want him to kick you in the head or knock you teeth out."*

A wave of nausea rippled through Doc's body. This was it. This was the end. This was where he would be killed. There was no way he could keep this guy from slaughtering him. He was scared like never before in his life, and he wanted to cry for help; but there wasn't anyone there to cry out to. He was all alone; and today, in this crowded room filled with society's rejects and reprobates, he would die all alone.

Chapter 7

"This is ridiculous. I am a grown man and a professional doctor. I'm not going to fight some Cro-Magnon mutant."

Doc turned away, but he was met by a wall of stern faces. He wasn't going anywhere. 'Wife beater' approached him again and said, *"Dude, everybody gotta fight when they come in. If you don't, then you will become somebody's bitch and they will take all your stuff and then they'll do a lot worse to you."*

Worse! What the hell could be worse than having your head bashed in and bleeding out on a cold floor in a place where the taking of a life is considered before dinner entertainment?

In a place where no one cares whether you live or die. Doc thought maybe it would be better if he did die. Maybe he should just antagonize this Neanderthal enough so that he would beat him senseless and end this misery. The crowd would have their blood lust fulfilled.

Doc was frozen and the crowd was restless.

He was a dead man.

"Just take your beatin', man". 'Wife beater' whispered in his ear. *"Get it over with now or you're going to be MY little bitch tonight."*

Chapter 8

Blood rushed to Doc's head. It had a dizzying effect on him. What was he going to do? Whatever it was he had better do it quick. 'Wife Beater' was breathing down his neck and the pigmy was moving in on him.

He was a dead man either way.

He closed his eyes for just a moment to clear his thoughts and to say a little prayer.

KA-THUNK! The pigmy had used that split second to ambush Doc with a sucker punch to the head. Doc's head was ringing like a gong. The punch had landed squarely on his temple stunning him and knocking him off balance. Doc was still stumbling when the next blow came. This time it was a straight missile to his right cheek bone. He heard the crunch of bone as his cheek gave way. Doc felt the hematoma begin to swell his right eye shut almost immediately. This was the real thing. This guy was trying to kill him. A kick to the ribs devastated Doc as several of them snapped and broke under the force delivered from the steel-toed boot, which the inmate workers used in the fields.

His right eye was swollen completely shut now and he could feel the pressure continue to build. He knew that it hurt but adrenalin was being infused into his body and the euphoria was taking over. His survival instinct was now fully engaged.

Flight, as an option, had been eliminated. Doc had never been in a real fight, but he had studied Jujitsu for sport and entertainment in his youth. He and his buddies had seen some Billy Jack movies and thought it would make them cool with the girls to know some killer moves.

At this moment, those few moves were all he could remember. The pigmy was being cheered on by all the black convicts. He was a demi-god in their eyes right now. The fucker even smiled. He was enjoying it. Madness married Doc's adrenalin and out of his one good eye all he could see was red rage. Pent up energy was pumping through him now. A beast deep inside him had been awakened.

The pigmy moved in to deliver his Coup de Gras, but Doc could now see that he was clumsy and cloddish. He was a street thug without any finesse or training. With his new heightened senses it was like watching the guy move in slow motion. Doc could see the pigmy's exact moves before he even did them. Doc evaded the first swing by a mile. The pigmy was surprised. He followed it with another attempt, which went swinging harmlessly past him, catching nothing but air. Doc recognized the opening when he saw it. His old training had come flooding back.

As the pigmy's arm went past his good eye, Doc saw that the diminutive brawler had made a critical mistake. He had left his midsection unguarded. Doc seized the opportunity. He planted his feet firmly. Back foot at a ninety degree angle and his other pointed in the direction that he was going to hit. He could hear clearly the old instructor's commands in his head.

"Look where you are going to hit. Don't aim at your target. Aim past your target. Lean with your body and follow your fist through the target."

The target in this case was one shocked little pigmy when Doc delivered a crippling right punch to his left kidney which put him on one knee. And the shock was even more noticeable on the black faces of the crowd when Doc took advantage of the situation and hit the disabled dwarf with a full power punch to his lower mandible. He didn't break the little freak's jaw, but one of his enormous lips exploded like a blood filled balloon. Red spray peppered the stunned crowd and cheering erupted from the white inmates.

The black convicts weren't used to this type of humiliation at the hands of some skinny and puny ass white boy. Their prize street fighter was clearly hurt and they were ready to take retribution on Doc. Doc had gotten lucky with a couple of well landed punches in a moment of desperation, but there was no way he could survive a complete onslaught from the whole gang.

And then he just blurted out, *"If you don't stop him, I am going to hurt him real bad!"*

Where the hell had that come from? The blow to his head must have really done some damage.

The crowd was stunned at the verbose declaration of this little puke with a purple swollen eye. A wave of indecision and indignation rippled through the black cons when suddenly a big voice exploded from the

41

back of the crowd.

"You'd better listen to my boy, cuz he be givin' ya some knowledge."

An instant hush.

Parting the gallery, then, *"Y'all got whatcha wanted, so this is the end of it. If any of ya lays a hand on m' boy again, I'm gonna lay my hands on you."*

'It was Farmer.

*****

"Chow Time."

The call to dinner empties the day room. Doc, left emotionally and physically spent, drops himself into the nearest bench. Conscious now of the exhaustion and pain, Doc is, never the less, aware of Farmers compassionate support, which gives him enough impetuous to stand, so that he can drift toward to his cell on his savior's out stretched arm. Farmer half drags Doc up the metal stairway. Doc doesn't even notice the new belongings sitting in front of the cell. The picket boss opens the single door. Doc limps in and collapses into the lower bunk.

"Thanks, man, for getting me here." Doc says.

"No prob." Farmer replies. *"I live pretty close."* Doc's one good eye brightens up at the prospect of having Farmer close by.

"Really?" Doc asks, *"Which cell are you in?"*

Farmer smiles a big toothy grin as he grabs his travel bag and mattress. *"I'm in this one, Killer. Don't cha know? You are MY boy now."*

Chapter 9

Doc's swollen hematoma resembled a big purple juicy plum. Any vision out of it would be days away. Farmer did a cursory check and confirmed Doc's earlier diagnosis of a cracked rib. The bruise on his left rib cage morphed into an ever expanding yellowish amoeba, but the pain racking his body was nothing compared to the alarm bells sounding in his brain.

'Take deep breathes.'

Doc told himself to take deep, deep breaths because he could feel an anxiety attack welling up. With his first deep breath, Doc almost passed out from the shooting pain that rocketed from his ribs to his brain.

Blood pulsed through his swollen eye even more fiercely, although with his good eye Doc noticed for the first time that the pigmy's blood now covered his new white prison clothes. Autonomic fear struck his heart. Blood was an occupational hazard in Doc's profession, but seeing it covering him so violently made Doc shake with horror. He knew that the pigmy and his gang of friends would try to get him again. They were not going to just let this go and sing "Kum-ba-yah".

Sure Doc had a protector now, but what did Farmer mean when he said, *"You're MY boy now"?*

Realization suddenly hit Doc, 'Oh lord God! Am I now his bitch?' His brain was screaming at him. 'What have I gotten into?' He was a straight guy, but he had heard how things were in prison and now he was indebted to this behemoth. He owed him. He owed big time. In fact, he literally owed him his life. Sure Doc was grateful, but just how grateful was he supposed to be?

What would he do if Farmer crawled into his bunk one night and demanded that Doc service him for pleasure? All Doc could see in his head was the enormity of Farmer's penis and his imagination went into a frantic panic.

What the fuck was he going to do now? He would rather kill himself than do the awful vile things that were running through his head. His choices were abysmally bleak. Either let the pigmy and his friends kill him in the most violent and painful way imaginable or let Farmer have carnal knowledge to violate him orally and anally until Doc wished he were dead.   These were not the best choices in the world.

There had to be another way. He was Dr. Bentley Braxton III. He wasn't supposed to be in a place like this or with people like this.

Sure he did drugs, but who didn't? He never hurt anybody. He never stole from anyone. He never sold the drugs. It wasn't fair. He didn't deserve to be treated like a common criminal. Where was his family? Where were all his friends? He wanted to go home. He wanted to forget everything that had happened to him, especially the last 24 hours. He wanted the pain to go away.

The pain was intense, and he didn't have any choice. He had to endure it according to Farmer.

"You can't go to medical, dude. If you do, then they're gonna give you a 'case' for fighting.   That's six months medium custody and loss of commissary privileges"

"But I was attacked," Doc said. *"I was the goddamn victim!"*

"Everybody here be a victim." Farmer retorted. *"That nigga will have twenty of his homeboys testifying that you jumped him and threw the first punch. Who you got?"*

Doc was silent. He knew Farmer was right, but it wasn't fair and it went contrary to everything he had ever learned. The adrenaline rush was wearing off and exhaustion began to possess his battered body. Darkness ate away at the edges of his consciousness until finally he was asleep.

*****

Small town court houses in Texas were famous for the beauty of their nineteenth century Victorian influenced architecture. Town squares were built around them and most had become bucolic parks as newer and more modern facilities were built to do the actual work of the county, however, there were a few old working courthouses that still dispensed justice from their antiquated halls.   Doc now sat in one of those old courthouses. Its majestic rooms were steeped with high ceilings, age-honed marble floors, and large deeply coffered windows, so designed to keep the sun from entering and thus keeping the old girl cooler on the inside in its earlier days. It may have been nostalgic and beautiful to the unaffected viewer on the outside, but right now, from Doc's point of view, it was as depressing and despicable a place as he had ever been in.

In a low guttural voice his name was called by the pot-bellied bailiff, who was holding his sawed off shot gun casually by his side in one hand and spitting chewing tobacco into a diet Dr. Pepper can in the other. No smoking had been allowed in the courthouse since someone had discovered so-called second hand smoke.

'What a bunch of commie pinko liberal crap that was,' thought the sweaty deputy.

'The country is going to hell on a cracker because of this new generation of God-hating, drug loving socialists. Thank god Lloyd county had strong Christian men like Judge Wesley Wood and Sheriff Hardon Johnson.'

Johnson, known as 'Red' to everyone that knew him and voted for him, was entering his 42nd unopposed year as Sheriff; but this year was going to be different because some outside Yankee transplant from Missouri or some such place had decided to throw his hat into the ring and oppose the good sheriff. He was 'rabble rousing' all over the county and saying terrible things about the department and the Sheriff. The deputy didn't know what 'official corruption' or 'maleficent' meant, but he knew that Red couldn't be guilty of it because he was a good Christian man and a deacon in his church.

'No sirree, this was Texas. God's country with honest and upright people.'

Doc entered the large hollow courtroom. This was obviously the prime courtroom and Judge Wesley Wood was the prime judge. Twenty five foot tall ceilings and moldings two and a half feet thick adorned the court room. Corinthian marble columns were gilded with gold leaf, and the acres of deep oak wood walls, seats and desks that had been polished by use for over a century had a permanent luster and a patina that could never be reproduced. This room was a standing testament to the old pioneer craftsmen that built these prairie castles; however, the old wavy glass windows that covered two complete walls on the corner of the building couldn't keep out the overcast gloom that was East Texas weather in November.

Cold winds swept down the plains and no living creature could escape its bone chilling wrath. Old ladies with their sheer silky scarves sat beside old men, who still wore hats, in the back on long courtroom pews. They came to impart diversion into their unexciting lives by watching the misfortunes of others. Doc thought about how ghoulish that seemed. They were wrinkled old vampires sitting there watching the court suck life out of whatever poor miscreant happened to be the illegal flavor of the day.

Doc was seated next to his Public Defender. The guy was so fresh out of law school that he still wore his alma mater jacket to court. He was a home town boy that had been given a scholarship, contingent on his returning and working for peanuts in the public defender's office for five years. All of the smarter students with much higher LSAT scores saw the deal for the indentured servitude that it was and politely turned it down. David "Duke" Putnam had been on his high school and college football teams. He didn't get a football scholarship to college and he would never play professionally. That was for sure. He was just an average home town Joe from Smallville, Texas. He wasn't an Einstein, but he had maintained a fair enough GPA to take the LSATs and was surprised that he scored high enough to get into law school. But he didn't have the money to go. So when the men of the county offered him a free ride, if he would come back and work, it seemed like a good deal. It would certainly be better than working in his dad's used tire shop and coming home with grimy hands every night. It would mean the difference between hamburger helper and Red Lobster. The decision had been a no-brainer for the former football player.

'Duke' Putnam, P.D. wasn't a bad guy, but he was in over his head. He may have graduated from law school, but he was definitely being schooled daily by the judge and receiving a lot of on the job training, since proper procedure seemed to be his inherent weakness. The prosecutor showed no mercy and pounced on every mistake. Each error was more detrimental to Doc than the previous one. Doc lost track of all the charges. At the end of the day, Doc was walked out of that courtroom with ten less years of his life. Well, at least the old wrinkled vampires could go home satisfied today.

*****

"How's my boy doin'?" Farmer asks.

Doc's eyes flutter cruelly as he is jerked into the present moment and becomes aware of his surroundings. Farmer had been watching his new "celly" for over an hour. He got worried when Doc began to jerk and toss from side to side. Prison cell bunks weren't like normal beds. Farmer had seen dozens of guys hurt themselves on the welded steel berths. There were no soft edges. There were no pillows or plush duvets to make sleep easy and pleasurable. Everything here was designed to make your life a living hell. Farmer had been in prison twice before. He knew the 'ins' and 'outs' of life here better than he wanted to. He was what they called "ol' school" or 'O.G.', for 'Old Gangsta'.

Over the years in a place like this you learned pretty quickly how to study people and to watch your own back because there weren't any real friends in prison. There were only people who wanted to hurt you and people who had not yet hurt you, so Farmer slept lightly and with the proverbial one eye open. He was constantly aware of and assessing his surroundings. Tonight his eye was on this white boy who didn't know' shit from shine-ola', as his granny used to say. Farmer normally didn't care about other people, especially the ones in prison. He figured nobody was innocent. People were just lucky or unlucky. The unlucky ones got caught and the lucky ones didn't. It was a total crap shoot.

So he was perplexed as to why he felt so drawn to this white boy. 'What made him different?'

Farmer had walked in the day room just as the pigmy ambushed Doc with a sucker punch. Farmer expected him to drop into the fetal position and to fold, but to his amazement the little guy summoned up enough courage to fight back and he actually put the pigmy pugilist on the ground. He had seen enough of these matches to know that Doc was

47

going to lose no matter what. Farmer admired the guy. He had heart and that meant something to Farmer. But now he could sense Doc's apprehension. He smelled fear. He could tell that Doc was uneasy and that he was scared out of his wits, even if he tried to hide it from Farmer.

"I feel like crap" Doc whispered. *"I hurt all over."*

"Yeah, well that's to be expected." snickered Farmer. *"You just had the livin' shit beat out of you."*

Doc blustered up a bit. *"I got a few good licks in too, you know."*

*"True, but you **look** like you had the livin' shit beat out of you."* Farmer said. Doc couldn't help but laugh despite the agony that he was enduring. Doc felt like the moment of levity would be the perfect time to confront Farmer.

"Look, Farmer," the nervous cracking in Doc's voice was obvious, *"I want to tell you how much I really appreciate your intervention today and I like you as a friend, but....."*

The awkward tension was so thick that Doc had to stop to swallow deeply in order to get the rest of his little speech out. Farmer was enjoying watching him squirm and fret. He loved the way he intimidated people. It gave him a rush to have that much power over others, so he sat there silently 'mean muggin', so that Doc's discomfort was ramped up a couple of notches. He knew what coming next and was already laughing on the inside. He was going to milk this for every drop of satisfaction that he could squeeze out of his new celly. This was going to be good.

"...I can't be your bitch." There, Doc had said it. Finally, it was out. *"I am straight and I can't.....you know, do those kinds of things with you."*

Farmer was about to explode with laughter on the inside. He knew that the little squirt was scared shitless, but he didn't get the chance to tease people very often. Everyone was so serious here. Most people would stab you in the back if they thought you had disrespected them or made them the butt of a joke; however, Farmer wasn't worried about his new celly doing anything like that.

"What do you mean you don't WANT to be my bitch?" Farmer puffed up his chest up and leaned in aggressive like. *"You think your mutha-fuckin' white ass has a choice. Bitch, I take what I want!"*

Doc winced because he knew Farmer was right and he was petrified. There wasn't going to be any lucky punch this time. There wasn't going to be another savior this time. No, this time he was going to have to lay down with the devil. He mentally prepared himself as best he could, but how did someone prepare to be prison raped?

Booming laughter erupted and filled the tiny cell.

"Dude, you ought to see the look on your face." Farmer was actually smiling. *"You were about ready to shit you pants."*

"What?" Doc realized he wasn't about to get violently anal raped and the relief washed over him in a wave. This was the only good news that he had in a month and he was on the verge of tears again, but this time they were welcome relief.

Farmer saw the liberated look on Doc's face.

"You aren't my bitch, bro." Farmer said *"You're my boy. You my little homey. Ain't no mutha-fucka gonna mess with you while I got your back."*

Doc wanted to believe Farmer, but if he wasn't going to rape him, then what did he want. Why was he being so nice? He knew enough to know nothing was free, especially in prison.

"Okay, I am supposed to believe you are doing all of this out of the kindness of your heart." Doc says sarcastically. *"What gives? What do you want?"*

Farmer's demeanor instantly changed. He sat at the painted steel desk that was welded to the wall looking away from Doc now. Doc wondered if he went too far or if he disrespected and 'dissed' Farmer in some way.

Farmer avoided eye contact and sat there quietly.

"Look, man, I didn't mean any disrespect. I am really thankful for everything you have done, but this is prison. You know what I mean."

Doc waited for a response, but all he received was more silence. This wasn't going well at all, Doc thought.

"If it is money you want, then I should let you know right now, I don't have any." Doc proclaimed. *"Everything I have has been frozen by the court or confiscated by the Sheriff's office. That's why I had to use that useless Public Defender."*

Doc was prattling on about his money problems when Farmer turned and stopped him.

"I need your help." Farmer said.

Had he heard him right? What could he do for Farmer? He was broke, financially and physically busted.

"I want you to teach me to read and write." Farmer softly said.

Doc was momentarily stunned. *"Of course, I will teach you."*

Farmer had been nervous about asking Doc for help, but he had to. He was out of options. He needed help, and opportunities in prison were slim to none, so when he got hooked up with this white boy, it was God answering his prayers. He had his pride, but he also had his needs.

"You can't mention a word of this to anyone else. This is to be just between you and me." Farmer said sternly. *"Promise me that you won't tell a soul."*

"I won't." said Doc *"I won't tell anyone."* Doc could see the concern on Farmers face. Doc wouldn't ever see that face or Farmer in the same way again.

Farmer saw the look of pity on Doc's face and he couldn't have that. He needed to put that 'weak ass shit' out the door 'quick like'. As a convict he couldn't have any of his weaknesses known. He liked this white boy for some strange reason, but he needed to keep him quiet and under his control. Big mouths were the biggest cause of problems and fights in prison.

" 'Cuz if ya do....." Farmer let it hang out there for a minute, so that Doc's imagination could soak it in. *"Well.....just remember I am the only one standing between you and the pigmy."*

Chapter 10

Guy was fresh out of college and interning for Sheriff's Candidate Joe-Don Lilly. He wasn't a true believer and he certainly didn't think that Joe Don had a snowball's chance in Hell of winning against the seven time incumbent, Hardon 'Red' Johnson. 'Big Red' had been running this county with his own brand of justice since before Guy was born. Guy needed a job and this was the only one in town. Every company that he applied to said that they weren't hiring anyone full-time.

Guy felt stupid now for swallowing all the political propaganda and supporting a new President. Guy had believed it all. All the lies.

Yeah,' Guy thought sarcastically, *'Things changed alright. From bad to worse.'* He truly thought the man would be different. He wasn't. He was the same or even worse than all the other lying politicians. Guy thought it ironic to find himself working for a politician like Candidate Joe-Don Lilly, since he felt so betrayed and hated all of them so much now.

Joe Don was convinced and obsessed with proving that Sheriff Red was profiting illegally or unethically from his position. Guy laughed because anyone over ten years of age in Lloyd County knew that much, but Sheriff Red was a slick old buzzard. No one had ever been able to get the goods on him with anything that resembled what could be called evidence.

The computer monitor gave an eerie glow to the darkened cubicle that was Guy's escape from his three roommates on this night, and many others previously, for that matter. His work spot glowed like a lone street light in the giant darkened room that had been transformed from an abandoned Piggly-Wiggly grocery store into the "Lilly for Sheriff" campaign headquarters. This place had become his late night refuge for needed solitude and reflection. He trolled cyberspace for hours without distraction. He had gotten a reputation as a loner; setting him apart from the other political cannibals that filled the campaign offices. He was an odd duck in their eyes, but he never cared one iota about the campaign anyway and he certainly didn't care what his co-workers thought about him. He was here for the paycheck. That was it. Nothing else.

Other campaign workers, hoping to get him fired, had tattled on him for his after-hours work sessions, but that plan had back fired on them badly when his boss had only praised him for being so diligent and hard working.

"We need a hundred more just like you, Guy." the campaign manager exclaimed about him in front of his detractors. Guy was pretty certain that she was infatuated with him and would like nothing more than to be his sugar mama. She had leaned in over his shoulder on the pretense of checking his work at the computer, using the close quarters to surreptitiously and ever so lightly push one of her pillowy bosoms against the side of his smooth, boyish face, while the other one strategically nestled in and hugged the nape of his neck in a very sexy and intoxicating embrace. She deliberately lingered there for a few extra seductive seconds. Yes, she knew what she was doing. This wasn't her first time at the rodeo and Guy was not the first stud that she had cut from the herd, but he wasn't accustomed to such blatant passes from older women and he flushed crimson red from embarrassment. It was awkward for him, as he was afraid of losing this job that he needed so desperately. Regardless of the number of labor laws that it might violate or how unethical it was, Guy was none the less extremely flattered and, if the truth be known even a little titillated by the old gal. She had to be at least forty, almost twice his age, but if this was the new women's lib in the modern workplace, then he was all for it one hundred and fifty percent.

The floor of the campaign headquarters was unaffectionately referred to as the maze by all who inhabited cubicles there. Infinite twists and turns coupled with the many numerous dead ends could keep an intern lost for hours. Guy didn't believe that anyone really knew what was going on in all these rat holes. It was as if they had all morphed into a mutant species of human rodents blindly performing useless tasks for politicos and making endless report after endless report that no one would ever read or use. Guy was disgusted with the whole system and all the people who worked in it. He was smart. He had a college education and a way, way above average I.Q., so *'What the hell was he doing here?'*

He asked himself that question a million and one times every day. The only thing his college education had given him so far was a lot of debt. And at his current salary, his grand kids would have to pay it off for him.

Strangely, it was his lonely nights that kept him going lately. They were really the only thing that he looked forward to as one boring day ran into the next. He didn't have a life and he didn't have anything to offer any girls that his roommates kept dragging home for him. They all wanted to be entertained constantly and Guy didn't have the funds his roommates had for that kind of companionship, which meant that he would spend his nights in the maze pouring over electronic blips in the dark. Since he had discovered internet radio on his computer, each night was custom programmed with perfect music for whatever task he was doing or whatever mood he was in. And if that wasn't enough, then a few swigs of some local moonshine, nicked from his roommate, was just what the doctor ordered to set whatever mood he desired. Tonight it was old 1940s Rhythm and Blues that fit the bill because he was having a pretty good pity party for himself. He was full of self-doubt lately.

Maybe he wasn't as smart as he thought he was.

It had been months and he had yet to discover any mistakes or uncover any corruption by 'Big Red' and his country bumpkins. They couldn't be that good, could they? Were they smarter than him? He was stymied at every dead end he came to. Night after night he stared with bloodshot rummy orbs at the computer as it blankly stared back at him refusing to give up any of the secrets that Guy knew were in there somewhere.

The Monkey Trap

He felt so useless.

Family and friends had always told him that he was meant for something great. Maybe he was an idiot for believing it, but he did want to do something great. He did want to set the world on fire, however, he doubted that he would ever do it while working for Sheriff's Candidate Joe-Don Lilly. The only thing he had discovered so far was his penchant for cheap homemade booze followed by copious amounts of self-pity set to music. Guy would lose hours absorbing the 180 proof sounds of John Mayall or Nappie Brown. They understood his torment. He reveled in the pain of every note and was buried alive in the blues almost every night with his wailing demons.

How he managed to get his work done some days was mystery to him.

He was missing something. But what was it? He had looked through every transcript and every expense report. He was a failure at this job. All he did was warm the seat every night. And that seemed to be all that most of the people here cared about. This was their fast track to the cushy lifetime government job of non-existent responsibility and zero accountability. It was the gravy train express for minority housewives and hen-pecked husbands that knew next to nothing about life outside their own county and cared even less about seeing anything new and different. Their television sets were as audacious as they got about the rest of the world. Earth shattering events across the globe took a back seat to little Johnny's Friday night football games or the church's bake sale down at the First Baptist.

It wasn't that Guy thought they were bad people, it was just that they had no ambition for anything better. But he did. He did want something better than what was in Lloyd County, Texas. This place was killing him. It was sucking the life force out of him and the only thing it was giving back was a slow alcohol dependency. And it wasn't even good alcohol. It was cheap rot-gut moonshine. It hardly seemed like a fair trade in Guy's mind as he sat there sipping 'shine' out of an old mason jar in an abandoned Piggly Wiggly.

Chapter 11

In the months since he arrived Doc had kept his head low and mouth shut on the advice of Farmer. It had been hard on him because he didn't understand the mentality of the other inmates nor could he seem to get a grasp on the seemingly irrational and disjointed logic of the guards either. Every day it was a new reality to him. Everything that he had learned the day before was obsolete or irrelevant twenty four hours later. He would be let out to go to work at 5:30 a.m. one day and not until 6:45 a.m. the next. Breakfast was called at 3:30 a.m. on Monday for runny unsweetened oatmeal, but on Tuesday they would be rolling the doors at 2:30 a.m. to go eat the three day old rubber pancakes. There was no consistency or continuity in prison life. He had been assigned to work in showers picking up the discarded underwear and sweeping up the used soap chips. It was as menial a job as any ever created by man. He spent the hours in the steam hunched over a broom picking up dirty dingy boxers with the broom handle while slogging mushy soap into a pastel pile of gooey filth. He hated it, but he resigned himself to his fate. At moments like this he couldn't believe that he had a medical degree and once pampered the most prestigious people in the state. He cried inside a hundred times. He had lost his life and his dignity. He felt that his life couldn't get any worse than this; shoveling up skid marked skivvies.

"Hey there, snow bunny." came a deep baritone voice

Doc turned to see a tall skinny black man standing naked and uncomfortably close behind him.

"I be checking you out, sugar" said the skinny black guy.

Doc couldn't help but notice the man's pendent as it swung from side to side slapping against each wet thigh. His purple lips were washed out looking in appearance compared to his dark onyx skin.

Doc did a quick side step to evade the swinging pendulum.

"I'm not interested, Dude." said Doc as he put his head down and resumed his sweeping.

"But I am" said the skinny black guy *"I am VERY interested."*

Just then Doc realized that life could get a lot worse as the skinny black guy grabbed Doc's hand and put it on his growing shaft. Doc tried to pull away, but the skinny black guy's grip was like a vice. Doc began to panic and his eyes dilated in fear. He scanned the area to look for help. His eyes locked immediately on a young guard standing in the doorway next to a very familiar short black pigmy. The guard smirked and turned his back disappearing from the scene and dashing any hope of rescue in Doc's mind as Doc was being forced to his knees.

The broom crashed to the wet floor and Doc slipped on the mushy soap. Attention from a throng of black guys, in various stages of undress, was completely attuned to Doc and his predicament. Upon the guard's departure, mob mentality shot through the naked crowd like a heroin rush. Whooping and hollering filled the showers as the horny horde amped up to participate in a good old fashion prison rape. Latinos and whites were rushing to the exits. There would be no witnesses to Doc's sexual assault. Naked black men were moving into Doc's peripheral vision on all sides. In a few seconds he was going to be brutally gang raped and left for dead. All he could do was pray. Pray for a miracle.

"You gonna like my kind of lovin', snow bunny." Said the skinny black guy as he smiled and used Doc's hand to stroke himself. Doc saw for the first time that the soon-to-be rapist was missing a front central incisor. In a momentary flash, Doc mind instinctually remembered the most frequent causes for lost and broken front teeth and in that nanosecond it was as if his brain had figured out a defense all on its own.

Doc's hand flew to the floor latching onto the fallen broom handle. The broom stick became his Excalibur as it sliced through the steamy fog to land with utter brute force on its squishy target with pin point precision. The fleshy pop echoed through the shower and every pair of legs in the place instinctively went together in sympathy to the excruciating pain that had just been delivered to the would-be rapist. Tears instantly formed and rolled down his face as he doubled over and wailed in inconceivable pain. In one single blow Doc had paralyzed and incapacitated the skinny rapist and the mob.

He lay on the floor writhing in agony and gasping for air between each long earsplitting scream. Doc had deftly delivered a crushing blow to the sexual predator's scrotum that exploded one of his gonads. Each blood curdling scream of the skinny black guy became more penetrating than the last as panic set in about his injured ball sac and it began to fill with blood. It had swollen to the size of a cantaloupe in a matter of seconds and didn't seem to be stopping. Such yelling couldn't go unnoticed by the security goon squad, which would arrive in moments with tear gas and in full riot gear. If he stayed, then he knew he would be sprayed first and asked questions later. He had seen big hardened inmates reduced to sniveling babies. Slimy green mucus and stringy white snot flowed in an unending stream out of their noses. Acid like tears couldn't be stopped as they cascaded over grotesquely red swollen deformed eyes. It was barbaric and inhumane, but the goon squad used it abundantly and indiscriminately on everyone in the area. Convicts were now in full stampede to get out of the shower room and as far away from the scene as possible. And that included Doc, who got up and ran as fast as he could, disappearing into the chaos and panic.

Chapter 12

After several pointless hours of research and even more pointless hours of drinking, Guy's eyes were bloodshot road maps. They hung heavy with fatigue. Exhaustion had dulled his senses and impaired his ability to get anything meaningful accomplished, except for a nice mellow buzz, so he gathered up his laptop and walked out the door. This night had been like all the rest. A big waste of time.

Guy staggered slightly to the old car that he and his roommates shared. It was beat up with rust spots and had a slow oil leak. The door creaked loudly as he pried it open. The bent key wobbled in the ignition as Guy turned it. Nothing. He turned it again. Same result. Nothing. He hated the old car and wished that he had the money to get one of his own.

He set the near empty jar of moonshine on the dash since it was too big for the drink holder. He popped the lever for the hood and got out. The slow oil leak had caked the engine with grime and grease from years of neglect. Guy removed his class ring and set it on the fender, so as not to dirty it up with engine oil and grease like the last time. He jiggled the battery cables and looked over the engine to see if there was any other obvious problem.

Blue and red strobe lights suddenly filled the parking lot and he was immediately blinded by an intense spot light. His heart rate accelerated in a matter of seconds and felt as if it was going to beat right through his chest.

"Whatcha doing there, boy?" came a distinct southern drawl from behind the powerful white beam.

"I'm just having a little bit of car trouble, officer." Guy said.

Armed with his own flashlight and looking inside of the old car the deputy stepped in front of the white beam as he slowly approached Guy.

"Well, it looks like you might have a little bit more than just car trouble here." said the deputy with his flashlight fixed on the jar of moonshine.

"Aw shit!" said Guy under his breath.

"Have you been drinking tonight, son?" asked the deputy.

"Yes, sir, but I haven't been driving" Guy said lightheartedly hoping that the deputy might respond to a little humor. No such luck.

"Are you trying to be funny, son?" the deputy asked rhetorically *"Because this is a serious matter."*

"Yes, sir" Guy said *"I know it is."*

"Why don't you just put your hands right up here on the car" ordered the deputy, *"for both our safety."*

The deputy frisked Guy roughly. Guy was placed in handcuffs and sat on the ground like a common criminal. This was outrageous. Guy told himself that the police were supposed to help people not harass them.

The deputy searched the car's interior and came out with a very old dried up 'roach' that Guy knew must have been left there by one of his roommates.

"You gotta drug problem, son?" asked the smirking deputy holding up the tiny piece of rolled paper.

"No" replied Guy.

This elicited a slight chuckle from the deputy, *"Well, I think you do now, son."*

Chapter 13

"What the fuck happened?" Farmer yelled as he came in the cell.

Doc just lifted his head, *"I don't want to talk about it"* and rolled over in his bunk.

"Well, you be the only mutha-fucka on the unit that don't." Farmer said *"Everybody be talking 'bout some shit that went down in the showers. They comin' up to me all day asking if I know about what my celly did."*

"Man, I am so fucking sick of this place" Doc yelled. *"I ain't going to be somebody's fucking punk. They can just lock me up now or kill me because shit ain't going down like that."* Doc's adrenaline was still pumping and he began to get more agitated with each breath. He hadn't even noticed that he had taken to using prison vernacular and lingo. Something he hated. But he was wound up tight and had a hundred scenarios going through his mind. It was racing with possibilities.

"Shhh." Farmer said. *"Calm down and tell me what the fuck happened."*

Doc told him everything. They spent hours going over every incident that had occurred over the past several months. Farmer listened intently and Doc was glad to get all the shit off his chest finally. When it was all over Farmer simply said.

"I wish ya woulda told me sooner. I will take care of this." And placed his hand on Doc's shoulder to give him a reassuring pat. Doc was grateful to have a friend like Farmer.

*****

Farmer had already put the word out. Nobody was to tell the guards or the investigators about Doc's involvement in the shower episode. They would lock him up in Segregation for sure and possibly give him a free world charge of aggravated assault, if they found out.

Farmer had friends wired in all over the prison unit. Both in white and gray uniforms. He was the unit painter and as such he worked directly for the big man.

The Assistant Warden.

He was known to be the Warden's 'boy' and as such it gave him a ton of 'stroke'; prison vernacular for influence and power. Farmer could come and go just about as he pleased any time or anywhere in the prison. All the guards knew that he was untouchable. One word in passing from Farmer to the Asst. Warden could get a guard, or even an officer, suspended. The guards hated him because he had more power and influence than they did, but they feared his power; thus they gave him a wide berth.

Instead of heading to chow, Farmer made a detour to the count room to talk with his buddy, Joey Flowers. Joey was doing forty years for shot-gunning four rival gang members in the face. He was a long timer who had worked his way into a very powerful and profitable position as the clerk for the count room. The count room was responsible for housing and job assignments for the entire prison and Joey was at the top of the food chain. For ten dollars of commissary or five squares, cigarettes, he could put you in any job you wanted or in any cell that you liked.

Farmer didn't get much money on his books on a regular basis, so he used his wits and his entrepreneurial skills to survive and get by. This made him the perfect prison hustler. Most of the time the stuff he was using to trade belonged to the prison anyway. He had ten different deals going all of the time, but they always ended the same with Farmer having a locker full of commissary. But tonight Farmer wanted something different and he wasn't going to leave until he had it.

Chapter 14

Adrenaline was pumping through Guy's veins now replacing his nice mellow buzz with a border line panic attack. His breathing was spotty and rapid. Two more squad cars had arrived as back up. It was a hot Texas night and Guy was sweating 180 proof from every pore, partly from the horrible humidity and partly from anxiety about going to jail for a roach that his brain dead roommates had left in the car. He could just hear his mother now as she lectured him to no end about every mistake he had ever made in his life, which of course would include his choice of roommates.

When he entered college he was forced to make a decision about where to live.

He could either stay at his mother's wonderful home and listen to her drone on nightly in her drunken stupor about how bad she had been mistreated by his father and all the rest of the sorry unappreciative fuckers in the world *or* he could meagerly subsist on Ramen soup seven nights a week and move out into a virtual slum apartment with two of the most utterly useless, spoiled and self-centered individuals on the planet.

 The choice had been simple.

He dreaded having to call his mother from a jail cell at this time of night because she would already be completely blotto and probably wouldn't even remember that he called. Of course that was predicated on whether she was sober enough to even answer the phone. He would probably be in for a long stay as a guest of the county. Lately, every aspect of his life seemed to be permeated by 'Big Red' Johnson.

Deputy Dawg, as Guy now referred to him, sauntered back to him with a cocky cop strut and with his right hand riding high on the butt of his revolver.

'What a prick.'

"Well, this must be your lucky night." crowed the deputy. *"I am going to let you go with just a warning this time, but I am going to do a little investigating on you, so you keep your nose clean and we can forget this ever happened. Do you understand?"*

"Thank you, sir" Guy was doing cart wheels in his mind.

"But," chimed the deputy as he picked up Guy's ring and cash from the front hood of the squad car *"I am gonna confiscate a few of these items because they might have been obtained from illegal drug sales."*

Guy loved that ring.

"Do I get a receipt, so I can get it all back when you are done?" Guy asked.

"Oh! You want a receipt, do you?" Deputy Dawg asked incredulously *"Well, that might be a problem. You see, all the receipts are at the station and if I take you there then I am going to have to charge you and book you."* The deputy let Guy have a moment to think before he quickly added. *"Is that what you want to do, son?"*

Guy knew what was going on now and that he would never see his precious ring or the $22.00 cash again.

"Uhh, no officer. I think it will be alright" Guy said meekly.

"Good decision, son," said the deputy as he pocketed the ring and cash.

Guy was left sitting on the parking curb as the squad cars drove off. He was as angry as he ever been in his life. The deputy had humiliated him and robbed him; and for that Guy swore to himself that somehow and someday he would get even with that cock-sucking son-of a bitch if it was the last thing he ever did.

*****

The fire of revenge burned hot like a coal inside Guy's gut. He couldn't let it go of it. No matter how hard he tried. He couldn't stop thinking about Deputy Dawg and his class ring. He hadn't been able to sleep or eat since it was stolen from him. The thought of that fat fuck wearing his ring; the ring that he had worked so hard for, was tearing his guts out. A thousand revenge schemes had hatched in his head, but Guy was an analyst and he knew they weren't realistic. They just made him feel better for the moment, but that hot lump of revenge was still smoldering in his belly on the long walk home.

The rage was still burning and his brain was turning. The seasonal night air cleared the alcohol cobwebs from his brain and his mind started processing information like never before. Suddenly, he was like a Cray super computer. Thoughts were so clear now. He was seeing things and organizing them in whole new ways. It was as if the rage had released some new super amino acid that made his brain fire on 32 freaking turbo charge cylinders. He was a new man.

No, he was motivated man. A very angry motivated man.

He had what some preacher called a goddamn 'purpose driven life'.

And that purpose was now....revenge.

Chapter 15

Joey Flowers sat at his work desk in front of his monitor. Prison 'sucked' no matter what, but you could make it suck a lot less, if you could land a plush job like his. On paper and to the rest of the civilian world, wardens may have been in charge of the prison, but it was the inmates who really ran it. There wasn't a single thing in the entire prison that wasn't done by the inmates, with the exception of manning the outside guard towers. If you wanted something done inside of prison walls, then you had to come to people like Joey. Twenty years of Joey's life had been spent inside this prison. On the outside he would already be eligible for retirement, but there was no such thing as retirement in prison and Joey was now at the pinnacle of the prison hierarchy. He had spent years in crappy grunt jobs working his way up by kissing up to one boss after another. He knew how the game was played and he played to win. Other prisoners may have called him a suck ass, but they were slaving away in hot crappy jobs and eating tasteless shit in the inmate chow hall. Joey still wore white, like all inmates did, but is clothes were now starched and pressed daily for him by other inmates. He sat in a cool air conditioned office and ate good food prepared to order in the O.D.R.., the Officers Dining Room. Plus, as an added bonus, the civilian ladies that worked for the prison, and that he flirted with, brought him extra free world food from the outside in their lunches. He especially loved when holidays and birthdays came around because he would eat like a king.

Yeah, he had it made. He was 'The Man'.

There was only one other person in the prison that could rival him in power and influence. And that person had just walked through his door. The two of them weren't what anyone would call friends, but they got along because he was the one guy on the entire unit that never once tried to muscle in and take Joey's job. He had never been a threat.

"Farmer!" Joey yelled with a big smile on his face. *"How's it hangin'?"*

"To the left." replied Farmer.

Prison pleasantries were like a dance. If you knew the right steps you would look great but if you didn't, then you could end up on the floor or looking like a fool.

Farmer was a dancer. *"Flowers, you look incredible. Shit, man, look at those guns. How much are you lifting now?"*

Joey was a body builder and Farmer knew that he spent hours on the weight machine in the gym pumping up his muscles. Joey was proud of his twenty four inch biceps and he loved to show them off. He even had his shirts tapered so that his muscles looked larger and more pronounced. Joey's entire upper body was tatted front and back, from waist to neck and wrist to wrist, so that even when he was wearing nothing at all he still looked as if he was wearing a skin tight dark tee shirt over his mounds of bulging muscle.

"I'm benching 315 lbs. now" said Flowers as he flexed his pecs for Farmer. They continued to exchange stories and complain about the officers whom they both disliked. With the obligatory chit-chat out of the way and a proper amount of respect paid by Farmer, Joey finally got down to business.

"Farmer, you didn't come all the way here to tell me how pretty I am or ask me out on a date, so what do you want?" Flowers asked, leaning back in his chair.

Farmer was grateful that he was ready to do business. *"I need a favor."*

"Don't tell me. Let me guess." said Flowers as he put his fingers to his head imitating a mind reader. *"Could it be the something involving your white boy celly?"*

Farmer had hoped to get here before Flowers had heard about the shower incident and his celly's involvement because he knew the price of a favor would be a lot higher. *"So you heard already, huh?"* It wasn't so much a question as it was a statement of the fact.

"Farmer do you know why I like you?" asked Flowers as he opened his desk drawer to pull out a piece of contraband free-world chocolate to offer Farmer. *"It's because you have never tried to take my job. You are the only one that never has tried to take it away from me. Why is that?"*

Only Farmer and his celly, Doc, knew the real reason that he couldn't do Flower's job and it was why he needed to keep his celly safe. He had been secretly working with his celly every night learning to read. He was actually enjoying it and he looked forward to their sessions every night with anticipation all day long. His celly had made it fun. His school teachers had never done that. Farmer felt silly at first when his celly had traded some tight whites for some tabloid magazines and brought them home for him to practice on. He was learning to read while he kept tabs on his favorite sexy celebrity girls. And the pictures made it a lot more interesting. Doc had really come through for him and

65

he wanted to come through for Doc this time.

"I am happy where I am at" said Farmer *"and you know that nobody could do this job as good as you, Flowers."* A little lying and a lot of flattery was what was needed right now, so Farmer laid it on extra thick. *"Besides that, I don't ever want to go up against you."* Farmers said humbly.

"That's the right answer," said Flowers cocky like *"so what you want today, Farmer?"*

This was it. Farmer knew that he was asking Flowers to give him the Holy Grail. Especially, since it was for a newbie and someone that hadn't paid his dues or put in his time.

"I need you to give my boy a new job right away." said Farmer.

"Sure, I can do that for an old friend" said Flowers. His attitude was all business now. *"It's $10 in commissary. Coffee and assorted pastries would be fine."* He glanced at the chart of job openings taped to the pristine wall that Farmer had only painted last week. *"How about a nice janitor job in Medical?"*

Farmer knew anything in Medical was greatly sought after because it was air conditioned. It was a nice job for anyone else, but Farmer knew where he wanted him to work.

"I was hoping that you could put him in the Law Library." Farmer replied.

Flowers froze and slowly turned his head to face Farmer to meet him eye to eye. *"Yeah, you aren't wanting much, are you?"*

Farmer remained quiet because this was the deciding moment. Experience had taught him that the next person to talk would lose the argument. The next ten seconds felt like ten years and it took every ounce of discipline that Farmer possessed to stay quiet.

"Well, that's a whole different ball game." said Flowers. *"That's going to run you more than just $10. You asking for best Cadillac job on the*

unit. I don't even know what kind of price to put on that. What have you got to trade for something that great?"

Farmer knew that it would cost him more than just $10 in sweets, so he didn't come unprepared. Farmer had done his homework and knew the one and only thing in the entire prison that Joey wanted, but couldn't get for himself.

"Casino." was all Farmer had to say.

Flowers froze.

Farmer knew from the look on Flowers face that he had pressed the right button.

"Bullshit!" said Flowers.

'Casino' was really Guillermo Rios, the most sought after homosexual on the entire unit. Flowers, despite being heterosexual and married, was completely and totally in love with 'Casino'. He was a small delicate Latino boy of twenty two that looked barely fourteen due to his smooth body and gorgeous looks. He had gotten the nickname 'Casino' because whoever got him had hit the jackpot. He had been the object of so many fights that he had had to be segregated and put on Safe Keeping by the administration. Flowers may have had the power to assign him to any cell he wanted, but he couldn't get him out of Safe Keeping. Only a Warden could authorize that.

Flowers was on his feet and standing right up next to Farmer now.

"If you could really do that, then I will put your celly anywhere you want." said Flowers, with desperate excitement.

Chapter 16

Clara served a big heap of biscuits with lots of wavy gravy.

Clara's Diner was an institution in Lloyd County that had been serving good food at cheap prices for over fifty years on the old town square. It was ideally situated across the street from the historic courthouse, which meant it was a daily favorite of deputies and lawyers before they headed to court. Like all small Texas towns it was also a place to gather and hear all of town's gossip. Guy couldn't think any better place to start his investigation than right here.

Being raise in Lloyd County meant that he wasn't a stranger to the people that filled the sparse dining room. Not to mention that he looked pretty darn good in his black cowboy hat.

Clara was furnished with typical cheap red vinyl chairs and brown Formica tables. They were chipped and had the occasional pieces missing on their edges from years of use by good old boys. Gray haired waitresses from a by-gone era still walked around in white hospital shoes. The youngest one was probably in her sixties, but just barely. They didn't believe in modern rules and convention. Waitresses and customers alike smoked as they pleased, and if you objected, then they were more likely to throw you out than the cigarette. Dishes clanked and orders were shouted back and forth through the kitchen window with the usual sass. Customers were greeted by name as they entered and left. A fat red headed teenager, who was most likely the owner's grandson, cleared tables as fast as they were left.

Guy's waitress poured coffee with both hands out of two different pots when she wasn't carrying four plates of breakfast on one arm. According to her puffy embroidered flowery name tag her name was Leona. Guy was amazed by the old waitress' skill. They didn't make them like her anymore. He sopped up the last bit of wavy gravy with biscuit and busied himself with the morning paper. He had purposely situated himself at a two top table in the center of the room. He had donned his has old cowboy hat and work shirt so that he would blend in with the rest of the farm hands that the frequented places like Clara's in every rural community. He was doing surveillance, but in places like this, he would have to do it while hiding in plain sight. A center table allowed him to easily eavesdrop on conversations all around him, something that a side booth or corner table could never afford him to do. It amazed him how much information freely flowed without any censorship in this kind of setting. People just assumed that the only other people that could hear their conversations were the ones sitting at their own table, but Guy was absorbing information like a sponge. He had been coming here almost every day for a week. The NSA couldn't do a better job than he was doing.

The booth diagonally behind him to his left had two of "Big Red's" deputies squeezed into it. They ate the large breakfast special as they passed the time before going to court. They were half way finished before Guy's attention was tweaked.

"Are you sure that we can get away with this?" asked the younger of the two.

"Stop worrying." said the big potbellied deputy as he stuffed another fork full of pancakes into his mouth. *"We been doing this shit since you were in diapers."*

"But what if we get caught or someone reports us?" implored the younger deputy. *"I can't afford to go to jail, Jonesy."*

"Relax, you worry too much, Salinas?" said Deputy Jones *"We ain't the only ones doing it. Everybody be getting a little bit. The key is just don't get greedy or sloppy."* He took a swig of orange juice to wash down the pancakes. *"And if someone complains, so what? It just gets covered up and Big Red announces that after a thorough investigation that they can't find any evidence of wrongdoing and that the complainant is just a disgruntled criminal trying to make trouble for honest upstanding and dedicated officers that put their asses on the line every day to protect innocent civilians of this great county."*

"But what if s....... the arrest s.....evidence sheet?" protested Salinas, but now they were speaking in hushed tones and Guy was having difficulty hearing them now.

"Can't happen." said Jones as he leaned in closer to talk to Salinas *"Nobody but the arr.......reports and that ain't gonna happen because we........to prevent that. So you ju........ing. Quit being a little pussy."*

Ooow! Yelled Salinas as he grabbed his cheek.

"Man, when are you going to go to see Dr. Shaddix and get that tooth looked at?" asked Jones as he ate the last bite of his flapjacks. *"He gives all us deputies a discount on account* of *his friendship with Big Red. The only thing you got to lose is that pain, you big baby."* And with that, they threw a tip on the table and walked out the door.

"Can I get you something else, sugar?" asked Leona, the waitress, as she stood there with a coffee pot in one hand and smoking a cigarette with the other.

"No, ma'am." Guy said. *"Just get my bill, please?"*

As she turned and walked away, Guy said to himself in a very satisfied way, *'I think I got everything that I need.'*

Chapter 17

Farmer wasn't done yet.

He had gotten what he wanted for Doc, now it was time for some payback.

Doc had told Farmer about seeing the pigmy in the showers and Farmer knew at that moment that it had been a set up. Doc had spilled his guts about every little incident that had ever happened to him and Farmer was now certain that pigmy was behind every dirty little trick that had been pulled. Doc was too much of a good guy and way too naive to know what was needed in this situation. Farmer had warned them to lay off of Doc and since they had chosen to ignore him, he was within his convict rights to retaliate. In fact, convict law said that if these incidents went unchecked and unchallenged, then it would be open season on Doc, and Farmer would never be feared again. And that wasn't going to happen. Not if Farmer could help it.

Pigmy would be expecting an immediate frontal attack, so Farmer had cooked up a much better revenge. However, revenge was a dish best served cold and that was exactly how it was going to get served.

*****

Prison was always gloomy, but at this time of year it seemed to have a distinctive sadness to it. Even in South Texas the holidays were cold and depressing. Family weighed heavily on the minds of convicts. There were no decorations denoting the seasonal festivities nor anything merry to raise their spirits. No cheery people wishing each other the best. Nothing like that at all. Prison had only bitter, angry and lonely men that wanted to get out to see their families or be with their old girlfriends.

Doc stayed to himself and in his cell, which was where he was when Farmer came in with a huge sack of commissary.

"Ho, Ho, Ho!" shouted Farmer as he dragged the big bag into the cell. Shouts could be heard from all up and down the run.

"Farmer, how did you get to go to store today" came one voice full of jealousy.

"Who cares" came another voice, *"Are you gonna hook a brother up, Farmer?"*

"Just calm the fuck down" Farmer yelled back, *"My mom sent me some love and I bought a little something to go around for Christmas."*

Shouts and hollers could be heard on the entire cell block for ten minutes following Farmer's announcement. Today he was a hero and Santa Clause, both rolled into one. Doc's eyes brightened up at seeing his celly and his friend show up. Farmer had a million watt smile on his face.

"I come bearing gifts." said Farmer holding up his bag and dumping it on his bunk. The goodies and treats cascaded out and Doc's eyes got as big as saucers.

"Wow!" exclaimed Doc. He had never seen so much stuff at one time since he had arrived. It looked like Farmer had bought out the entire store.

"That ain't all of it." said Farmer as he reached deep inside his pants and underwear to produce a huge baggie full of sugar. Doc was stunned and bewildered.

Farmer saw the confusion on Doc's face and before he could even asked, Farmer said, *"Don't ask. It's for Christmas."*

And without any more explanation he began to put most all of it on his two small shelves, except for the sugar which he put in his locker for safe keeping. Doc knew that it was contraband that it had been gotten on the black market from the kitchen and that Farmer could catch a major case if he was caught with it. Sugar was like gold in prison because it was the main ingredient needed to make "hooch".

Farmer was meticulous in how he arranged his stuff, but when he was done he opened a package of chocolate cupcakes and handed one to Doc. They sat in silence and savored every delicious bite. Doc smiled and thanked Farmer profusely.

"Shut up" Farmer said *"just remember me when you get a come up sometime. Besides I need you to help me make up my Christmas cheesecakes for the whole cell block."*

"What?" Doc said, *"How do we do that?"* Doc had never heard of such a thing.

"Don't you worry that little smart brain of yours about that. I will do all the work and you can just hand me the stuff that I ask for." Farmer said confidently. *"And you might learn a little something from this big dumb nigger."*

They stayed up half of the night making one prison cheesecake after another. Doc had taken chemistry in college, but he was astounded by what he learned watching Farmer make cheesecake crusts from crushed up vanilla sandwich cookies. The most amazing part was when he mixed dry milk powder, a cool-off drink powder packet and a half can of warm Sprite together to make the cheesecake itself. The introduction of the warm soda caused an immediate bubbling thermal reaction that surprised Doc every time Farmer did it. It looked like a high school science experiment that created a lava flow. Doc wanted to try it, but Farmer was adamant about doing it himself. They made ten cheesecakes before the night was over.

The next day was Christmas Eve and Doc was glad that he didn't have to work, especially after what had happened the day before. Farmer had left and returned many times during the day. By evening time most everyone, except all the black Muslims, were settled into their cells awaiting the Christmas gift sacks from the local prison ministry to be passed out. The Muslims separated themselves into the day room for this while the Christian convicts celebrated the birth of Christ. The Muslims always made a big fuss about how they should be treated special and separate.

Farmer had managed to trade his sugar to the hooch maker on the cell block for some booze that had already been made. He and Doc sipped the homemade holiday cheer and talked to one another as real friends that cared about one another for the first time.

The Muslims weren't supposed to consume alcohol, but they were convicts, not choirboys. They had already broken innumerable laws and ended up in prison anyway, so one more wouldn't really matter in their eyes or the eyes of Allah. Besides most of them were just jailhouse converts that only declared themselves Muslim in order to get alternative meals and to get out of work for the additional Muslim holidays. They were simply doing what they always did. They were scamming the system.

And tonight they were all gathered together in the day room. Somehow they too had gotten a hold of some hooch and every one was in a jolly mood. Spirits were high and inhibitions were low. The stupid grin on the pigmy's face grew larger with each sip of alcohol.

*****

Farmer had sliced up all ten pies and had them distributed to each cell as a Christmas gift from him and Doc. Shout outs were given to them in abundance. At precisely nine o'clock the count bell went off and no movement whatsoever would be allowed until it was over, except for the janitor sweeping the wing; but even he couldn't leave the wing.

Once the count began, the tipsy Muslims noticed that everyone in the cells had gotten some of Farmer's cheesecake.

"Farmer." came a cry from the day room *"You ain't gonna show us no love?"* Convicts would be anyone's friend to get something that they wanted. Blacks were the worst and the most hypocritical of all. Once they got what they wanted from you, then you were just a piece of shit again.

"Where's that Christian charity?" shouted one of the Muslims.

To Doc's surprise Farmer was up and shouting back to them, *"I am a decent mutha-fucka and I treat everyone the same on Christmas. I made enough for everyone, including you niggas. I will have the janitor bring it to you, so shut the fuck up or you won't get shit."*

"Hey man" came another slurred voice, *"we cool. We appreciate it, man."*

Doc was shocked by the whole conversation. He had just spent a couple of hours getting to know Farmer better and spilling his guts out to him. And now he is being nice to some of the very sons-of-bitches that tried to rape him. What the hell was going on? Doc felt a little betrayed by his so-called friend and celly.

To Doc's amazement Farmer pulled out another cheesecake and slid it under the sliding door so that the janitor could take it to the day room. When he turned around he saw the hurt on Doc's face.

"Man, I don't care what you think. It's Christmas." Farmer said *"You have to trust me on this. And don't give me that look. I am your friend."*

They sat and ate their cheesecake and sipped their homemade wine. The radio was on and playing unending Christmas carols one after the other when a ruckus could be heard from the day room. At first it was just a single voice, but within moments a cacophony of urgent shouts could be heard coming from the day room. Some of the screams were panicky in nature. They were screaming for the guard, who was nowhere around, to come open the day room door and to let them in their cells.

"It's an emergency, goddamn it." screamed a familiar voice. *"Open these mother fucking doors now."* It was the pigmy and it sounded as if he was on the verge of tears.

Over the next few minutes the screams became louder and louder and more and more desperate.

Doc was up out of his bunk and next to the bars trying to hear what is going on, but Farmer continued to lie on his and enjoy the home made hooch. The noise had risen to a desperate crescendo and had become more and more frantic when Doc heard one of the Muslims scream at the top of his voice.

"Someone get a mother fucking guard to open this god damn door or else I am gonna shit my fuckin' pants here"

Doc quickly turned his head and saw Farmer grinning from ear to ear as he lifted his cup of cheer up to Doc and said, *"Merry Christmas, little buddy."* And with that he turned his cup up and drank the whole thing with complete satisfaction as the competing screams of panic became sickening shouts of disgusts by the arriving guards responding to the screams of the now freshly soiled Muslims.

The smell of feces wafted up to the cells nearest to the day room and now everyone knew that the entire Muslim congregation had defecated on themselves and all over the day room.

"You people got me fucked up with someone else" shouted the janitor *"I ain't cleaning that shit up. You nasty mother fuckers."*

Within minutes the goon squad arrived to quell the supposed uprising, but since it was count time and there wasn't any visible violence, they refused to open the day room and let sullied Muslims out. They obviously had no desire to intermix with the offensive smelling inmates that had crapped their pants. Doc could hear the Islamic inmates hurl vindictives at the guards. The inmates in their cells were now laughing and taunting the day room captives, which only compounded the embarrassment for them.

The entire wing was in an uproar.

In time, the Muslims were told to strip out of their soiled clothes and were escorted in mass to the shower room and allowed to finish their bowel movements and to shower themselves clean.

Then they were all summarily marched to lock up and given cases because when the goon squad did enter the day room they had found contraband hooch in all of their cups. However, the one thing they didn't find was one single piece of cheesecake anywhere. It had been completely consumed. The administration had attributed the entire mess to a bad batch of homemade hooch. Only Doc and Farmer knew the truth and that would be how it would remain.

Chapter 18

Guy felt like a new man.

Gone was the aimless post college slacker. He now had purpose in life. He was up at the crack of dawn and worked until late every night. He was a dynamo at the maze these days and he had caught more than just the attention of Jewels, the campaign manager.

"What do you have for me today, Guy" came a voice from over his shoulder.

Guy turned and craned his neck to see none other than the big man himself. Joe-Don Lilly. Guy nearly fell out of his seat trying to get up, but Joe-Don put a hand on his shoulder.

"Stay where you are, son." Commanded Joe-Don.

"Well, sir," Guy began *"I think I might have stumbled upon some discrepancies between the Sheriff's records and the court records."*

Joe-Don's friendly and casual demeanor noticeably changed to serious and interested. *"What kind of discrepancies?"*

"I am not quite sure yet, because I can't get access to the court records, but the arrest records don't seem consistent with the charges against the defendants." Guy explained as he held up several printed sheets and pointed to the computer screen.

Joe-Don's face remained stoic and impassive as he listened and questioned Guy about each police report that he had uncovered. Guy had been methodical and exhaustive in his research after what he had overheard at Clara's cafe and Joe-Don paid attention to Guy's entire presentation. When it was over Joe-Don didn't say a word to Guy, but he simply turned to Jewels and said, *"Find out if there is anything to all this. This is priority one."*

He started to walk away, but before he got two steps he stopped and pivoted on his polished oxfords to tell Jewels, *"And I think we need give this young man an office"* Joe-Don said it loud enough for everyone to hear. *"And a raise."*

"Something more befitting the new Director of Research." Then he looked right at Guy. *"Does that sound okay to you, son?'*

Guy almost sang, *"Yes, Sir!"* as he sprang to his feet to salute the Sheriff's candidate. *"I won't let you down, sir"*

Joe-Don laughed. *"I know you won't."* And with a wave of his hand he was gone leaving Jewels and Guy standing there.

"Well, that was quite impressive." Jewels said. *"You might have given me a heads up about it, you know."*

Guy could see that she was a little perturbed at him for capturing all of the attention when he was supposed to be working for her. He knew that she would have liked a little recognition too. *"I didn't know that he was coming by and I didn't think I was ready to let anyone know of my findings yet. There is still a lot to do. I mean, it could be a big fat dead end."*

"Well" she said with one eye brow raised *"it better not be, because as of*

now you make almost as much as I do. Which means that you are sitting at the grown-ups table now."

She let the gravity of that sink in for a moment. She saw the frightened countenance of Guy's face before she added, *"but don't worry, I am here for anything that you might need."* To which she gave him a little wink and quick pat on the butt before she left.

Now he was really scared. And a little excited.

Chapter 19

Farmer and Doc laughed and laughed. The more they drank, the more they laughed. The more they laughed the funnier it got. Farmer told Doc how he had made an extra cheesecake especially for pigmy and his brothers and how he had given the hooch maker five pounds of sugar to give the Muslims enough hooch to lower their guard so that they would eat the cheesecake. And just to make it more convincing, he had made enough real cheesecake for the entire cell block so that they wouldn't be suspicious. In fact, they had even begged for it. This made Farmer and Doc laugh even more. Doc thought Farmer was a genius. Even though he couldn't read or write yet, he was still a genius. Doc knew he could have never pulled something like that off.

The alcohol had begun to make him melancholy and he ruminated on how lucky he was to have such a great friend as Farmer.

They had completely forgotten about the Christmas gift bags that were to be passed out. It was almost midnight and the lights had already been dimmed, when they arrived and had been slipped through the bars. Their wing had been the last receive the gifts due to the incident in the day room with pigmy and the Muslims.

Doc laid in his bunk in the semi-darkness and opened his bag. It contained a bar of free world soap, three blank Christmas cards, a small New Testament bible and one small hand wrapped piece of hard candy that had been tied with a small piece of delicate ribbon. Attached to the ribbon was a small stenciled angel with childlike lettering below it that said, "You are loved."

Doc's eyes filled with water and the tears flowed. Doc couldn't think of anyone who loved him right now and his only friend in the whole world was now asleep and snoring in the bunk above him. He had never felt as alone or as abandoned as he did right now. Doc wasn't the least bit religious, but he prayed for the first time since he was a small child. He prayed that God would help him out of this horrible situation and give him the strength to endure the wretchedness of this place. And then, before he too drifted off, he thanked God for sending him Farmer.

*****

Joey Flowers was having the best Christmas in years. Farmer had delivered on his promise and tonight Joey was enjoying a romantic Christmas Eve in his cell with Casino. Joey hadn't been this happy in years. Despite being in prison for the past twenty years he had managed to get married twice while he was locked up. His last wife had been a guard. He had flirted with her for over a year and had even managed to steal a couple of moments of private time when no one else was around for some over the clothes action. She had pulled him out for extra duty and special projects whenever she could. Joey wasn't a fool. He knew that she wanted him and when the work was over she would take him to the showers and would watch as he teased her with his muscles and his exceptionally large manhood. She enjoyed watching him make it dance and jump for her under the wet showers. As time went on she got bolder and bolder until the opportunity presented itself for them to have intimate relations during a count period when they were alone and wouldn't be walked in on. It hadn't been very romantic, but Joey hadn't had sex with a female in over twelve years and it didn't matter to him. He had managed to nut up three times and she convulsed almost continuously. After that, she was a puppy dog that did everything that he wanted. She brought in contraband, put money on his books and even gave him oral sex about on demand.

Yeah, she was sprung and he was taking advantage of the situation. She even quit her job as a guard so that she could marry him. It had lasted about two years, but she found some ex-con on the outside, had his name tattooed on her right breast and left Joey with a quickie divorce.

Joey wasn't bummed out by it. After all he got a year of pussy and two years of fairly steady money, so it was a pretty good run. But she was a fat hag compared to the exotic sexiness of Casino. Casino was the prettiest human being that Joey had ever laid eyes on. Male or Female. It was love at first sight for Joey, but he was under no delusion that a gorgeous twenty two year old would ever be in love with him. Sure he had a huge piece and a great body, but he was now forty years old with average looks. He wasn't any Brad Pitt. That was for sure, but he was cute in his own way; however, to Casino's surprise, Joey had a sweet and funny personality. Casino found himself actually attracted to Joey. He liked the way Joey teased him and treated him 'normal'. The thing that he like the most was that Joey treated him with love and respect and not like some punk the way others tried to do, which he hated. Joey was different. He didn't care what other people thought or said. He was proud to be seen with Casino. He would openly hold Casino's hand in the dayroom when they watched TV and call him 'Babe' in front of everyone. He made Casino feel special and not like a prison punk or piece of meat. In a single word, Joey Flowers was 'Wonderful'.

*****

Christmas morning had arrived and Farmer was surprised when he woke up to find Doc awake and packed up.

"What the hell?" Farmer said as he looked down from the top bunk. *"Where the fuck are you going?*

Without looking up, *"I'm moving."* Doc replied.

Farmer began to protest, but Doc cut him off, *"And nothing you say can change my mind."*

Farmer was dumbfounded and he was more than a little angry. What a sorry ungrateful little son-of-a-bitch. After all that Farmer had done for him now he was 'catching out' on him. He was about to verbally unload on Doc when he noticed the grin on Doc's face.

"Merry Christmas!" Doc yelled as his smiled at Farmer. He was also holding out a small package that had been crudely wrapped with a piece of cloth from the Textile plant where weaving fabric for the inmate uniforms were done. It was tied with a single shoe lace from a work boot. Farmer was touched. In all his years in prison no one had ever surprised him with a Christmas gift. Despite its simple wrapping it looked like the most elegant gift in the world to Farmer.

"Okay" said Farmer taking the gift from Doc *"but why are you all packed up?"*

"Just open your present." chimed Doc.

Farmer delicately and slowly untied the package and slipped the fabric piece from the gift. Doc had given him a very nice mechanical pencil and a book of Crosswords. Farmer was touched.

"Read the card." said Doc.

Farmer found the card tucked inside book. It was one of the cards that they had received in their gift bags, but it had been written on.

"Go on." urged Doc. *"You can read it."*

Farmer instinctively looked around to see if anyone could see him. Satisfied that they were alone he put finger to the card and slowly sounded out each word.

"Mer-ry - Christ-mas - to - my- best - friend - in - the - whole - world."

Doc was on the verge of tears. He was extremely proud of Farmer as he read the rest of the card one syllable at a time. Doc had intentionally written it all in one syllable words, except for Merry Christmas, so that Farmer could read it.

"Grab - your - bed - and - move - it - down." Farmer smiled and jumped down to give Doc a hug. Giving up the lower bunk was a big deal and

the gesture wasn't lost on Farmer. He really appreciated it and it meant a lot to him. Farmer choked up on the inside, but he held it all in because that was just what he had to do. But he loved this little white boy like he was his own brother.

"Man, I can't believe that you be given me your lower bunk." said Farmer.

Doc just looked at him. *"Well, you better hurry up and move your stuff before I change my mind."*

"Oh, hell no! This is my crib now." Farmer said mockingly as he pointed to the empty bunk. *"You ain't ever getting this sweet spot back."*

As they helped each other move their junk to each other's bunks Farmer handed Doc an envelope. *"I got you a little Christmas gift also. I didn't get ya no card and it ain't no good until tomorrow, but I hope ya like it."*

Doc opened the sealed envelope with three big letters scrawled on the outside. "D.O.C." All that was inside was a thin slip of computer generated paper. Doc read it over but before he could finish it, Farmer chimed in. *"It's a fucking job change. No more slopping soap in the showers. You, my friend, now have the best Cadillac job on the entire unit. You are going to be working in the Law Library"*

"What?" Doc said *"I don't understand?"*

"Well, maybe you can understand this" Farmer shouted *"Merry Fucking Christmas from your best friend in whole world!*

Chapter 20

Guy's new office was in the fresh produce section.

But he didn't care if they put him in the men's room. Anything was better than being stuck in the maze. There were no frills in the new office. It possessed only modular furniture with coordinated gray fabric and gray Formica that covered all of the snap-in style office accessories. It was still a cubicle by definition, but at least the walls went up eight feet and it had a door.   Not one bit of color could be distinguished anywhere in it, but it was still an oasis to Guy's eyes. He was really moving up. It was all happening so fast.

Sleep had been almost non-existent to him the previous night.   Anxiety had kept him awake. He spent two hours of tossing and turning while listening to one of his roommate's nocturnal escapades with a girl that he had drunkenly dragged home after trolling his favorite bar.   It had become too much to endure. He could only take a certain amount of sexually muffled, "oh yeah, baby's", through the thin apartment walls. And apparently, that magical number was thirty-two, because that's when Guy threw his covers off and took his laptop to the Hot Biscuit, the local all-night restaurant.   He could use their free Wi-Fi and drink copious amounts of coffee while he 'phished' around the Internet for more evidence against 'Big Red' Johnson.   Guy now viewed every cop that came into the place, whether they be city, county or game warden, with suspicion.   He noticed that they came into Hot Biscuit regularly since it was probably one of the only restaurants in Lloyd County that stayed open all night.   He was hunkered down in his favorite old worn 'Chevrolet' ball cap when he heard that voice. That unmistakable voice. There was no other one like it.

It was Deputy Dawg.

Guy sank lower into the booth and pulled his cap further down, so as not to be recognized by the crooked cop. He couldn't believe his eyes when he saw his ring on Deputy Dawg's fat pinky. He burned hot. He wanted to take a meat cleaver and hack off the plump pinky and cram it down Deputy Dawg's fat throat after he had retrieved his precious ring. The fantasy played itself over and over in his head, becoming more gruesome and violent with each re-enactment.

Guy was sitting there fuming when his day dream was disrupted by Deputy Dawg's cell phone. Guy strained to listen.

"Hey, baby!" crowed Deputy Dawg *"Are you missing me?"*

Guy's stomach was nauseous at the thought of this pork butt being amorous with anyone. The picture of rooting pigs was the visual that filled Guy's brain, which in turn caused him to no longer want the link sausages on his plate.

"I am over getting a little something at the Hot Biscuit, but I'll be there in fifteen minutes." said the deputy *"Are you at the Budget Motel?"*

He motioned to the young waitress to lend him her pen. *"Alright, what room is that again?"*

"103. Okay, baby, I will step on it and have my big nightstick ready for you?" Deputy Dawg cooed into the phone with sickening smooching noises.

"Hurry up with those biscuits and eggs, Darlene. I gotta go!" Hollered the horny deputy as he pocketed his phone.

"Just hold your horses, Ernie, it will be ready in 5 minutes." Darlene screamed back from behind the service window.

Deputy Dawg sauntered back to the men's room and Guy shot out of his booth like a bullet. He was out of the door in a flash. He looked left and then right. There it was. He immediately ran and dived under the front bumper of the patrol car. He prayed that no one would drive up in the next thirty seconds. That was all he needed. Scrambling onto his back, he removed the tiny flashlight key chain from his pocket, swearing that the next time he saw his mom that he would kiss his her for all of her crazy late night purchases from the Home Shopping Channel. He lit up the bottom of the squad car's radiator with the tiny beam of light, something he had done many times on the old Junker that he shared with his roommates. He could have probably done it in the dark, but the small LED flashlight made finding the drain plug effortless. He turned the screw a couple of quarter turns with the attached wrench/screwdriver attachment of the flashlight. Boy, was his mom going to get a big kiss. This wasn't what she had envisioned him doing with it when she bought it, but she was right when she said, *"You're going to thank me one day when you need this."*

Well, she was right. He was going to thank her for sure. Water began to slowly drip out of the cooling system. Guy snapped off the light and shimmied out from under the patrol vehicle and jumped to his feet. He quickly looked around. Still clear. He quickly walked to the left rear and leaned over and efficiently unscrewed the two shorter antennas from the car's roof. He stuffed them into his cargo pants pocket and then circuitously walked all the way around the building and stopped at the corner opposite where the patrol car sat.

He removed his cellular phone from his pocket and opened the back so as to remove the GPS chip. After reassembling his phone he dialed 911.

Moments later Deputy Dawg came rushing out of the Hot Biscuit. He jumped in the patrol car and spun out of the parking space throwing a plume of gravel for ten feet behind it. When the car reached the road the red and blue emergency lights came on. The rear tires caught traction on the asphalt and they began to smoke on the two lane highway as they grabbed the road with a vengeance.

The speeding patrol car disappeared over the horizon and Guy couldn't help but smile as he notice a long wet streak between the pair of black lines that the patrol car left on the deserted highway.

He strolled back into the Hot Biscuit. Darlene, the waitress, emerged looking around with a bag from the kitchen.

"If you're looking for the deputy, he just left." Guy said twirling his keys and motioning to the empty parking lot.

"Damn!" Darlene said as she put the bag on the counter. *"Well, I am sure he will be back"*

"Oh, I wouldn't bet on it." said Guy. *"Could I get a warm up on my coffee?'*

"Sure, sweetie." She picked up the coffee pot and as she filled his cup, *"Well, that sure is a snazzy little key chain you got there. I bet that comes in handy at times"* she said.

"You can't imagine." Guy said as he tore open a packet of sugar to put in

85

his coffee. *"You just can't imagine."*

*****

Deputy Dawg, aka Deputy Ernie Sinclair, was pushing the old police car hard. He had the pedal down and the speedometer was hovering near ninety mph. The emergency lights were all on and the siren was wailing at full blast. Deputy Dawg's adrenaline was also pumping full blast. He had both hands on the wheel and both eyes peeled on the road as it rushed past him, which meant that he wasn't paying any attention to his instrument panel. If he had been, he might have noticed that the temperature gauge was rising at an alarming rate. The needle had moved out of the safe green zone and was quickly rising through the yellow and the squad car was making a calamity of different noises. The sirens were raging. The dispatch radio would burst in with its usual discord and the engine was revving as it never had before.

Deputy Dawg couldn't wait to get to this call. These were the kind of calls he loved to get. He knew that he would be able to make some money tonight. Greed consumed his thoughts as the temperature gauge exited the cautionary yellow zone and crept into the red danger zone. He was now pretty far out into the rural area of the county but almost to his destination. He failed to notice that the dispatch radio had finally dissipated completely and the siren's wail had also distracted him from the growing growl of the car's engine.

Deputy Dawg did notice a light vapor of fog that had begun to roll over the squad car as it ripped its way down the country road. Light rural fog was not an unusual phenomenon late at night in rural areas of Lloyd County, so he was unfazed by its sudden appearance. He was just about to arrive at the call's destination and he was already thinking about what charges he could trump up against these 'girls'. They would be so easy to shake down. They would give him anything to avoid going to jail. Easy money. And maybe more.

He slowed to turn into the narrow drive of the private club's parking lot. As he did the hand painted phallic sign that was the club's logo was obscured from his view by a billowing cloud of white smoke erupting from his patrol car's engine.   He was engulfed in hot steam and immediately stopped the car. Unfortunately, that had caused the car to die completely on the small bridge that crossed the rural culvert. The hot steam whistled as it escaped the hot engine with ferociousness. Its high pitch shrill filled the quiet night and competed with the still wailing siren.

The parking lot commotion had caught the attention of the club's patrons. They poured out of the club by the dozens. Deputy Dawg immediately grabbed his shoulder radio and spoke frantically into the microphone as he fled the smoking vehicle.

"Dispatch? Dispatch? Officer needs assistance!" the panic in his voice was evident. The crowd began to laugh openly at his desperation.

"You gonna have to scream louder than that, Sugar, if you want your mama to hear you from out here." came a high pitched falsetto voice from the crowd.

"DISPATCH! OFFICER NEEDS ASSISTANCE, GODDAMN IT!" Deputy Dawg was screaming into his shoulder mic, but no one responded. He was all alone and now he was surrounded by a bunch of fruitcakes and fairies. This place was the 'Snake Ranch'. It was a private club, built out in the boonies of the unincorporated part of the county for queers and deviants to congregate without fear of persecution from the local church going folks of the town. Deputy Dawg had been on a few late night calls to this place and had been able to shake them down pretty easily; however, they wised up and began hiring their own security, so Deputy Dawg nor his buddies got calls to come out here anymore. Since it was a private club on private land, they weren't even allowed to enter the parking lot without expressed permission. So tonight Deputy Dawg assumed that he was on solid legal ground. He saw the growing crowd and tried to regain his composure and the upper hand.

"Who called the police?" He yelled into the night crowd. Silence. *"Did someone here call for the police?"* he yelled again, but this time the confidence in his voice had wavered.

A short man with a paunch and a bald head parted through the crowd. *"You know ain't nobody here called for you, so I suggest you get your porky pig butt off my property."*

"Do you know who you are messing with, Little Man" said Deputy Dawg. His courage rose up when he saw the short stature of the man.

As he approached the small man he heard the cranking of motor cycles and the crowd began to split away as they rode up to flank the small man. The riders spread out and formed a line thirty feet on each side as they continued to rev their hogs to intimidate and drown out Deputy Dawg every time he attempted to speak. The crowd continued to caterwaul and taunt the deputy.

The short man raised his hand and the engines quieted and a hush came over the crowd. The short man didn't even have to raise his voice to be heard. *"I don't think you know who you are messing with, Deputy. So I am going to give you thirty seconds to get in your car and get off this property."*

He looked back at the car totally defeated. *"Well, as you can see, my car won't move right now."*

"Well I think we can help you out with that, Little Man" said the short man sarcastically. He then turned to the bikers and said with a big waving gesture of his arms, *"Girls, do you think you might help the deputy with his problem?"*

Laughing erupted from the crowd.

And with that, the left flank of bikers got off their bikes and walked over to the right side of the patrol car and squatted down to grab the under carriage.

Deputy Dawg was about to object when the short man commanded, *"Heave!"*

"Ho!" came a collective groan in unison from line of bikers as they lifted the car all the way over onto its left side. The crowd cheered and whistled.

All the bikers, except one, backed away from the upturned car and remounted their Harley-Davidsons as the crowd whooped and hollered.

Deputy Dawg watched as the remaining biker removed his helmet and stood beside the short man. Only it wasn't a dude. Realization that his car had just been turned over by a bunch of lesbians hit Deputy Dawg like a sledge hammer in the gut and in his pride.

He turned in disbelief and screamed, *'Look what you bitches did!'*

The crowd went silent.

The woman next to the short man lowered her head and slowly walked over to the patrol car. Then with a single shove from her stiletto boot she sent the car rolling off of the narrow bridge and into the culvert upside down causing the roof to crush like a cheap aluminum beer can. The red and blue lights were still going until they began to sizzle and spark in the dirty water of the drainage ditch.

"That's what a BITCH did to your car and I can do worse to you, Porky Pig, so you might want to get to stepping on down that road while I am still in a good mood." said the female biker before she turned on her toe and remounted her motorcycle.

Deputy Dawg was infuriated to the point that he moved his right hand to his hip to unsnap his service pistol. He would show these women who was boss, but before he even cleared his holster, the entire right flank of bikers had a dozen guns on him, pulled and cocked. Most were semi-automatic handguns, but his attention was now focused on the double barreled sawed off shot gun that was aimed at his junk. He froze as the lesbian who kicked over his car slowly pivoted around 180 degrees. She walked up to him and she removed his gun from its holster. She put her face up next to his, nose to nose. Deputy Dawg thought that she was going to kiss him and he parted his lips to receive her. To his shock, what she gave him was a crippling knee to his groin, which sent him into the dirt in agony. She stepped over his writhing mass and removed his cuffs from his utility belt and expertly grabbed one wrist and snapped it around it. As impressive as that was, she then put her knee in his back, to put him into complete submission, as she latched up his other wrist behind his back.

"Don't kill me, pleeeeaase." Deputy Dawg blubbered into the dirt.

Everyone began to laugh again.

"What a little bitch" some screamed.

"How would you like me to put a little cinnamon on those big sweet buns." came another voice with a lisp.

"I am a chubby chaser. Let me have him." Shouted someone else.

The lesbian biker pulled him to his feet and kicked him in his ample ass and saggy uniform pants. *"Get out of here and don't ever come around here again."*

Chapter 21

"I am crazy."

"I've been tested" said the long haired man *"Twice."*

The man had introduced himself as Big Bad Bubba Jesus. He definitely looked like a Bubba. After all it was Texas, but the resemblance to Jesus was a bit more tenuous unless Jesus had a big beer gut, had his whole body covered in black hair and had two humongous pink hams for feet. Bad Big Foot Santa Clause seemed more accurate, but it certainly didn't seem to roll off the tongue quite as eloquently.

"I have already had two court ordered psychiatric evaluations" said Bubba Jesus with his distinctive Texas twang. *"So why the hell can't I get out of this God forsaken place?"*

Doc loved being in the Law Library. He felt like he was really helping people. It had been hard at first because he didn't know which books to refer people to, so he was relegated to just sharpening pencils and re-shelving books when people were finished with them.

However, Doc was able to catch on quickly because his brother, Boyce, had gone to law school and he picked up some legal knowledge by academic osmosis from helping him study for exams. Cases and precedents came flooding back. It felt like it was only yesterday since he had sparred with Boyce at exam time. If Boyce got an answer wrong, then Doc would have to read him the correct answer with case law. And if he got it right, then Boyce had to recite the case law back to Doc.

"Just because you are crazy doesn't mean that you are going to get out." said Doc.

"What!" hollered Bad Bubba Jesus.

Doc backed away and held the thick law book that was in his hands up to his chest to protect himself if necessary. *"It only means that they will probably put you in a prison psychiatric facility with other crazy people."*

Big Bad Bubba Jesus was incarcerated this time for having a wild west shoot out with his brother at the Pierre Gardens Motor Court and RV Camping Grounds near Lake Sam Rayburn. From all the reports that Doc had read it had been a doozy and like most incidents of this nature, alcohol was involved. Apparently, lots of alcohol.

Police reports and numerous witnesses at the scene had reported that the brothers had been bickering all day long during the St. Patrick's Day lake festivities. The brothers were always arguing and needling each other about one stupid thing or another. And the more nasty green beer they drank the more ridiculous the arguments became. Most of the people were shuffling around from party to party in their dirty feet and rubber flip-flops when the first shotgun blast pierced the festive trailer park soiree. Illegal fireworks had been exploding on and off all day, but none had compared to the immense 'Boom' that ripped through the Pierre Gardens.

"You crazy 'sum-bitch'!" came a yell from the single wide trailer. A hole had appeared where the mouth used to be on the porch statue of poor St. Patrick. The once happy fellow from the shamrock isle now resembled a blow up pornographic sex doll clad in weird green suit.

Suddenly, another blast filled the air. The crowd began to scatter and run for cover. Moms commanded their children into their trailers with no more urgency than if they were calling them for dinner. The second blast had amputated the little leprechaun statue's index finger and completely obliterated his corn cob pipe, so that the green clad porno midget was now flipping the bird to the entire motor court.

"That's it, Bubba." came a voice from inside the mobile home. *"You asked for this."* Four quick shots rang out in secession from inside the front door of the single wide. The men of the camp grounds ducked for cover, but not before they hoisted the keg of green beer to safety.

Big Bad Bubba Jesus sought refuge behind the 1972 lime green AMC Gremlin sitting on cinder blocks in the yard. He took another swig of green beer from his red cup before breaking the breach of the shotgun and loading two more shells of double ought buckshot.

"You never could hit shit." yelled Bubba Jesus as he popped up and blasted away the satellite dish.

A half dozen more shots rang out from inside the trailer. The two brothers traded insults and barbs between each volley of ammunition. Big Bad Bubba Jesus attempted to get up to fire another round in the general direction of his brother, but slipped on a pile of green vomit causing him to fire his shotgun prematurely and shooting out the right tire of the mobile home. Air hissed as it escaped from the wounded tire and the house sank down six inches.

"You sorry bastard" came a drunken yell from inside the trailer. *"Look what you have done to my house."*

The elevated wooden porch now blocked the front door of the sunken mobile home. "I can't get out you crazy fool." And with that Bubba's drunken brother emptied the rest of the clip into his own door.

"Here let me give you a hand with that." hollered Bubba Jesus and with that he raised the shotgun to his shoulder and unloaded two shots into the trailer. However, his missed the front door entirely and blew out the kitchen window and beheaded the poor plastic pink flamingo.

The Monkey Trap

The brothers continued to hurl insults and hot lead at one another until the local the police finally arrived and found the two brothers inebriated, exhausted and out of ammunition. In all, the pair of psycho siblings had fired a total of fifty-nine shots at one another from a distance of only twenty feet. Miraculously, no one was hit or injured in the entire ordeal, but the 1972 lime green AMC Gremlin had sustained $142 worth of body damage from 33 bullet holes and was thus considered totaled.

"What the hell were you two fighting about?" asked Doc.

"Nub threw up green beer and nacho cheese all over my wife's Pancho" said Bubba Jesus.

"Why didn't you just wash it?" said Doc.

"Don't you think I would have done that if I could have?" said Bubba Jesus *"I couldn't get it out from under the trailer."*

"He threw up on it under the trailer?' Doc asked confusingly.

"No" said Bad Bubba exasperatingly. *"The little fucker ran under there after Nub hurled green puke all over him."*

"I thought he threw up on your wife's poncho." said a very confused Doc.

"He did" yelled Bubba Jesus. *"Pancho is my wife's Chi-Waa-Waa dog. Only now he was my wife's green chi-waa-waa."*

Doc snickered out loud.

"It's not funny, Doc. My wife, Vatra, loves that yappy little mutt. She said she couldn't find a shampoo strong enough to get the green out of that dog and that puke green 'chi-waa-waa' was unholy looking for weeks." explained Bubba Jesus. *"Hell, Vatra was so mad at me that she refused to post my bail."*

"Shit," Bubba Jesus continued *"she even used my bail money to hire a damn dog whisperer to find out what kind of psychological trauma that her poor little Pancho had suffered from at the shoot out."*

At this point Doc and everyone in the law library was rolling on the floor with laughter. Prison was depressing, but on this day it was made just a little better by Pancho, the Green Chihuahua.

*****

Doc's quickly gained a reputation as the go to guy in the law library and was considered the best jail house lawyer in the prison. He was writing motions and his success rate was astounding. He consistently found errors that helped his fellow inmates get new hearings or reductions in sentences. Other inmates where now offering to pay him to work on their cases, which meant that he was able to enjoy the occasional pint of ice cream or even go in on a spread with Farmer or some of the other guys on the wing. People he didn't even know would even acknowledge him or wave to him in the hall. At first he didn't know what to think of it, but Farmer had explained how he was now getting a reputation. He now had 'stroke' of his own. Farmer would also come to the Law Library to work on his own case and to sneak in a little extra time with Doc on his writing lessons.

"I think you should write a letter home to your Mom." said Doc.

Farmer responded, *"I don't think I am ready for that."*

"Yeah you are." said Doc *"Trust me."*

"I don't know what to say" Farmers said bowing his head to his friend.

Doc looked over his new reading glasses at Farmer with disbelieving eyes. *"You have been wanting to do this for a long time, buddy."* said Doc with compassion. *"And I know that are ready."*

Farmer's stomach was in knots. He had been practicing for months and he really did want to write a letter home with his own hand, but now he was more scared than he had ever been in his life. Doc could read the consternation on Farmer brow so he put hand his friend's shoulder. *"You can do it"* said Doc *"I will be right here, if you have any problems."*

Farmer had never had a friend like Doc and he found himself relying on him more and more for encouragement. He never had anyone reassure him and praise his work the way Doc did. He couldn't believe how much of a difference it made. He was actually liking the lessons that Doc had come up with. Doc told him that skills as an artist had given him superior penmanship.

Farmer started with the date and progressed to the salutation, but stopped after that. He sat there for a minute and didn't move.

Doc saw this and asked *"What's the matter?"*

"I don't know what to say." Farmer said.

"What do you want to say?" queried Doc.

Farmer thought for a second and then with the most earnest voice that Doc had ever heard from him said, *"I want to tell her that I love her and that I am really sorry about everything."*

Doc felt a hard lump come up in his throat come up immediately and tears well up in his eyes. *"Then why don't you make that your first sentence."* And that's what Farmer did.

After that, everything else came so easily. He was shocked and amazed that in no time at all he had an entire page written, but more than that, he felt good about himself.

Doc's emotions welled up in him. It had been so easy to tell Farmer what to do. Doc had been in this horrible place for a year. He had been bitter. He had been angry. And he had definitely been lonely. He had never received a single letter from his brother, but as he sat watching Farmer he realized that he had never written a single letter either. Pride had gotten in his way. He had been stubborn and resentful.

The past year of his life had been a waste in the eyes of the world, but he understood now that he needed that lost year to detox and to examine his life without the influence of pharmaceuticals on his brain. He needed that time to get honest with himself He felt regret. He felt remorse. He realized that he was like a monkey caught in a trap. He had held onto false comforts and he had gotten so wrapped up in his own falderal that he had forsaken the one person that did care about him. His brother. Boyce had been both father and mother to Doc. He had also been his best friend until Doc got so full of himself and so full of drugs that he drove Boyce away.

The look on Farmer's face when he finished his letter was different.

'Why?' thought Doc.

There was something tangibly different about him.

'What the hell was is it?' Doc wondered.

Doc couldn't take his eyes off of Farmer. In that moment Doc realized that he was seeing contentment and peace on Farmers face.

He was seeing release. Release of guilt. Release of burdens. And the release of his inner demons. He was no longer trapped. Sure, he was still locked up and in prison. They both were. But Farmer was no longer trapped by his mind. He had been freed. He freed himself with something as simple as a letter home.

That was it. That was definitely what it was. And that is what Doc wanted too.

"No," he told himself. *"That is what I needed."*

He needed to be released from his own mental Monkey Trap.

Chapter 22

Guy had gathered up his laptop and got into the old Junker only a minute after Deputy Dawg had torn away from the Hot Biscuit. He pressed the gas pedal down and had the old car going as fast as he could. Black smoke was puffing from his tailpipe, but it got him to the 'Snake Ranch' just in time. He parked on the side of the road and grabbed his digital video camera as he flung himself from the car and ran towards the newly gathered crowd from bar. His feet landed in the muddy water as he jumped the culvert. He wiggled his way through the barbed wire fence before he broke into a dead run through the waist high Texas brush. He broke through the bramble weeds and blended into the right side of the growing crowd. He worked his way up to the front and lifted the camera to his eye.

He relished watching what the lesbian biker chick had done to Deputy Dawg. Sure he had made the fake 911 call and loosened the drain plug on the radiator and removed the car's antenna, so the deputy couldn't call for help from this far out but he regretted not being the one to kick the fat son-of-a-bitch in the nuts.

The camera had caught every humiliating minute of it on video.

The lesbian kicked him in the ass and sent him walking down the road with his hands cuffed behind his back. This was better than anything he could have imagined. Revenge on the fat fucker for stealing his ring was all that he had done this for, but as he watched the deputy begin his slow shuffle down the road his mind began to work over time. Those lesbian bikers had just given him a gift and they were beautiful to him right now. He didn't know if he had the cajones to go through with the plan that had just entered his brilliant brain. If it back fired he would be in a whole heap of shit, but if successful he would then be a freaking hero.

*****

No cars had come down this road in the hour that Deputy Ernie Sinclair had been walking down it. He was in tears and his arms hurt like nothing he had ever experienced. Walking had blistered his swollen feet and he wanted to just sit down, but with his arms cuffed behind him, he was certain that he would never be able to get back up again. He would just die there. So he staggered down the road on his aching feet.

He heard the old car chugging and clanking on the old dark road before he ever saw its headlights crest over the hill, the smell of the black exhaust fumes accompanying it.

Guy had let him walk for more than an hour in order to soften him up and to make him mentally pliable. When Guy drove up, Deputy Dawg was exhausted and weak.

Deputy Dawg was so glad that someone had come down this road. He knew it was a miracle. He dropped to his knees and tears were streaming down his cheeks. The car rolled to a slow stop. The deputy was illuminated in the car's head lights.

"Thank god." he wailed. *"Help me, please!"*

The car just sat there. No one got out. His pleas had gone unanswered.

"Is anyone there? Why don't you show yourself?" Deputy Dawg blubbered as total despair overtook him.

"You having a problem here, boy?" came the voice from behind the headlights.

Deputy Dawg looked up, but the car's headlights blinded him from seeing the person.

"Oh my god, are you here to kill me, aren't you?" And with that he bowed his head to the asphalt highway and gave up.

"I have thought about killing you a thousand times, you worthless piece of shit." said a voice above him. Deputy Dawg just stayed down on the ground in defeat.

"Well, you certainly look a lot less high and mighty now, don't you, son." Guy added the word 'son' on the end as gig to the crooked deputy for the way he had treated Guy on that fateful night in the parking lot.

Guy stepped up, but not so close that Deputy Dawg could see him. *"Well, I guess this is your lucky night because I am here to give you a choice, you sniveling little worm."*

"W-W-What?" cried Deputy Dawg through his tears.

"Listen to me carefully, you maggot." instructed Guy in his most distasteful voice. *"If it were up to me I would just let you die out here and leave your carcass for the wild hogs to eat, but someone else thinks you might know something useful."* Guy was really laying it on thick now.

"So here is the deal. You can spill your guts and tell everything you know for which I will let you live and give you a nice free ride home. Or if you refuse to tell what you know, then I will simply walk you out into these dark, hungry woods and leave you there, only to be eaten by feral hogs and never to be seen again. Hell, I bet them hogs wouldn't even wait until you're dead to start gnawing on you." Guy said while poking him in his gut.

Deputy Dawg began to blubber, *"But I don't know nothing. I swear."*

"That's what I thought" Guy said as he grabbed Deputy Dawg by the arm.

Deputy Dawg began to wail pitifully.

"C'mon, die like a man," Guy whispered in his ear.

"Okay, okay, okay!" screamed Deputy Dawg *"I will tell you whatever you want."*

"That's better. And I know that you are going to be totally honest with me, aren't you?" asked Guy. *"Because if you aren't then we are going for a long late night walk."*

"I promise. I will tell you whatever you want to know." swore the deputy.

"Oh, I have no doubt that you are going tell me everything that you know." said Guy.

*****

Guy set up the video camera and made use of the car's headlights for lighting. He cleaned the deputy and gave him water to clear his throat.

Guy remained off camera and asked Deputy Dawg question after question. With no resistance left in him, he freely answered questions about anything and everything. Even his vile personal proclivities. Guy wanted everything he could get on this guy. The more he talked the deeper Guy had his hooks into him. He told about what he had personally stolen. He answered questions and named names of people in the sheriff's department that where doing illegal things. He surprised Guy when he also named government officials. He told about different busts and how they went down and who profited from them. And who he thought profited from them. He was just a little fish in an ever enlarging pond, but it was solid information. Guy continued on and let Deputy Dawg continue to incriminate himself and to tell about all the misdeeds and illegal activities that he ever participated in.

When it was over, Guy covered Deputy Dawg's head with a reusable grocery bag and stuffed him into the passenger seat to drive him to town. Along the way he used the time to drill some reinforcement into the deputy's brain.

"I know you are smart enough to know to keep your mouth shut. But if you should tell anyone of this, then a copy of this tape will be sent to the people you squealed on first. If by some miracle you are still alive a week later, then we will send a copy of your personal confessions to the District Attorney, and the press just to make sure it doesn't get buried somewhere" Guy kept his voice deliberately monotone to add to the seriousness of his threat. *"And after we have ruined your professional life and have you on the way to a lengthy prison term then we will release the entire video of you getting your ass handed to you by a bunch of lesbian biker chicks; for which your life will be completely and utterly over, because you will either be someone's butt boy in prison or dead in your cell."*

"Do I make myself clear, Deputy Sinclair?"

The deputy just nodded his head.

Guy pulled the car over to the side of the road a block from the police station. He pulled the depleted deputy from the car. As he started to unlock the cuffs he noticed his ring still on the deputy's pinky.

"This sure is a nice ring." said Guy menacingly into the deputy's ear.

"Take it." said the crying deputy. *"It doesn't mean anything to me"*

And with that Guy left the deputy sitting on a bus bench with the grocery bag still on his head and minus one ring from his fat finger.

Chapter 23

The Law Library was quiet.

Doc would sit for hours all alone sometimes. The warden had received complaints from the prosecutors all over the state about the sudden rash of successful motions coming from his prison. That was their subtle way of telling him that they wanted something done to stop it because it made them look bad, and it was creating a lot of work for them to do. The warden was a typical Texas bureaucrat. He was a definite believer in the good old boy philosophy of 'you had to go along to get along.'

The warden knew that he couldn't just close it down; the ACLU and those federal do-gooders would be crawling all over his ass, so he did what all the wardens in Texas did. He just made it impossible or unbelievably difficult for inmates to go to the Law Library.

He changed the hours so that it was only open from 2-5 A.M or 4-7 P.M. The option was that if you went to the Law Library, then you didn't get to eat breakfast or dinner. He knew what every Warden knew. Food trumped everything.

The desired effect was immediate and Doc was left with nothing to do, except think about his life.

*****

Boyce was four years older and Bentley had lived in his shadow all his adolescent life, which had never been easy. Boyce was an over achiever and excelled at every academic thing he did. He wasn't superior at athletics. So he never tried out for the school teams but he would play them for fun with his friends. They did attend the games and pep rallies to support them. When it came to the sciences and the liberal arts, however, Boyce was exceptional. Normally, that would have branded someone a nerd, but Boyce had charisma. People loved him. He could talk to anyone and be totally interested in what they were saying. He could make whoever he was talking to feel like the most special person in the room. It was as if they were the only person in the world that mattered. He was mesmerizing when he spoke and everyone wanted to be his best friend. He was in almost every social club and invited to everyone's parties.

Every year Bentley would hear the same thing from his teachers when they discovered they had Boyce's little brother in their class.

"Oh, your brother, Boyce, was such a delight," the new teachers would fawn over Bentley with excitement in front of all of the other kids, *"I just know that you will be too."*

Of course, this set him up as an immediate favorite of every new teacher and as an immediate leper to the other kids in the class for being the teacher's new pet. After several years of this, Bentley began to try and break out of his brother's shadow and create his own name and reputation. Bentley knew he was smart, but he was never going to be as driven as Boyce about academics, so he went the other way. He went out for sports. He didn't do well at team sports, but he excelled at golf and tennis. So he joined the school teams. And since they were individual sports, he was able to join teams whenever he had to change schools. He could play them also at the country club as much as he wanted.

He started hitting balls in the seventh grade. By the time he got to High School he had his own reputation and Boyce had newly graduated and left to go to college.

High School was Bentley's time to shine. Puberty and two years of playing tennis and swinging a golf club had turned Bentley into a hunk. The little scrawny guy who graduated from the eighth grade was not the handsome jock that walked into the new high school three months later. Bentley had grown four inches in height and ten inches in the chest and arms. He turned every girl's head in the school. When he entered his first class the room literally went silent. He took his seat and heard whispers from groups of girls all around the room.

"Who is that?" A giggly voice asked.

"Do you know him?" came a high pitched voice.

"What's his name?" said another female with a sultry and sexy tone. This caused Bentley to grin because he was enjoying all the attention and the spotlight for a change. It felt good not to be in Boyce's shadow for once in his life.

"I don't know, but I sure want to find out." Said a male voice, which made
Bentley almost break out laughing. 'Oh well', he thought, 'he was only interested in the first three, but he would be lying if he didn't admit that he was flattered by the fourth.'

High School was great, but he still felt empty inside despite having lots of girlfriends to do things with. He went out with girls, but they were never really serious and he never felt close to them. He hated to admit it, but he was really missing Boyce because most of the guys in school felt threatened by his good looks and so they snubbed him. He hardly had any guys to just hang with or talk to, and the ones he did have just wanted to get near the girls he knew or near his money.

It had gotten out like it always did that Bentley and Boyce were orphans because their parents had been murdered when Bentley was only nine years old. They were bounced around from one conniving relative to another. Each thought they were going to hit the jackpot and get rich off of the little boys' inheritance. Their father had provided for the boys very well and very cunningly. Their parents' will was iron clad at their deaths and it remained that way to the very day that Boyce turned twenty-five and took control of all seventy eight million dollars.

Bentley had been provided for in the will, but Boyce was left as the sole administrator and executor of the estate when he became of age and would remain so until death. Bentley would be cared for by the estate but never in control of it as long as Boyce was alive and competent, and Boyce was extremely competent. No one could ever dispute that.

Boyce had been competent since the day they had been picked up at school and pulled out of class by the principal and handed over to Mr. Fuhrmiester, their father's attorney. He had held both of their hands as the three of them walked down the echoing halls of the school in hard soled shoes.

He didn't say a word until he had gotten them all the way home. He sat them both down on their mother's Mario Buatta chintz sofa and informed them in his matter-of-fact tone of voice that both of their parents were dead. He wasn't uncaring, but the delivery of the tragic news had been a bit sterile. Boyce and Bentley just stared at him in horror and disbelief for what seemed like forever to Bentley, but the gravity of it finally hit the youngest Braxton boy and he began to tear up and cry. Bentley buried his face in Boyce's shoulder. Boyce put his arms around Bentley.

"Go ahead and let it out." said Boyce as he comforted his younger brother. *"I am here for you. I will always be here for you."*

Boyce, however, never cried. Not even at the funeral. He had been stoic and in command of his emotions. He had always been the master of his emotions, but now he was in command of his own destiny also. It had come unexpectedly soon for Boyce at thirteen years of age, but anyone who ever knew or encountered the young man came away with a sense of respect for the boy. He was not one to be railroaded or intimidated. He was not the average adolescent, and anyone who attempted to tangle with him quickly found themselves outwitted and outsmarted in a very skillful and subtle way by an extremely charming and polite young man. It made for a very disconcerting experience for those who tried.

Most boys his age idolized or emulated sports figures or celebrities but not Boyce. The oldest Braxton was not swayed by such superficial notoriety. His role models were Queen Victoria, Napoleon and Ghangis Khan. He had memorized Sun Tzu's The Art of War, by fourteen and conquered his High School student government before he was a sophomore. He remained its President for the rest of his tenure in High School. He was voracious in his academic pursuits but only if they lead to power and control. His parents had been ripped from him, and he vowed that their premature deaths were the last random acts that would ever take place in his life. He was not going to be a victim of serendipity ever again.

The only thing he hadn't been prepared for was being Bentley's full time guardian and protector. He hadn't ever foreseen being responsible for anyone else. It was definitely a curve ball in his grand plan, but it wasn't insurmountable. Besides that, Bentley was a good kid who idolized Boyce.

How could he not like and adore the little stinker?

So thanks to Sun Tzu and the U.S. Marine Corps manual, he Accessed, Adapted and Overcame.

Boyce had mapped out his path to success, and he made Bentley a part of it, but as Bentley matured, he surprised Boyce with a spurt of independence. He didn't know why or what brought it on, but he was relieved because he was just entering Southern Methodist University. It was his father's alma mater, but he didn't want to ride his father's coat tails. He was aiming higher. Much, much higher.

He wanted to run the state.

He wanted Texas.

And he wanted it before he turned, thirty because he had even bigger plans for his thirty-fifth birthday.

*****

Bentley sailed through High School. Even with his yearly move from one home to another, he had been able to stay at his private high school for the entire four years. He had been popular and he treasured them as the best years of his life.

The Monkey Trap

Prom had been magical for him. He went with one of the prettiest girls in school. Sandy was a new cheerleader that had moved from Odessa with her older sister, the new English Lit. teacher at the school. He had been smitten the moment he saw her. Auburn shoulder length hair cascaded to her voluptuous breasts that set off her skinny neck.

She was a knock out in Bentley's eyes, and he had been nervous about talking to her, but she didn't wait for him to rustle up the courage. She wasn't like the other girls. She was bold and unafraid.

She saw him in the hall between classes one day and just walked right up to him at his locker.

"Hi! I'm Sandy and I am new here." she said *"and I think you ought to buy me lunch today and show me around."* Then with a peck on the cheek she pivoted on her blue and tan saddle oxfords and was gone.

Bentley was stunned. *"What gall she had,"* thought Bentley, *"but man she was beautiful"* and with that he knew that he would most assuredly be buying her lunch that day and for as many days as she wanted him to.

She had been so easy to talk to and wasn't at all stuck up like he feared she might be. She didn't care one bit about his money. Money never seemed important to her. If they had money to go out, that was great, but if they didn't, she made those times great too. He had never met anyone else like her before. He told her of his tragic and turbulent life, but she reminded him that he had her now and that everything was going to be okay. She liked him. She was fun to be with and he felt intoxicated when he was around her. Sandy wasn't ever pretentious. She loved to do anything and everything as long as they could do it together. She never smothered him but was right there with him when he needed her. She adored Bentley and he was truly happy. He now had a sense of contentment that had been unforeseen, unfelt and heretofore unrecognized. He now had what he had been missing his whole life. He finally had love. He felt real true love for the first time in his crazy life. He felt the kind of love they wrote song about. She was the real deal.

They cavorted like two puppies. Sandy had an irreverent sense of humor that made him laughed a lot as they lolled about in the sun or under the clouds. All they wanted to do was to be in the same space, touching each other, often quiet and content for hours. Their relationship wasn't always sensual or sexual by any means. She was sensitive to his feelings, when others around him didn't notice or care much that things might not be going exactly his way. When they were together they shared a safety zone that no one in the world could penetrate. It was something that they both needed. They talked easily to one another about their early years. They shared and compared stories. Sandy like to say that they were "damaged goods". They both had endured brutality, dysfunction and secrets.

Bentley thought to himself, 'If I could hold her in my arms close enough and long enough, then I might be able to eventually absorb and drain away all of her hurt'.

Nothing seemed to be absent or wanting when they were together. He felt fulfilled. No one else seemed to be needed and time meant nothing. All of life's question had answers. Why would he ever need or want anyone else or want to face his life without Sandy?

She completed whatever he had been missing all of his young life.

*****

"I want this prom to be special." she whispered in his ear.

It was the last slow dance of the prom and she laid her head on his shoulder, so as not to let him see the small tear drop in the corner of her eye.

Bentley had been with girls a few times before, but it had never been like it was on that night. It wasn't just the love-making that had been wonderful. It had been the whole night. It had been perfect because it was Sandy. She filled the hole in his heart. She supplied what had always been missing in his life.

Before the night was over, he made the biggest decision that he had ever faced. He decided to ask her to become Mrs. Bentley Braxton III after their graduation.

The Monkey Trap

Graduation day had finally arrived. He couldn't believe that he was going to finally do it. They were graduating tomorrow. They would be done with High School.

He knew they were young, but he trusted the feelings he felt and knew he wanted, no, he needed, that contentment for the rest of his life. He had money, which eliminated the hurdle of most young marriages. He envisioned the two of them going forward, having a family, growing old together.

He saw Boyce and Marla Smith like grand-parents to his as yet unborn children. Utopia had to be just the way he dreamed this marriage would be. He had asked himself all of the questions that he could think of, and all the answers were that he should marry Sandy. And Sandy seemed to always be in total sync with his feelings.

He was conflicted only by the wish to savor their every moment together and the anticipation of their future moments, which he could only see as just better and better. Any obstacles to their happiness could never be more than hiccups to hot peppers.

He was going to propose to her in his cap and gown on bended knee in front of all of their friends and her family. And Boyce. The marriage proposal was going to be as dramatic as the birth of Jesus. All their friends and families would be there to bear witness and to heap approval on their perfection as a couple to be united as one.

He had told Boyce what he was going to do the day after the prom. Boyce had tried to talk him out of it. Everything he said about why Bentley shouldn't get married was absolutely true, but all of them put together couldn't overrule the one reason that he should. He loved her. He loved her with all his heart. He knew Sandy loved him.

And try as he might, Boyce just couldn't win against love.

Bentley's diploma was in his hand and the ring he had so carefully chosen was in his pocket. The big moment had arrived. Bentley had butterflies in stomach. Thank God no one could see his knees shaking underneath the royal blue graduation gown. Sandy's family had gathered so that each relative could have their photo taken with the new graduate. Boyce was following Bentley. He may not have approved of the marriage, but he would be damned if he wasn't going to be beside his little brother for the biggest moment in his life.

"Oh, I am so glad you are here" said Sandy as she ran up and kissed Bentley. *"You are just in time to get your picture made with me."*

Boyce and Marla Smith, Sandy's sister, both clicked away with their cameras to record the moment for the inevitable scrapbook that would hold it for their children one day to laugh and make fun of many years from now.

"Can I have your attention, folks?" Bentley asked with a voice loud enough to quiet the small group. He took Sandy's left hand and went down on one knee. A real hush came over the group.

"Sandy, you know that I love you and you mean the world to me. I didn't understand what happiness was until I met you and now I don't think I could live my life without you. So," Bentley fumbled to get his right hand out of the cumbersome robe *"Sandy Smith will you marry me?"*

Astonished looks were on everyone's face as he professed his love to Sandy on bended knee, and a chorus of squeals erupted from Sandy's girlfriends as they jumped up and down and grabbed one another.

Sandy's eyes were filled with tears of joy. Shaking with excitement she grabbed Bentley's hand. The very hand that he had slipped a gorgeous two carat ring on her finger with and pulled him up to her. As he stood she leapt into his waiting arms and wrapped her sinewy legs around his small athletic waist. She latched onto both sides of Bentley's face with her tiny hands and nails that she had impeccably done in Corvette red. Bentley was immediately smothered with a barrage of kisses from the luscious lips that had been painted to match her silky nails. This was the happiest moment in the world for both of them. Sandy couldn't let go of Bentley and Bentley never wanted to let go of Sandy. This was their moment and nothing could change that, they thought. She excitedly accepted his proposal and pledged her total and consuming devotion. Tears of happiness filled her eyes.

Everyone had huge smiles on their faces and were jumping up and down with the exuberance of the momentous occasion, except for two people----Marla Smith and Boyce Braxton.

In their eyes, this was a disaster. Boyce had talked to Bentley until he was blue in the face. He felt helpless to stop this impending marriage, but Marla didn't. She felt no compunction about letting her feelings be known and she wasn't going to wait to let the happy couple know it.

"Uhh-Uhm" came the familiar voice.

That voice was Marla's.

Marla stepped forward.

The sunny and loud laughter from the gaggle of Sandy's girlfriends came to an abrupt and haunting death silence that smothered the joyful celebration.

"Bentley" she said in a low even tone. *"You are a fine young man, but Sandy cannot marry you----now"*

"Well, why not?" he asked as he looked from Marla's gaze to Sandy's wet, tear stained face. *"Besides, it's not your decision it's hers."* he said grabbing her other hand and squeezing it tight.

"No, I am afraid it's not." informed Marla as she turned to Sandy *"Perhaps you need to tell him Sandy."*

"NO!" yelled Sandy. *"I am going to marry Bentley."*

"No you're not, young lady." retorted Marla, using her teacher's voice. *"You have accepted early admission to Princeton University and that will be where you will be going as of next week."*

"WHAT!" screamed Sandy. *"You can't stand it that I want to be happy. You want me to be just like you. Old and miserable. I hate you!"*

Sandy heaving with sobs could not speak anymore and was now crying uncontrollably. Bentley leaned in to comfort her but she pulled away and disappeared into the crowd of graduates weeping uncontrollably.

Bentley was left standing there confused.

Marla Smith put a gentle hand on Bentley's arm and said, *"Sandy is only seventeen and I am her legal guardian until her eighteenth birthday. I want her to go to college and receive a top notch education. She agreed to do that and I am committed to seeing her go, so I will not allow you to marry her at this time."* She took a deep sigh.

"You are both too young and have so much time ahead of you."

It was Bentley's turn to cry now. And once again the shoulder that was there for him was Boyce's.

*****

WHOOOOOP! WHOOOOOP! WHOOOOOP!

"Get down on the floor now!" yelled the guard as he ran to secure and lock the door, but before he could turn the key the door came flying open and crashed right into his shoulder. The mighty and unexpected force of the blow threw the portly guard against the painted cinder block wall with a resounding thud. He was a guard in name only. Like so many of them, he was nothing more than a glorified baby-sitter. An empty shirt filled with a warm body for $10.50 an hour and all the free food that one could eat.

He screamed out in terror as two black convicts stormed their way into the library. The lead thug reared back his fist at the sniveling sentry and, with all his might, he pummeled the fat man in his face. Copious amounts of bright red blood flew from his wounded face and splattered the guard's life fluid all over the gray wall.

Doc watched in stunned horror as the guard's cheek opened up and burst like a crushed tomato. The second thug piled on with even more punishment as he too delivered several more head blows. The guard was on the ground trying to get into a fetal position to defend himself from

112

the onslaught of brutality that he was receiving at the hands of these two thugs.

Doc wondered what this guard had done to deserve such a savage beating.

The two convicts relish the cowardly pleas of the guard. The more he cried the harder they beat him. His assumption of the fetal position only inflamed them more. The taller one began to stomp on the guard's head as his partner unceasingly kicked the guard's upper torso and buttocks.

Doc was petrified. This was insane. What was he supposed to do? They were going murder this guard right before his very eyes if he didn't do something. But what? There wasn't anything that he could use against these animals. They were like hyenas in a feeding frenzy. Blood was everywhere.

Suddenly, they just stopped. The guard's body was now just a lump of bloody meat lying in the floor. Lifeless and unmoving. The two black jackals turned and looked at Doc with the coldest eyes he had ever seen. Fear consumed Doc instantly as they zeroed in on him.

"Oh my God!" said Doc. He backed away as fast as he could. Chairs and empty tables were all that he had to put between himself and these homicidal maniacs. He was defenseless.

The shorter one sneered at him with his cheaply made gold teeth, which compounded his menacing look and Doc's fear. Doc could feel his bowels loosening when the taller one threw a chair across the room that had been in his path. It bounced off Doc's shoulder and forearm, but it grazed Doc's head as it went cascading to the floor. Doc felt a warm trickle run down his face. Sticky red blood was smeared across his face as he wiped it away.

"Hey, guys, I didn't see anything. I am cool." said Doc as he moved back against a table.

"Fuck you, punk!" screamed the taller one. *"Ain't nobody in here to save your white ass this time, mutha fucka."*

"Yeah" said the shorter one with his gold grill. *"You messed with the wrong brothers, punk. You don't fuck with us without paying the price. You think you can just kick our homey in the nuts and get away with it?"*

The realization that they were here to kill him caused Doc's breathing to become so rapid and panicky that he almost fainted from hyper-ventilation. The twosome spread out and began to circle around in opposite directions to cut off Doc's retreat. The short one put his foot up on one of the library chairs. Doc's fear shot up to his throat as he watched the thug pull a ten inch metal shank out of his sock.

"That's right, mutha fucka" hissed the short one *"we gonna feed you your nuts."*

Crashing chairs came from behind him as the taller one made his move to grab Doc from behind. Doc felt him grab his collar as he fought to get away with his life. Doc did the only thing that was available to him. He dived under a table and scrambled on his hands and knees to escape, but the tall man wasn't giving up so easily. Doc was almost under a second table when he felt a hand grab his ankle and pull him back. Struggle as he might, the only thing he was able to latch onto was the table leg, which only pulled the table back with him. A second hand grabbed his calf and now he was being pulled back with ease. Panic consumed Doc as he flipped himself onto his back. He was being pulled out from under the table and sliding on his rear now. Doc could see the taller man grimacing like a Halloween pumpkin as he dragged Doc from under the table. Doc used the only weapons he had at his disposal. His feet and legs. As the snaggletooth face came into view Doc drew back his right leg and delivered a horrific upper cut to the soft under side of the taller man's jaw snapping it closed with unbelievable force. Doc heard the thug's remaining teeth crush like glass. Blood gushed out of his mouth as the meaty lump of his tongue landed on the floor. The thug instantly released his grip on Doc's leg. Gushing arterial blood filled his mouth and he began to gag and choke as he cried out in agonizing pain.

Doc turned over and began to scramble crab-like under the tables again. He had to get out of here. He had to get to safety. He could hear the shorter thug jumping and pushing over tables. Doc had to get help. Only a few more feet to the door.

"Oooaaffff!" screamed Doc, as the smaller guy jumped over the last table and landed on Doc's back. All of the air was knocked out of Doc's lungs. He could feel the strength in the thug's arms as he took Doc's head between his hands and raised it up off of the floor. Then he rammed Doc's head into the concrete floor with all his might. All Doc saw was blackness and stars. He slammed Doc's head a second time and Doc could feel his consciousness starting to slip away.

Now the thug was up on both feet straddling Doc. He never let go of Doc's head. He lifted one leg over Doc's head and began to drag Doc by his hair. Doc was lifted up and felt himself being placed on the smooth table top. His consciousness was slowly returning, but when he opened his eyes he recognized instantly that he wasn't on a table top. His head was on the paper cutter. The long shiny blade was raised to it full height. Doc's hand instinctively grabbed for the handle to save his own life. The homicidal thug had his hand on it as well trying to pull the sharp blade down onto Doc's jugular. Doc was fighting with everything in his might, but he could already feel the cold razor's edge on his throat. Just a millimeter more of pressure and his throat would be sliced wide open. He could see the yellow hatred in the thug's eyes. Doc was resisting with his whole being, but it was a stalemate. The thug didn't have much more time before the place would be swarming with the goon squad. He moved his body to reposition his feet in order to give him enough leverage to defeat Doc and to slice his head completely off.

Doc felt the minute shift and used that moment to shove the thug off balance. The thug over compensated and stepped into a puddle of blood that had flowed from the lifeless guard.

The thug, losing his footing, was forced to let go of his death grip on the blade handle. Doc pushed off to remove his head from the guillotine. However, the thug reached out and grabbed Doc's hair to try and pull Doc's head back onto the chopping block. Doc could actually hear his hair separating from his scalp as it was being pulled out by the roots. The pain was excruciating, but Doc knew that if he let himself be pulled back under that blade, he was as good as dead.

Doc had his hand on the thug's hand and felt himself being pulled back under the blade. Then he felt it, his saving grace. He felt the rigid handle. Doc grabbed the handle and brought it down with all his might. He felt the paper cutter's guillotine arm slice its way into the thug's wrist. The thug let out a horrible scream, but Doc held onto the blade's handle with every ounce of strength that he had left. He pulled the handle down even harder as the thug's grip began to waiver. Doc was exhausted. He didn't know how much more energy he had in him. He had to get away from this thug. His assailant's screams became more intense as Doc increased pressure on his wrist with the blade. Doc could hear it cutting through cartilage.

Then Doc saw a glimmer out of the side of his vision as the thug's ten inch shank came zooming through the air. The tapered metal shank pierced his arm and felt like fire entering his bi-cep.

"Oooowwww!" Doc cried out loud.

Doc didn't know where the strength came from to hold on to the handle, but he knew that he couldn't let go, so he pulled it down farther using all the strength that he had left in him. The thug screamed louder as Doc increased the downward pressure of the blade. The thug's bone finally gave way and Doc heard the tendon of the wrist snap as the blade did its dirty chore.

Suddenly the pressure on his hair was released and Doc was catapulted back onto the floor.

What he saw next was his attacker standing there absolutely still with his mouth and eyes wide open. He was staring at his handless arm. He was clearly stunned and was going into shock as he witnessed stream after stream of his own blood shooting out from his body with every beat of his blackened heart.

Doc felt as if he might be going into shock, too. His vision was coming and going. This was too much. He wanted to go home. He needed to get out of here. He couldn't take this place anymore. This was insane. He had just severed one man's tongue and cut off another man's hand.

"What kind of crazy, fucked up place is this?" Doc yelled to no one.

Just then he felt a heaviness on his head. He was covered in blood and his hand was still wet as he reached up and realized that the homicidal thug's hand was still holding onto his sticky hair and dripping blood down Doc's forehead and into his eyes.

Chapter 24

Guy tossed his keys on his new desk and smiled.

He looked all around the maze and the office. He couldn't believe that he got away with it. He even drove around the block surrounding the campaign headquarters just to see if the police were in the area waiting to pick him up. His heart had been pumping like crazy during the entire ordeal.

The night's reverie started as only a coffee fueled prank to get revenge on the dirty deputy for stealing his ring, but it had escalated to a quasi-kidnapping and assault. Guy was still trying to get his mind around it all. He didn't know whose cajones he was using last night, but they must have been made of steel.

'What the hell had I been thinking?' was the phrase that keep repeating itself in his head.

In the light of day he imagined a thousand different things that could have gone wrong. Guy thought that he must have been out of his mind to have done what he did to Deputy Dawg. He could be in jail right now. Hell, for that matter, he could be under the jail. Guy was still paranoid that the police where going to swoop in and bust him.

"There is nothing keeping them from it," he told himself, but then felt the small disk in his pocket, and he knew why he would be safe, at least for a while. The video card that he held in his hand was his stay-out-of-jail free card, but he knew that time was of the essence. He needed to get some proof and he needed to get it fast.

He plugged in his laptop and downloaded Deputy Dawg's confession so that he could go through every bit of it. He wouldn't ever be able to use it in court as evidence due to how it was obtained, but he could get the information off of it and find other ways to prove it. Knowledge was power and the Intel from the Deputy Dawg was what he was going to use to get as much knowledge as he could of Big Red Johnson's corruption.

Guy felt like he was the cock of the walk now. In the last 24 hours he had become Director of Opposition Research with a new office and had blackmailed and threatened a confession out of a dirty cop that would make him famous when it was all finally exposed. The sight of Red Johnson being perp walked to his own jail was too delicious for Guy to think about. He would be a hero. Hell, they might even interview him on CNN or Fox News.

Yep, things were definitely looking up for Guy

Not bad for his first day.

*****

Guy scribbled notes furiously on an old used yellow pad as he watched and re-watched and re-watched again the video confession of Deputy Dawg. It was grainy and the lighting from car's headlights made the image of Deputy Dawg on the highway shackled with tears running down his fat cheeks, look even more pathetic and terrified than Guy remembered. There was no way he could ever let this video be seen by anyone else. They would think that the nice, smart and sweet Guy that they all knew and loved was some sort of crazed schizophrenic psychopath.

Maybe that was exactly what he was, Guy thought. A psychopathic monster. Because as he watched the video he couldn't believe that he was the one who was responsible for it all and that it was him saying such vile and gruesome things to Deputy Dawg. It was like he was watching someone else. He didn't want to believe that he was saying all of those horrible things, but it was.

'Oh God', thought Guy to himself, *'do I have the nerve to really do*

118

this?'

These were powerful men and it wasn't some game to them. If they felt threatened, he knew that they would push back hard and probably even kill him because this kind of evidence, if Guy could prove it, would put them all in prison for a long, long time. They knew better than anyone that cops in prison didn't last very long. He realized that he was playing in the big leagues now, and he was playing with some very dangerous people; and if he wanted to get out of it alive, he was going to have to play to win.

*****

Guy didn't know who all the people were that the deputy talked about on the video, but he did recognize the name Dr. Shaddix. He remember the two deputies in the coffee shop talked about a dentist friend of the Sheriff's by that name.

'Why is this dentist so well known in the department and what is his part in the corruption scandal?' That question was nagging at Guy's mind.

Guy decided to take a closer look at Dr. Shaddix, the dentist. It was time to take a big bite out of crime in Lloyd County.

Chapter 25

"If you move a muscle, I will kill you." said the guard.

Frantic yelling back and forth could be heard over the guard's radio. He was sweating. Fear was in his eyes. Doc was on the floor.

"Lock down! Lock down!" came the voice screaming over the radio.

Now it was Doc's turn to be scared. This was surreal to him. How had his wonderful life come to this? This was insane. He had to get out of this place. There was blood everywhere. He had to get out right now. Frantic voices could be heard from all over as the prison was being locked down.

WHOOOOOP! WHOOOOOP! WHOOOOOP!

The siren kept getting louder and louder. Doc could see the sweat on the obese guard's forehead. He was desperately listening to the coded distress calls that were squawking on the radio. Doc's panic was growing worse with each wail of the siren. Doc began to think about all of his college days and his life as a doctor. This was crazy. This had to be a dream.

"No," he said to himself, *"it is a nightmare."*

He had to wake up, but to do that he had to get out of this room. He had to tell someone that he wasn't supposed to be here. He didn't belong in a place like this. He wasn't one of these kinds of people. Someone had made a big mistake sending him here. Somebody needed to listen to him. He needed to go home.

"Get your ass back on the ground, god damn it!" screamed the guard, but Doc could only hear the incessant wailing of the alarm and of the voice in his head telling him to get out. He was breathing harder than he ever had. He was feeling light headed and blood was racing and pumping through his body. His brain was telling him to get up and get out.

The guard, the radio and his brain were screaming at him, but he couldn't seem to understand any of them. He had to get out of here. His body was telling him to get up and run, but his legs felt like they were in cement. He couldn't move. The voices were getting louder and louder. He had to get up.

His brain was screaming at him now, *"Run!"*

"Down Now! I said." screamed the guard, but Doc could only hear the panic in his own head as he rose up off the concrete floor and dashed for the door.

"Run, Run, Run!" said the voice in his head. *"Just get out of here and everything will be okay."*

Doc never saw the blow come from the guard's night stick. He felt a sudden impact to his left kidney, which immediately brought him to knees gasping for breath. The next blow hit him in the head, and blackness overtook Doc's eyes and all of the voices fell silent as he crashed face first into the floor. The last thing he remembered seeing were shoes. Big shiny black shoes and then everything went dark.

*****

Bentley's first two years were spent at SMU with his brother. Upon Boyce's graduation from Law school, Bentley was left alone again. With the loss of Boyce to his new job in Austin, Bentley sought refuge in the bars and comfort in the bottle. He was the eternal sad sack until he knocked a few back. Then he was the life of the party and everyone's best friend. His friends were the regulars of Cardinal Puff's bar, and they were always glad to see him. The bartenders knew what he liked and had it at the ready when he walked in the door. And everybody knew his name.

He continued on with his classes, sometimes sober and sometimes not, but he did manage to muddle his way through his junior and senior years. Within two weeks after High School graduation, Sandy and her sister, Marla, had moved away and dropped out of touch, but Bentley had never forgotten her. No matter how hard he tried he just couldn't get over her. He dated girls in college but inevitably ended up comparing them to Sandy, and they always came up short.

She was his first true love and everyone else paled in comparison. So without Boyce's constant presence and guidance, he drifted to drink. He had graduated with a decent enough GPA, but had no idea what to do after he graduated. He didn't want to be a lawyer and live in Boyce's shadow again, so he decided to become a doctor. Since his grades were good enough to get him into Baylor Dental School right away, so that's where he headed next.

Three years later he was ready for his little black bag. He was surprised when it came with and endless supply of amphetamines to stay awake and barbiturates to sleep. Good ol' boys in Texas took care of one another and his buddies were making sure that he was able to stay up and cram for his exams. He loved how they made him feel and his grades shot up from C's to A's and high B's despite the higher competition in graduate school The emptiness that he had carried around with him just disappeared. After a while he didn't miss Sandy anymore because 'love' was lavished on him by one amped up girl after another. He was sexually insatiable, and the number of girls throwing themselves at him was endless. One girl blurred into the next one. Girls in nice dresses. Girls in bathing suits. Girls in bikinis. Girls in nothing at all. Lots of girls at once in nothing at all. It was great. He was having the time of his life. He was acing his exams and was on top of the world.

After he graduated it, only got better. Boyce gave him some of the money from their inheritance to start up his practice and he became Dallas' new golden boy. He partied with the social elite and traveled with the jet set. He cruised the Caribbean with celebrities and flew to Europe on private jets with super-models. He was a platinum member of the mile-high club. When he combined sex with the amphetamines and cocaine, it was the perfect storm, the perfect trifecta of addictions. Nobody got hurt and everyone had a good time. Besides, he and his friends weren't some street junkies. They were the 1%. They couldn't be touched. Regular laws didn't apply to Dr. Bentley Braxton, III, and his friends. Those laws were made for other people, the masses of poor, but not them. He loved all of the attention and adoration. He couldn't get enough of it, but the thing he liked best were his road trips to Florida. He hit the road in his racing yellow Porsche that had been a gift from Boyce when he graduated from Baylor. Boyce had taken Bentley to the showroom and let him pick any car he wanted. The minute he saw it, he knew it was the car for him.

That night after graduation from dental school, Dr. Bentley and his buddy Dr. Malcolm had gone to Cardinal Puff's and picked up three drunken coeds.

"Let's go get 'Righteous'" yelled a drunken Malcolm as he slapped his buddy on the back and one of the drunken coeds on the ass.

Getting righteous was their euphemism for getting high and screwing until their eyes popped out of their sockets. After two days they went beyond righteousness and entered the holy land.

******

Doc's eyes fluttered from the light as he strained to open them. The blurriness slowly sharpened into focus as he concentrated and awoke. God almighty, his head was pounding and his back was aching like crazy. He was racked with pain.

Doc started to rub his temple, but as he tried to raise his hand it was snapped back by a hard grab around his wrist. His eyes darted down.

"Fuck!" He muttered to himself as he jerked his hand again and again at the handcuffs that attached his hand to the rail of the bed.

"Take it easy, Esse." said the laughing Latino voice in the next bed. *"You keep jerking it like that you won't be able to use that hand to jack off for a very long time."*

Prisoners in the other beds began laughing. Doc threw his head back against the pillow and went limp. The medical ward was as stark and impersonal as everything else in prison.

"Well, you are finally awake" said the prison nurse as he walked up.

"Why am I here?" asked Doc.

"What do you remember, Mr. Braxton" asked the nurse as he took Doc's wrist and began to take his pulse.

"I don't know." said Doc *"I was in the law library. Alarms started going off and then I don't remember anything after that."*

"Uh-huh" said the nurse as he let go of Doc's wrist and began scribbling on Doc's chart.

"I am really hurting though." said Doc *"Do you think I might get some Vicodin for this pain."*

The room erupted in laughter and the nurse just looked at Doc over his

123

glasses in a condescending manner. *"I don't think so, but I will get you some aspirin."* he said as he walked away.

The room stayed silent until the nurse left.

"Yo, Esse!" came the Latin voice in the next bed. *"If you be wanting something for the pain I can help you out."*

"Have you got some Vicodin?" Asked Doc because his head was pounding like a hammer and his back was on fire. He was desperate and he would welcome anything.

"No, Esse, I got something better." said the Latin guy *"I got some pills here that will take care of any pain you got."*

Doc turned to look at the guy. The Latin guy did a double take. *"Hey you're that really smart guy from the law library, aren't you? Man! I have heard of you. You are like famous, Esse."*

He pounded on the bed and yelled out. *"Hey everybody! Look who this is. It's the library dude who fucked up Pigmy and his crew."* The round faced Latin and everyone else craned their necks to Doc. *"Dude, you are legend around here. I can't believe that you are here. What happened, Esse?"*

Doc's brow furrowed as he tried to actually remember what had landed him here and handcuffed to this bed. His brain was throbbing with blinding pain, but no matter how hard he tried he couldn't remember what happened. He just wanted the pain to go away.

"I don't remember" said Doc. *"but I need something bad."*

"Sure. Sure." said the Latin guy *"Anything for a legend."*

He looked around and removed the plug from the end of the bed rail. He peeped over at the door one more time before he pulled out some white pills wrapped in a piece of blue plastic.

"Here you go, Esse." said the Latin guy handing him one of the pills. *"My name is El Diablo, by the way. You just remember that name and I*

124

will take care of you."

Doc knew that he shouldn't do any kind of deal like this, but the pain was all that he could think of. He just wanted it to go away, so he took the pill from El Diablo and swallowed it right away. He would deal with everything else later after all the pain was gone.

"What was that?" asked Doc after a minute as the pain began to drift away. He felt so light headed and his body began to feel a wave of warmth and peacefulness. Everything was so wonderful. He didn't have a worry in the world. His eyes got heavy, but he could feel his face smile with happiness.

"Morphine, Esse." said El Diablo laughing at the woozy Doc. *"Don't worry about anything now. We will talk when you wake up, Esse."*

Chapter 26

The place was a shit hole.

Guy hated going to the dentist's office, but this one seemed exceptionally bad. The decor was crappy and the magazines were ancient. The receptionist was ninety years old, if she was a day. She coughed and wheezed like an old sick car. He filled out his paperwork in the depressing waiting room with its cheap clown paintings. He had no idea what the frequency of his masturbation had to do with his dental appointment. He filled in all of the blanks and handed it back through the sliding window.

"Just have a seat. It shouldn't be long." said the old receptionist between hacking fits.

A young ginger headed child had scattered Highlight's magazines all over the floor and now turned his attention to the dirty aquarium that stood neglected in the corner of the room. There were only two fish in it that were still alive. The persistent ginger boy tapped on it repeatedly to get the fish's attention and then put his mouth on the glass and blew air into his cheeks to puff them out. Maybe he was trying to scare the last remaining survivors to death. Whatever his motivations were, he never tired of it, but Guy sure did. Guy was already extremely uptight and anxious about being here, and this kid was tap dancing all over his last nerve. Guy bit his tongue and resisted the urge to go over and just smack the kid.

'Where are this kid's fucking parents?' Guy wondered.

Guy picked up a Time magazine that had Bill Clinton on the cover.

"What a shit hole!" Guy mumbled to himself again. It was bad enough that the dentist still carried magazines instead of having a television in the waiting room, but the least he could do was to get some magazines from this century, that was if they still published any.

The door opened and it seemed as if a spotlight suddenly beamed down on a cute little thing with big wide-spaced, wide-opened eyes who cooed, "Mr. Guytana Canova?"

Guy shot out of his seat in order to get away from the blow hard kid who was also momentarily arrested by the captivating beauty of the girl standing at the open door. After seeing the old wheezer at the reception desk Guy had not expected to see someone so young. Guy felt as if cupid had pierced his heart right in the dental office.

"Come on back, Mr. Canova" she said. "My name is Lola, I am the hygienist." To Guy's ears she sounded like an angel, or the weather girl, as she whispered his name with her soft southern drawl.

She seated him in the Biscayne blue dental chair and put a dribble bib around his neck with alligator clips on a cold silver chain. Guy couldn't take his eyes off of her shoulder length chestnut hair or ruby moist lips. As she sat down in her chair, she leaned over him and for the first time Guy got to stare into her smoky brown eyes. He began to feel a tightness grow in his pants and he was mortified that she might see his obvious excitement.

"Do you think I might get a blanket?" he asked. "For some reason I am

126

kind of cold."

"Certainly" she said *"The doctor likes the office fairly cool"*

"Thank you" said Guy. He was now fully engorged in his khaki trousers and he prayed that she would not notice as she covered him up. If she did, she was professional enough not to have mentioned it. Guy could feel the hot blush of crimson on his cheeks that came with his embarrassment.

She laid the old soft blanket out to cover him. Stretching it all the way to his feet.

'She did a quick and almost imperceptible double take at his crotch before she quickly changed direction and began tucking in his feet. *"Oh, my God, this is so embarrassing."* thought Guy. He was really mortified now.

She instantly placed a sterile package of instruments rolled in a white towel held together with a tape that changed colors during the heat sterilization leaving no doubt about the perfect protection of her patients, but she couldn't help but be flattered that such an attractive man would be so interested in her.

'Wow!' she just admitted to herself that she thought he was attractive too. That was a first. Now all she could think about were his beautiful green eyes. She found herself getting aroused and rather excited. That certainly wasn't very professional, but she caught herself daydreaming about what it would be like to be with such a cute guy. She hadn't been on too many dates and most of them had been blind dates and double dates set up by her brother, Santos. He was a deputy with the sheriff's department and he was always setting her up with his buddies from the force. Inevitably, they would just end up telling stories about things that had happened on the job. Lola was so bored by them. They were all the same to her. In addition, most of the guy's that her brother set her up with were kind of fat and sloppy. She wanted a handsome hunk. She wanted someone like this guy----"Guy". And it seemed like he wanted her too. He was so nice compared to all of Santos' friends.

127

Guy's embarrassment caused his mouth to dry up, so he cleared his throat. The sudden noise broke Lola's daydreaming spell. She raised up quickly; catching her arm on the drill and causing the dental mirror to drop into Guy's lap.

Up until that moment, Guy didn't believe that the situation could get any more awkward. The mouth mirror dropped right on top of his erection. He was surprised by how heavy the little instrument was.

"Oh my gosh!" Lola screamed as the instrument fell.

Instinctively, she reached out to try and catch it, but instead she ended up hitting her patient's stiffened manhood. With that realization she jerked her hand back immediately so as to try and maintain her composure and not to cause her patient any more embarrassment. Dr. Shaddix would be furious with her if he found out. He was such a stickler about not having any problems in the office. He chewed them out regularly for the most menial things. She knew that he would throw a fit and she didn't think he would excuse this at all. He would fire her for sure and she needed this job badly. She didn't have a pretty yellow Porsche to drive around in. She was barely making ends meet.

"Oh, I am so sorry!" Lola said.

Guy could see the panic on her face and he forgot all about his embarrassment.

"It's alright." Guy said.

This ordeal was going badly. Guy wanted to get out of the chair and run away from the office. There was no way he was going to be able to get any information now. She probably thought that he was some pervert who liked to get his jollies in dental chairs. This was just awful. He had really screwed up this investigation. She would probably throw him out at any minute and call the cops. He thought he might as well get out as quickly as he could, so he began to get up from the chair.

"Oh no, please, don't go." Lola pleaded with him.

'What?' Guy thought. 'She wants me to stay?'   Now he was really

128

confused. 'Maybe she isn't going to call the cops after all.'

"Please, Mr. Canova, if you leave, Dr. Shaddix will fire me for sure." she was begging him now. Guy could see that she was almost in tears. *"I am so sorry."*

Now Guy was really confused. 'She is sorry? For what?' He was the pervert that couldn't keep it in his pants and she was apologizing to him? This was crazy, but how could he refuse those beautiful brown eyes. So he eased back into the chair.

Lola was visibly relieved and she began to shake with relief that he wasn't going and that she wouldn't lose her job. Guy saw her shaking and he reached out and took her hands in his. They were soft and delicate and he felt like he never wanted to let go.

An electric jolt went through Lola's body when he touched her. She had never in her life had a feeling like that with a man. His touch calmed her instantly and she wanted nothing more than to be held closer and tighter by this gorgeous man with his emerald green eyes.

"Just what is going on here?" came a loud authoritative voice from the open door.

Guy was surprised, but he could see the fright in Lola's eyes. She froze like a small deer in a hunter's headlights. Guy thought that she was going to speak. He could see her lips moving barely perceptively but no sound came out of her beautiful and terrified face. She seemed paralyzed with fear. Guy wanted to take her into his arms and comfort her. She was the sole picture of innocence and virtue. He wanted to do whatever he could to save her.

"OOOOhhhh noooo! Are you the dentist?" cried out Guy in the most hysterical high pitch voice that he could muster. The dentist and Lola were both startled as they immediately turned to see this wild man screaming hysterically.

Guy turned back to Lola and grabbed her harder and pulled her towards himself. *"I told you that I don't think I can go through with this."* He said with a sly wink to Lola. Then he began to jerk the blanket off and tear at the paper bib to yank it off.

Lola was a smart girl and she didn't miss a beat in putting her hands on his shoulders and pushing him back into the dental chair. She knew what Guy was doing immediately.

He was saving her job.

"Now, now, Mr. Canova," she cooed *"I told you that Dr. Shaddix is the best in town and that you won't feel a thing."*

Upon hearing his assistant's praise Dr. Shaddix puffed up like a peacock. The doctor's demeanor changed noticeably as he deduced that Guy was just another scared patient.

Guy continued his panicky charade. *"I have changed my mind. I don't think I can do this. . I am scared to death of dentists."* He was really pouring it on thick now. He saw Lola snickering behind the doctor's back.

"Its okay, Mr. Canova," said the puffed up quack.

Guy caught Lola's eye. Without verbalizing a single word she silently gave him the biggest thank you in the world with those beautiful brown eyes. He was the happiest guy in the world at this moment, but only on the inside because on the outside he was still hamming it up for the doctor.

"Now just relax for a moment and when you wake up you will be as good as new." And that was the last thing he remembered as he sucked in big gulping breaths of nitrous oxide. Stars shot out in every direction and he felt his body float off the chair into the air. His last memory was the *Whump! Whump! Whump!* as his eyes began to spin around.

"Relax, Mr. Canova" said the doctor. *"Don't smile so big."*

As he looked into Lola eyes he couldn't help but smile from ear to ear.

Chapter 27

Farmer ran down the hall as if his life depended on it.

He sprinted past each crash gate and ignored every cry from the guards.

"Hey, asshole! Slow the fuck down." someone yelled.

Farmer ignored them. He had to get to where he was going. His life didn't depend on it, but someone's might. The Sergeants working the hall didn't dare stop him because of who he was and who he worked for.

They had been up against him before and it never turned out well for them, so they just let him go by unimpeded.

Farmer saw in the distance that Lt. Sharp was sitting at the central desk. He slowed down to a fast walk.

Lt. Aloysius Sharp was a no nonsense ball breaker. A total prick. Farmer knew that any case that the tight-ass Lieutenant might give him would be thrown out and end up with the Lieutenant being dressed down by the Warden for "interfering with his boy".

As a 36 year old black man, Farmer hated being called the Warden's 'boy', but if it got him what he wanted he would just suck up the indignation he felt deep inside his gut.

Lt. Sharp may have known who Farmers boss was, but that didn't mean that he couldn't still jam Farmer up in the hall and fuck with him just for his own pleasure or entertainment.

Lt. Sharp was the boss and there was no way to get around that, so Farmer slowed himself and blended into the one-way traffic heading south. He needed to be invisible for the next few moments because each second was precious. It could mean life and death.

Doc didn't know it, but his life depended on Farmer now. Farmer had ears everywhere and they had told him that Doc was about to get "sprung" over a debt for morphine pills. If that happened then there was no going back for Doc; and he would never be under Farmer's control again. If Doc let himself be compromised sexually it would be the end of his usefulness to Farmer. He would just be another prison punk who would be passed around getting his ass hole stretched out for a little white pill.

Farmer should have seen this coming, but he was old school. And old school meant that you didn't get involved in someone else's life. The unwritten code in prison was to mind your own fucking business and not to get involved in someone else's. People ended up dead in a place like this for a hell of a lot less.

What was about to happen was Farmer's business. If he lost Doc, everything he had worked for would be for nothing; and this little white boy was way too important to him to let him just piss his life away. Especially right now. He could throw his life away later, Farmer didn't care, but not right now. Farmer needed him too much.

*****

Doc had been wounded seriously in the Law Library. Farmer had seen the stitches and the bruises, but what he hadn't seen was that Doc had become addicted to morphine. Farmer had seen a lot of black addicts, but he had to admit that this white boy had 'game'. He had fooled Farmer for over a month. The 'niggas' that Farmer knew were straight up junkies. They were easy to spot. Drugs were their everything, but Farmer was in unfamiliar territory with Doc. Doc was white and intelligent and he knew how to hide his addiction. Farmer had never been around anyone as sophisticated as Doc. He would never admit it to anyone, but he was more than a little intimidated by the white boy. He hadn't suspected anything about Doc's sudden affinity to be alone in the cell and his penchant for sleeping for long periods of time. Farmer just attributed it to his healing, but word had finally got back to Farmer that Doc was buying as many morphine pills as he could get his hands on.

'Preposterous!' Farmer had thought.

Everyone in prison constantly 'hated' on other people. That was just the way it was. They made up shit up all of the time. Besides that, Farmer knew that Doc didn't have any money because the District Attorney had frozen all of his assets and confiscated all of Doc's funds. Farmer lived with Doc and he seemed like the same guy that he had always been. Sure, he slept more and he was a little depressed but that was normal in prison. Men had those times that they wanted to be by themselves a lot more. Everyone went through that from time to time. After all, it was prison, not summer camp. A man had reasons to be down, and a good celly didn't question it or get nosey because next time the shoe might be on the other foot. No one wanted to be seen as weak. So a good celly just left you alone. That's just what Farmer had done.

That proved to have been a big mistake. He should have kept a better eye on Doc. He should have kept Doc on a shorter leash.

*****

Doc had relapsed and spiraled out of control. Morphine was a sexy, but ugly lover. She whispered sweetness in your ear, casting her intoxicating spell on a man, and then became a hungry and seductive witch. She would make a man do anything to feel her beguiling warmth and loving embrace. Literally. Anything.

Doc was no different than all of her other lovers. He had quit caring about anything or anyone else anymore.

"Fuck it and fuck everyone." He said.

He just wanted to feel that all-encompassing morphine euphoria. That was all he needed now. Nothing else. He started out by hiding his addiction and leading a double life, just as he had done in the free world. But after several weeks of being cuddled and loved by the narcotic nymph, he didn't care about anything or anybody anymore. He was in prison and what other people thought didn't matter to him anymore.

'Screw 'em all, goddamn it.' he thought 'What is the fucking point?'

He was in prison now and that was that. He was going to be here for a very long time and nothing was going to change that. Why shouldn't he just let go of all the bullshit and just do whatever the fuck he wanted to.

133

Right now, he wanted to get high. Real high.

He couldn't get out of this hell hole physically, but he sure could mentally. Morphine was like a time machine in pill form. Time just evaporated when he was high.

Morphine had become his temptress; his sweet lover. Everything was alright when Morphine kissed him. Her warm lips felt like such sweet comfort. She made the pain evaporate and his problems didn't matter anymore. Morphine understood him and his new buddy, Hillbilly, didn't judge him either like others did. Hillbilly had become his new home-boy.

Hillbilly liked to shoot up in his arm. He had what he called his sweet spot on the inside crook of his elbow. He had tried to get Doc to shoot up also, but when Doc saw the 18 gauge vet needle Hillbilly was using and the giant infected hole in Hillbilly's arm, he decided to pass on what was most assuredly a case of Hepatitis-C or AIDS. Doc opted to just pop his pills and wait for Nirvana to wash itself over him.

He hated coming back to reality. He loathed being reminded that he had lost everything that was important to him and pushed away everybody who loved him. Now his only love was Morphine. Sandy had abandoned him because of her bitch sister, Marla. Boyce had abandoned him after two stints in rehab and countless interventions. Doc figured that his big brother had finally given up and washed his hands of him with his constant troubles. Doc didn't blame Boyce. Look at where he had ended up.

However, Doc had never abandoned Boyce. When he wasn't high and being stupid, Doc had kept up with his brother's meteoric rise in Austin. Boyce never did anything wrong. Boyce was always fucking perfect. He was the Golden Child. A damn choirboy. Doc loved him deeply, but he could never equal his brother and he was tired of trying. He had given in and gave up. Given in to his addiction and gave up competing with his brother. It was just a lot easier.

Boyce had become one of the most influential people in the state. He was a mover and a shaker. Jerry Bass was the Governor of Texas, but everyone knew who really made the decisions in the Governor's office. Bass was a tool, a stuffed shirt. He was only a puppet. Everyone who was old enough to tie their shoes in the State of Texas knew that Boyce Braxton was the real power in the Capitol Building. He was the man who decided what the Governor ate for breakfast or what oil companies got to drill in Texas. Some men wanted titles and others wanted power. Boyce was a power man.

Right now all Doc wanted was another little white pill.

All he cared about was getting a fix. He was hurting. Hurting badly. He felt cold and clammy. Nausea had set in and he could no longer stand the sight of food. The food here would turn a man's stomach anyway, but in Doc's current condition, the sight of it made him violently ill. He spent an hour hunched over the stainless steel contraption that was a drinking fountain, a sink basin and a toilet all-in-one. Doc hated drinking out of it. The water tasted like the stuff that someone had just flushed, and to add insult to injury, it was always warm and disgusting.

Doc lay in the floor with his head deep in the stainless steel toilet bowl retching up nothing except bitter yellow bile mucous.

'Where is my salvation and escape from this hell hole?' Doc asked the putrid smelling toilet.

All he wanted was to get out of the fucked up place. For more than a year he had endured the vilest reprobates on the planet. They were animals and scum. They had tried to rape him, beat him, starve him and kill him. And this was only his first year. He couldn't take it anymore. He certainly couldn't take nine more years of it. They had broken him. They had finally taken everything. His life. His career. His car. His money. His hope.

They had it all, except for his dignity. In prison that wasn't worth a damn thing. These cretins had nothing and had never done anything close to being responsible. They were just the dregs of the world. They killed. They stole. They maimed. They hurt people.

They were trash. As he lifted his head up and wiped the spittle of yellow wretch off his face, he realized that he was just trash, too. If he wasn't, he wouldn't be here with them, would he?

Why hadn't Boyce answered his letters? Why had Boyce abandoned him this time? The only answer that he kept coming up with was that Boyce hated him now? Well, that was fine because now Doc hated him also for letting him rot in this putrid stink hole.

In fact, Doc hated the whole world right now, including God.

The only thing he loved now was the one thing that loved him back. That was Morphine. She was his sweet temptress and his loving mistress. She was the only thing that made him feel safe and kissed him tenderly while she held him in her warm and seductive arms. She was the only one that cared about him, and he would do anything to see her right now. The gnawing in his gut was getting worse and worse. He didn't know how much longer he could stand the pain.

Doc's celebrity status had run out after a month. Now El Diablo wanted money before he would give Doc anymore morphine pills. His new drug friend, Hillbilly, had been able to score a few hits here and there, but it wasn't enough to feed both of their growing appetites. Hillbilly's addiction was becoming exceptionally voracious. He couldn't ever seem to get enough. For a while Doc's celebrity status gave him the ability to acquire drugs for the both of them, but it just wasn't enough. Doc could have been selfish and kicked Hillbilly to the curb, but Hillbilly was his buddy while they were both laid up in the infirmary. Hillbilly always shared his pills with Doc and vice-versa. They had established a bond; a silent brotherhood, if you will. It only seemed natural for them to maintain their alliance once they got out. Hillbilly also had an innate and infectious sense of humor that Doc loved. He was fun. Pure and simple. He helped Doc forget for just a few moments what a horrible place he was in.

There were really no other words to describe Hillbilly. He was just a silly and sweet-natured southern boy. He was as dumb as a box of rocks, but he was also sweet as homemade pie and funny as hell. Those were two qualities that Doc didn't see much of in here. Hillbilly kept him laughing, and Doc was grateful for the blonde hick from the sticks with his male patterned baldness and white skin so translucent that you could almost read a newspaper through it. That skin was one of the reasons Hillbilly could hit his veins so easily. Doc had told him that he could probably hit Hillbilly's vein from across the room and in the dark.

They were total opposites, but Doc had never felt as comfortable with anyone in his whole life. In his euphoric morphine transitions he would ruminate for hours about why he and this simpleton were so simpatico. They were oil and water, the prison odd couple some would say, but Doc was absolutely fond of this albino red-neck. Even though the only thing they had in common was their fondness for Morphine, Doc felt like Hillbilly was the only person that understood him and liked him for who he really was. Warts and all. He knew that Doc was insecure, weak and indecisive, but he didn't judge Doc. He still liked him and wanted to be with him. Doc had never experienced that with anyone but Sandy. And she was gone.

Geez, she had been gone from his life for more than a decade. Why couldn't he get her out of his goddamn mind? How long would her memory continue to haunt him? The State of Texas had incarcerated his body, but they would never be able to free his mind. There was no parole from her memory and no Governor's reprieve from the recurring death that was his daily memory of their love affair. She had been the only person that he had ever loved with all his heart and soul. The pain was still just as awful as the day she was ripped from his life. No others had ever come along to replace her. Nothing had ever made him forget her. That was for sure.

No one before Morphine had freed him from his mental snare. Some called it a Monkey Trap-----a trap that has within it the very thing you want more than life itself, and you can't get out unless you let go of the very thing you want more than life itself. Without that thing, you believe that your life will have no meaning or value to it, so you hold on as tight as you possible can. But it is a false trap. A trick. Because it is that 'very thing' that will end up killing you.

So you had to ask yourself, "Do I die holding on to something I love but can never have or do I let go and live everyday wishing that I could die because without it I am so damn miserable that I can't stand living another day?'

Doc just wanted to be free. Free of this wretched place, but as much as that he wanted to be free of the memory of Sandy. He was so tired of hurting. Peace and happiness were what he craved, but that wasn't possible, except when he was on drugs. Except when he was on morphine.

*****

Doc joined Hillbilly at his cell. Hillbilly had the most perfect cell on the block, the very last cell on the very top tier.

The one thing that you could count on in prison is that the guards would do as little work as possible and they would take as few steps as they humanly could to do their jobs. They rarely walked their immense and overweight bodies up three flights of stairs and down the football field length of the run. They didn't really give a rat's ass what these convicts did with each other or to themselves. It was just a job and they wanted merely to collect their money and go home.

The collective thought was, 'just let them kill one another. Who would really care? Just as long as they do it on someone else's freakin' shift. '

"It took me two years and twenty five bags of coffee to get this crappy cold ass cell." said Hillbilly as Doc sat shivering on the toilet.

In the tiny cell the toilet was the only place to sit other than the lower bunk, because sitting on another man's bunk was considered a cardinal breach of prison etiquette. The only people who would ever be allowed to sit on a man's bunk would be his celly--- or an incredibly close "friend". It just wasn't done, so Doc didn't take any offense when he wasn't offered a seat. He was taking the huge risk just being in someone else's cell. If he got caught in here, he would most assuredly get a major case and spend a couple of weeks in lock up, but it was a chance he was willing to take if it meant he could get a hit.

"Hola, hotos!" yelled El Diablo as he quickly stepped into the cell. Doc was shivering and felt like total dog shit, but even in his current state he perked up at the thought of getting a hit.

"I got a little something for you, mi amigos." And with that said El Diablo tossed a few pills to Hillbilly and then to Doc.

Doc was jonesing like crazy and he wanted to just gobble up the white pills like Hillbilly was already doing, but he felt compelled to tell El Diablo, *"Dude, I don't have any money right now."*

"Hey, man, don't insult me." said El Diablo as he twisted his face up with indignation. *"You are my homie now and homies do things for each other. Go ahead and enjoy yourselves and we will talk when you wake up, mi amigos."*

Doc thought about it and hesitated for a moment, but Hillbilly hadn't hesitate at all as he jabbed the giant needle into his arm. Doc watched him register it. The blood spiraled like red smoke into the syringe and Hillbilly pushed the plunger down until every last drop was gone.

The euphoric release was immediate. Hillbilly's eyes glazed over and rolled back into their sockets as his jaw slackened and his tongue lolled sideways to rest on his lower lip. Doc knew that wonderful feeling and he began to crave his hit of the wonder drug as he watched Hillbilly's head leaned back against the wall. He knew that feeling of ecstasy and he wanted to feel it too.

Hillbilly hadn't even had time to pull the needle out of his arm. Doc watched as a dark red trickle ran down Hillbilly's arm leaving a hematoma trail like a small snail. It would have grossed out the average person but it only made Doc's skin itch with anticipation. He knew the total euphoria that Hillbilly was feeling and he wanted that feeling for himself more than anything else in the whole world at this moment. The thought of so much pleasure and seeing Hillbilly enjoying himself made the craving in Doc's body so intense that tears formed in the corner of his eyes as he reached up and dug deeply into his face with his nails because of the intense desire to be on the same plateau as Hillbilly was. That was all that Doc wanted at this moment. That was all that he could think of.

It was all that he could feel.

"Man, look at you, Esse." Said El Diablo licking his lips. *"Go ahead, hit it, homey. You're hurting, dude, and I am here to help you, so go on."*

He was right. Doc was hurting. All he could think about was how good he would feel. He didn't care what the cost would be. He wanted to get high and he would cover the cost somehow. All he wanted was a hit, so he would find a way to pay. He wanted to feel that perfect euphoria. And he wanted to feel it now.

Nothing else mattered to him at this moment. The high was all he could think of. Fuck the money or whatever it cost. He would pay it or do it. He didn't care what it was. Whatever it cost, he would pay it.

This was the new Doc. The practical Doc. The Doc that said, *"Fuck it!"*

And with that last thought he glanced over at Hillbilly one last time and then threw the pills into his open gullet.

The last thing he remembered was two hands helping him down and helping him up into bed.

*****

Farmer entered the cell like a raging bull. He was snorting and gulping breaths.

The first thing he saw was that El Diablo was exposed and completely naked. His prison whites were crumpled on the ground around his left ankle. His right foot and his leg was hoisted up onto the desk next to the toilet; accentuating his muscular smooth thigh that was stretched taut with sinewy muscle. The scene was pornographic and disgusting to Farmer.

The two star tattoos on El Diablo's shoulder blades and smooth hairless buttocks were the first thing that Farmer noticed as he busted through the cell door. El Diablo had not expected to be interrupted and he had definitely not seen Farmer barge into the cell.

The Monkey Trap

Farmer could see that El Diablo was fumbling with Hillbilly's unconscious and lolling head trying to steady it with one hand, while he grappled pointlessly with his uncircumcised cock in the other. The stocky Mexican was trying to force his swollen and engorged cock into Hillbilly's unconscious mouth.

Farmer grasped El Diablo by the necklace that he wore to hold his gold cross and yanked him backwards. The sudden thrust of the necklace being pulled back against El Diablo's larynx caused him to gasp and choke with surprise and astonishment.

Farmer was strong and he pulled El Diablo back with such force that he yelled out loudly as his fully erect penis was being torn out of the albino's mouth. What Farmer couldn't have known was that El Diablo's fragile and tender foreskin had caught on Hillbilly's rotting right central incisor and was literally being ripped out of Hillbilly's mouth.

A spray of penile blood arced its way across the high gloss gray wall of the cell and splattered Doc's whites like a Jackson Pollack canvas. Farmer was still in his painter's coveralls and the blood couldn't be distinguished from any of the other stains and colors that already covered him. However, Farmer felt the hot fluid across his face and despite his best effort to turn away from the spray, it had gotten into his left eye. For the first time in his life he was actually seeing red.

Farmer was responding and acting on pure adrenaline as he pulled back his enormous fist to hit the shocked and whimpering Puerto Rican with all his Nubian might, but despite his best shot, his fist was too saturated in the Latin spick's cock blood for the hammering blow to be fully effective. The blood covered El Diablo had managed to duck his head so as to avoid what would have most assuredly been a direct shot to the Puerto Rican rapist's face.

The Puerto Rican was trying to get out of Farmer's grip in order to pull up his pants and to staunch the flow of blood gushing from his penis. The cell was small. Doc and Hillbilly were both oblivious to the bloody struggle that was going on over them.

Farmer regrouped himself internally. He aimed for a second shot to the rapist's face. This time he connected and hammered the slime ball drug dealer across the bridge of his nose causing it to split right down the middle and to splay wide open. Farmer heard the cartilage pop like a chicken bone.

El Diablo let out a horrific scream, but Farmer's black fist immediately smashed into the bald Puerto Rican's mouth and silenced him immediately. Farmer's knuckles were cut and bloodied from El Diablo's teeth.

Farmer felt no remorse as he continued to beat the smooth bodied and naked Puerto Rican into a bloody pulp. El Diablo was still on his feet, but Farmer had bent him over so that the scumbag was facing the floor. Farmer was forced to grip El Diablo by the back of his neck because he lacked any hair for Farmer to grab onto. Farmer swung the Latin drug dealer around and in one last move to finish off the Puerto Rican and to end the fight. He ran El Diablo's bloody skull directly into the cell bars.

The Latin molester fell defeated and completely limp onto Hillbilly's lap.

Farmer had exhausted himself exponentially with every punch. He was amazed at how tired he got after only a few hits. In a freaky momentary flash, he realized that even though he was still a big guy, he was getting old. Old age was a cruel bitch. It certainly wasn't for sissies that was for sure.

By the time he finished pummeling Diablo, the Puerto Rican's coco latte coloring was a thing of the past. His face was now swollen purple and yellow and covered in the red sticky ooze of his own perverted blood.

Farmer looked down at his hands and saw the same sticky red liquid was covering his own fists and arms completely. He began to feel panic enter his body as he gulped in one deep breath after another.

"Yes!" he thought to himself, '*I am was scared shitless and about to crap my own pants. But I don't have a choice. I will hold it together, Goddamn it!*'

However, time was imperative and he had precious little of it left.

He had to get Doc and himself out of this bloody cell. If they got caught here, there was nothing that anyone could do. It wouldn't matter who Farmer worked for. They would both be in lock up for a very, very long time.

He wanted to get the blood off of his hands, but that wasn't going to be possible now. In for a penny, in for a pound, as his old granny used to say.

He grabbed Doc under the arms and started to pull him out of the cell. Doc was 150 lbs. of dead weight and Farmer's arms were beginning to burn with fatigue.

Farmer had Doc almost completely out of the cell, when he felt a hard crack across the back of his head. He dropped Doc and was thrown forward into the railing of the third floor run. It was tubular steel, the typical style of prison railing, and Farmer had to catch himself so that he didn't go through the two rails and end up hurling himself forty five feet straight down onto the concrete below. Complete blackness was all he saw until he started seeing white stars shooting in his brain. While it sure didn't feel very good to his head, he knew that the shooting stars were a good sign because it meant that he wasn't going to lose consciousness. Doc was a crumpled heap at Farmer's feet, half in and half out of the cell.

El Diablo had regained consciousness while Farmer was trying to pull Doc and himself out of the small and narrow cell door. Farmer's attention was on the task of getting himself and Doc out of the bloody cell and away from the trouble that would definitely be coming. El Diablo seized the moment that Farmer had turned and was no longer facing the inside of the cell. He leapt up off of the comatose red neck and grabbed the first object that he could find, a prison coffee pot.

With all of his might and with every ounce of strength left in him, he gripped the handle and brought it down as heavily as he could on Farmer's head.

The hard clear plastic coffee pot shattered with a mighty crack and pieces flew everywhere. It wasn't a great weapon by prison standards but it had gotten the job done. Farmer was sent down to his knees and almost went head first through the railing to the first floor, but by sheer luck he had caught himself. He was still stunned and stumbling but he wasn't going to be like that forever, so El Diablo made his move.

El Diablo knew that he couldn't whoop him, but he could kill him, so he searched the ground until he found what he was looking for. He needed a weapon against this giant nigger and he picked up the biggest piece of the broken coffee pot that he could find. It was sharp and long. It was perfect.

'I gonna stab this nigger hard.' El Diablo thought to himself. He didn't know where yet but it was thin enough that it would slide easily between the nigger's ribs and sharp enough to slit his throat if he needed it to.

No one beat El Diablo like this and got away with it. He wasn't just some prison punk. He was a made member of one of the most ruthless and feared gangs in prison. Star tattoos marked both of his shoulder blades. Going back to his home boys looking like this meant that the other guy had better be dead. If it got out to the gang members that he had let himself get beat down this badly, he would be made somebody's punk within twenty four hours or killed for disgracing the gang. He would rather be killed than be disgraced. He had nothing to lose by killing this big nigger. In fact, his reputation would probably go way up in the eyes of his gang buddies. He would be a fucking hero.

He was still naked and that bothered him a lot, but he didn't have time to worry about it. He had to kill this nigger now or die trying.

He gripped the plastic shiv so hard that it was cutting his own hand. He lunged over the limp body of Doc in the doorway and brought the clear plastic knife down as hard as he could towards the nigger's slumped body. He saw Farmer's neck and aimed straight for his jugular. He would cut this nigger so that he would bleed out like a stuck pig. He wanted to see Farmer's life blood run out of his body and over the edges of the run until he was dead. When it was over El Diablo would cut the nigger's dick off for what he had done to him.

Farmer was dazed, but years of fighting in prisons had given him a second sense when it came to danger. El Diablo let out a blood curdling scream as he leapt over Doc's body. An amateur move. Farmer didn't know what the Puerto Rican had in his hand, but he didn't want to wait find out either.

El Diablo had committed to his thrust at Farmer's throat; and since he had to straddle Doc's body to get to Farmer, he had past the point of no return. He was committed now to killing this big nigger.

Farmer saw the naked rapist while he was in mid-air.

El Diablo screamed. *"AAAAhhhhhhh!"*

Farmer couldn't stop the naked Puerto Rican since he was already in mid-air and coming straight down at him. Farmer was in the worst position possible. Nothing he could do would defend him against the oncoming attack, so he hunkered down further into a tight ball and put his hands over the back of his head and neck. He prepared himself for the coming onslaught of pain. He hated pain and would do anything to avoid it.

On the descent down El Diablo saw Farmer retract himself into a tighter ball and raise his hands over the back of his neck to protect himself. El Diablo felt the rush of victory over this nigger when he saw the big strong African cower into a ball. He decided to raise his arm further back to give him even more thrust to stab this mullah in his neck. In doing so, he landed with his feet first.

Farmer felt the drug dealing rapist's naked body land squarely on his back. Without thinking or waiting, he sprang his body straight up.

The attacking Puerto Rican was stunned at the sudden turn of events. Before he could plunge the make-shift dagger into Farmer's jugular El Diablo felt himself being lifted up off his feet.

Confidence of victory was suddenly swept aside by the absolute fear of certain death. El Diablo had miscalculated and underestimated the African giant. He tried to grasp the rail as he was lifted high and tossed through air. He didn't have enough time to think about his life or family as he plummeted to the concrete floor below. All he could think about was the pain he was going to feel on impact and that he would be found naked. He was right about being found naked, but he never felt any pain because he was killed instantly on impact. His neck broke in five places and his skull opened up like a watermelon thrown off a roof.

Farmer never heard a sound until the little naked pervert's head hit the cement. The breaking bones sounded like a splintering bat. The sounds that brought him back to reality were the screams of inmates on the first row who had blood and brains splattered all inside their cells.

"Aaaaaaaahhhhh!" screamed someone.

"Someone call a guard, goddamn it!"

"Oh my God! What the Fuck?" voiced another cell.

Farmer snatched Doc's arm and began to drag him down the run as fast as he could. Doc's head hit half a dozen stiles on the way to their cell. His head was going to hurt when he woke up, but Farmer had to get them into their own cell before they locked the place down.

Screams were coming fast and frantic from the entire wing. The calls for help were deafening. Farmer heard the main gate to the cell block open. The guard didn't wait to get to the body before he screamed out for re-enforcements and for the wing to be locked down.

Farmer heard the picket boss running across the catwalk from the other side of the hall. Farmer was dragging dead weight and Doc's arms and legs kept catching on every other stile. The picket boss could be heard jumping down the metal stairs two at a time. He opened the control panel and hit the panic button. All first floor doors began to close. Farmer wrestled to get Doc's shoulder loose. The picket boss could be heard bounding up to the second row. Farmer and Doc were running out of time. The doors on the second row had been activated and were closing. Farmer had only a matter of seconds. He could hear the picket boss' boots as they began their climb to the third tier. Each step pounded like a striker winding up in an old clock. Farmer was counting the boss' steps and comparing them to his own. It was going to be close, but

Farmer couldn't win a tie. Not dragging Doc he couldn't.

"Goddamn it" screamed Farmer. He was so fucking close to lose like this, but he wasn't a quitter. He had to try. He couldn't give up.

Farmer's muscles were on fire. He was only ten feet away, when he heard the guard top the stairs. Farmer was almost there. Only five more feet. He could save himself and just leave Doc out on the run, but then everything would have been for naught. He couldn't believe that he had gotten this close only to lose everything. He had done his best but there was no way he was going to be able to drag himself and Doc into the cell before the picket boss hit the panic button and slammed the doors shut.

Then Farmer heard it. The picket boss tripped on the open grated floor. Farmer heard the guard cussing and swearing in pain. Farmer reached his cell and turned to jump in, but Doc's arm pit caught on the railing just outside their cell.

"Fuck me!" yelled Farmer. He just couldn't catch a break.

He jumped out of the cell and jerked Doc's arm free. He didn't fucking care if Doc hurt tomorrow.

"He deserves to hurt. This was all his fucking fault anyway" said Farmer to himself as he up ended Doc into the cell; throwing Doc's feet in over his head.

Farmer heard the pissed off picket guard hit the panic button. All of the cell doors on the third tier began to electronically shut. Nothing would stop them now and Farmer was still on the wrong side.

Farmer made a dive into the cell on top of Doc's body. Doc was still oblivious to everything. Farmer's foot was grazed by the cell door as it finally clanged shut.

*****

The trip down the run hadn't been what anyone would call a clean get away in any sense of the word.

Thankfully, it was the middle of the afternoon and most inmates had decided to go to Rec or to watch re-runs of <u>Law & Order</u> in the dayroom.

Farmer was panting like a dog. It would only be a matter of minutes before the guards started looking in and checking each cell. Just because Farmer had gotten them into their cell didn't mean that they were home free yet. Doc was unconscious and Farmer was covered in blood. Farmer had to think fast and work even faster.

He yanked back the covers on his lower bunk and dropped Doc into it. He pulled the sheet up over Doc. The guard would assume, correctly, that Doc was asleep.

'Not much of a stretch there,' Farmer thought.

Now came the hard part. Farmer could hear guards filing in through the crash gate and onto the wing. It would only be moments before the first one would make his was up to the third level and begin a cell by cell visual inspection.

Farmer pulled up his privacy curtain. It was only a sheet that was strung up to give a little bit of privacy when an inmate was taking a shit. His feet could be seen while he was sitting on the stainless steel crapper but the rest of his body was covered. Farmer shucked blood soaked coveralls and sat down on the toilet.

He heard footsteps ascending the metal stairs.

The guard had his clip board and was counting the number of people in each cell. Farmer wrestled to put on the clean white shirt that he had grabbed at the last moment. He could hear that the guard was only one cell away.

"304. Show yourself." came the command from the guard as he looked into Farmer's cell.

Farmer shoved his last arm into the shirt and pulled back the privacy sheet to expose himself fully to the guard. The guard had no desire to gawk at Farmer's immense manhood and quickly checked off cell 304 as 'okay' on his clipboard.

Farmer sighed with relief as the pubescent guard moved on down the line.

Just then Doc began to stir. Farmer leapt up from the toilet and rushed to the bunk where Doc was. He placed his hand over Doc's mouth and leaned in next to Doc's ear.

"Whatever you do, don't say a fucking word." Hissed Farmer into Doc's ear.

Doc's eyes grew wide. He had no idea how he had gotten here and he was even more confused as to why his very large black celly was sitting next to him half nude and holding his hand over Doc's mouth.

"You don't know nothing. Not a DAMN thing" said Farmer. *"Do you understand?"*

Doc didn't understand anything, but he nodded in the affirmative to Farmer when he looked at the hand covering his mouth and noticed a gold tooth stuck into Farmer's fourth knuckle.

Doc thought to himself. 'Maybe this is a good time to just agree to whatever Farmer is saying and to ask questions later'. Because, frankly, that tooth in Farmer's knuckle was freaking the crap out of Doc.

"Good," said Farmer. *"Just lay there and pretend to be asleep. Okay?"*

Doc started nodding off again, but just then he heard someone at the end of the run scream out at the top of his lungs.

"WHAT THE FUCK!"

"Oh my fucking God! Someone call the Lieutenant." screamed the guard as he came running back down the run.

Farmer leaned down to Doc's ear. *"Remember, stay down and pretend you are asleep. You don't know anything. Both of our lives depend on that. Is that clear, Doc?"*

He nodded to Farmer, but in reality Doc wasn't clear about anything. All he knew was that he woke up in a shit storm. He knew nothing as for what was going on or how he was involved? He had no idea whatsoever.

But he was about to find out.

Chapter 28

Prickly Springs wasn't what anyone would call cosmopolitan in any sense of the word, but you could find a few nice restaurants, if you tried really hard.

And that is exactly what Guy had done.

"Wow," said Lola as she sat in the rounded red velvet booth, *"I don't think I have ever been in a place this fancy before."*

She was like a kid at the fair. She was looking at everything. Nothing escaped her notice. She was impressed which was exactly what Guy had wanted to do. He was in love with Lola and he wanted to really make the best impression on her he could tonight.

"Yeah, it's one of my favorites." Guy said nonchalantly. The truth was he hadn't been here in years.   His mother had brought him on his thirteenth birthday because she said, "he was a man now and that he needed to know about such places because one day he would want to impress a young lady". She had taught him all about which fork to use with which course and about how to keep is left hand in his lap. Elbows on the table were a big No-No. He thought that it was all so silly then, but at this moment he was so grateful for all of her repeated brain-washing about etiquette and manners because he wanted Lola to be impressed.

Lola's brown eyes grew as big as a full moon as she perused the menu. *"Are you sure you can afford this. These prices are really high."*

"Don't you worry about it. I got a promotion at work recently. Get whatever you want." He wanted to sound like a big shot. He had been

so enthralled with looking at Lola that he hadn't even bothered to look at the prices until she said something.

He opened his menu and silently gulped at the dollar figures on the right side of the page. As a kid he had never had to pay the bill, so he never noticed what anything had cost.

The meals had been absolute perfection. Lola was a delight to talk to. She was interested in everything, but the thing that Guy liked about her was that she had ambition. She told how she wanted to move away to a bigger city and to travel to places that she had only seen in magazines. Their conversation never stopped. This was the best date Guy had ever been on and he didn't want it to end.

"Could we see the dessert menu, please?" he said to the passing waiter.

"Oh, I couldn't eat another bite" protested Lola.

"Please" Guy pleaded *"just split something with me."*

How could she resist those sexy green eyes? Lola thought to herself.

"Okay, I can do that."

They held the one menu between them and Guy couldn't help but be intoxicated by the wonderful scent of Gardenias that drifted through the air from Lola. They chose the warm chocolate melting cake and the waiter delivered it with two spoons. It was so decadently chocolate and Lola had never tasted anything so delicious. Even though she thought that she couldn't eat another bite, she was shoveling huge spoon full of chocolate pudding cake into her mouth.

"This is so incredible." She exclaimed.

"It must be" said Guy *"because you have it all over you mouth."*

"What!" Lola grabbed the pressed thick white napkin out of her lap and dabbed her mouth. She was mortified. Guy was laughing at her now. He probably thought she was some hick girl who didn't know how to eat properly.

151

"Here, let me help." said Guy *"You missed a spot."*

He leaned over close to her; and with his napkin, he dabbed the corner of her mouth. Then time and space just seemed to freeze. His face was right next to hers and their eyes locked on each other.

Lola couldn't move and then she realized that she had stopped breathing.

Guy had frozen too. He didn't want to move. He didn't want this moment to ever end; and if he moved, he might jinx it forever. He knew that Lola was the right girl for him. She was perfect. She was the girl of his dreams.

But he couldn't just stay like this forever. It was already getting to be awkward. He had to do something.

So he did.

He leaned in and pressed his lips to Lola's. She didn't pull away. He saw her eyes close and felt her soft lips part to accept his kiss. He tasted the sweetness of her love. And a little bit of chocolate.

It was pure heaven.

It ended with a light smack and from that moment on Guy knew that his life would never be same.

*****

"You are so different than all of the other guys I have gone out with" said Lola.

"Do you go out with a lot of guys?" asked Guy jealously.

"Oh no, it's not like that." said Lola *"They are just guys that work with my brother, Santos. He is always trying to set me up, but all they want to do is talk about their job and arresting people. I get so bored with them, but not with you. You're different. You didn't talk at all about your work. You were a perfect gentleman and you were only interested in me all night long."*

At that moment Guy felt like a heel because he knew exactly why he had gone to the dentist office in the first place. He went to find out information. He hadn't expected to meet Lola and to fall in love. He was in a real predicament. What was he going to do now? If he asked her a lot of questions about her boss, she would think that he didn't really care for her and that he was just using her to get info. He couldn't risk that. He had just found the love of his life. He loved her too much to lose her like that. He knew that Dr. Shaddix was involved in something shady, but he didn't know what yet, so he would just have to keep it all to himself for now and keep his eyes and ears wide open.

*****

Guy drove Lola home in his new vehicle. He had gone to Honest Hal's used car lot the day before and found a reliable and fairly late model truck. The best part about it was that the inside didn't smell like an old pair of sweaty gym shorts, and he didn't have to stop every hour to fill it with oil. Compared to the piece of junk that he had been sharing with his roommates, it looked and drove like a Cadillac.

Lola had hopped right up into the cab of the truck like she had been doing it every day. On the way home she even moved over to the center and put her head on Guy's shoulder. It was just like something in a Hollywood movie.

He pulled up to her house and turned off the engine, but Lola didn't make move to get out of the truck. No, she stayed right where she was and squeezed his arm even harder. Guy turned his head and their lips began to kiss each other deeply. He put his arm around Lola and pulled her into him tighter. He could feel her breast against him. Her hand moved to his thigh and he felt his pants begin to tightened and his breathes begin to shorten.

No girl had ever had this much of an effect on him. He was in uncharted water here. He knew what his body was wanting to do, but his head was telling him to slow down and be careful because he loved this girl. This girl was everything he ever wanted. He didn't want to blow it on a few minutes of heavy groping on the seat of his truck. He wanted a lifetime of groping and heavy petting.   And children too.

'Wait a minute!' he thought to himself. 'Where the hell did that come from?"

He was doing some serious future tripping. The windows of the truck were completely fogged up. Lola's hand was slowly climbing its way north on his thigh and Guy found that his self-control was going out the window. Guy slipped his hand between the buttons of Lola's blouse and she let out a gasp as his cold hand cupped her tender breast. He felt her heart and it was beating as fast his was. Their kisses became hard and frantic. Guy let out and audible moan of ecstasy as her hand grasped the outside of his manhood.

'This is it.' thought Guy.

All of the sudden red and blue flashing lights filled the night. Guy and Lola jumped apart and began to frantically pull themselves together and straighten themselves up.

A tap came on the driver's side window and startled Guy. He rolled the window down and was immediately blinded by a white light.

'This just can't be happening again.' he thought, but just then an even worse thought shot into his brain. What if this was Deputy Dawg and he recognized Guy from the deserted road by the gay bar. Guy was in full panic mode now. He was about to be beaten or humiliated right here and right now and in front of Lola.

"What's going on here, folks?" Came the voice from outside the truck. It was a familiar voice to Guy, but it wasn't Deputy Dawg's voice. Guy was racking his brain to remember where he had heard that voice. Before he could figure it out or answer the question, another voice screamed from inside the truck.

"None of your damn business, Santos." Yelled Lola.

The light moved from Guy to Lola and the officer leaned in further to peer into the truck. Guy recognized him. He was the young deputy from Clara's cafe.

"Sis!" the deputy exclaimed in total surprise. *"What the hell are you doing out here and in a truck."* The deputy looked at Guy again incredulously. *"And with this guy?"* he said with obvious derision in his voice.

"That IS the part that is none of your damn business." said Lola *"And turn off that light too."*

Guy was trying to soak it all in. The deputy was definitely intimidated by her and he clicked the light off immediately. This girl had fire when she needed it.

"Why are your clothes messed up?' he inquired sheepishly. Then in a more protective kind of voice. *"Is this guy trying to get funny with you?"*

"Well, Mr. Nosey Pants, if you really need to know," she said scoldingly, *"I was trying to get funny with him. So why don't you just put that in your little book and get back in your little police car and leave me alone"*

"But...." the young deputy started to say.

"Santos," she screamed *"I swear if you don't get out of here I am going to hurt you so bad when you come in to get that tooth finished that you will wish you were dead. Do I make myself clear?"*

"Yes, Sis." Said an embarrassed Deputy Santos Salinas as he turned and walked back to his car and left.

*****

"Oh my God!" said Guy *"You were magnificent."*

Lola beamed with pride as she nestled up next to Guy. *"I think you are the one that is magnificent, Guy. Do you think we could go out again?"*

"Are you kidding?" said Guy *"I would like that very much. Besides after seeing how you handle that deputy I would be scared to say No to you."* And with that he pulled her into him and kissed her more deeply than he had ever kissed any girl in his life.

This was the girl that he wanted for the rest of his life, but would she want him after she found out who he was and who he worked for.

*****

Deputy Santos Salinas loved his sister. She was his only sister and he loved her very much. He had done what she wanted, but he was still a cop and he was going to make sure that she wasn't dating some dirt bag.

He couldn't understand why she was seeing this scrawny little piece of shit when he had set her up several of his buddies from work who were way bigger and better than this runt.

The truck had paper plates on it and Santos tried running them but nothing came back yet, which meant that the state hadn't had time to issue a real license plate yet. He hadn't had time to even get the guy's driver's license so he didn't know the guy's name or where he lived.

He would just have to do some old fashion police work. Hell, that was why he had wanted to become a cop. He wanted to catch bad guys and to help his community, but the job hadn't been what he expected. He was seeing a lot stuff going on in the department and with some of his co-workers that he didn't think was right. They told him that it was alright, but it made him feel uneasy. He couldn't do anything about it because he was just a rookie.

Santos parked his car a block away and sat in the dark. He saw his sister slide over and begin to make out with this little creep. He wasn't good enough for his sister. No one was good enough for her, but she apparently liked this guy a lot because she had never yelled at him like that before.

She was serious about this dude, so Santos decided to appoint himself her secret guardian to make sure that this guy wasn't some pervert or criminal. After all that's what brothers were supposed to do. Right?

For all Santos knew this guy could be a deranged psycho or a member of some terrorist gang. Santos and everyone on the force had heard about how some gang had ambushed Deputy Ernie Sinclair. They had stolen his car and left it turned over in a ditch. They had kidnapped him and handcuffed him with his own cuffs. He had only been able to escape after they all got high and passed out. He had been in tears when he told how he had escaped with a bag over his head and made his way through the woods by looking down to the ground and out of the bag.

The other deputies searched high and low for where Deputy Sinclair had escaped from; but since he could not see out of the bag, he had no idea where it was. He was on psychological/medical leave due the hours of torture that he endured at hands of the whole biker gang. Deputies were now stopping every bearded motorcycle rider that came into the county. The deputies had made it their mission to find these dudes.

Santos knew that this wimp of a guy wasn't a member of any motorcycle gang, but he could still protect his sister from him.

*****

Guy was so busy reliving every minute of his fantastic date that he didn't notice the patrol car that was following him in the distance.

Guy detoured through the city to stop at his office. H was too keyed up to go home. If he couldn't sleep, he thought he might as well get a little work done. After his visit to Dr. Shaddix, he decided to do a little electronic digging on the good doctor. There was something about him that Guy didn't like. He had met both a doctor and a used car salesman this week; and of the two, he definitely trusted the used car salesman a lot more than the good doctor. Especially one that was driving a vintage racing yellow Porsche 911. Guy didn't know any dentists making that kind of money, at least not in po-dunk Lloyd County. After visiting Dr. Shaddix's office and listening to Lola describe how bad business was, he knew that the good doctor had his hands in more things than just people's mouths.

He felt a little guilty using information gleaned on his date, but he knew that he couldn't let Lola know about what he was doing. She would think that he was just using her to spy on her boss. She would never believe that he actually loved her. He couldn't bear it if she weren't in his life. In one night she had changed him forever. He wanted to give her all of the things she wanted and take her to all of the places she wanted to go. He wanted to be her hero. To do so he was going to have to be another kind of hero. He needed to find out and expose the corruption in Sheriff "Red" Hardon Johnson's office. That was his and Lola's ticket out of this place, and now he was more motivated than ever. It was a perfect plan. Now all he had to do was keep Lola from finding out.

Why couldn't love be easier than this?

*****

Santos pulled into the shadows and watched as Lola's new boyfriend walked into the campaign headquarters of Joe Don Lilly. On any given day, Sheriff "Red" could be heard screaming expletive's about "Mr. Lilly White", as he called him. It was a nasty campaign and Sheriff "Red" seemed to be worried about losing his first election ever. The tension in the department was thick because all of the old guys knew that if Joe Don Lilly won, they would all be out of a job and their extra incomes would evaporate.

Santos was new and idealistic. He wasn't as jaded as the old guys and he didn't agree with some of the things they were doing; but he knew if he said something he would be shunned and frozen out. Or worse.

He had been struggling in his mind about what to do. He had become a cop to do good. To help people. He didn't want to be a part of anything like what they were doing anymore. He was still bothered by what they had done to the dentist from Dallas, but they had given him a fat envelope of cash and told him it was his part of the "confiscation" and that it was all legal under state law for the police to take anything that they wanted from drug dealers. Santos didn't believe for a minute that the dentist was a drug dealer. He might have been a user, but he was no dealer. Santos had seen lots of them, and the doctor wasn't anything like them. His partner Jonesy had justified it and explained it over and over to him, but Santos still knew that it was wrong. Confiscating peoples bank accounts and cars only to have it directly profit the pockets of the same deputies, prosecutors and judges that arrested and tried that person wasn't right. He knew the difference in right and wrong, and this was wrong; but he was a part of the long blue line now, and that meant that he couldn't tell anyone. God, it was eating him up inside every day.

He didn't know what to do, and now this guy starts dating his sister, too. He had secretly thought things might be better if Joe Don Lilly did win. Maybe the new Sheriff would get rid of all of the bad deputies, but Santos knew he had taken the money and he was now one of those bad deputies. So what could he do, except keep his eyes open and his mouth shut and that is exactly what he was going to keep doing, about his job and his sister's new boyfriend.

*****

Guy ran a complete background search on Dr. Shaddix. Through corporate tax filings, he knew what the good doctor made each year. The county tax assessor told Guy what property the doctor owned. In addition, he had run a credit report and discovered that the good Dr. Shaddix's credit wasn't very stellar. He was behind on all of his bills, and he had declared bankruptcy only three years ago. He remembered Lola telling him that Dr. Shaddix had only gotten the vintage Porsche 911 recently. He searched the credit report but found no evidence of a purchase or lease for a vehicle of any sort. His tax filings indicated that Dr. Shaddix hadn't made enough money in the past five years combined to afford such a vehicle. Hell, he was even in arrears for his employer taxes. Somehow this guy owed money to everyone on the planet money and yet he was driving $100,000 sports car. How was that possible? This guy couldn't even pay for his dry cleaning.

Guy searched high and low and kept coming up with goose eggs. The answer was out there somewhere. He knew it. He just hadn't found the right rock to look under. Yet.

*****

Santos was tired and he wanted to go by the Hot Biscuit for a cup of coffee and something to eat. Darlene always had something good on the grill this time of night and he was getting hungry. His late night visits were becoming the high point of his boring nights, and he enjoyed her company. She always had a smile and a new joke for him.

He turned the engine over and put the patrol car into gear. Just as he was about to pull away, another car whipped into the parking lot of the Lilly campaign headquarters.

"This sure is a busy place at night" Deputy Salinas said to himself as he slipped the gear shift back into park. *"Maybe I should stick around a little longer."*

****

Jewel's iPhone had notified her that someone had entered the campaign headquarters. She activated the inside remote cameras of the campaign offices and was delighted by what she saw.

Guytana Canova.

He was by himself and working late. She liked the young buck for both his mind and his body. He was definitely easy on the eyes, and she wouldn't mind a little office romp, if she got the chance; and this evening had 'chance' written all over it.

Jewels was on the backside of forty with an attractively slim build. She was still a very desirable woman and her face had yet to show any signs of wrinkles. Her hair was like wavy red fire which highlighted her silky smooth white skin; however, despite all of this, she was beginning to notice that more and more of her nights were being spent alone in her apartment with only a bottle of Yellow Tail wine for company. She was good at what she did and not many women had reached the level she had in her profession. She had been a pioneer for woman in a profession previously dominated by good ol' boys when she started. She had run many successful campaigns across the state and had become a tough-as-nails, no nonsense street fighter when it came to politics, but after a day of cut throat deal making and lobbying with imbecilic politicians, what she really wanted was to come home to someone who would care about her wants and her needs.

She solved everyone else's problems and made their lives better, but no one was there to pamper her when she came through the door at night licking her wounds from a day of hard fought battles with one special interest group after another. No one was there to rub her shoulders or just hold her in silence after she had been mentally beat down by selfish labor unions. She had foregone a family and a relationship in trade for her career. She wasn't sorry for that decision; but when she was out of the political arena and away from the prying eyes of her opponents, she wanted to be able let her guard down to someone without fear of being attacked. She was a successful and strong woman with needs.

And she wanted someone for her needs.

'Is that too much to ask?'

Jewels jumped into her car and sped to the campaign headquarters. She had risen to the top of her profession by knowing how to recognize opportunities when they appeared and then knowing exactly when to seize upon them.

Tonight was the time to strike. It was time to penetrate the innocence that one Guytana Canova wore like suit of armor.

Jewels hopped out of her car. She hadn't bothered to dress and was still in her turquoise nightie and flimsy Penoir robe. She had seen the Victoria's Secret show with the sexy angels that floated down the runway. She had rushed to the Northpark Mall in Dallas to buy it the next day. She had been enjoying a little Merlot and soft music alone at home when the alert came in from her new cameras at headquarters. She hadn't needed to change because it was the perfect outfit for the full frontal attack that she had mind.

Guytana Canova wasn't going to know what hit him.

Chapter 29

Sirens wailed ferociously.

Doc couldn't hear himself or anything else for that matter.

Jack-booted footsteps ran heavily down the walkway causing the metal catwalk to vibrate like a tuning fork.

Doc lay as still as a dead man in his bunk.

"This is not good," he told himself. He had no idea what "this" was, but there was no way that it was going to end well for the inmates, no matter what it was.

Farmer stood at the sink behind the flimsy make-shift curtain and scrubbed himself as fast as he could. He desperately scrubbed at the dried blood that was heavily caked on his hands.

As Doc lay there, his anxiety built up to the point that he just couldn't stand lying in the bunk for another second. He had to know what the hell was going on. He threw the covers back and swung his feet around to get out of the steel bunk.

"Get your fuckin' ass back in that bunk" Farmer hissed *"and do exactly as I told you to do"*

Doc froze. Farmer had never spoken to him in such a vicious manner. Doc had seen him mad before, but this was different. Farmer was scared. Truly scared for his life.

'But why?' thought Doc. He was so confused.

"I mean it." Farmer said threateningly *"If you don't want to end up with a murder charge, then you had better start listening to me quick. You think you are so god damn smart, but you are just a spoiled little fuckin' brat who don't know shit."* Farmer had gotten right up in Doc's face and sprayed spittle over him with every word.

Doc was now terrified. 'What did he mean by murder?'

Doc couldn't remember anything. His mind was a complete blank. He wasn't a violent person. What the hell had happened? Why was Farmer so hostile? And why couldn't Doc remember anything? And why did the back of his head and his arm hurt so badly?

Farmer's huge wet hand grabbed onto Doc's forehead. Farmer's grip was immense. Doc could feel Framer reach from ear to ear with only one hand as he wrapped it around Doc's head. Doc wondered if that tooth was still in Farmer's hand, but what he really wanted to know was, 'Where the hell did it come from?'

Doc wanted to scream back at Farmer because he hated being treated like a small child, but he didn't dare say anything right now. He was scared of Farmer and he was frustrated at being in the dark. Farmer thrust Doc's head back into his makeshift pillow.

"If you want to go to lock up, then just go ahead and open your fuckin' mouth." hissed Farmer.

Screaming could be heard all over.

Prisoners were screaming down below because they were drenched in blood and splattered with pieces of El Diablo's brain. Inmates were now locked in and were becoming more and more hysterical as pools of blood began to run into their cells. Guards were screaming everywhere for more help and the remaining one hundred and twenty prisoners on the other rows were yelling back and forth trying to find out what happened and who was lying naked and dead on the first floor with his head cracked wide open.

Lt. Sharp and several of his minions ran by Farmer and Doc's cell. Farmer finished scrubbing the blood off his face and arms and quickly cleaned up the sink basin. He swiftly glanced onto the run; and when he was sure that no guards were around, he opened up the side of his mattress that he had carefully cut a hole in several months ago and stuffed everything inside of it that had blood on it. He distributed it around evenly and carefully patted down any lumps that popped up. He sealed it back up and then he lay on top of it to give it just the right indention's in all the right places.

Farmer and Doc lay there in total silence as it sounded like the world was collapsing around them. Guards had come around several times looking in each cell and checking off who was in each one.

The morphine was wearing off, and Doc's head began to throb. He also noticed that a huge bruise had come up where his arm was aching. This scared him even more.

'What have I done?' thought Doc. 'Why can't I remember anything?'

Doc was on the verge of tears as he lay in his bunk and watched each officer go by.

There was a fear in his heart at what was happening to him. 'How has my life come to this and why can't I remember what happened?'

He knew from all the yelling that someone was naked and dead on the first floor, but what did that have to do with him? And what was going on up here on the third row?

Guards and officers were running up and down the run, but they stepped back and cleared out of the way as two paramedics made their way down the run with their heavy orange equipment boxes. They would have normally wheeled it all down on the gurney, but there was no way to get their gurney up to the third level of the cell block due to the narrowness of the stairs and the runs.

The cell block suddenly got unusually quiet as inmates locked in every cell quieted down so as to try and hear anything they could about why the paramedics were on the third row when it was so obvious that the dead guy was splattered all over the first. Apparently, there was more to the story, and convicts loved stories. Every ear was peeled to catch anything they could overhear from the officers and paramedics.

Doc wanted to get up and press his face to the bars to see what was going on. Somehow he knew that it had something to do with him, but for the life of him, he didn't know what. He couldn't remember anything.

Guards started clearing the run and officers began to shout orders to clear the way. Someone was coming through. Doc lay in his bunk with his eyes wide open to see who they were going to walk down the run.

"Get that gurney ready at the bottom of the stairs." shouted someone from above to the guards down below on the first row.

Doc could hear heavy lumbering footsteps coming down the run. There were several sets plodding slowly towards Doc's cell. Doc could hear them stop ever so often and he could hear people talking as the procession passed their cells, but he couldn't hear what they were saying.

They were almost to Doc's cell. Doc could hear them talking now.

"Do you need to rest?" Said a voice.

Well, Doc thought, the person is alive at least because he is obviously walking down the run and the guard just wanted to know if he needed to rest. Doc was becoming more and more intrigued because maybe whoever it was would help him figure out what the hell was going on and why Farmer was acting like such a crazy man talking about murder and stuff.

Doc could hear them very plainly now since they were in front of the next cell. The first thing Doc could see was the back of a guard's uniform. That seemed a little strange to Doc. This was prison and he hadn't seen anything yet that didn't seem strange or ass backwards when it came to how to do things. The guard obviously had his hands full and was holding something. Doc couldn't see what it was yet, but he was really struggling to get it down the narrow run. It was obviously heavy. The guard was now in front of Doc's and Farmer's cell.

Then Doc saw what it was. It was a body. But whose? Doc couldn't see the face. The guard had grasped the body under the arms and the head was between the guard's arms and was lolling towards the railing away from Doc.

"Who is it?" Doc asked himself. It was almost too much to bear. He wanted to jump up to the bars and see who it was, but he was frozen to the bunk on Farmer's orders to stay there no matter what.

But just then a lightning bolt struck Doc's heart as the arm of the corpse came into view. Doc saw the 18 gauge vet needle still stuck in the sweet spot.

Panic swept over Doc. 'Oh, my God!' thought Doc. 'It's Hillbilly.'

The sudden crash of Hillbilly's body on the catwalk like run brought Doc's mind back into the present.

"I asked if you needed to stop and rest." said the irritated guard still holding Hillbilly's feet.

Doc could see his friend's face now. His lips were blue from the lack of blood, but other than that he really didn't look much different since he had always been so pallid and white. However, there was no mistaking that he was dead. His eyes were wide open and they stared directly at Doc now. They couldn't see him anymore, but Doc could see that they were accusing him of killing him. Doc had seen cadavers before in his anatomy classes, but this was the first time that he had ever seen a fresh corpse. He certainly had never seen a friend that was dead and lying on the floor like some discarded piece of trash.

"Pick him up, damn it!" yelled the officer from behind.

The pudgy and sweaty guard indelicately grabbed Hillbilly by whatever he could grasp and began to drag him down the stairs.

Doc was crying now.

What had he done to his friend, and why couldn't he remember any of it?

He pulled the cover over his head and wept into his pillow for his dear dead friend.

*****

Farmer watched in terror as the brutish and clumsy guards dragged Hillbilly's limp and lifeless body down the stairs. It was an undignified way to treat someone, but to prison officials, he was simply a piece of meat that they needed to discard. After all, to them all prisoners were pieces of meat. The only difference was that some were walking around and some were being dragged down the stairs.

'Prisoner's don't deserve any dignity; dead or alive.' Thought Lt. Sharp. 'They forfeited that right when they got themselves sent here.'

The Lieutenant marched down the stairs and watched as Hillbilly's body was wheeled off the wing unceremoniously and down the long hall. He turned his attention to the next matter at hand.

'Who the hell was the naked dead Latino that was splayed out all over the concrete floor of the first run?'

The face was unrecognizable. The fall had crushed the entire skull, but it was apparent that the man had taken a pretty good beating first. The only way that the Lieutenant knew that it was a Cholo was because of his tattoos.

They had done three counts on this wing and everyone was accounted for, so who the hell was this mystery Mexican who was lying here dead and naked with half of his dick ripped off and what was he doing on this cell block if he didn't live here? Heads were going to roll for this. No one is supposed to be on a wing that they don't live on.

"Lock the whole farm down and do a special count until we find out who this guy is" screamed Lt. Sharp *"and plan on being here for a while, because no one is going home"*

*****

Doc had bawled like a baby and Farmer heard every bit of it. Farmer wanted Doc to really learn his lesson this time. Farmer had stood by for too long and watched idly as Doc had spun out of control. He wanted Doc to stew in this misery for a long time so that he would understand the consequences of what he had done and what was in store for him if he continued to use those worthless drugs. His buddy was dead now. Maybe it would finally sink in.

Farmer wasn't some prude. He liked to smoke a little weed every now and then, but he had seen how hard drugs had taken over and killed so many of his friends. They had OD in crack houses, heroin dens and even in the gutters of the streets. If it didn't kill them directly, then the drug business and the thug life associated with it killed them just as sure as if they had shot it directly into their arm. He hated it, but he hated even more to see someone like Doc, who had everything in the world going for him, lose it all because of some pharmaceutical junk. Hell, that was what got him sent here in the first place and now he was riding that roller coaster again.

'Well, it's time for him to get off of it for good.' Farmer thought to himself.

Chapter 30

Guytana Canova was all alone. Nights like this just didn't come along very often in his life. He was remembering every minute of it in his mind's eye. He could still taste Lola on his lips. He never knew that innocence had a taste, but it did. And it tasted like Lola.

He wasn't walking through the office anymore. He was floating. Everything seemed to be magical. He had met the girl of his dreams and nothing could go wrong. He had never been this happy in his life. This was a great feeling. It was as if his brain was full of rainbow pudding. He saw something good in everything that he thought about. He was incapable of having a bad feeling right now. Everything was perfect. Nothing could spoil this night.

"What's going on here?" came a familiar and foreboding voice from the darkness.

'Fuck me!' thought Guy. 'I spoke too soon.'

He had just spent the past several hours with the most perfect girl in the world and now he had to deal with Jewels. God, why couldn't he have just gone home and been happy in his bed? Why had he decided to come to the office and let this woman ruin his night? He should have anticipated that she would know that he was in the building. He had seen the men installing the new security cameras for the past several days, but he had been so wrapped up in the thought of Lola that he had completely forgotten about all of the new cameras that had been put in the building. So now here she was. The Cougar.

"Oh, Jewels, you scared me." Said Guy, as he feigned being startled. *"What are you doing here so late?"*

"I was about to ask you the same question." replied Jewels.

It was Jewels' voice alright, but it sure sounded different tonight. He thought that he must have woke her up because it sounded raspier than usual. She sounded like that old movie actress that his mom liked named Lauren Becall.

Jewels stepped slowly into the glowing light of Guy's office. She was softly silhouetted in the computer's illumination. Guy saw immediately that he must have awakened her because she was in a flimsy gown. She obviously raced here in a panic because she had forgotten to close it all the way. The emergency exit light illuminated her from behind and Guy could see every little outline of Jewels' very curvaceous body. He was mesmerized for a moment as his own body began to react to the sight of her nakedness through the sheer nightie and flimsy robe.

After spending the evening with Lola and making out with her in the truck, Guy's hormones were still popping and exploding all over his body. He was one big sexual nerve.

'My God!' he thought to himself as he looked over Jewels' body. He felt his breathing become rapid and shallow. As he stared at Jewels' silhouette, there was no denying that he was more than a little titillated. She was a very sexy woman. She was right in front of him now, almost naked.

But what about Lola, damn it!

He loved Lola. He knew that to be true with all his heart, but it wasn't the organ that was yelling to him right now. It was another part of him further south that was screaming to his brain right now. He felt flushed and he could feel his cheeks begin to warm with excitement.

"I am just, um,..." stammered Guy *"looking over a few new things that I wanted to examine a little better."*

"Really?" said Jewels as she slowly moved from the doorway where she had been perched. She seductively sashayed over to Guy's chair. She leaned in on Guy's left side. She hadn't bothered to close her silk robe. As she bent over, it opened up and brushed Guy's arm. It felt like a bolt of electricity as it grazed his bicep. He felt his mouth go dry and he tried to swallow. Her breasts grazed against him. He could see them clearly through the sheer nightie. They were round and very firm. His breathing was so rapid and short that he was on the verge of hyperventilating.

"Well, what is it that is so interesting that it brings you here in the middle of the night, Guy?" she cooed in her seductive voice. She could see that Guy was definitely interested. His body language was virtually shooting off flares.

"I, umm." Guy was sweating now. *"I think, um,...uhhh"*

Guy couldn't take his eyes off of her breasts. God, they were magnificent, but most of all, they were so close.

Jewels leaned in further. Her lips were only millimeters from Guy's ear. He felt her warm breath as it cascaded down his neck. The tightness in his khakis was becoming unbearable. His male member was so tingly that it was about to explode at any moment. Blood was rushing to every extremity, and he couldn't remember what she had asked him. All he could think about was her breasts with those hard nipples straining at the flimsy fabric. The raised dots around her areolas were now visible. When her hard pink nipple touched his arm, fireworks exploded in his head and almost in his pants.

He grabbed Jewels around the waist and spun his chair around. He spread his legs and pulled her in on top of himself. She ground her pelvic bone into him as he thrust his trapped maleness up to meet her. He felt her grasp the back of his head as she pulled his face to her chest. His smooth hands slipped under her short nightie, and he accepted her full bosom into his mouth.

She whimpered and groaned with each and every nibble on her swollen breast. She felt her thighs quiver as he suckled and ravaged her breast with the uncontrolled lust that only came with youth.

It had been a long time since she had had such a vigorous and unconstrained young man. She felt like she was twenty years old again and she liked the way he made her feel. She felt young and alive for the first time in many years. She felt like a sexual succubus draining his carnal energy. His man-youth was restoring her by the moment. She felt like a real woman again.

And she wanted more. Lots more.

"I can't do this!" screamed Guy as he tried to tear himself away from her breasts. He knew that his words sounded hollow since he continued to squeezed each bosom and lick each nipple like an insatiable infant. He couldn't help himself. He wasn't the most experienced man in the world, and right now he couldn't control himself.

"Oh you are doing great." exclaimed Jewels as she writhed in ecstasy. She needed this. She wanted it badly. This was the thing she had dreamed about on all of those lonely nights at home. Guy was fulfilling her cougar office fantasy.

He was clumsy and a little rough, but his tenderness and innocence offset his youthful inexperience. What he lacked in technique, he more than made up for with enthusiasm. For that Jewels was extremely grateful. She needed to be reinvigorated and re-energized. Here was just the Guy to do it for her. She was going to teach him a few things about what a woman like and needed.

She was going to turn little Mr. Guytana Canova into a big 'Casanova'.

*****

Santos was really getting hungry. He had seen the woman in the flirty little negligee go into the building almost an hour ago. He had expected

171

her to come right back out, but to his dismay, she had stayed inside the headquarters of Joe Don Lilly.

He wondered what was going on, especially so late in the evening. This was really strange. Sheriff Red's people never worked this late. Hell, they were mostly his friends and his deputies, so they usually never worked past 3pm. Santos wondered what working under Sheriff Joe Don Lilly would be like. He liked being a cop but hated the things he saw going on in Sheriff Red's department. Deputies would brag to each other in the locker room and in the halls about how much they had 'gotten off of' one criminal or another. Santos's partner, Jonesy, had bought a brand new fishing boat at the sheriff's auction last week, and he was crowing about how he had gotten it for only $100. The auctions were rigged so that the officer who was responsible for the bust got first choice of the confiscated goods. Last year, Jonesy had been upset because he didn't get to buy the yellow Porsche he wanted which had belonged to the dentist from Dallas he busted. Sheriff Red had made it clear that Dr. Shaddix was to get it.

Santos was getting tired of sitting. His mind was on the banana pancakes that Darlene would be cooking right now at the Hot Biscuit. He loved the way she piled the fresh whipped cream on top. Her banana pancakes were truly decadent and delicious. Jonesy would undoubtedly be there by now and shoveling them by the fork full into his fat mouth.

What were they doing in there? His sister had better appreciate all this.

*****

Guy was spent.

He was sweating profusely. It seemed like every drop of fluid had been expunged from his body. He didn't think he could move a single muscle. He was so tired. Yet he felt so great. Jewel had taught him things he had never even imagined. His roommates had talked about how older women knew things that they would teach younger guys; but until now, he thought it was just talk.

Boy, had he been wrong. Jewels had showed him exactly what to do to her and how fast or slow to do it.   She had changed his world.

But so had Lola and now what was going to happen with her?

Had this changed everything? Jesus, what had he done?   He loved Lola.
How could he have done this to her? She was everything that he wanted.

If that were true, then 'Why did I sleep with Jewels?' he asked himself.
'God, was I that freaking weak?'   He had always thought himself
different than most other guys.

Jewels didn't know anything about Lola, and Guy wanted to keep it that
way.   He had heard about how women got possessive about men after
they had sex with them.   He didn't want her running to Lola and ruining
everything just because he had made one little mistake. He didn't love
Jewels. He knew that much. He didn't know what he was going to do or
how he was going to let Jewels down easily when he told he couldn't be
with her. After all, she was still his boss, and he wanted to let her down
gently.

Guy opened his eyes and was astonished to see that Jewels wasn't lying
beside him anymore. What the heck? Where had she gone? The sex
had been great. He would cuddle a little bit before he let the poor
woman down.

"Jewels?" he shouted into the dark.

"Yes?" she answered. Appearing out of the darkness.

He was surprised to see that she was already dressed in regular clothes
and had several sheets of papers from his desk in her hands.

"What is all of this?" she questioned *"Who is Dr. Shaddix. Why are you
running reports on him?"*

Jewels felt she had been blindsided by Guy before. She wasn't going to
let it happen a second time. Sex was sex. This was business, and that
was all that mattered to her. She felt sexually gratified now, but she
wouldn't let Guy sandbag her again with the candidate, Joe Don Lilly.
She was in charge, both in the bed and in the office. That was the way it

would stay. She would lay down the law and let him know what she needed and when she needed it. Right now, she needed to know what he was working on.

Guy stammered for a moment. He was still on the floor naked and he was more than a little caught off guard at how Jewels was fully dressed and had switched gears so quickly. He felt vulnerable and more than slightly embarrassed lying on the, floor exposed and naked while Jewels was towering over him fully dressed.

"Where did you get those clothes?" Guy asked.

"I always keep an extra set in my office. You never know when you might need to change." she said matter-of-factly. *"Now, who is this Dr. Shaddix and why are we interested in him?"*

"He is my girlfriend's boss." Guy said before he could stop himself. Geez, now it was going to hit the fan. He just knew that she was going to be mad at him and jealous of Lola.

Jewels lowered the papers and looked into Guy's eyes. *"Again, what does he have to do with the campaign?"* Her voice was stern and even.

"I think he might be involved in something shady with Sheriff Red." said Guy as he hunted for his pants, hopping on one leg while trying to put them on.

"I didn't know you had a girlfriend, Guy." Jewels said mockingly.

'Oh, boy, here is comes' thought Guy. Jealousy. The old green-eyed monster.

"Well, actually, I met her while I was investigating the doctor's office. I took her out to dinner tonight to pump her for information. She's not really my girlfriend." Explained Guy. He hoped that it would be enough to keep Jewels from doing anything crazy.

'Uh-huh.' mumbled Jewels.

Guy decided to lay it all out and to tell her what he had overheard at the dinner concerning the doctor's new yellow Porsche. Anything to get her focus off of Lola.

She listened intently to every word and didn't interrupt a single time. Silence hung in the air when he finished. He could see that she was thinking about something. Was it about the campaign or about them? Was he her sex slave now? Her boy toy? Would she still respect him? Was she going to get all hysterical and mad because he was seeing Lola? She could make his life hell now. He knew that sleeping with his boss would have some consequences. He didn't want one of the consequences to be losing Lola. That would just be too much to bear. He would quit if he had to. He wasn't going to be made to forego the girl of his dreams just because of one night of meaningless sex. Yeah, it had been great in a way he had never experienced before, but he loved Lola, not Jewels.

"Well, you sure have been busy, haven't you?" She said. He couldn't tell by her voice if she was mad or not. She was a hard woman to read. Not that Guy was any good at reading women anyway.

"Look, I don't want you to be mad," he blurted out, *"but I kind of like this girl. I mean, don't get me wrong, I think you are just great, and what we did was fantastic. But I don't want you to be jealous,"* he paused to look her earnestly in the eyes *"but we can't go on in a relationship together. I hope you understand and that we can still be friends."*

Guy noticed that Jewels eyes widened with each word he said. Her lips pursed together. He just knew that she was about to explode with jealous expletives hurled at him for leading her on, but he was shocked when she burst out laughing.

She was laughing----at him, no less.

After a few moments, she caught her breath and said, *"Guy, let's be clear. There is no relationship between us. What we just did was a one-time thing. It's never going to happen again. I am your boss."* She paused for a brief moment to look him in the eyes and said, *"I hope you understand."*

175

'What?' Guy was gutted. He was relieved. But then a little insulted too. He thought what they had done together was pretty spectacular. Now she wasn't at all interested in him. She had just used him for a booty call. It was every guy's dream to find a woman that just wanted to have great meaningless sex, but he had to admit to himself that he was more than a little hurt that he had meant so little to Jewels. He was just her late night snack.

Jewels was back in 'boss' mode now. *"Now, here's what I want you to do. I want you to continue seeing this Lola girl and get as much information as you can. If you need money from petty cash, let me know. I don't care what you have to do. Find out what is going on and report back to me."*

Guy was more than a little stunned. He was off the hook with Jewels. She was ordering him to take Lola out, and the campaign was going to pick up the tab. He stood there slack jawed, not knowing what to say.

"Is that clear?" Said Jewels.

"Uh, yes ma'am" he said.

"Good, now put the rest of your clothes on and go home." she said.

Guy bent over to put on his shoe and felt a hard slap on his ass.

"By the way, good work tonight," said Jewels as she winked at him, *"on everything."*

*****

Santos was so hungry. A late night chill had filled the night air and had fogged up his windows. He had turned on the patrol car's heater to warm it up. He had been passing the time by trolling Facebook on his smart phone and periodically clearing the windows of condensation.

He was wiping the driver's side window with his shirt sleeve when Lola's pretty boy exited the building. From a distance, he looked tired and sweaty. He almost raced to his truck. 'He sure is in a hurry to get out of there', Santos thought, but there was no sign of the woman.

Santos's felt he faced a dilemma. Should he follow the guy home to see where he lived? Should he stay and find out what happened to the scantily clad woman who showed up?

For all he knew, pretty boy was some psycho killer, and the lady in the flimsy nightie might be in there with her head bashed in. As a rookie, he was new at this kind of thing. So confused and conflicted. If he let the guy get away, Santos knew he might never find him again until the next time his sister went out with the guy. On the other hand the lady in the hooker outfit might be in danger and need his help. He had joined the force to help people, and his job was to protect and to serve. He decided to stay.

As Guy drove away in his truck, Santos watched his tail lights disappear into the inky moonless night. Santos was reaching for the keys to turn over the engine when a mighty roar came from the other end of the street. His attention was immediately refocused.

Thirty motorcycles crested the ridge and were headed down Main Street. They passed directly in front of Deputy Santos Salinas. He was transfixed on the loud choppers. They were beautiful works of American Iron, but his attention was really on the riders. They all wore complete face covered helmets, and they were wearing 'colors' that he had never seen before. They were definitely new in town. He would have to remember to tell someone about them.

They rode by peacefully, and he couldn't find one infraction or a single reason to stop them. Actually, he didn't want to mess with that many bikers on a dark night. He was all alone and had a fresh memory of what some outlaw biker gang had done to Deputy Sinclair. He didn't want his genitals tortured and then have to find his way home through the woods hog tied, with a bag over his head.

'Yeah,' thought Santos 'say what you want, but no man goes looking for that, especially alone and at night.' The thunderous hogs turned the corner and disappeared.

'Damn it!' he cursed. 'It's time for some banana pancakes. That woman never had come out of the building though and now he was going to have to go inside to investigate.'

*****

Jewels watched Santos remove his Mag Lite from his utility belt and begin to shine it into the windows. The new camera system was integrated so that she could see everything on her iPhone. She could even maneuver the cameras and zoom in from her iPhone. She had system installed first to catch Guytana Canova, but tonight it was catching a lot more. She watched as the officer got out of his car and walked slowly around the building. She recognized the sheriff's outfit immediately.

'Hmmm?' she thought. Possibly Sheriff Red up to no good?

She had met many of the good Sheriff's minions at different functions and debates, but this deputy was new. She didn't recognize him. She did notice that he was young and very handsome. He had huge arms and looked as if he spent a lot of time in the gym. Jewels had a weakness for young muscle men. She felt herself beginning to get aroused again. Her inner thighs started to ache with desire. She knew this feeling and there was only way that it was going to be quenched.

*****

Santos rapped on the glass doors.

He was peering through them into a black void when a vision appeared out of the nothingness of the night. The voluptuous angelic vision materialized in a flowing and feathery turquoise penoir.

Santos was startled at the sudden appearance, but he seemed paralyzed and unable to move. She was unlike any woman that Santos had ever encountered. He was enraptured.

"Oh, hi there, deputy." Jewels said. *"Can I help you?"*

Santos stood there.

He couldn't take his eyes off of her. He had never seen a nightgown like that before.

"Deputy!" Jewels repeated more forcefully as she snapped her fingers in front of Deputy Salinas' face.

"Oh, uhhh....." Santos couldn't think of what to say.

"Are you alright?" asked Jewels.

"Uhh, yes ma'am." Santos said as he shook the mental cobwebs away. *"I was just checking the area, and I saw a car in the parking lot, and I just wanted to make sure everything was alright."*

Jewels could see the perspiration on the young deputy's temple. *"Well,"* cooed Jewels as she pushed her breast out against the flimsy nightie. She purposely exposed her long inner thigh and crossed her right leg over in front of the left. She watched the deputy's eyes wander all the way down to her freshly painted pink toe nails in her puffy house shoes.

"Does EVERYTHING look alright to you, Deputy?" Whispered Jewels.

Chapter 31

The chow line snaked its way out the door and into the main hall. Doc was nauseated and didn't want to be there. Farmer had become his shadow ever since Hillbilly died. He felt like a damn child. He couldn't do anything. He didn't ever have a minute to himself. Farmer stuck to him like glue. He couldn't go anywhere without Farmer being right beside him. It was embarrassing having a big black Sambo as a shower shadow. But Doc was too depressed to care anymore that his constant moroseness had strained his relationship with Farmer.

Hillbilly was dead. It was all Doc's fault.

Doc had finally been able to piece the entire episode together. It had taken several weeks.

The Monkey Trap

He could still hear Hillbilly's infectious giggle. He missed Hillbilly's constant enthusiasm. He was always mischievous and happy. Now, because of Doc, he was dead.

Doc was the one that had kept getting the pills and he kept giving Hillbilly more and more. He was a doctor. He was supposed to know better, but ever since he had gotten to prison all he had done was whine and complain and feel sorry for himself.

In the month since Hillbilly's death, all he had done was wallow in his bunk and his own self-pity. Doc hated himself, and he hated the world. He was tired of being a victim. He was more tired of being miserable. He had enough of feeling like this. He felt like everyone's punching bag. He wanted to be free of looking over his shoulder for another nine years.

His emotions were swirling. He wanted his life back.

"Coming through." came a voice as Doc was shoved aside into the wall.

It was a peckerwood. Doc had seen him around. The guy thought he was some kind of rock star that could do anything he wanted. He was always cutting in the commissary and chow lines. He would always break in front of people to join a group of other peckerwoods. No one challenged him or said much because he was always with a bunch of other peckerwoods. They seemed to run in packs. People normally grumbled and let him go by, but today Doc had had enough. This was the day that Doc decided that he wasn't going to stand by and let people run over him anymore. He couldn't take it for another minute. He was fed up with being a wimp. He wanted to be taken seriously.

This guy and his buddies would probably beat him to a pulp and kill him, but at least he would die like a man with some dignity and a little bit of backbone. Anything would be better than living the way he had been or the past year and a half. It was time to man up. Even if it was only going to be for a few minutes until he was killed.

"Hey, Neanderthal," shouted Doc. *"Why don't you take your sorry inconsiderate ass to the back of the line and wait in it like a real man?"*

People had been talking and the timbre of the chow hall created echoes off of the fifty foot concrete walls. Because of Doc's outburst to the peckerwood, everyone around them came to a hush. People began to squeeze up next to the wall and started moving away from both of them.

"What did you say, motherfucker" said the obnoxious white guy as he snapped his head around.

People at the nearby tables picked up their trays and hauled ass. If a fight broke out they knew that they wouldn't be getting any replacement meals for whatever was lost.

The peckerwood lunged at Doc. Doc felt an adrenalin rush through his body like nitrous oxide through a car's engine. This was it. He was ready. He had thought about fighting back a million times. He visualized it daily in his mind. He hadn't ever had the guts to do it before, but now he did. In fact, he found himself itching for the confrontation. He didn't care what happened. He was wasn't going to be a scared little mouse anymore.

He would never be big in size, but he knew that he could be deadly. Doc knew more about the human body than anyone else in the prison. The state had taken his license, but they couldn't take his knowledge.

Like a typical bully, the peckerwood advanced straight at Doc with his arms pulled back and his chest puffed up. Doc knew the routine. The peckerwood would jump up in Doc's face and try to intimidate him with a standoff. Doc had seen it a thousand times. Two guys would bump their gums at one another, daring the other to throw the first punch. Most of the time other people would break it up before the guards came. The result was always the same. The bully invariably got his way and the victim got humiliated.

'Well, not this time.' thought Doc.

Doc planted his feet firmly when the peckerwood raged in. Doc balled up his right hand and knuckled up to deliver a pinpoint stabbing blow with his third knuckle to the white boy's soft sternum bone between his rib cages.

The peckerwood was completely stopped in his tracks. He had been utterly immobilized. His mouth was wide open as he gasped for air that just wasn't there. Panic set into his eyes as he realized that he wasn't able to draw a single breath.

The crowd stood stunned. Doc saw the fear in the peckerwood's eyes. Normally, he would empathize and feel sorry for anyone with that look, but that was the old Doc.

That was Doc the victim.

The new Doc grabbed the peckerwood and bent him over. As he did so, he put the bully into a head lock with his right arm and turned him completely around in a circle to the left. At the completion of the circle, Doc use the peckerwood's skull as a battering ram into the cement block wall. The blow triggered an auto response to allow the peckerwood to breathe again. However, the cranial impact had stunned the white boy into a daze.

Doc stood him upright; facing the dining room. The bully was wobbly. The peckerwood's friends had been so stunned at how quick their buddy had been defeated, all they could do was stand motionless as Doc let go of him. .

"You gotta be really careful when you cut in line." Doc's voice had an eerie calmness to it as he slowly lowered his head and looked over the tops of his eyes.

Doc waited a beat until he knew they were all paying attention. Then with the flourish of an executioner, he shoved his left hand in between the bully's shoulder blades. He forced the bully forward as he used his right leg in a backwards sweeping motion. Removing the peckerwood's feet from under him.

From the distance of twenty feet away, his buddies saw what was going to happen to the peckerwood before he did. Doc had positioned the bully perfectly; a torso's length away from the tubular rail that divided the serving line from the dining room. With his feet removed and his body being deliberately propelled forward, the dazed peckerwood was headed for the top rail. The woozy white boy landed exactly the way Doc had planned it. The bully hit the rail directly, crushing his larynx with a sickening squish. Inmates all around let out a collective groan as the peckerwood's head was snapped back from the impact. He hit the floor and immediately began to fish flop as he gasped and grottled for breath.

Doc turned to a slack-jawed Farmer.

"I am feeling a lot better now, but I don't want to eat here anymore. How about we just fix a spread in our cell. I feel like having a birthday party"

'What?' thought a flabbergasted Farmer. *"What birthday?"*

"My birthday." Said Doc. *"My new birthday."*

With that he turned and walked out of the chow hall.

Doc continued to amaze and confuse Farmer. He just took out a guy in the chow hall in front of 500 witnesses in less than 30 seconds and now he was acting like it never happened. The most amazing part was that the beaten peckerwood didn't have a single mark on him. There was no blood. No marks. No scrapes. No evidence. No proof.

There was nothing. Nothing to connect Doc to almost killing the guy. It was the perfect assault. Other than the 500 witnesses.

The chow hall began to empty out as guards began to arrive with pepper spray to stop a fight that had been reported. All they found was a group of white guys huddled around their fallen buddy. Farmer knew no one would snitch to the guards. Other than a few peckerwoods, everyone had cleared out of the chow hall, including Doc and Farmer.

Doc walked with a new slow and deliberate pace. Inmates were passing him in the large hall, making sure they gave him a wide berth. Doc was surprised at the number of people that gave him the thumbs up as they walked by and went around him. He was the victor. He was a hero.

Most of all, he was a man again.

*****

"What the fuck just happened, celly?" Asked Farmer, as he followed Doc into the day room.

"I don't know what you are talking about." replied Doc.

"What! Are you kidding me?" Farmer exclaimed. *"You just annihilated a peckerwood in the chow hall in front of five hundred people, and you don't know what I am talking about?"*

Doc sat on one of the stainless steel table tops. *"Yeah, well maybe I just finally got fed up taking everyone's shit."*

Farmer looked at Doc closely. This wasn't the same guy that Farmer rode the bus with over a year ago. He wasn't the same timid and scared little puke that Farmer had been sharing a cell with for all of this time. Farmer was looking at someone else. He was looking at a completely new man.

More than that, Farmer was looking at a dangerous man.

Doc's eyes had a different look. Gone was the sheepish little nerd. The man sitting on the table in front of him was confident and fearless. Farmer had seen this guy stroll back from the chow hall with a swagger. This new Doc was someone to be reckoned with. Farmer felt something well up inside of himself.

It was pride.

Farmer was actually proud of his little buddy.

Doc felt like he had been set free. He had never felt like this. It was exhilarating. He was still reeling from the adrenaline rush of beating the crap out of that peckerwood. He knew he shouldn't be happy about it, but he was. And it felt good. It felt really good. It felt powerful. And he liked it.

He had gone to that chow hall a scared little rabbit and had come back a fearless lion. It was as if a switch had been flipped, and now his life truly belonged to him.

All of the moping and silent bitching for the last year and a half had only cost him precious time. It was a year and a half that he would never get back, but he was a new man now. Doc knew now that he was the only one who was going to get him out of this place. No one else was going to do it.

It was time to get serious.

Doc had been hoping and praying that his big brother would come riding in and save him. Well, that wasn't going to happen. It was time for him to get upon the horse and do it himself. It was time to get busy and go to work.

"Farmer, why are you my friend?" Doc asked matter-of-factly.

Farmer was speechless. Where had that come from? What was he supposed to say? Was this some sort of trick question? What was he wanting to hear?

"Because you are my celly and we gotta stick together." said Farmer.

"Horseshit!" said Doc. *"You could've had anyone you wanted as a celly. I am not stupid."*

"I know you're not stupid." Farmer replied. Then he paused and began to look down. His brow furrowed, causing his forehead to crinkle, *"but I am, Doc."*

The words coming out of his mouth were as much of a surprise to Farmer as they were to Doc. Farmer had never said those words about himself. He began to tell how proud black men just didn't admit to that kind of thing to other people, especially to no white folks.

Farmer didn't want to be just a proud black man anymore. He wanted to be an educated black man that his family could be proud of for a change. He had run around all his life with nothing but proud ignorant niggers and the only thing he had to show for it was being the warden's boy in a prison at almost fifty years old. Those niggas had been so cool skipping school and making fun of all the white kids who were stupid enough to go to class every day. He and his homeboys shot hoops all day on the basketball court, and they would smoke a few blunts before going down to the park to hit some 'poo-nah-nah' from some of the girls that liked to get high. He knew that over the years he probably fathered more than half a dozen kids, but the only two he knew were living with his wife.

Raising those kids had been a struggle on his wife since he was in and out of prison so much. He had tried to do the right thing so many times. He would get a job and do really well at it until he couldn't advance beyond minimum wage. He hadn't known how to read or write. That was why he had latched onto Doc and now that he had learned to read and write he wanted something even more. He didn't want to merely go back. He wanted to go back to do better and to have more than just a thug's life.

"I want to get the fuck out of here, Doc." said Farmer *"Even though I knows how to scribble my name now, I still ain't got the book smarts like you do. I knew you was book smarts the first time I met ya. You didn't have a lick of street smarts back when we got shackled together on that bus,"* Farmer raised his head to look at Doc in his eyes *"but today, I think you grew up."*

Doc thought deeply about all that Farmer had just told him. Farmer had never opened himself up that sincerely and showed his vulnerabilities that way before. The old Doc would have been moved to tears and embraced the old Nubian giant, but the new Doc was a different kind of man.

"Well, you got that right." Doc said as he hopped off of the dayroom table. *"I certainly grew up. Now let's get the hell off this pitty pot and go figure out what we are going to do to get out of this mother fucker."*

Chapter 32

Jewels definitely had an extra little pep in her pump this morning. After a night of back-to-back love making she felt alive and ready to conquer the world.

Jewels' morning routine consisted of sipping Mandarin orange hot tea while she perused the morning papers.

"Jackson, where are my papers?" hollered Jewels.

Jackson was a cute twenty something intern who could type like the wind. What had gotten him the job was his skill at making a good cup of hot tea. What kept him employed was his ability to keep Jewels abreast of all the office gossip and latest news. Jackson was a southern Oklahoma boy who had fallen in love and decided to move to the Great State of Texas to be with his true love, a cute little blonde number with a turned up nose by the name Kelly. He hadn't completely fallen in love with Texas, but he had fallen for Kelly. In a twist of strange irony, after only three months, Kelly moved away to Oklahoma to attend university. Leaving poor Jackson destitute and all alone in Lloyd County. Jackson eventually got a job and enrolled in the local college. He was pursuing the seven year Drama degree and a new love by the name Blake Rivers.

"Here you go, Your Highness." Said Jackson. *"I got your hot tea and some even hotter news."*

"Jackson, for the millionth time," she sighed with mocked exaggeration *"I have no interest in the Twilight Rapist. I swear I don't understand your obsession with some sicko who gets his jolly's by raping old grannies. If you ask me, it is probably some teenage weirdo who didn't get spanked enough as a child."*

"I am not obsessed." retorted Jackson *"But at your age you can't be too careful."*

"What!" exclaimed Jewels as she feigned indignation at Jackson's jib about her age.

Oh, settle down, Mary, and snap those bloodshot baby blues on this." said Jackson as he threw the Washington Post newspaper down on her desk.

Followed by The Austin American-Statesman and the Dallas Morning News. The headline was the same on all of them.

"TEXAS SENATOR ASSASSINATED"

"What?" Jewels was in shock. She knew Senator Chris Carona. She had been on his staff in Austin when he was the Texas Land & Railroad Commissioner. It had been right out of college, and she owed her first state-wide campaign to him. He had recommended her. She felt sad at the loss of such a great man. The Washington Post story told how an RPG took out the Senator and twenty two Marines while on a fact finding tour over Afghanistan in a V-22 Osprey.

"Send Barbara Corona some flowers from me," said Jewels *"but let me write the card."*

"Will do, but" Jackson pulled the Dallas Morning News from the bottom of the pile and put it on top *"you might want to turn to page eight and read who the front runner is to fill the vacant seat until the next election."*

Jewels quickly turned the pages and the photo jumped off the page before she ever read a word. *"Oh my God!"* screamed Jewels. *"You have got to be kidding me."*

"Yup! None other than your old classmate." said Jackson. *"Mr. Boyce B. Braxton."*

This was huge. Boyce Braxton. For seven years he had been the thorn in her side. He was Mr. Wonderful, Mr. Perfect and Mr. Rich, all rolled up into one. Everyone loved Boyce.

Including Jewels.

No one was as brilliant, as gorgeous or as smart as the illustrious Mr. Braxton. Even back in college everyone knew that Boyce Braxton would be someone big one day. Jewels knew that he had everything that it took to be President. As she read the editorial from the Dallas Morning News she could see that this was Boyce Braxton's move to achieve that goal. He had always been the behind scenes guy. He had never held a public office, which now made him the perfect person to fill Senator Corona's seat. The country's sentiment had turned against career politicians and they were "looking for fresh faces", said the Dallas Morning News.

"Well, they don't get any fresher than Boyce Braxton." said Jewels. *"That's   for   sure."*
"Uhhhhh-huhhhh!" cooed Jackson, as he ogled the newspaper photo. *"I only got three words for him. DEEE-Lish-OUS! And I'm outta here, Ms. Thang."* Jackson snapped his fingers and swished out of Jewels office.

Jewels had served on the University of Texas Law Review with Boyce. He was ambitious. That was for sure, but he had enough brilliance to go all the way to the White House.

So did Jewels. She began calculating in her head. Senator Corona's vacated seat still had two and a half years left on it. Then there was a Presidential election two years after that. The timing was perfect. If she could win this election for Joe Don Lilly, she would be the winningest campaign manager in the state. Boyce would be absolutely crazy not to hire her. She was already strategizing how she was going to be Boyce Braxton's next campaign manager. There was only one minor little problem that she could foresee.

That problem would be Boyce Braxton.

*****

"You are going to have so much fun" said Lola.

Guy had agreed to go with Lola to the Sheriff's auction. He didn't really care what he did just as long as he was with her. He had never seen her this excited. They had looked over all the auction lots and she had showed him all of the things that she liked. It was almost like they were married. They got their bidding paddle and sat down on the center aisle.

This was his first auction. At first it had been confusing. There was so much going on and the guy up front was talking so fast that Guy couldn't understand a word he was saying. It sounded like the time he went to the Pentecostal Church with his Aunt, and they all started praying in tongues, except this time he was able to eventually understand the auctioneer after about thirty minutes. Sometimes he would see a paddle go up, but most of the time he didn't see anyone bidding. Guy figured the auctioneer must have better eyes than he did because every time he said, 'Sold', and banged his gavel, someone would whoop with joy.

"Our next item is Lot 23. A fifty-five inch HD TV with full surround sound system. Who wants to start the bidding?"

The bidding started at $10 and Guy was shocked that by the time it got to $50 no one else bid on it. It was a nice TV and Guy thought he could definitely use a new television, so he raise his paddle a little so that the auctioneer could see him. He even smiled as he caught the auctioneer's eyes.

"Fifty dollars, going once." shouted the auctioneer.

'I guess he didn't see me.' Thought Guy, so this time he raised his paddle up higher so that he would be seen for sure.

"Fifty dollars, going twice." shouted the auctioneer as he turned away from Guy.

This time he shot his arm all the way up into the air. There was no way anyone in the whole place could miss it this time.

BANG! *"Sold for fifty dollars to Deputy Jones"* shouted the auctioneer. *"I am so sorry sir, but I didn't see your hand and I already banged the gavel. Better luck next time."*

Guy was fuming. He knew the auctioneer had seen him all three times. There was something fishy going on.

The man sitting behind Guy leaned up to whisper in Guy's ear. *"Don't let it get to you, son. He often goes blind like that when the deputies want something."* said the old man before he eased back into his seat.

Guy watched and listened, but he couldn't detect anything. The problem was he couldn't see what was going on behind him. Guy laid his paddle in his chair and excused himself to the men's room. Guy was an analyst and he was going to figure out what was really going on here. He stood against the back wall and surveyed the entire auction house.

Lots came and went without so much as a whiff of anything suspicious. Guy decided to relieve himself and to go back to his seat.

Guy entered the handicap stall because he was pee shy and couldn't use the standup urinals. The restroom was a busy place. Guy could hear people coming and going.

"Hey, Jonesy," screamed someone who had opened the door. *"Your next item is coming up, so unless you want that outsider poaching your diamond ring, you better pinch it off and move your butt."*

*****

"Lot 66 is a beautiful 4.83 carat solitaire diamond ring. This is a beauty folks. Who would like to open the bidding?" asked the auctioneer.

"One Hundred Dollars" was the bid from the large potbellied deputy standing to the side of the room and near the men's room.

Bidding inched its way up a little bit, but the large officer was still the highest bidder at Two Hundred and Twenty Dollars when the bidding suddenly ground to a halt.

Guy's mother had a ring almost as large as the one on the auction block, and he knew that it was worth much, much more than two hundred and twenty dollars. There was something strange going on here. Guy raised his hand to bid on the ring.

The auctioneer immediately turned away.

"Two Twenty going once." yelled the auctioneer.

Guy knew that the auctioneer had seen him, but was deliberately looking away so that he could pull the old 'I didn't see you trick again'. This was a crooked auction for sure, but they couldn't be too obvious in front of all these people.

"One Thousand Dollars!" screamed Guy,

The Monkey Trap

The room went silent and the auctioneer turned red faced. He was obviously caught in a serious dilemma. He couldn't ignore Guy's bid. Everyone in the room had heard it. If he didn't acknowledge the thousand dollar bid, he would definitely lose his auctioneer's license. The sweat was beading down his forehead, and Guy glanced toward the fat deputy near the Men's room. The deputy was snorting like a wild pig and cheeks were crimson red with rage.

"I have a thousand dollars bid." informed the auctioneer in a slow and calm voice as he turned to the large deputy and raised his eyebrows. *"Do I have any other bids?"*

Everyone in the auction pivoted in their seats to see what the deputy would do. All of the attention almost required that he make another bid just to save face in front of all his friends and co-workers.

"Eleven Hundred" said the deputy as his buddies slapped him on the back.

The auctioneer didn't even ask for any other bids. *"I have eleven hundred going once."*

Guy saw what was happening. He wasn't a fool. They were trying to get the gavel down for the sale as quickly as possible. The old man had been right. It was obvious that the deputies were favored customers.

'Well, let's see how bad the old fat man wants it,' Guy thought to himself.

"Twelve Hundred." yelled Guy.

The deputy was seething with rage. Guy was secretly enjoying the moment. The fat deputy was so angry he looked as if he was about to explode at any second. His friends huddled with him; encouraging him to bid again. Everyone in the room could see that they were discussing money as several of his buddies opened their wallets to count how much they could loan the potbellied deputy.

"Twelve Fifty" said the deputy popping his head up from the huddle.

The Monkey Trap

"Twelve Fifty going once." screamed the auctioneer. And in the same breath he yelled. *"Twelve Fifty going twice"*, but Guy knew that they were tapped out when the deputy halved the standard raise by only fifty bucks. It was a 'tell', a sign of desperation that he had reached his limit.

The old auctioneer already had his gavel high in the air, but before he could get it down and yell, "Sold", Guy shouted at the top of his voice, *"Fifteen Hundred Dollars."*

The deputy and his friends all started screaming and stomping their feet because they had come so close. The large deputy tore his bidding card in half and stormed out of the room.

The auctioneer sheepishly asked. *"If there are no further bids then I have fifteen hundred going once, twice and sold. May I see your number, sir?"*

"I don't have it with me." Guy said. *"Just a minute."*

The auctioneer brightened up. *"I am sorry, sir, but the rules of the auction say that you must have your number in order to bid. I am afraid I will have to accept the next highest bid."*

The deputies in the back whooped and hollered as they called the deputy back. Guy was flabbergasted. They were going to screw him over on a technicality. Any lingering doubt about an honest auction went out the window. It was rigged from top to bottom. The potbellied deputy was going to get the ring after all.

"Excuse me, Mr. Auctioneer." came a sweet voice from the seated audience. *"But that is not right."*

The entire auction hall was dead silent now.

"I am sorry, little lady," said the auctioneer, *"but those are the rules."*

Lola could see that he was trying to intimidate her. *"No! What I mean is that you are incorrect."* The auction room was silent now. *"According to the rules printed right here on the bidding paddle."* Everyone was listening to her now. She was being feisty, but polite, and no gentleman in Texas would dare cut a young lady off from speaking. *"It states here that the bidders paddle must be available to the auctioneer or on the bidding floor when the final bid is accepted."*

Lola then picked up Guy's paddle and lifted it high into the air. *"As you can see it is in Mr. Canova's chair, which is obviously on the bidding floor, and it is definitely available to you."*

The audience began to clap. Guy rushed to her side and he kissed her deeply. The clapping grew louder and Guy saw, out of the corner of his eye, the group of very unhappy deputies exit out the door to the parking lot.

This had been a good day.

At least that was what Guy thought.

*****

Jewels had tried repeatedly to reach Boyce Braxton.

Every time she called his office every one she spoke with swore that they would give him her message. She hated getting the brush off. She knew what was really going on. Boyce Braxton was still pissed off.

Boyce had a long memory and apparently held a long grudge.

'Jesus,' thought Jewels as she hung up the phone for the sixth time 'surely, he can't still be mad at me for what happened between us in college. That had been over twenty years ago. The man must have a memory and carry a grudge like an elephant.'

Boyce Braxton had been a shoe in to be the youngest member to ever be selected to be on the University of Texas Law Review. It was comprised of one hundred of the university's best minds. Every year the fifty longest serving senior members would retire and fifty new junior law students would take their place, and the previous junior members would move up to be senior members in order to assure that the board always had continuity and experience with the older half of its members and fresh blood and ideas with the incoming younger half. Every year three to four hundred of the universities' best and brightest minds applied and fought viciously for the fifty positions on the prestigious Law Review Board. Being on the Law Review could mean the difference between working in a D.A.s office for five years of plea bargaining traffic tickets for peanuts or getting recruited by a top law firm and making a six figure salary. The competition was cut-throat among junior law students. However, there was the occasion shooting star that was able to make it in their sophomore year. That year it had been Boyce Braxton. He was charismatic, good-looking and knew how to politic better than anyone. Noone could ever beat him in Moot Court. As a debater of the law he was a rock star on campus. He had beaten everyone he had ever gone up against. That was until he went up against a second semester freshman named Jewels Sapphire.

Jewels Sapphire was cute and sexy. She had flaming red, curly hair that bounced off of her shoulders when she walked in her four inch platform heels. She wore nothing but mini-skirts and tight blouses that showed as much cleavage as she could get away with. Her skin was porcelain white, and her lips and nails were always painted 'Jungle Red', just like she had seen in an old movie from the 1930s that depicted strong women with style. Her body was amazing, and it opened every door she ever knocked on, but it was her brain that delivered the knockout punch. She was brilliant.

She had applied for the Law Review at the very last minute and had beaten the deadline by less than a second. She had carefully calculated it so as not to give her competitors enough time to mount a unified defense against her. She wanted to be the youngest to ever be accepted to the Law Review.

The board had picked forty-nine juniors to be on the new board but the fiftieth position had come down to Boyce and Jewels. Only one would make it on to the Law Review this year while the other would inevitably have to wait until the next year. Campaigning had been intense for both applicants, but the voting had ended in a tie.

The decision was made to hold a Mock court to debate and re-argue the Lincoln-Douglas debates of 1858. To be fair, they had drawn lots to see who would argue which position. Boyce had drawn the short straw and had to take Stephen Douglas' pro-slavery position while Jewels, the red bombshell, got to play the heroic part of Abraham Lincoln in a hot little mini-skirt while defending his anti-slavery position with a more than ample amount of persuasiveness and cleavage.

Stephen Douglas had originally won the debates and the Illinois senate seat in 1858, but there had been a civil war and over a hundred years of civil rights since then; and it had been an almost foregone conclusion that Jewels would be the winner of the debate and the next member of the Law Review. No one was going to stand up and vote pro-slavery in this modern day, even if it was a mock debate.

Jewels won and Boyce was forced to wait another year to make the Law Review. Apparently, he had never forgotten it, and now Jewels knew that he had never forgiven her for it either.

Convincing Boyce Braxton to let her be his campaign manager was going to be tougher than she thought, but she wasn't deterred. She had pulled off harder things.

*****

Guy and Lola left the auction house in his new truck. Lola was now a permanent fixture in the middle of the seat and under his arm.

"This was what love was supposed to feel like." Guy told himself.

Guy had waited for love all of his life. He never had a girlfriend in high school. He had been a computer geek. He never played on the football team nor had he been invited to go to the cool parties. He prayed that things would change when he got to college, but after a few weeks, he soon realized that the people in college were the same ones that he had been with in high school. Needless to say, his romantic experiences in college had been pretty dismal. If truth be known, he had given up all hope and resigned himself to being a perpetual bachelor. He had never expected to have Lola fall into his lap, and now he couldn't imagine his life without her in it.

Guy couldn't get the auction out of his mind. It was obviously rigged, but he was still trying to figure out what was going on. Why were all those deputies at the auction? They didn't buy much, but Guy had watched long enough from the back to see that when they did bid, either the auctioneer subtly ignored bids from the other people or everyone else just stopped bidding against them. It was as if the people were too intimidated or scared to bid against them.

What the hell was going on? What did they know that he didn't?

He would have to figure it out later.

CRASH!

Guy's head was thrown violently forward towards the steering wheel. His hand instinctively grabbed onto Lola. He clutched her to him before she was propelled face first into the truck's dash.

Guy had barely recovered when he saw the big SUV racing towards him in the rear view mirror. It was painted camouflage and rigged with spot lights all the way across the top of the windshield. The large black tubular grill rushed up to fill Guy's rear view mirror. This time Guy braced himself for a second impact.

The collision of the SUV forced Guy's rear wheels off the ground momentarily. The trucks momentum was halted as the bed of the truck was driven into the air. Lola screamed as she was propelled into the truck's floorboard.

The truck's wheels hit the ground while still spinning at sixty miles per hour. The tires grabbed onto the rural blacktop road causing the truck to fishtail back and forth. Guy turned the steering wheel violently to the left and then back again to the right in order to keep the truck from careening off the road and into the deep culverts. Lola struggled to get off the floor, but the force of the truck being jerked from side to side catapulted her head into the truck's passenger door.

"Lola stay down," screamed Guy *"they are coming for us again."*

"Who are they, Guy?" asked Lola with frightened tears in her eyes and

blood running down her face.

"I don't know, baby!" yelled Guy as he guided the truck with both hands. Tightly grasping the steering wheel and watching his rear view mirror at the same time.

As Guy's truck tacked back and forth erratically across the road, the driver of the SUV assumed that Guy would end up in the ditch so he backed off. Guy seized the opportunity and used the momentary relief to reacquire control of his truck.

He reached out with his right arm to offer it to Lola so that she could get off the floor of the truck.

"Buckle yourself in quick!" screamed Guy as he looked over his shoulder. *"They are going to hit us again."*

The SUV raced toward them. The driver had been disappointed that he hadn't been able to crash the truck on the first two tries. This time he was putting the pedal to the metal. Guy saw that the camo SUV had picked up speed and was serious about hurting them. Guy put his foot down and gunned the gas. The pick-up truck's V-6 roared to life. He had been able to surprise the SUV by putting a little bit of distance between them and thus had thwarted the SUV's third attempt. Guy knew they were seriously trying to hurt them. This wasn't an accident. Whoever was in that SUV was trying to kill them.

"But why?" Guy asked himself. It didn't make sense. Why did anyone care about him? He was just a computer analyst from a little hick town.

The SUV's engine was screaming and Guy could hear it grow louder and louder in his ears as it closed the distance between them. If he didn't think of something to do soon, these crazy nut jobs were going to succeed in killing him and Lola. It was one thing if they wanted to kill him, but he would be damned if he was going to let them hurt his Lola.

He assessed everything around him. The only hope he had was a half mile ahead. It was an old Farm to Market road. It wasn't even visible yet, but it was their only option. All he needed was a little bit of time, so he stomped on the gas and said a prayer.

Lola was looking back giving Guy expert information about the camo SUV. It was gaining on them with its larger V-8 engine, but she and Guy were able to maintain the moving distance for a little bit. Guy wondered if they would have enough time to reach the old road before the SUV was able to run them down?

As they approached the old FM Rd, horror struck Guy's heart. A line of motorcycles were coming down the road. There was no way he was going be able to slow down enough to make the sharp turn.

He had to think of something quick. He needed to turn the tables on this guy. But how? He was tired of being the rabbit. He wanted to be the fox. What would the fox do?

"Hold on!" Guy screamed as he stood up and stomped on the brake. His arms were stiff and fully extended as he held the wheel steady and braced for the inevitable impact.

The truck tires smoked and screeched as they locked onto the asphalt highway. Guy had decided to take the offensive and turn the tables on the camo SUV.

The driver of the SUV saw the smoking tires of the truck and knew that his plan to run Guy off the road had turned on him. If he hit the steel bed of that truck now, he would go flying through the windshield. He had seen enough accidents to know there would be nothing but eyeballs and teeth left for the accident team to scrape up off the road.

The SUV driver jerked the wheel right at the very last moment. As he jetted past the truck, the rear view mirror was ripped from the side of the SUV and pieces of debris shattered the side window showering him in glass. The driver began to dip into the right culvert of the road. After he cleared the truck, he yanked the wheel left and shot past a line of motorcycles waiting on the side road.

Guy had almost come to a complete stop when the SUV flew by him. He jerked the steering wheel and made a hard right turn onto the old road.

"Are you okay?" asked the female cyclist.

Guy recognized the woman. The last time he had seen her had been in the dark, but he remembered her vividly.

"I think that guy is some kind of maniac who is trying to kill my girlfriend and me." said Guy. He felt like he was talking ninety miles an hour. Guy's adrenaline was pumping and he was scared that the SUV would turn around and come back after him.

The motorcyclist looked over at Lola with blood oozing from over her eye and covering her beautiful face.

"You go get her taken care of and don't worry about that SUV." said the motorcyclist. *"We will take care of him. We know just what to do with guys who like to hurt women."*

Chapter 33

Gray ostrich cowboy boots reverberated off of the marble floors of the old Lloyd County courthouse. Those boots belonged to none other than Sheriff Hardon 'Red' Johnson. He still had a ceremonial office on the first floor for the tourists and press conferences, but the Sheriff's department now had a new twenty million dollar jail and headquarters two blocks away. Today as he ascended the smooth marble steps of the old courthouse, he was proud of this old building. It had been his for the past forty two years.

Gone were the metal detectors and x-ray machines that the federal government had purchased for them following September 11, 2001. They had been an eyesore in the grand and majestic old courthouse, and he wasn't going to have his beautiful building sullied by a bunch of nancy boys from the government who couldn't handle a couple rag heads.

'We know how to handle 'em down here, and if any of those sand niggers come into Lloyd county', thought Sheriff Johnson, 'we don't need no machines to protect our town.' We keep it safe the old fashion way, the way that made this country great.

Over the course of thirty years he had run more than a couple of undesirables out of town at the end of his great-grandfather's 1898 Colt revolver. His great-grandfather had met Teddy Roosevelt at the Menger Hotel in San Antonio in 1898. Teddy filled his grandfather and several other patriotic fellows standing around the hotel bar that night with several drinks and more than a few stories of heroic adventures. Before the night was over, they had all agreed to join some group that Teddy was putting together to fight the Spanish in Cuba. In their drunken revelry they had even come up with a name for themselves, "The Rough Riders".

Hardon's great-grandfather shot over sixty Spanish soldiers with the old revolver in the charge up what he referred to as a couple of old dirt mounds called Kettle Hill and San Juan Hill. He returned home a hero but died several months later of "Cuban Fever"; however, on his death bed, he bequeathed his most prize possession, the revolver that Teddy Roosevelt had given him, to his youngest and favorite son, Harlan, Sheriff Hardon 'Red' Johnson's grand-father.

"Good mornin', Sheriff." said the clerk with her deep East Texas twang.

"Why good morning, Belinda." responded the Sheriff. *"I swear if you get any prettier I will have to arrest you. Is Wes in?"*

Belinda blushed. *"Yes. He is expecting you. Go right on in before I call your wife up and tell her you're flirting with me again."*

Judge Wesley Wood's private chambers were the stuff that Hollywood movies recreated. Filled with law books strewn everywhere and century old tiger wood oak that gave the room a mellow glow. It had been meticulously cared for by inmates since it had been built in 1894. It had been restored and renovated in 2003, but Judge Wood was emphatic that his chamber be left exactly the way it had been built by the founding fathers. Tradition was important to him, and he was determined to preserve it.

"Damn, Wes. " said the Sheriff as he took off his Stetson *"Do you know what time it is?"*

Judge Wood never missed an opportunity to school somebody in county history, even if that somebody was the county Sheriff. It was his passion.

Why no, I don't. " said the judge. *"And do you know why that is, Sheriff?"*

Oh, dear lord, here it came. Another boring history lesson. The judge waited for the sheriff to respond. He always did that even though he was going to tell you anyway.

"No, I don't, judge, but please tell me, why don't you know what time it is. " said the sheriff sarcastically.

"Well, I am glad you asked. " said the judge as his eyes brightened at the opportunity to bestow on someone his vast knowledge of obscure historical facts. *"When they built this magnificent building, they erected an enormous clock tower, which was the custom and architectural fashion of the day for these grand castles on the Texas prairie. "*

"However, " He paused for a deep breath, *"the original holder of this very office refused to have a clock put in that esteemed tower after the good folks of this county had spent a considerable amount of money to erect it. "* Said the judge with unbridled enthusiasm.

"And do you know why he refused to have a clock put in that tower?" The judge got his jollies at doing this type of bantering.

"No, Wes, please tell me why. " said the sheriff in dead-pan monotone. He had heard a million of the judge's stories. However, the Sheriff's sarcastic response was in no way acknowledged and had absolutely no effect in deterring the judge's enthusiasm.

"Because, he said, if a man gets up when the sun rises and goes to bed when it sets, then he doesn't need no damn clock. "

The judge sat there with a satisfied look on his face. *"There sure were some smart old fellas back then. Much smarter than ones running around today. That's for sure.* The judge's mood noticeably changed as he put on his reading glasses and picked up a sheet of paper off of his desk.

"You got a problem, Red."

*****

The vein in Doc's head protruded.

His face turned crimson and his eyes bulged. He struggled with every bit of might that he had left. Stars began to encroach into his periphery vision as blackness tried to take over his consciousness, but he wasn't about to give up.

"Hurts, don't it, Hoto?" Said the voice above him.

Doc's arms were shaking as he fought back against the black rusted pipe that was almost at his throat. He didn't know how much longer he could hold out. His windpipe was about to be crushed.

"What a little bitch." a harsh voice said mockingly. *"Fight it back."*

The taunt made Doc madder. He wasn't a quitter. That was the old Doc. The new Doc was a fighter. He pushed back with everything he had until the cold pipe began to push away from him. He felt his rage begin to take over.

"Ahh! C'mon, is that all you got?" taunted Joey as he placed his hands on the black pipe bar and put his face directly over Doc's. *"My abuela can lift more than this."*

If Joey's grandmother had arms like he did, then Doc could believe it. The teasing from Joey spurred Doc on, and he gave the bar one last push with all of his might. The weight began to move up as Doc's whole body shook until the weights of the bench press had cleared the hooks. The struggle had been so epic for Doc that his feet left the ground.

Doc dropped the weight bar onto the steel cradles, and with the sudden relief of the weight off his arms, he let them collapse completely out to the sides. Salty sweat burned as it ran into his eyes, but he was so exhausted he didn't care. The burn in his muscles hurt far worse. He couldn't move either arm, but he could feel his muscles twitching involuntarily.

"That was pretty good." Joey said as he tossed Doc's t-shirt over his face.

The new Doc had decided to change everything in life. He had become a new man on the inside so he decided to complete the transformation on the outside as well. At first he was only going out to recreation. He started out by doing what most of the other convicts were doing; walking around the worn down dirt track, but after a couple of times that got monotonous as hell to Doc.

'Walking around a dirt track with old geezers wasn't what bad asses do.' thought Doc, so he looked around for something else.

The young Mexicans played soccer and the blacks dominated the basketball courts. Doc saw a couple of guys playing handball, which looked like fun, but the scarce availability of handballs didn't make that a viable option.

Doc stood around the weight lifting equipment. It was old and primitive, but it was always there. Doc looked at the guys on it and thought how much he would like to look like them. They looked powerful, and Doc knew that it was exactly what he wanted his new image to look like. If he wanted to look like the best, then he needed to be trained by the best.

Doc spent several days standing around the equipment watching and observing. Most of the blacks weren't serious body builders. They mainly wanted to front for their buddies. None of the whites seemed to really know how to sculpt their bodies. They just threw on weight and lifted without much other consideration or dedication.

The best on the yard was the big Mexican that they called Joey. He worked out every day, but Doc noticed that he had a very precise routine and regiment, unlike most of the other inmates. His body was magnificent. He was big, but he was not grotesque in size nor did he have veins that stuck out like arterial road maps. His muscles were smooth and well rounded. It was exactly the look that Doc wanted. With that kind of look, no one would mess with him anymore. That was for sure.

As the new Doc, he was willing to stand and fight, but he wasn't stupid. Fights brought you unwanted attention and trouble. If he could deter his enemies before fists went flying, that would be a preferable strategy. Everything Doc did and every thought he had now was calculated to making himself stronger and to getting out of prison.

Doc had approached Joey and asked him to be his trainer.

"What's in it for me?" asked Joey.

Doc hadn't thought about that, but he should have. Everything in prison had a price tag. Even friendships.

Doc didn't have any commissary except what he got for helping people in the Law Library.

"Wait a minute." said Joey as he looked at Doc more closely. He smiled. *"You that white boy that they all been talking about, ain't cha'?"*

"I don't know." said Doc.

"Yeah, you do." Said Joey. *"You is Farmer's boy."*

"I am not anyone's boy" said Doc defensively.

"I heard that too." said Joey *"I think we can work out a trade. I could use a little legal work."* as he stuck out his hand and smiled. *"Deal?"*

With Joey's help, Doc's body had changed drastically in only two months. Gone were the soft, doughy edges. Doc was now lean and hard. He couldn't believe how fast Joey had been able to transform him. Doc would look into the polished metal mirror in the cell for over an hour sometimes; checking out every minute change and new muscle that seem to appear every day.

Doc liked Joey. With his friends, Joey was a jokester; always laughing. The only wrinkles on Joey's body were on his forehead from smiling so damn much. They were so big and so deep that he reminded Doc of one of those Shar-pay puppies with all of the wrinkles.

"Well, that's enough for today. I don't want to kill you." said Joey as he put out his hand and pulled Doc up from the bench. *"I don't want you to keel over before you get my parole packet finished.*

Doc had agreed to help put together Joey's parole package. Joey had spent twenty years of his life behind bars. He had only been nineteen years old when he was convicted of shooting to death four rival gang members. The black gang bangers were trying to take over his gang's neighborhood in El Paso.

*****

On a beautiful spring day in April, Joey and his buddy, Tito, were celebrating the Quincenera of his niece. It was a perfect day. The air was filled with white puffy clouds and festive Tejano music. Beautiful girls with flowing black hair swirled and danced with Mexican boys in their finest cowboy boots and hats.

No one noticed when a car load of black gang bangers rolled by and, without any notice, opened up with automatic weapons and began spraying deadly lead indiscriminately into the party.

Panic consumed the crowd as people dived for cover to escape the barrage of deadly gun fire. Joey heard at least a dozen shots before he was able to move. He felt a bullet whistle by his head as he dived behind Tito's low-riding '69 Chevy Impala. Detroit still made automobiles from steel in 196, and Joey heard several shots ricochet off of the old car that would have sliced right through any new car made today. He knew that the old girl had just saved his life.

Joey heard the squeal of car tires as the black Buick Grand National hit the accelerator and peeled off to get away. The entire incident had only lasted a few seconds, but it had seemed like an hour. It was as if time had only moved forward in slow motion.

Joey lifted his head up. Everyone he loved was lying on the ground. He didn't know if they were alive or dead. Some began to move. Some didn't. Joey jumped to his feet to see who was okay.

Girls beautiful party dresses were now covered in blood. The butchery was massive. Blood was everywhere and on everyone. Even the piñata had been hit and massacred with stray bullets. It had spilled out its candy guts into the bloody carnage.

He saw Tito struggling to stand up and ran to help him. Tito fell into his arms. He had been hit several times in the chest. Bright red bubbles of blood seeped out of the corners of his mouth as Joey cradled him in his arms. Tito looked at Joey with confusion. To this day, Joey still couldn't get the image of Tito's eyes out of his mind. He was desperately pleading for Joey to help him, but Joey couldn't do anything, except cry out for someone to call an ambulance.

Joey felt Tito's grip on his arm loosen. Then Tito's eyes stopped blinking. His head suddenly became heavy, and his tongue lolled out to the side. He had died in Joey's arms.

His life had just slipped away. There were no trumpets. No fanfare. No choir of angels to herald him to the next life. No one to shout to the world what a great guy Tito was and how much he would be missed.

Joey thought that there ought to be something more to living and dying than this.

But there was nothing.

One moment he was singing and dancing, being the life if the party, and the next one he was gone. Just gone. His best friend in the whole world was now a corpse. He had never felt so angry or helpless. It was at that moment, with his dead friend's lifeless head still cradled in his arms and the smell of released bile; choking at his swollen throat. Joey vowed not to rest until he had avenged his friend. He swore to make those black bastards pay for what they had done.

They would pay with their lives and they would know why they were going to die. He would make them beg like dogs for mercy. It would not be given. Not today. Not ever.

Joey and his homeboys had scoured the city for a week without any luck. He had gone over to Juarez to take his abuela shopping in the old Mercado that she loved so much in old Mexico. He had just dropped her off at home when he spotted the black 1987 Buick Grand National pull into the drive-thru of Church's Chicken.

He was all alone and didn't have time to go get any help. The only help he had was the shot gun that was under the seat and the pistol that he kept in the glove box. If he didn't do something now, he might never get another chance at these guys. He knew he shouldn't try to take them down alone. They probably had a lot of weapons and fire power in that car. They probably still had the weapons that killed Tito.

Joey's blood boiled with hatred.

He wanted these guys bad, but he didn't want it to be a suicide mission. He struggled to decide what to do. All he could think about was Tito. He had sworn, in Tito's dying moments, to avenge him, and that was exactly what he was going to do.

The black Buick pulled out of the drive-thru, but instead of driving off, it pulled around and parked. He could see through the windows that they were all grabbing at the box of chicken like a pack of wild hyenas. Joey pulled the Glock 9mm out of the glove box, checked the clip and stuck it in his waist band. He slipped the car into gear and eased into the parking lot behind a mini-van. He was just another person stopping by to pick up some chicken.

Nothing suspicious about that. The four blacks were in the car with their music turned up and chomping on their chicken when Joey pulled into the next space to the right of the black Buick. Joey eased out of his car just like any other chicken customer, except that when he turned around, all four blacks in the Buick were staring at a big black hole in the end of his Mosbacher riot shotgun.

Everyone in the car froze with their chicken still in their hands. They never had a chance to go for a single weapon. Joey got into the car and told the three passengers if they let their hands let go of their chicken he would shoot them in the balls.

He wondered what everyone must have thought when they saw a car driving down the road with three black guys in the back seat holding pieces of fried chicken up in the air.

Joey drove them close to the border. He forced them to get out of the car and to strip down out of their clothes. They refused, so Joey, without so much as a sound pulled the 9mm Glock out of his waist band and shot the closest one in the leg.

They couldn't get naked fast enough after that.

He piled up their clothes as they stood nude and sweating in the hot El Paso sun. He told the one that was the most scared to tear his silk shirt into strips and to tie the others up with their hands behind their backs. They continued to curse and threaten him until he forced them down onto their knees.

The realization that they were about to die came over them collectively.

Threats were replaced by pleas for mercy and for their mommies. They were scared. Shit had just gotten real for them really fast.

"Man you ain't gotta do this." Whimpered the biggest one. *"Can't we talk about this?"*

"Talk?" said Joey. *"You didn't want to talk when you shot up my niece's party last week, Puto!"* Joey was screaming into the big black guy's ear and holding his pistol up to the man's mouth.

"I don't know what you talking about, man. You got the wrong dudes, Esse." said the black guy. *"We don't know nothing about no party. Please don't kill us."*

Joey was seething on the inside. This guy must have thought he was some kind of chump.

"Well then, Negro, it is just your bad fuckin' luck to be in that piece of shit ride today, ain't it?" said Joey.

"Suck my dick, bitch!" The light skin black next to the big one spouted out. *"That's a GNX Turbo"*

"Oh, I am a bitch now, am I?" said Joey as he got right into the light skin's face. *"Well, how about if I make you into MY bitch?"*

Joey let his eyes drop down to the light skin's crotch. *"Oh, but you got too much junk down there to be my bitch."* Joey took light skin's penis into his left hand and pulled it straight out as far as he could.

Joey pulled the 9mm Glock out of his waist band and put the cold muzzle right at the base of light skin's penis shaft.

Then he whispered, *"Guess who's the Bitch now?"* and pulled the trigger.

The shot had been thunderous. Light skin's screams were earsplitting.. Now all of the blacks where begging for mercy as tears came running down their cheeks.

The blast had severed the man's penis. Joey still held it limply in his left hand. The partial black powder burn was clearly visible. Light skin had ceased his screaming and was sucking in huge gulps of air. Shock was beginning to set in, but his eyes were focused on his dangling penis that was no longer attached to his body. Joey held it up in front of light skin's face.

"You are nothing but a goddamn, cock-sucking, murdering bastard who doesn't deserve to live." Screamed Joey as he violently stuffed light skin's freshly severed penis into his gaping and gasping mouth.

Light skin began to choke on his own cock. Bloody bile spewed as he vomited all over Joey, which only enraged him more.

Joey was out of control. He couldn't help himself. These animals had shot up his niece's party and killed his best friend, Tito. He wanted them to suffer. He wanted them to hurt like he was hurting. He wanted payback. He wanted to kill them all.

Joey didn't have a bit of compassion for these animals. They had wounded eleven of his friends and killed six others, including Tito. They deserved to die horrible and painful deaths. Joey was going to make sure that was exactly what they were going to receive.

Joey stepped back and raised up the shot gun to the first big black man's face and pulled the trigger.

Time slowed again for Joey. The shot exited the shot-gun barrel at eleven hundred feet per second. The choke had been set wide open so that the shot would open up as much as possible as it left the hot smoking barrel.

One moment the big black man was begging for his life and in the blink of an instant, his face, that used to have two eyes, a nose and a mouth, had been totally obliterated into freshly ground hamburger.

That's what it looked like to Joey.

One second a face, the next second bloody stringy hamburger meat fresh out of the grinder.

Joey calmly and methodically went down the row and eliminated each of their existences and their faces with a simple pull of the trigger from his shotgun, but he saved light skin for last.

Light skin was still gagging and puking on the juices of his own penis that Joey had crammed so violently into his mouth. He was lying on his side trying to breathe in any amount of air that he could.

Joey rolled him onto his back with a harsh shove of his boot. Horror and absolute terror filled light skin's eyes as Joey stepped over and straddled his prone body. Joey lifted the shot gun in front of light skin's face.

Light skin closed his eyes.

Joey pulled the trigger.

Light skin's pain and suffering were over.

And so it was for Joey's.

Tito had been avenged and Joey had kept his promise.

*****

"You got a problem, Red." resolutely stated Judge Wes Wood.

"And what might that be?" chuckled Sheriff 'Red' as he took the piece of paper that Judge Wood shoved toward him.

Sheriff Red read it while Judge Wood stayed silent.

"What the Hell!" yelled Sheriff Red taken by complete surprise.

"Shit is about to hit the proverbial fan, Red," said the judge, *"unless you do something about it. Now this case was all your doing, but the blowback on it could hit all of us."*

"Why didn't you stop this from going out, Wes?" asked Sheriff Red.

"Because the request went through the county records department and not this court. It was sent out automatically, and I was simply notified as a courtesy. It's a good thing too or else we would be in deep do-do." said the judge as he cleaned his glasses.

"Well, what do you want me to do?" asked the Sheriff. *"I have been stopping and intercepting his mail coming and going ever since we put him there. How did this get here without going through my people?"*

"It was sent through the prison's internal mail system, which inmates can use for their legal work. Somehow he knew enough to go through the records department instead of this court. Most inmates aren't that smart, but this one is." said the judge.

"Well, shit fuck, Wes!" said the Sheriff. *"What the hell am I supposed to do now?"*

The judge put his glasses back on and looked at the Sheriff sternly. *"I want you to do whatever you have to do to make this problem disappear."*

There was silence between the two men. *"I think I have just the man to handle it."* said Red. *"He has been under some stress lately. I think he may need to take a less stressful job in Huntsville. I'll see to it that Dr. Braxton won't be requesting anymore records."*

"I knew that I could count on you, Red." said Judge Wood. *"It's always a pleasure seeing you."*

*****

Deputy Ernie Sinclair was surprised when the Sheriff himself stopped by to see him at home. The Sheriff told Deputy Sinclair that he wanted his help with a delicate situation. Now he was on his way out of town to a new job. Deputy Sinclair had jumped at the chance to get out of Lloyd County and away from the lesbian biker gang and the guy who videotaped him. He worried constantly that the tape would suddenly appear on the Internet and that he would be exposed. Now he was getting away from them, and he had a new job where he didn't have to worry about that kind of stuff.

Sheriff Red had told him that if he did a good job he would make Sergeant.

"Sergeant Ernie Sinclair."

Deputy Dawg kept saying it over and over in his head. It had a nice ring to it.

*****

Guy dropped Lola at work the next morning with a loving kiss. Lola turned and entered the converted house. Guy had spent several hours with her in the emergency room getting stitches above her eye. It pained him to know that she had been hurt because of him. He was going to find out who had rammed them on the highway, and he was going to make them pay. Lola's injury had put Guy's motivation into overdrive.

It had all started at the auction.

His intuition told him that it was the best place to begin. Guy nonchalantly passed by Dr. Shaddix's freshly washed Porsche.

He jumped into his truck and quickly jotted down the VIN of the beautiful automobile. Times like this made him grateful for his eidetic memory. He sped towards the campaign headquarters.

He floored the old truck. It didn't fail him. He was playing the previous day's events over and over in his head when he noticed the red and blue lights in his rear view mirror just as he turned into the parking lot of the Lilly headquarters.

"What the fuck?" he said to himself.

Guy slid the truck into park and slid out of the truck just as the deputy was exiting his vehicle.

Guy told himself to stay calm and not to get nervous. He knew he hadn't done anything wrong, but that hadn't stopped someone from trying to kill him and Lola the day before, so he was weary.

The deputy physically bolted the patrol car. Without warning, Guy felt the impact as the deputy dived at him and drove him hard to the ground. This was insane. This was wrong.

Guy knew that no righteous deputy would tackle him like this with no reason and with no warning. Guy landed on the ground with a heavy thud. He felt the wind rush out of his lungs as the uniformed deputy landed on top of him.

Guy felt the first blow as it drove his head into the ground with amazing force. 'This son-of-a-bitch could hit.' thought Guy. 'If I don't get away from this crazy man now, I may not survive.'

It was Deja-vu of the day before.

'Why is everybody after me lately?'

Guy shoved the deputy away and used every muscle and limb to kick at the mad uniformed assailant. Then Guy saw his opportunity. The deputy was fighting with blind emotion. Guy delivered a devastating blow to the deputy's temple with his elbow. He followed it with a kick to the groin that left the deputy writhing in agony.

"STOP IT!" came a scream.

Guy scrambled backwards like crab to get away from the contorted deputy who lay parking lot next to his truck.

Jewels stood above them. *"What the hell is going on here?"*

Chapter 34

All prisons have a pulse.

The ability to perceive minute changes becomes instinctive in prison. Inmates can feel when something isn't right.

The weird glance. An unusual gathering that you haven't seen before. Maybe a new guard. Just someone different lingering by himself in the wrong place.

Doc couldn't put his finger on it, but there was something.

The Law Library was full of inmates, mostly black Muslims since the chow hall was serving pork patties for dinner. It was always amusing how they would eat pork chops like starving cannibals, but when it came to pork patties, the prison version of Spam, they developed a convenient religious conscience, invariably causing several of them to end up in the Law Library.

This group had a strange vibe. Law books were laid out on the table in front of each one, but no one was looking at them or writing anything down.

Doc felt extremely uneasy. With his new body, he knew that he could defend himself against one or two with no problem but not against the whole bunch.

Fear was nibbling at the edges of his psyche. Something just wasn't right. Suddenly the door slammed opened. Doc jumped in his chair. Heads turned and Doc felt every eye in the place on him. He swallowed hard.

"Alright, time's up. Get ready to go, Legal Eagles." announced the guard, who was new, and Doc hadn't seen him before.

Doc watched warily as the Muslims all got up from their seats. There was no way that he could watch all of them. They mingled and crossed each other's paths. Some were shuckin' and jivin' in the corner. One was coming out of the toilet. Another was under the table looking for his I.D. card. They were are all over the place and Doc watched closely whenever anyone came near him. Doc had learned that survival in prison meant you never took your eyes off of people. You had to always be aware of your surroundings.

"I will be back in thirty seconds," said the new guard. *"Everyone be ready."* With that he closed the door, and Doc heard the loud action of the lock seal them in the Law Library.

Doc thought that it was strange; but he had learned that every boss was different, and it was best to just go with the flow. The flow was going pretty well for Doc lately. Everyone seemed to have a new found respect for him. No one had tried to mess with him, and he had made several new friends. He was actually starting to fit in. He had buddies on his wing and watched TV and played games with them in the day room. One friend had even given him a 'T-Vadio'. It was a prison radio that he had re-engineered to pick up the local television stations. Doc was now able to listen to television shows and the news in his cell. For over a year he had hardly known anything that had happened in the outside world. His ritual was to go to work from 2:30am til 6:30am. Farmer would be leaving just as he came in, so Doc was able to sit at the desk and work on his appeal every morning while listening to the news and the network mornings shows.

The past several months had been the best he had spent in prison thus far. He thought he was getting used to life behind bars. He was beginning to accept his situation.

That is until last week when he heard on the news about who the Governor was appointing to be the state's newest senator----Boyce Braxton.

His big brother was now a U.S. Senator.

Boyce was in the big leagues now. No wonder he hadn't ever answered any of Doc's letters. Everything he did would be scrutinized. He couldn't give the appearance of impropriety. He certainly couldn't be seen visiting or communicating with a prisoner, especially his own brother. Especially his brother the drug dealer. Now Doc knew how Whitey Bolger must have felt.

Doc accepted that he was entirely on his own.

Any hopes he ever had in the recesses of his mind that Boyce would come to the rescue were dashed and extinguished. Still he was proud of his brother.

Bang! Bang!

Doc's attention was diverted immediately to the glass separating the Law Library from the Main Hall.

Bang! Bang! Bang! Bang!

Now the Black Muslim at the window was fanatically banging at the window like a crazy man.

"What the fuck are you doing?" asked Doc from his desk. The black guy was banging maniacally now.

Doc noticed that all the black Muslims were becoming agitated. Something definitely had them scared.

'What the hell is wrong?' Doc thought.

Now he was starting to get spooked. Something was happening. Everyone in the place was jumpy. Doc's eyes felt irritated. He was blinking and squeezing his eyes. They were starting to burn.

A Muslim, hacking and coughing by the bookshelves, began to rush to the door. Moments later several of them joined their comrade and began pounding at the window. It became more panicky and more frantic with each passing second.

"Where's that mutha-fucka?" said one.

Another banged his fist on the prison glass as hard as he could. *"That fat fucker said he would be here. Where the hell is he? He gave us the signal."*

'Signal? What signal?' thought Doc. 'What are they talking about?'

"We have already put the shit in the cans, man." screamed another window banger. *"Let us the fuck out."*

The Muslims were apoplectic at the window; banging like crazy. They knew something that Doc didn't. Doc's lungs began to burn. Every breath he took was like breathing fire down his throat.

Poison Gas!

All Doc could hear were hacking coughs and people pleading for help. Panic was spreading wildly throughout the room

Instinctively, Doc dropped to the floor. 'What the hell is happening?'

His eyes, nose and throat were on fire. People were screaming in agony now. No one could stand long enough to bang on the windows anymore.

Several people crawled blindly and in agony to the open restroom. Doc noticed through his blurred and stinging vision that they had removed their shirts and had immersed them into the toilet and the sink. The first one wrapped it around his face like a mask.

Just then Doc smelled it. Chlorine gas.

"Noooo!" screamed Doc to the men in the restroom, but his warning was drowned out by the agonized screaming of the two men as they inhaled water into their lungs with the chlorine gas. Until this moment Doc had only read about the horrendously painful deaths brought on by poison gas attacks. Chlorine was soluble in water and when mixed, it instantly becomes hydrochloric acid, which immediately destroys the tender membranes of the lung in the most tormentable death imaginable.

That was why it had been banned as a chemical weapon since World War I; over a hundred years ago, but today Doc was seeing it used first hand. The two men with their wet shirts tied around their faces screamed in agony unlike anything Doc had ever witnessed. Their bodies writhed on the cold concrete floor. They convulsed until they death finally eased their agony.

Doc was consumed by panic. Everyone was dying around him. He was next if he couldn't come up with something quick.

Doc just wanted to run away as fast as his feet would take him, but the door was locked and no one was getting out. No one would make it out alive if they couldn't escape this room.

In his peripheral vision, Doc saw one guy forcing himself up to one of the book shelves from which he pulled out a can from behind one of the law books. Light smoke was erupting from the can. The man was gagging and coughing as he held the can at arm's length and raced it to the toilet.

Doc perceived what the man was going to do, but the man obviously didn't have the knowledge that Doc had. Even though the man had good intentions, his actions would only hasten death to all of them.

Doc ran for the door, but there was no escaping the gas explosion, especially in an enclosed room. Death was certain.

The man had dropped the can into the stainless steel toilet with a flourish. Prison toilets operated with minimal water until they were flushed. He pushed the silver button with gusto and the toilet was instantly filled with high pressure water that filled the bowl.

Violent smoke exploded, and the man was completely engulfed in a poisonous yellow cloud.

Doc ran as fast and as far as he could, which wasn't far at all.

It certainly wasn't far enough.

Guttural sounds of pure agony could be heard. The man's esophagus was swollen shut with fiery pain. The man's suffocation wasn't silent nor was it painless by any means. The man's face reappeared as the yellowish cloud dissipated. He no longer possessed the smooth cocoa colored skin. Instead, his handsome face was now disfigured with pustules and blisters. Enormous bubbles grew erratically on his face. Blood oozed from his eyes and his tongue swelled to the size of a grapefruit. Screaming for Allah's mercy were the man's last intelligible words. Death came as a blessing in a matter of moments.

Doc tripped over a casualty; landing on the floor with a painful plop. The dead man's blank eyes stared right into his soul. Doc saw red blisters on the man's skin that had erupted from contact with the poisonous gas. They remind him of a massive outbreak of pimples or boles.

He remembered the acne problem in his youth, that he had tried everything to get rid of, but this was beyond compare.

That was it!

It hit Doc's brain like a ton of bricks.

Activated charcoal.

It was used in all sorts of everyday products from acne creams to vitamins, and it was also used to counteract the effects of poison gas.

Doc looked around. His eyes were stinging. Opening them felt like hundreds of needles were being jabbed into them simultaneously. The pain was too much to endure for more than a millisecond at a time.

Somebody had to have what he was looking for.

Doc blinked his eyes rapidly; it looked as if he was watching an old Nickelodeon. Everything had a strobe effect as he viewed the room one disjointed frame at a time. He would open his eyes and he was forced to close them almost immediately. While they were closed he tried to process in his brain what he had seen.

He desperately searched the room. He assessed it one fragmented frame at time. Dead body after dead body was all he seem to see. Everyone was dead or praying to be. Doc was using his feet to spin himself around like a pinwheel until to see what he was looking for.

Doc pushed himself as low as he could and desperately made his way to a dead man lying beside the bookshelves.

With his eyes closed and breathing as little as he could, he yanked off the dead man's 'Jackie Chan' shoes; removing them from the ashy, knurled and crusted black feet.

Doc began tearing out the cloth insole.

'Please let it be there!' whimpered Doc in his head. 'It has to be there.'

There it was.

The prison version of an Odor-Eater. It was thinner than a free-world Odor-Eater and it had been glued into the shoe; but Doc pulled the shoe pad out with a violent and desperate yank to free it from its blue canvas cocoon.

Odor eliminators contained super-activated charcoal as a main ingredient to absorb sweaty feet odor.

Doc ripped and tore at the insert. No matter how hard he tugged and pulled he couldn't get it apart with his hands. Time was of the essence. Time was running out. The clock was ticking with a deadly vengeance.

Time was up.

Doc closed his eyes and stuffed as much of the rubberized shoe insole into his mouth as he could and began to chew on it. The gas was stinging his nostrils, but all that his tongue could taste was the foul stench of the dead man's feet with each and every chomp of the old rubber insert. Doc gagged involuntarily as the taste of rancid toe jam and foot sweat inundated every taste bud his mouth. It was too much to endure. Doc laid his head down on the floor and continued to chew.

His head felt as if his brain was trying to push its way out of his skull. He wanted to just give up. He could feel the bile coming up his esophagus. He swallowed hard to keep it down. He knew that his life depended on ingesting as much of the activated charcoal as possible.

Doc inched his way slowly over to the door to try and put his mouth up to the crack under the door. Any amount of fresh air would help alleviate the fire in his lungs. Someone else had same idea. Doc crawled his way up beside him. At first Doc thought the man was dead because he seemed so lifeless.

The big Muslim opened his eyes, but there was no whites left in them. Blood oozed from the corners down over his blistered cheeks to drip into the yellow creamy puss that had pooled onto the floor. Death was ugly in all of its forms, but Doc hadn't realized just how awful it could be until he came face to face with it.

The big Muslim raised his head slightly and whispered, *"You're s'pose to be dead."*

Doc tried to ask what the big Muslim meant, but his mouth was so full of odor absorbing rubber that it just came out as unintelligible garble. Doc began chewing on the rancid shoe insert as fast as he could as the big Muslim's head dropped onto the ground. His swollen tongue fell out of his mouth and into the bloody and yellow puss puddle on the floor.

Doc wondered if that would be how he would be found.

Chapter 35

"My nuts feel like bruised oranges." said Deputy Salinas. *"Where is that*

little prick? I'm going kill him."

"I sent him away, and your nuts feel fine to me." Said Jewels as she reached down between his legs to cup them in her hand. She began to slightly rub and massage them. *"I know what would make them feel a lot better."*

Deputy Salinas shoved her hand away. *"What the hell?"*

He looked around the empty parking lot. *"What if someone sees you doing that?"*

"Relax and don't worry. I sent everyone back into the building to work." she said.

She liked making men feel uncomfortable. It gave her a rush to know that she had that kind of power over them. It was a control issue. Admittedly, it was a small one right now, but it was still fun.

"Relax, hell." shouted Santos *"that son-a-bitch hurt my sister."*

"Well, I don't think that is true, I think he is in love with your sister." said Jewels. *"Listen, why don't you calm down and come by my place tonight and talk about it?"*

"Really?" said Santos as he eyed her deep cleavage. *"You want me to come to your house?"*

"Yes, I do" replied Jewels.

The invitation seemed to calm him down. He was like a puppy. It was just too easy for her to manipulate him. Men were so easy to control. Well, most men.

She knew of one man that wasn't as malleable to her charms as others were.

*****

Guy dusted off his pride. He wanted to punch Lola's brother for sucker punching him with a blindsided ambush, but Guy knew that while Santos

223

was in uniform there was no way he could win. Besides, he had more important things to work on. There was something sinister going on at that auction. Someone was threatened enough to try and kill him and Lola.

He hacked into the DMV data base and quickly input the Porsche's Vehicle Identification Number before he could forget it. With his eidetic memory, he knew that wouldn't ever happen; but he was always afraid that one day his memory would just disappear, and he would never remember anything ever again. Logically he knew that it was irrational and silly, but he couldn't help himself. Weird people have weird fears.

He leaned back and rubbed the bruise on his head. There was lump. It throbbed and it hurt. It didn't hurt nearby as much as the fear the he had seen in Lola's eyes when they were being chased. He was thankful that the motorcycle riders came along when they did. He couldn't get them out of his mind.

'Who are they?' he thought.

To him, they were guardian angels. The first time he had seen them, they had humiliated old Deputy Dawg pretty well and allowed him the good luck to video a confession from him. Now they appeared out of nowhere and saved his and Lola's life. He had left them on that road, and he had no idea what had happened after he left.

He wondered if they caught the camo SUV; and if they did, what did they do to the driver?

Guy didn't know who the cycle girls were or how to get in touch with them. It was all so frustrating.

The computer began to print. Guy's wool gathering was interrupted. His attention was focused now on the page in the tray. He picked it up.

There it was. One name.

Bentley Braxton.

*****

"Have you got a minute?" Guy asked as he stuck his head into the office door.

Jewels looked up with her usual look of disdain. *"Yeah, what's on your mind?"*

"I need you to sign off on some travel money from petty cash." Guy said.

"Travel money?" asked Jewels. *"I meant for you to take that girl out to dinner and to a movie, not to take her on a trip."*

"What?" said Guy, but then it hit him. Jewels must have thought he wanted the money to take Lola out. *"No, no, no, boss. I think I have found our smoking gun."*

This got Jewels attention. She was out of her seat in a flash and running around her desk to grab him by his arm. *"Don't just stand there, boy. Show me what you got."*

Guy found himself being dragged to a chair. *"Well, I found out about a dentist from Dallas that the Sheriff's department arrested and convicted."*

Guy spent the next two hours telling Jewels about the auction and how he and Lola had nearly been run off the road. He showed her everything he had on Dr. Shaddix and his shady dealings. He told her everything he knew from Deputy Dawg but kept to himself the fact that he kidnapped and videoed taped the deputy. Guy didn't see any reason for incriminating himself, unnecessarily.

Jewels listened intently, taking in every juicy detail. Guy felt like a real detective telling her about it. He carefully walked her through it step by step and when Guy finished, she sat there stone faced and silent. He could see imaginary wheels turning in her head; but for the life of him, he could not read her face. She was like one of those stone monoliths on Easter Island that he had seen in National Geographic magazine.

The silent suspense was about to make him burst at the seams until she finally looked at him. *"Who else knows about this?"*

"No one." Guy responded.

"Are you sure?" Jewels asked him again. This time she was extremely emphatic with him as she reached out and grabbed his arm very firmly.

Guy winced as her sharply manicured nails dug into his flesh.

"Yes. I am sure." he said.

"And you are positive about the name of the dentist from Dallas?" She asked insistently.

"Absolutely positive." Guy said. *"And you are hurting my arm."*

Jewels hadn't even noticed that she still had the boy by the arm. She turned him loose and walked around the desk.

"I want you to go to Huntsville right away." instructed Jewels. *"You are not to tell anyone, and I mean ANYONE, about what you just told me. Do you understand?"*

"Not really, but I will keep my mouth shut." Promised Guy. He knew that exposing the corruption of the Sheriff's department was a big deal for Jewels and the campaign, but Jewels seemed a little too excited.

Jewels reached into the bottom right drawer and pulled out a small lock box. Guy was surprised to see that it was loaded with cash. She handed him several thousand dollars.

"I want you to pay cash for everything and use another name whenever you can. I don't want anyone to know that you were ever there." She said. *"This is big. If you are right, your life could be in danger. They've already tried to kill you once, so be careful. There is no telling how far up the line this goes."*

Guy left the office feeling like James Bond. This was some spooky shit.

He loved it.

*****

Jewels reflected on the gift that Guy had just dropped into her lap. It was all she could do to keep from screaming with joy at the top of her voice. The Gods must really be on her side.

If Guy's info turned out to be true, this was exactly what she needed to end up on top and eventually in the White House. Timing was going to be critical. She needed to make sure everything was kept close to the vest. If any of this new information got out, she could kiss off ever being Chief of Staff.

"Jackson," Jewel's screamed.

"Yes, your highness," lisped Jackson as he swished into Jewels' office.

"Clear your calendar for the week. We have a lot of work to do and a big trap to set." said Jewels as she pulled out a yellow legal pad and started writing on it. *"I want you to pick up a few things for me."*

Jackson looked at the list of things that Jewels had given him. *"Well, from the looks of this list, I think you are setting up a big ol' man trap."*

*****

"Why can't you tell me where you are going?" asked Lola.

"It's business." said Guy.

"It sounds more like monkey business to me." Said Lola with a pout.

"Oh, baby, don't act like that." he said.

"Well, how do you expect me to act? You and Santos are both acting strange." she said.

"Really? What is that asshole brother of yours up to?" asked Guy. *"You know he tried to beat me up this morning, don't you?"*

"Well, I wish he had because now I feel like doing it myself." Lola said with her cute and petulant look. Guy knew she wasn't serious. He loved the little girl face that she made when she wanted him to fawn over her. *"Why can't I go? We could have a little time alone together."*

Guy could see that she was sincere. *"Baby, it's not that kind of trip."* He said as he jumped on the bed beside her to kiss her gently. *"This is all business and I can't have any distractions."*

He kissed her tenderly again on the lips. *"And you are definitely a distraction."*

*****

Jackson had worked all afternoon and Jewels was amazed as what she saw before her. She had to give her gay assistant his 'props', because Jackson had really come through for her this time. He had turned her dull rental house into a total pussy palace. Aromatic candles filled the air with the scent of sweet strawberries and seductive vanilla. Tiny flames shimmered in every room. Walls were illuminated and danced with golden light. Red sheer scarves were draped over every lamp in the place. New colored bulbs enchanted each room. Every surface had been covered in soft textiles; furs, chenille's, satins and silks. Sexuality oozed from every piece of furniture.

But Jackson didn't stop there. He had worked his limp-wristed magic on more than just Jewels' house. Jewels was now a diva dominatrix. She was delighted as she gazed into the mirror. She couldn't take her eyes off of the red patent leather bustier that she had to squeeze her bosoms into. Her ample breasts had been forced and literally man-handled into the rigid corset-like contraption. They looked enormous as they were pinched and pushed chin-ward. The pink areola of Jewels' right breast peeked its way out of the blood-red patent leather that shackled her voluptuousness, and it stared back at her in the ornate gilt mirror. Black laces crisscrossed back and forth up the center that cinched her breasts together. The shiny red beast that was strapped around her had transformed her from a naughty little cougar into a true sexual wench of erotic danger.

Jewels always liked playing the bad girl more than anything, but she especially loved all of the sexy clothes. Jackson had really outdone himself this time. This was the best outfit yet. She didn't know where he found these pleasure pieces, but she loved the way they transmogrified her physically and emotionally.

As Jewels admired herself in the mirror, she actually felt herself beginning to get titillated at her own image. She was hot and she knew it. She turned right and then left; admiring the way the corset flared out over her hips to enhance her curvaceous waist. Black frilly lace panties cascaded over her slender thighs from underneath the leather chastity belt that was draped with decorative chains and a small padlock that dangled back and forth erotically like a shiny stainless steel clitoris.

Black thigh-high patent leather boots completed the kinky ensemble with cut-outs and silver medallions running up the entire outside edges. The six inch heels were forged entirely of silver and spiked to the tiniest sharp point she had ever walked on. However, the true masterpieces of this exotic art were the hand-sculpted erotic silver tongues that covered the toes of the boots and protruded out several more inches in a suggestively seductive lick. As she strutted, one would lick the ground as the other licked the air, alternating with each seductive step.

Jewels began to sway her hips. Grinding and posing to the music. It was rhythmic with its hardcore thumping base beat. Very sexual, but it also had an ethereal essence that would come in and seduce the listener with a sensual softness. The mood of the music had mysteriously made her loins begin to come alive.

She began to grind harder to the beat as she closed her eyes and imagined the effect that she would have on her dark and exotic deputy. He had just been a lark in a moment of weakness at first. She had seduced him in her office the first time. She liked it when he ravaged her on the desktop, while he had kept his uniform on. Even the squawking of his radio had heightened the illusion. At one point, she pulled out his night stick and put it behind his neck to pull his mouth onto hers as he drove her orgasm home with every powerful thrust of his strong and muscled hips. The deeper he went, the deeper she kissed him. She thought she was going to bite off his lip by the third orgasm. She had been left sore but unbelievable satisfied.

They had met several times at the local no-tell motel for fun filled fantasy romps. The scenarios were always similar with him being the cop that came to her rescue and with her showing her gratitude by servicing him for his gallantry. The last time they had met was on an old country road where her car had broken down and he had showed up to rescue her. They had done it on the hood of his patrol car. The flashing of the red and blue patrol lights had naturally quickened her pulse rate to heighten the sexual encounter. But the piece d' resistance was when he pulled out and grabbed her ankles to lift her legs high into the air. It was a cool night. The warm hood felt good on her back and her soft white buttocks. Santos was gentle but powerful as he separated the warmness between her legs with his tongue. She had never experienced anyone with his kind of lingual strength. So much intensity in it. Jewels' began to writhe on the warm vibrating hood of the patrol car. She felt the whimpers escape her tiny red lips as wave after wave of convulsions overcame her. Finally, the big one came and she couldn't keep the screams of ecstasy inside anymore. Jewels' back arched up off the hood and her pelvic region began to convulse vigorously; but Santos never stopped. Her screams seemed only to spur him on and on and on. She could feel her wetness dripping down his face. He was like a madman as he shook his head from side to side between her thighs. She couldn't stand it anymore. It was too much pleasure. If she climaxed one more time she thought she would go insane.

"P..p..please, Ss.s.s.s...stop!" were the only words that Jewels had finally been able to get out in between gasps of air and squeals of ecstasy.

Santos stopped and raised his head up from between her slender thighs with a smile. Yeah, he was pleased with himself. And Jewels had been pleased also. Only she was in such a state of exhaustion that the only thing she could do was collapse onto the hood like a dishrag doll.

Totally spent and helpless.

Santos appeared with a blanket to cover up her naked body and to warm her from the chill of the night air. Her hair was a tangled mess, drenched in sweat, but it had been the best sex of her life. No one had ever made her orgasm that intensely or that many times.

"Oh my god," said Santos *"did I hurt you? Is that a tear in your eye?"*

Jewel closed her eyes. 'No, silly boy, you didn't hurt me.' she thought to herself. 'You have just given me the best tonguing that I have ever had'.

But he could never know that, she told herself, because he could never know how much power he had over her now. She had to maintain the control in this relationship.

The doorbell snapped Jewels out of her reverie.

'Yes', she thought, 'tonight the power is going to shift back.'

Chapter 36

The door flew open and fresh air rushed in. Doc could feel the coolness envelope him. His body involuntarily gulped at the abundant oxygen. It was as if the ghost of life had rushed in to resurrect his dying spirit.

Too late. Tears rolled down his face.

Mucous oozed from his nostrils as his head laid down, and his whole world went black.

*****

"It's done." said the new guard into the phone. *"You won't be having any more problems from this end, sir. I guarantee it."*

"No sir," replied the guard *"I left them all in there. There are no witnesses left. It will look like a prison gang retaliation gone bad."*

Bentley Braxton had been easy to set up. The Muslims had it in for him already. All they needed was the opportunity to hit him. They had come up with the scheme to gas him all on their own. Some had entered the Law Library with soda cans half filled with liquid ammonia procured from the janitors, while the others had smuggled in dry bleach from the laundry. During the session, the inmates with the cans of ammonia had discretely place them behind law books and in various concealed places around the library. Upon his signal, "Legal Eagles", the Muslims were to drop the bleach into the cans while acting as if they were re-shelving their books.

The plan had been for him to be back within 30 seconds to let everyone out, except for Braxton. He would be told to stay behind for a moment to clean up.

But the new guard had left them all in there. He couldn't leave any witnesses who might shoot off their big mouths about what they had done. Black prisoners couldn't ever keep their mouths shut. Invariably, they always bragged about getting even with someone so they could front for their buddies.

'Too much pride and not enough brains between them,' thought the new guard.

No, it had never entered his mind to let them out. It had been the perfect plan. Guards got away with murder all the time in prison. With so many at once, he knew they would have to go through the motions of an investigation. He would stay here for about a month and then quietly quit. No one would ever be suspicious.

The new guard hung up the phone. He had finally paid his dues and was going to be in the inner circle. In a month, he would be Sgt. Ernie Sinclair and set for life.

This called for a celebration.

*****

Guy pulled into the old roadside motel. The Palace Motel had been one of the thousands of motor courts that had been built on the two lane highways of America after WWII. Little motels wrapped around center court yards and parking lots. The old pool had been filled in with dirt many years earlier. Rusted monkey bars and swings now sat idle. Tribute to half-hearted attempts to draw in long gone family vacationers. Hookers and drug addicts now rented the dilapidated rooms by the week, and steel cages had been erected around the vending machines.

Guy stepped up to the check-in window and noticed that it too had been reinforced with steel mesh. A small hole, big enough only to pass money or a room key through, had been left open at the bottom. Guy had a sneaking suspicion that room service wasn't offered at this motel.

Guy peered through the wire mesh and into darkness.

"Can I help you?" came a voice from behind the window.

Guy had been startled by the unseen voice, but quickly recovered. *"Uh, yeah"* said Guy *"I need a room."*

"Are you sure you got the right place?" asked the bored voice. *"I think you might be looking for someplace else."*

Guy reached into his pocket and pulled out his money. *"I got cash."*

"Well, that's good because that is all we take, Slick." said the voice with a little more enthusiasm. *"What are you looking for?"*

"I need a room." said Guy.

"A room?" said the clerk *"Hell, we got a lot of those. What do you want for? Girls? Boys? Drugs? We got it all around here."*

"I just need a place to sleep." said Guy.

"Well, that would be a first." Said the invisible clerk. *"Are you sure you want to stay here? There is a nice Holiday Inn down the street."*

"No" said Guy *"this will be just fine. It seems perfect."*

*****

Guy pulled his truck into the parking spot in front of Room 9. It was situated towards the back corner of the Palace Motel, next to the non-working ice machine. Several people were standing around, and there seemed to be quite a bit of activity as people quickly came and went from certain rooms. Guy deduced that they were probably buying and selling drugs.

As he pulled his small suitcase from the back of the truck, he noticed an unusually tall black female that was casually, but purposefully, leaning against an old decorative wrought iron column under the breezeway.

"What are looking for tonight, sugah?" said the black woman with an unusually deep voice. *"The Diva of Desire can supply whatever you be wanting."*

Guy put his head down and started for the door.

"I don't think you have what I am looking for?" said Guy as he fumbled with the door key.

"Oh, honey," said the deep voiced black woman *"I am Dion, the Diva of Desire and I have what all of you white boys are looking for."* She laughed at her own humor with a big booming laugh that carried effortlessly across the motor court.

Guy quickly jammed the key into the door and slammed it shut. He leaned his back against the door. A hard knock from the other side scared him so much that he jumped a foot into the air.

He fumbled to put the latch on the door and opened it slowly. To his surprise it was the hooker. He was speechless. What could she possibly want? He was happily committed to Lola and now he was about to be raped by a six foot five inch black drag queen. He stared out of the cracked door unable to speak.

Dion, the Diva of Desire, stared back with huge eyes surrounded by yellow and orange eye makeup. Guy was mesmerized by the length of her lashes. They sparkled. In fact, Dion's entire body sparkled with glitter. The flickering yellow 'P' of the motel's neon sign caused the Diva of Desire to twinkle like a disco ball in his doorway. It was as if Guy was hypnotized by this glimmering black showgirl.

"I think you forgot something." said the enormous drag queen as she held up his suitcase. Her giant hand possessed the longest nails that Guy had ever seen in his life.

"Oh my God!" screamed Guy as he fumbled with the latch and threw open the flimsy door. He lunged for the little suitcase. He had hidden most of the money Jewels had given him inside a sock.

'How could I have been so careless?' he thought.

"Easy there, Cowboy," said Dion, *"boosting is not my thing. But you are lucky it was me that found it. 'Cuz any of these strung out Ho's around here would have sold it for a dime rock before your head even hit the sheets."*

"Thank you so much." said Guy clutching the bag.

There was an awkward silence.

Guy was out of his element. He didn't know what to do. Should he give her a reward or something? But before he could make up his mind,

"You know the polite thing to do would be to invite me in and to give me a drink for being so nice." Said Dion, the Diva of Desire.

"Oh, uhm, uh...sure" said Guy *"Where are my manners? Please come in."*

The giant drag queen sashayed around him with amazing grace. Guy wondered how she walked in such high heels. Then he wondered,

'Where the hell do you buy shoes that big'?

Her feet were enormous.

He nervously shut the door looking to see if any one saw the transvestite hooker enter his room.

This was going to be a very strange trip.

Chapter 37

Strange was the only word that could describe how Deputy Santos Salinas felt as he was being handcuffed.

It was usually the other way around.

Santos tensed up as cold steel clamped around his wrist. Each click of the cuff's jaws ratcheted down tighter and tighter around his sturdy brown wrist until he felt the tickle of the pink fluffy feathers. He wondered where in the hell Jewels had found them. They looked silly and harmless, but they definitely were real handcuffs and all of sudden he felt a little bit of panic deep down in his gut. He loved the sexual games and fantasies he and Jewels played, but this time it was different.

This time it was real.

As the last handcuff clicked into its final position, he realized he was now at her complete mercy. What the hell had he gotten himself into? His brain was in overload now. He couldn't do this. This was just too crazy. That was what his brain was telling him, but he had other body parts that were screaming things to him also.

'Holy Shit!' Santos thought as he struggled within himself. He had never done anything like this. He had never let himself be put in a position where he couldn't get himself out. No matter how much he liked Jewels, he just couldn't let himself be constrained like this.

"Jewels, I have change my mind." Santos said as he jerked at the handcuff on his right wrist and at then one on his left. *"Just let me out of...."*

Santos' words were abruptly cut off by a sudden zinging of a riding crop slicing through the air. The hide leather whipped across his smooth, brown bottom.

"Oooww! What the FUCK!" Santos screamed, but before he could complete his expletive, a firm hand reached around the left side of his neck. Jewels' hand had five perfectly polished red finger nails that gripped like iron as they clutched his chiseled masculine jaw. His head jerked to the left. Jewel's face was now next to his right ear. He felt her

warm breath on his neck and the wetness of her tongue in his ear.

Santos' loins surged and swelled as an instant inferno of desire shot through his brain and straight to his manhood. She had zeroed in on his second biggest weakness. She was good. Extremely good. And that just made him want to be bad.

Really bad.

As she removed her sweet tongue from his ear, he heard her say,

"You will address me as Mistress Rojo. If you call me anything else, then I will punish you like you have never been punished before." she said, as she ran her riding crop slowly down his body from the cleft of his lower lip to the treasure trail of peach fuzz that led from his navel to the shaft of his growing member.

Santos was both titillated and scared shitless. She was serious, and he couldn't do a damn thing about it.

"You are not to say a word unless I tell you to speak or ask you a question. Do you understand?" Asked Mistress Rojo.

"Yes, Mistress Rojo." said Santos.

What the hell else could he say? After all he was naked and handcuffed to the most enormous barbell he had ever seen. There had to be a thousand pounds on it. However, it had been covered in ruby rhinestones and painted the color of Pepto-Bismol. Santos now noticed that in addition to being bedazzled, both ends had been capped with two enormous flashing dildos.

Theoretically, he could leave any time he wanted. All he had to do was simply lift the bar bell up and walk out the door.

'Yeah right,' thought Santos.

Who the hell could lift one thousand pounds and just walk out the door? And what the hell would he do if he could? It's not like he could get behind the wheel of a car with the damn thing. If he did make it out the door, he would be butt naked locked to a thousand pounds of tacky pornographic gym equipment. Even now he could feel the dildos vibrating the bar. But if that wasn't weird enough, they were humming.

Surely anyone who stopped to help him would call the police. How would he even begin to explain why he was shackled naked to a thousand pounds pink porno pig iron with ruby sparkles and humming dildos?

He listened more closely.

'Oh my God. They aren't humming.' Screamed Santos' brain. 'They're moaning.'

This was insane. This was crazy. This was fucking awesome!

Mistress Rojo swatted his bare buttocks with such force that it widened his eyes.

"*Are you ready, my little Sancho?*" cooed Mistress Rojo as she tickled his sack with the tip of her riding crop.

Playing with his ball sac was his biggest weakness. His 'Numero Uno!' His most powerful erogenous zone. She was a vexing witch, and she knew exactly how to make his libido dance like a Russian Cossack. His engorged member was already a trickle with premature excitement.

No, Santos didn't want to go anywhere now.

"*Yes, Mistress Rojo,*" growled Santos "*I am ready.*"

He had fantasized about what it would be like to be with a dominatrix since he was a teenager. He had some fears, but those fears and uncertainties were exactly what heightened the sexual experience. Yes, he was definitely ready to submit to whatever Mistress Rojo wanted him to do.

Santos knew now that this was going to be the best night of his life.

*****

Guy hadn't ever been to a prison before.

It seemed like he drove forever in the middle of nowhere. It was all just two lane black top country roads that meandered and wound through the Texas back woods. If it hadn't been for the constant prompts from his GPS app on his phone, he never would have found the place.

The thick forest of piney woods suddenly disappeared. A giant patch of scalped land appeared before him. It had been laid bare, and the only thing remaining were the rows and rows of fences topped with shiny concertina wire, more than he had ever seen in his life. It sparkled and glistened in the early morning Texas sun. Concentric rows were broken only by the occasional towers that encircled the entire prison.

Guy could see the silhouettes of the tower guards standing post near the rails with their rifles in hand. Guy couldn't help but think that everything looked just like it did in the movies. Except, there was no mistaking this was real life. He pulled up and was stopped at the outer check point.

The guard approached Guy's truck.

Guy couldn't help notice that kid couldn't be any older than himself.

"I need the name and number of the prisoner that you are you here to see?" said the guard.

"Bentley Braxton" said Guy. *"690479"*

The guard took down the information and disappeared into the guard shack. He returned a moment later with a very different and a more noticeably hostile demeanor.

Guy's truck was searched inside and out before he was allowed to proceed to the visitors' parking lot where he was put through another vigorous interview about who he was there to see and searched yet again. He finally made it to the entrance of the prison building where he was strip searched and x-rayed once more. Guy noticed that no one else was being strip searched. He wondered why he was being singled out.

The Monkey Trap

Guy used the time that he waited to redress himself. After so many interrogations and searches, Guy felt like he was the prisoner. Guy wasn't allowed to bring anything in with him except for his ID and some coin change, which he could use to buy candy and soda pops from the vending machines. Guy was nervous because he had taken the ID of his roommate. At a quick glance, he could pass for him. It had worked at the bars last year when he was too young to get in, so he hoped that it would work again now. Jewels had made it clear that she didn't want anyone to know he was down here; so he had used it to check into the motel room also.

The bored female officer gave it the same cursory glance that the bouncers had at the bars. She simply wrote his name on the clip board and handed it back.

"Thank you, Mr. Parris. You can go through now." Said the guard.

He had only seen Dr. Braxton's mug shot, which was almost two years old. He assumed the doctor would look a little different after being in prison for a year and a half, but he wasn't prepared for what he saw when Dr. Braxton entered.

Bentley Braxton was a beaten man. He was obviously a very sick man. Guy wondered what had happened to change him so drastically in only eighteen months and why he was now in a wheel chair.

Guy stared at the slumped figure as another inmate pushed him up to the glass. Bentley Braxton's eyes were blood shot and full of hardened mucus in the corners. His face was blotched and red.

"Dr. Braxton?" said Guy.

Doc looked up to the stranger. He hadn't been called Dr. Braxton in years. It felt strange to his ears.

"Who are you?" asked Doc.

"My name is Guytana Canova." said Guy. *"I am here to help you."*

*****

240

Blake Rivers came down to visit his little brother every other month. Blake faithfully put money on his account and wrote him twice a week. Even though they were only half-brothers, they had been close growing up. When Blake's mom divorced his dad, she changed his name from the Spanish surname of Rios to the Anglo version of Rivers. Despite the split up and the name change, the boys remained close. Guillermo had always been the wild and adventuresome one. Blake was the consummate do-gooder. So it came as no surprise when the police caught Guillermo one Friday night joy riding while naked and high with some other guys in a stolen car.

Guillermo had a little girl, and Blake always took pictures and brought them down to show him at their visits. Despite some of the physical changes that prison had done to Guillermo, it never changed how he and Blake felt or acted with each other. They were still solid, and they told each other everything.

Guillermo, now AKA Casino, told Blake about his new man, Joey, and Blake told Guillermo all about his man, Jackson.

The room was filled with people visiting their loved ones because no matter who they were or what they had done, they were still someone's dad, brother, son or husband.

Guillermo loved to go around the room and point people out and tell Blake about them. Everyone was on their best behavior around their families, but Guillermo would tell Blake what they were like and what they really did when their families left. It was how they filled the time after they finished looking at photos and ran out of things to talk about. The visits were two hours long and no one ever left early because that was all the time that inmates had to feel normal. Afterwards, when it was over, inmates had to go back to their cells and back to their prison life. That was when they felt their lowest. No one wanted the visits to end.

Blake pointed over to a sad looking guy in a wheel chair. *"Man, that guy looks like hell. Did someone beat him up?"*

"Dude," exclaimed Guillermo *"that is the Doc. He is legend in here.*

241

Man, put down a black midget mooley and a big ass white peckerwood. He cut some guy's hand completely off with a paper cutter; and when some other nig tried to get him in the shower, he almost bit off the guy's dick when he tried to use the Doc's mouth as a pussy.   And a few days ago, a whole gang of Muslims tried to kill him in a poison gas attack. All seventeen of them died.   He was the only one to survive.   They said he saved himself by eating some dead guy's shoes, but I don't know if I believe all that crap. People in prison make up all kinds of shit."

"*You're fucking with me, bro!*" said Blake as he looked at the guy again in disbelief. "*That is just crazy.*"

"*That's not all.*" said Guillermo as he leaned in closer to his brother. "*Word on the block is that a guard was in on it; but since everybody is dead, nobody can prove shit.*"

"*A guard?   Which one?*" said Blake incredulously as he swiveled his head around looking at every guard in the room.

"*I don't know his name.   Some new guy.*" Said Guillermo looking around the room. "*I saw him a minute ago.*"

"*There he is.   That's the one.*" said Guillermo pointing to a large portly guard sitting at the check in desk.

"*OMG!   Are you serious?*" Asked Blake. "*I know that guy.*"

"*What?   Dude, you don't know no guard.*" said Guillermo.

Blake turned and gave his brother a condescending look.   "*Bitch, he wasn't a guard when I knew him.   His name is Sinclair. He was some flunky deputy. I saw him around the courthouse all of the time, but then he got kidnapped by a gang of Hell's Angels or something. Word around the courthouse is that he went a little crazy; and they put him on psych leave because they couldn't trust him with a gun. It sure seems strange that he is down here now.*"

*****

"*Help me? How are you going to help me?*" asked Doc. "*You are just a*

242

kid."

"I may be young, Dr. Braxton, but I have information that might get you out." whispered Guy. *"But if you aren't interested I can just call the guard to let me out."*

Guy began to scoot his chair back.

"No! I'm sorry." said Doc. *"I didn't mean to be rude, but I have had a very hard time lately."*

"Let me guess." Said Guy. *"From the information that I know, I would venture to say that someone tried to kill you. And from the state that you are in, I would guess that they nearly succeeded."*

Doc couldn't believe what he was hearing. *"What is it that you know?"*

"I know quite a lot, but I need your help to prove it." Said Guy.

"Whatever it is, if it will get me out of here, then I will do it." Doc was on the verge of tears.

Guy felt sorry for the man, but he needed Dr. Braxton to be indebted to him and to rely completely on him, so that he could prove all of the things he had found out.

He needed Doc to be motivated. He knew that dangling the faint hope of getting out of this place would do that. Guy didn't even know if that was a possibility, but he did know that the doctor was the key and that if they tried to kill him once, they might keep trying until they succeeded. Dr. Braxton was no good to him dead.

Time was of the essence. He needed Dr. Braxton's cooperation, and he needed it immediately.

Guy spent an hour telling Doc about the corrupt cops and the confiscation racket. He told how he suspected that they rigged the auction so that they could get the things they confiscated in trumped up drug busts.

He told about how some dentist was now driving his Porsche, how he had traced it back to him and then found the court records that led him to Huntsville; and Doc listened with total fascination until Guy was completely finished.

Doc sat there for several long arduous minutes and digested everything that the young man had told him. He couldn't believe that this young guy sitting in front of him was here to help him. He was thoroughly impressed with the young man and with how he had managed to put all of this together by himself. He was a smart kid, but Doc still had a few things nagging at him.

"I have two questions, kid. First, what's in this for you?" Doc asked. *"Hell, you could probably make a tidy sum of cash from the Sheriff just to keep quiet and go away. What do you get out of helping me? Nobody does anything for free."* said Doc. He had learned that in prison. The hard way.

Guy took a minute to think about it.

"I get the girl." said Guy.

Guy told him all about Lola and how they planned to leave Prickly Springs and Lloyd County. He told Doc about all of the hopes and dreams and things that he and Lola would talk about. He told about his ambitions to do big things. He didn't know what, but that wasn't important to him as long as Lola was by his side.

Doc liked the young man. He was a romantic, and he had met the girl of his dreams. Nothing else in the world mattered when you were young and in love. Doc remembered how he and Sandy use to do the same thing. He began to get a little sad. That perfect summer had been so long ago, yet the thought of her still made him ache.

"Okay, my second question is, what fucking dentist has my car?" Doc asked.

"Some guy name Shaddix." said Guy. *"He is a real slimy kind of guy."*

"Shaddix?" Doc screamed so loud that several people in the room turned their heads to see if the inmate in the wheel chair was going to go

crazy and cause a scene.

The guards looked around ready to pounce and the room settled back down.

"Shaddix?" said Doc again, except he hissed it through clinched teeth in a much more subdued manor. Guy could see the rage in Doc's eyes.

"Do you know Dr. Shaddix?" inquired Guy.

Now it was Guy's turn to listen.

*****

Blake and Guillermo both heard Doc's outburst and turned simultaneously to look. Anything could happen in prison, and it usually did. For the first time they both got a look at the guy talking to Doc.

"Oh my, isn't that a great big ol' butch treat?" chimed Guillermo.

Blake took a moment and agreed that the guy was cute. He was about their age too. He had a little bit of a nerdy quality about him. A lot of gays were looking like him these days. They called it Geek Chic.

*****

Visits ended.

Inmates were herded back to their cells, and visitors were escorted out. Blake stood in line to put money on Guillermo's commissary account. As he reached the pay window he noticed the nerdy guy was at the next window filling out a deposit slip. The guy was cute but had that poor college student look. Faded and well-worn jeans, an old soft tee with his college logo and the school's mascot emblazoned on the front of it. He wore a blue pin point oxford button-down as an over shirt and scuffed up Cole Hann loafers. The poor college kid may not have had money, but he did have enough style to look like he might have come from it.

*****

Guy arrived back at the Palace Motel.

To his surprise Dion, the Diva of Desire, was sitting in front of his door. Only this time, she wasn't a she. She was a He. Sort of.

He was no longer dressed in women's clothes and any glitter he had had on was long gone. But he still possessed that flowing hair and most of his long finger nails. Guy noticed that several looked as if they had been broken in a fight.

Guy exited his truck with more than a slight bit of trepidation. Dion sat as stoically as he could while dabbing his face with a tissue that was completely stained and dotted with either mascara or blood. Guy hoped it was the former, but unfortunately as he drew closer, he could see that Dion wasn't wearing any mascara.

"Oh, I am so glad that you are here." said Dion as he sniffled and dabbed his face.

"Why?" asked Guy.

"What do you mean, Why?" said Dion as he stood up with his Louis Vuitton shoulder bag and hoisted the handle of his luggage. *"Look at me, I am a mess and I have to get ready for my show."*

"I can't just let you stay in my room. How would that look?" said Guy looking all around *"I mean, what would people think?"* He whispered to Dion.

"Well, I would think that you are a kind and decent man for taking in a girl in her time of need after she has been thrown out in the streets upon discovering her two timing scum bag of a boyfriend shacked up with a trifling little two-bit ho with a weave that is so cheap that it looks like it came from the hind end of horse." replied Dion to Guy. However, midway through her diatribe she was screaming it out loud to someone who was obviously in another room of the Palace motel.

Guy was in shock.

What the hell was he going to do? People had opened their doors and windows to see what the commotion was all about. Everyone was beginning to stare.

Guy quickly unlocked the door. He put his hand on Dionne's hip and hustled the large drag queen in the door. He wished that Lola was here with him, but then again, he didn't want her to know about all of this. How was he ever going to explain this without her thinking that something happened? She already showed him that she could be very jealous. Couple that with the fact that he wouldn't let her come with him. Oh boy, she would hit the ceiling if she knew he had another girl in his room.

Dion wasn't a real girl, of course. However, when he played it back in his mind, it sounded even worse. Guy thought about it carefully and came to the conclusion that some things were better left unsaid and untold.

No one could ever know about this.

*****

Blake had driven down early that morning to see Guillermo. Jackson had to work for Jewels' that morning, but had driven down later to meet Blake, so that they could have a night together away from Suffocating Springs, as he called it. This was going to be their night to go out together to a real bar and to have some real fun away from everyone they knew. In small towns everyone knew everyone else, and, frankly, Jackson was tired of seeing the same old people.

He checked into a third rate place that was close to the bars called the Palace Motel. It wasn't much to look at, but it was cheap and had a tawdry sort of tackiness to it that made it kind of campy. No sooner had he got his suitcase in the door of Room 15 on the second floor when Blake called to say that his visit was over.

"Well, that's just great, Honey," said Jackson, *"because I just checked into the motel. It's the Palace Motel on Avenue Q, just past the Jiffy Lube. It's a bit of a dump, but there is lots of color here. I just saw some enormous drag queen catch her boyfriend in bed with her best friend. So if the bars get boring, then we can always just come back to the motel for some excitement."*

247

"You just love drama." said Blake. *"If you don't have drama in your life, then you are running to get in someone else's."*

"That's right, Honey." said Jackson with a big high finger snap. *"And tonight I have a surprise for you, but first I have to see what is going on in the courtyard because now the big drag queen is in front of some room with a cute boy yelling about someone's bad horse hair weave."* Jackson was peeking out the window. *"Oh, honey, now she is moving into that fine little boy's room."*

What Jackson didn't tell Blake was that he recognized that fine little boy. It was none other than Guy Canova, head of Opposition Research for Joe Don Lilly.

'Well, well, well.' thought Jackson. 'Little mister computer nerd has a big, big secret.'

Jackson loved having knowledge, but he especially loved knowing secrets. Having dirt like this on someone was exceptionally juicy. What he needed now was to figure out how to use it to his advantage. He scrolled through the pictures that he had just taken of Guy leading a drag queen into his motel room.

They were sharp and clear.

This trip was going to be full of surprises.

Chapter 38

Farmer had deliberately stayed under the radar since Hillbilly's death. Doc was a changed man. He became obsessed with improving himself. He had begun to work out in order to develop his body and his chances of getting out. He had requisitioned all of his court records and was pouring through the transcripts of his trial every night.

The Monkey Trap

"Farmer," said Doc excitedly, *"this testimony from the trial is wrong."*

Farmer was lying in his bunk with the sheet pulled over his head trying to nap.

"I had more cocaine than what the officer testified to." said Doc. *"I left Miami with exactly one pound and one ounce. I weighed it myself on the scale. It was precisely half a kilo. And I know that because our third investor dropped out, so Malcolm and I ended up splitting it in half. I saw it myself, but this transcript from the trial only shows half a pound. Not half a kilo."*

Farmer was still amazed at Doc's naivety. Farmer told him that no evidence sheet was ever correct.

"Cops skim confiscated drugs all of the time, man." said Farmer. *"Where do you think they get the fucking drugs to plant on people or in cars when they search them? They can't go to no damn drug store and just buy them."*

Farmer let that sink in before he added. *"And if they aren't planting them on people, then they are selling it to people. They are using it to supplement their incomes or snorting it up their nose. Believe me, there ain't no such creature as a good cop."* emphasized Farmer. *"There are only degrees of stink, it all smells like pig shit; however, if you are hell bent on proving it, then you gonna have to get a hold of the evidence sheets. Plain and simple."*

After his talk with Farmer, Doc had bombarded the court with records requests of every type. He had requested the officer's initial report and any notes taken at the time of arrest, but he was told such records didn't exist or that they were no longer available. Every request he had made to the court was rebuffed and rejected with the same innocuous form letter from Judge Wood.

It had been an old jailhouse lawyer that had advised him to bypass the court and request what he wanted directly from the County Records where everything is archived, and it had work the first time. He had gotten the evidence sheet from the trial, which backed up the officer's testimony; however, his subsequent requests for the initial confiscation sheet and the officer's initial incident report came back with the same form letter, again from Judge Wood.

Someone had caught on to his tactic.

He thought he had hit a dead end and that he would never be able to prove that he had been jacked by the cop if he couldn't get the original confiscation sheet to compare it to; and without that, he would never be able to get a new trial or a reduced sentence. He had resigned himself to the fact that he would spend the entire ten years behind bars.

The attempt on his life from the Muslims by gassing him only reinforced the belief that he was getting close. Real close. He was making waves. Someone wanted to silence him, and they obviously had enough pull to do it inside the prison.

Doc knew he was a sitting duck. If someone was brazen enough to plan an attack on him once, they certainly could do it again. Seeing that he was trapped and without anyone to help him, he knew it was just a matter of time.

Since Doc had begun working out with Joey Flowers, he physically felt like a new man, but since the gas attack, he felt like a dead man walking.

Doc lay in his bunk like he did every Saturday, trying to think of some way to get out.

"Braxton." hollered the picket guard. *"Get dressed and come out. You gotta visitor."*

The loud metal doors slid open and the floor guard pulled him out. Naturally, Doc was suspicious and on alert for anything out of the ordinary. A sudden visit from someone after a year and a half was definitely out of the ordinary. That was for damn sure.

He had been weakened by the attack and had stayed in the infirmary for one only night, but the prison doctors had confined him to wheel chair for a week. He fully expected to be wheeled to some secluded area of the prison without any witnesses to be ambushed and killed.

What he hadn't expected was to be wheeled into the visitation room full of civilians and families.   His mind was reeling now.   He was totally caught off guard.

'Did he really have a visitor?' he thought. 'Who could it be?'

Doc was dizzy from the sudden rush of excitement.

'Could this really be happening, or was he being set up?' Doc kept asking himself over and over again.

As much as he wanted to hope that he had a visitor and as much as he wanted it to be Boyce, he knew that it was an almost near impossibility.

Yet, hope was niggling at the back of his brain.

The rest of his brain was on high alert, and his body was ready for any kind of ambush.   It would be the perfect time.   They would be counting on Doc to be so excited about a visit that he would have his guard down; but Doc was wound tight.   They would get quite a surprise when Doc rose from the wheelchair like a phoenix rising from the ashes.

They wouldn't be expecting that.

However, what he hadn't expected was the kid sitting on the other side of the glass who was actually there to see him.

Chapter 39

"Mistress Rojo" graveled Santos. *"May I suck your delicious big toe?"*

"No" replied Mistress Rojo petulantly. *"Not yet, my naughty pet."*

Making Santos plead for privilege of pleasuring her was like emotional heroin to Mistress Rojo.   Santos had become her most willing servant, an eagerly submissive sex slave.   They had begun the evening with a little bit of bondage.   Some light paddling.   And a tidbit of titty twisting.

The Monkey Trap

Mistress Rojo placed her red patent leather thigh high boot with its solid silver stiletto on the bar bell between his cuffed wrists. Santos was suddenly confronted by an enormous erotic tongue as Mistress Rojo seductively twisted her foot, so as to devilishly make the boot's silver tongue lick his right cheek. She slowly passed it by his lips and languidly caressed his left cheek. Suddenly, she stuck the rigid sterling tongue in his mouth. Santos tasted the metallic lingua as she probed him orally.

"Tonight" stated Mistress Rojo breathlessly, *"We are going to play a new game."*

'Oh my lord,' thought Santos, 'this has been a night full of firsts.' He didn't know how much more he could take. Just when he thought that she couldn't go any further or do anything new, she pushed him to an ever higher level of sexual revelry.

There seemed to be no end to her insatiability. Nor to her imagination. She was a sexual goddess, and she was making sure that he knew it. He worshiped her, and not just because she ordered him to. No, she had unleashed the beast and it would never be put back in its cage. He was a changed man. The scales of innocence had been lifted from his eyes and he now could see that Jewels' was the woman for him. No other woman would ever be able to satisfy him like she did.

He had met girls and had sex with so many that he had lost count, but none of them had ever entered the realm of seductiveness that Jewels' had with him. She was a once in a lifetime find; a soul mate, and he would do anything not to lose her. Anything.

He was willing to sell his soul to the devil in order to keep her.

"Are you ready for my little game?" asked Mistress Rojo, as she delicately tickled his anus with her blood red painted nails.

Santos was almost speechless.

"YES!" Exclaimed Santos as she touched a nerve.

Without warning or provocation Mistress Rojo caught Santo's scrotum in her grasp and tugged on it until her grip was like an iron fist holding his manhood and squeezing his sanity. Santos didn't know whether to scream from the pain or to cry out in ecstasy.

A tear came to Santos' eye.

Heaven and Hell at the same time.

'How does she know the things that she does?' Santos asked himself as he gulped in short breathes of ecstasy. She moved her delicate digits to his virgin sphincter. Another tear rolled slowly down Santos' cheek. She touch him like no other person ever had.

He felt her soft ruby lips press gently against his.

Any reservation or apprehension instantly dissolved as her lips touched his.

He was aware, suddenly, that her other hand had ever so lightly begun to graze the hairs of his sack with her immaculately manicured nails.

Her tickling touch was so light, hardly more than a whispers breathe, like that of an angel's wing fluttering.

Mistress Rojo knew exactly what Santos was feeling and how to keep his horned beast enthralled and under her complete control.

If you controlled the penis, then you controlled the mind.

'Simple creatures.' thought Mistress Rojo.

She had him under her spell. Now and forever, he would do whatever she wanted. The rest of the night would be spent doing the things that reinforced her dominance and that would insure his total devotion to her. That was imperative.

After all, that was the sole purpose of tonight's soiree, sexual debauchery coupled with emotional dominance.

"Tonight's game is called," Mistress Rojo announced with whispered authority. *"Toe Job or Blow Job?"*

Santos loved to play Mistress Rojo's games, because even if he lost, he ended up a winner in his book.

"Are you ready, my little darling?" quizzed Mistress Rojo.

"Ooohhh, yes! Mistress Rojo." exclaimed Santos with eagerness.

But no sooner had the words left his lips when the ornate silver tongue of Mistress Rojo's boot flipped back to reveal five of the most beautifully manicured toes that he had ever seen. They were painted fiery red with white French tips. They looked like sweet candy.

Santos' lips quivered. He wanted to hold every one of them in his mouth. He would be as new born babe suckling to its mother for the very first time. He would start with the smallest and work his way up, slowly, one by one. He would give each delicate digit the loving attention that it deserved.

"Mistress Rojo, may I pleasure you by sucking your sweet toes?" Santos asked most humbly, but he could not hide the hunger in his eyes.

"Yes you may, my pet." cooed Mistress Rojo used her riding crop to outline his lips playfully.

"For the game is now afoot!"

*****

Officer Sinclair spotted the two queers pointing at him, but he couldn't be bothered by a couple fruits kiki-ing and kawkaw-ing about him. He was too enthralled by Dr. Bentley Braxton and his visitor. Dr. Braxton hadn't ever had a visitor, and now he had one out of the blue. It was a strange coincidence, and Ernie Sinclair didn't believe in coincidences.

Sinclair scanned the clip board to see who the visitor was.

Pete Parris from Prickley Springs. Never heard of him.

Sinclair wrote down the name and address. He would pass the info to Sheriff Red the next time he called, but right now he was waiting for an opportunity to finish the job that he was sent down here to do. Sheriff

Red had been irate when he learned that Braxton was still alive, and said that if Sinclair didn't finish the job, he would be stuck down here in this shit hole job for the rest of his life. He would be banished from Lloyd County and would never be Sergeant Sinclair.

"Code 42, Visitor's parking lot." came the alert over Officer Sinclair's radio.

Code 42 was an unknown disturbance usually associated with arguing inmates. Sinclair, nor any of the other officers that were responding, had ever had a Code 42 in the parking lot. The only thing that he could figure was that two visitors were fighting.

Officers ran out of the front door and hustled their way through the double security gates, a few at a time; However, when they reached the parking lot, there wasn't anything going on. In fact, there wasn't even anyone around.

"They are over here" said the female guard. Despite the urgency of the situation, Sinclair could not help but notice that she had the most enormous ass he had ever laid eyes on; and every inch of it was covered in skin tight uniform gray polyester. Her hair had obviously been wrapped around beer cans and stiffened with a glossy blue colored lacquer.

She waddled like a duck as she led the small platoon of guards to an RV parked in the lot.

"There." she screamed pointing at the old motor home with her three inch finger nail ornamented with a painted rhinestone bug.

As the assembled group looked on, they could see that the RV was rocking back and forth. A short distance away inmates could be seen gathering by the dozens in the cell block windows and others raced by the hundreds from the Rec yard to the fences.

Chants from the inmates reverberated through the air.

"Go! Go! Go!"

The Monkey Trap

"Y'alls need to put a stop to this nastiness in my parking lot." hollered the female guard with the big booty.

The male guards stood for a moment just looking at one another. Most of them were barely out of high school, and most were snickering like they still were on the playground. Sinclair was already starting to sweat and he didn't want to be out in the heat all day. In addition, Sinclair was probably the oldest and the most mature one of the bunch, so he stepped forward and pounded loudly on the door. Disturbance calls were nothing new to him. He had knocked on many a door in his years as a deputy. This wasn't going to be any different. This was probably just two amorous teenagers having a little fun.

"This is Officer Sinclair with the prison." shouted Sinclair *"Would you mind opening the door, please?"*

The motion in the RV stopped. A few seconds later the door opened a crack.

"Can I help you?" asked a sweet voice from inside the RV.

"Yes ma'am, could you and whoever else is in there please come out here right away." commanded Officer Sinclair.

The door creaked open wider to reveal an elderly gray headed woman in a flimsy house coat. Behind her stood a small bald man stooped over in faded checkered boxer shorts and black socks. Every male guard began to snicker and chuckle while the squatty female guard just glared at them.

"This ain't funny." she screamed at her co-workers.

But it was funny, because the little old man had a boner sticking straight out as hard as a baseball bat. Upon seeing it, they all busted out laughing with unbridled guffaws. As the old man emerged from the RV, the inmates all began to cheer and caterwaul. Whistles and cheers erupted from the fence line in celebration of the old man's woody.

Officer Sinclair stepped back to avoid being poked by the geriatric's giant swinging schlong.

"Uhm..uh..I am so sorry ma'am, we thought something might be wrong when we saw the RV shaking." said Sinclair sheepishly. This was so embarrassing. He just wanted to run, but he had to stay professional even though his colleagues where busting a gut and laughing only ten feet behind him.

"Oh no, everything is just fine." said the old lady with all the dignity and composure of a royal queen.

"Ma'am, this is a prison parking lot. Were you looking for a camp ground?" Sinclair thought that they might have gotten confused and parked in the wrong area by mistake. Old people did that kind of thing all of the time.

"Oh no, we have a spot at the KOA, but Henry took his testosterone shot and for two hours he is like a porn star, so we were just having a little alone time together while our daughter is inside visiting her boyfriend." The old woman was actually beaming with pride. *"I hope we weren't causing any trouble, young man."*

Henry just stood there in silence with knobby knees and a sheepishly silly grin on his face. He was seemingly oblivious to the huge erection in his baggy boxers.

Sinclair was dumbfounded by the old woman's honesty. No embarrassment. No remorse. No trying to hide anything. Just totally forthright and honest. What was he supposed to do? As far as he knew, they weren't doing anything illegal and, God knows, they were past the legal age of consent.

Normally, he would scold a couple, give them a stern warning about such behavior and tell them to move on, but Sinclair couldn't bring himself to chastise the old couple. They reminded him of his grandparents. It was apparent they were well into their seventies. Hell, at their age, it might be the last time ever.

"Well, I am sorry to have disturbed you." Sinclair said as he turned to leave red faced.

"That's it?" screamed the squat bodied female guard. *"You aren't going to do anything?"*

"Nothing I can do." stated Sinclair as he continued to walk back to the building as fast as he could. All of the other guys were laughing and having a field day with it. He was sure that it would be all over the prison within minutes. He could just hear the jokes now.

"Hey, Sinclair, the way he was swinging that thing at you, maybe you could charge him with attempted assault." Hollered one of the guards. The uproar was raucous and Sinclair was mortified. He had been the butt end of jokes all his life. He was never going to live this down. He was fuming on the inside.

Someone was going to pay for this.

*****

"Did I catch you at a bad time?" asked Guy as he fumbled to push the speaker button on his iPhone.

"No" said Jewels as she sat on the pink bar bell between Santo's shackled wrist. Her legs straddled his broad, muscular shoulders and his head rested easily between her ivory thighs. *"I am just sitting down with an old friend. He's getting something to eat. What do you need? Did you meet with our friend?"*

Santos was spent. He was grateful for the momentary relief. Jewels was relentlessly insatiable. He had never met anyone so sexually focused.

"Yes, I did," said Guy *"but we may have a problem."*

"I didn't send you down there to find problems." stated Jewels in a displeased tone of voice.

Guy informed Jewels about everything that Doc had told him.

"But it all means nothing if we can't get our hands on the initial arrest reports and the confiscation records. We have to prove that the drugs are missing and that the Sheriff and his deputies are profiting personally

from these drug busts. Otherwise, Joe Don Lilly is going to lose the election and we will be out of a job."

'The kid was smart' thought Jewels. They had each hitched their proverbial wagons to the other. It was all or nothing for both of them. Guy knew what was at stake and what it was going to take to win. What he didn't know was that the solution to their problem had literally dropped into Jewels' lap.

Too bad. Because that was an important little tidbit of info to know.

Jewel hung up her phone and smiled as she lifted Santos' sweaty face and wiped his wet cheek with her delicate hand.

"Mistress Rojo, is sad now." Said Jewels as she pouted childishly by sticking out her ruby red lower lip. *"I don't think you love me anymore."* She turned her head to her left shoulder. Her curly red locks draped loosely about her exposed areola.

Guy was hypnotized by her sweet girlish charms. Even if she were all dressed up as a whip wielding dominatrix.

"I love you, Mistress Rojo." Stated Santos devotedly.

"If you mean that, then you will have to prove it to me." cooed Mistress Rojo

And that is just exactly what he began to do.

Chapter 40

The Blue Poodle.

Guy had never been to a drag bar before. He wondered if they were all like this. Smoke and mirrors. That's what the Blue Poodle had lots of. And people too.

Guy was amazed at how crowded it was. Dion had gotten him what passed for a table. It wasn't much bigger than a postage stamp.

"What'cha sucking on tonight, cutie pie?" Came a lispy rasp.

A startled Guy Canova turned in his chair and looked up.

It was Dolly Parton in a Duck Dynasty beard.

Even after watching Dion meticulously apply his makeup and fret over each and every hair and every single bugle bead, he was not prepared for the creature now towering above him and holding a cocktail tray. The waiter/waitress was some sort of freakish diabolical hybrid. Guy contemplated how much psychological help this person needed and how much he might need himself just for seeing him. Or her. Whichever.

Dolly wore a knot-tied green gingham checkered halter top ornamented with what could only be described as wooly wild chest hair and a strand of bubble gum-sized pearls. But to her credit she was a nice C cup.

Guy ordered a Coors Light Beer.

Dolly pivoted in her red chunk pumps and Guy was suddenly faced with his first set of hairy mud flaps.   As Dolly sashayed away from the table, Guy noticed for the first time that she was sporting the shortest pair of shorty shorts that he had ever seen. Until that moment, he had never fathomed that Daisy Duke's even came in a men's size forty four.

"Is someone sitting here?" Asked a nice normal looking kid.

"No" said Guy.

"Do you mind? The place is packed and I hate to take up a whole table when it's just me." said the kid.

"Of course." Guy was relieved to have some normal looking company for a change. So far his trip to Huntsville had been very unusual.

"My name's Blake." said the kid as he pulled out the chair and sat down.

"Well, it didn't take long for you to snag one, did it?" said Dolly as she set Guy's beer on the table. *"And what would you like tonight, besides*

cutie pie here." asked Dolly to Blake.

Blake looked at the bottle with droplets of cold sweat running down the sides. *"You know, that cold beer looks great. I will have one of those, also."*

"Oooohhhh! Two butch boys. One table. I can tell already that this is going to be a popular table tonight." Once again Guy received a face full of hairy mud flaps as Dolly retreated to the bar in her size thirteen red sling back chunk pumps.

"I saw you today at the prison. I was there visiting my brother." said Blake.

Guy was caught off guard. Jewels was very clear that he wasn't to be seen nor recognized while he was down here. He didn't know this kid, and this kid didn't know him; but he had checked in as Pete and Dion knew him as Pete. This could get awkward if he changed anything now. Guy really felt like James Bond now.

"Yeah, I was there visiting my uncle." That was so lame, thought Guy, but it was the first thing that popped into his head. Guy stuck his hand quickly across the table. *"My name is Pete. Nice to meet you."*

Blake grabbed Guy's hand and was impressed by how firm, and manly, it was. *"I couldn't believe it when my brother told me what happened to your Uncle. He was lucky to have survived."*

Doc had told Guy about how the Muslims had tried to kill him with poison gas, but Guy hadn't thought about how it must have been the talk of the prison. Prisons were micro communities that were full of people, and the one thing that all people and all communities did was gossip. Guy realized that his unexpected encounter might just be a blessing in disguise.

"Yeah, he was lucky." said Guy. *"But he was so weak and out of it that he couldn't tell me all of it. What did your brother tell you?"* It was a lie. Doc was fine and was playing opossum. He had told Guy what had happened, but Guy was anxious to see what the gossip was around the

prison. Gossip could be notoriously unreliable, but it usually had some truth in it somewhere. So Guy listened closely as Blake recounted everything that Guillermo had told him.

"And I couldn't believe that the guard that tried to kill him was right there in the visitation room today." said Blake. *"And that he is still working there."*

The story had been almost the same, except for the last part. Doc hadn't mentioned anything about a guard being in on the attack. This was new, and Guy knew that if it was true, Doc was still in danger. Serious danger. But if it was just prison gossip, he was going to look like a fool if he told Jewels about it.

Guy was struggling with what to do when the lights went down.

"Ladies and Gentlemen........."

*****

Farmer never minded working late. He hated being cooped up in the cell, and he didn't like the day room unless there was a big game on the TV. It was always so damn loud with sixty plus people on average in there. People would be screaming out loud just to be heard on the pay phones. Inmates would be slamming dominoes on the stainless steel table.

SLAM!

"Nigga, why you be doin' all that shit? You ain't even making a fuckin' point."

SLAM! SLAM!

Farmer couldn't stand it, so he worked as much as he could. Being the Warden's boy meant that he could stay up in the main offices. They were air conditioned. He worked a lot in the evenings. He painted after the secretaries and clerks had left for the day, which meant that he was all alone. Well, almost. His co-worker, Pookie, was with him and they would turn on the secretary's radio and listen to the Crocket Cruisers as they painted. Hell, Farmer must have painted everything in these offices at least five or six times in the past year. Prison was a monotonous place. All work was usually busy work to keep the inmates occupied. People that worked in the prison got to where they just didn't even see inmates anymore. They were like black servants of the Old South. They were there, but they weren't. They were just a part of the furniture; and unless it was something new or unusual, no one really noticed it. That was how Farmer felt. Guards would talk about niggers, mooleys, kikes, spics, wetbacks and crackers to one another, as if Farmer and his partner weren't even there. Nothing was filtered or held back.

Farmer didn't care as long as they left him alone. Since learning to read Farmer pulled the newspaper out of the Warden's trash can each night. He started with the Sports section, but with nothing else to do, he soon found himself reading the whole thing from front to back. The Huntsville Item wasn't much of a newspaper compared to the bigger city papers, like Houston and Dallas, but they reported a lot of local interest stuff. Huntsville had seven prisons, so most of the county was employed by the Texas Department of Criminal Justice, which meant that anyone and everything that was in the paper had some kind of tie to the prisons.

The big news for the past month had been the rash of rapes that had occurred. The victims were all between the ages of sixty and eighty. Farmer wondered what kind of sicko got his jollies from molesting old women. Some pervert like that wouldn't last a day in general population before he was killed. The victim said that the rotund rapist had stolen into their homes at night while they were sleeping and once during the day while the old lady napped in her easy chair.

"You know, Pookie, I would love to have just five minutes with this guy." said Farmer to his co-worker.

"Man, guys like him are always put on Safekeeping." Pookie chimed in. *"They wouldn't last a day in population."*

"I hate guys like this." Said Farmer shaking the paper. *"My granny got attacked once and if I could ever get close to this guy, I would rip him a new ass."*

*****

Guy stared in amazement.

They looked so real. He had never seen these kinds of drag queens.

"First time to ever see female impersonators?" asked Blake.

Guy sat stunned as each one paraded out across the small stage.

"Yes" said Guy. *"Except for Dion. But these look a lot different than her."*

Blake giggled to himself.

"...And now, The Blue Poodle is proud to present your host and star of the show, Miss Dion Martell!" said the announcer as the crowd jump to their feet in thunderous applause and cat calls.

Dion suddenly appeared out of the smoky darkness as spot lights lit up the stage. She looked even taller on stage.

Something Guy didn't think was possible.

Dion was draped in a short red fringe dress that barely covered where his hoo-ha should have been, but where the dress ended, two miles of incredibly smooth and long legs began. They did not end until they got his six inch silver sequined platform pumps and all topped off with a Tina Turner wig.

"Girl," exclaimed Blake as he furiously clapped his hands, *"she has done beat that wig to filth!"*

Guy had no idea what that meant, but from Blake's excitement level, he assumed that it was something good. Sirens blared from every speaker as they started with a low bass and crescendoed to a treble decibel that set the room into a frenzy. As the excitement and the music level rose, so did Dion's arms.

Guy and everyone else's eyes were glued to the two bottles that Dion was twirling in her hands. By the time Dion's hands got to the top, the noise in the place was deafening. The crowd seemed to know what was coming, which only increased the havoc.

The music peaked and Dion was now gyrating around the edge of the dance floor on one leg. Her wrists were still spinning and the other leg was high kicking up in the air, shaking from side to side.

Guy had no idea what to expect, when suddenly the siren of the pulse pounding music exploded just as Dion released the tops of the bottles. Champagne could be seen showering the throbbing mob and spraying bubbly all over the club's patrons in the colored disco lights. The crowd was screaming and yelling like it was a rock concert.

'All of this hoopla over the homeless drag queen that I brought here tonight' thought Guy. 'This is without a doubt the strangest experience of my life.'

No one in Prickly Springs would ever believe this. If he dared to tell anyone.

However, he knew that he was going have to tell one person everything.

And another person absolutely nothing.

*****

Darkness.

Huntsville was what people called a sleepy little town. Big box stores were all along the highway. The seven prisons spread throughout Huntsville caused most of the residents to be dispersed across the whole county on rural lots. The adjacent neighboring areas were filled with small towns. Madisonville was its closest neighbor to the north. The only reason anyone would take notice of it was because it had a decent country radio station and a Buckee's truck stop.

"Home on the Range" RV park had seen better days despite the fact that it looked as if it was in a perpetual state of unfinished construction. On a regular basis, the owner's three dogs and seven chickens ran wild, which included one very loud rooster.

At this time of night, the dogs were inside and the feathered livestock was asleep. The moonless night was clear and still. Stars twinkled through the leaves of the trees. Despite his girth, the stranger moved stealthily through the woods and up to the old Jamboree motor home. Old people were so complacent and docile. That was why they were the perfect targets.

The big man bided his time and it's wasn't long before his patience was rewarded. The old lady opened the door and stepped out in her tattered terry cloth robe with embroidered sea shells pockets. She followed the old worn dirt path to the distant shower. He had scouted this place for weeks and chose it specifically because of its remote shower location. It was rarely used by the monthly residents, and the park had only a couple of overnight spots available. Madisonville wasn't what anyone would describe as a big tourist draw on the Texas map.

However, tonight the corpulent creepster was drawn to this stark and lonesome shower. Steam began to rise and seep through the jalousie windows of the cinder block building. The pudgy pervert closed in on his prey, poking his head in to peak at his saggy unsuspecting spoil as she soaped herself.

The door's lock silently turned.

Chapter 41

Fucking Rats.

They were everywhere in the old courthouse.

In old buildings like this, they had hundreds of holes. Santos could hear them scurrying inside the walls. He hated coming in here. Especially at night. The old place gave him the creeps.

The basement was dark and dank. Musk and decay permeated the air. He could smell the mold growing all around him. Dust could be seen floating in the ether as it passed through the dim beams of light that were spaced throughout the court house dungeon.   Officially, it was the archived records room where old reports were sent to die so they didn't take up space at the new administration building, but to Santos it reminded him of something that prisoners from the Spanish inquisition might have been tortured and kept in.

Huge rough cut blocks of Texas granite lined the underground walls and created the mammoth subterranean support columns for the old building. It really did look like something from another era of time, thought Santos, as he rifled through mountains of boxes.   The dusty files had begun to affect his allergies.   His eyes were now itching and burning. His sinus felt constricted and packed full of snot.

He hated feeling like this, but Jewels had insisted that she needed some old arrest records from two years before.   Santos had initially refused. He didn't want to get into trouble.   He could get fired for doing something like that.

Jewels said that she understood.

"But, honey," she said softly in his ear as she nibbled on his lobe.   *"If I had that information, then we could be together forever.   And if you got this vital piece of evidence for me, I can virtually guarantee you right now that you would be the new Assistant Deputy Sheriff in the new Sheriff's administration."*

What she was asking him to do was tantamount to treason.   She knew who he worked for and he certainly knew who she worked with, but until this minute neither had broken the Chinese firewall that they had put up. Jobs were supposed to be off limits.   Yet, she had just crossed the DMZ and asked for Santos to defect; and not only to be a traitor, but to be a thief and a spy also.   People just didn't cross the Thin Blue Line, especially, not with Sheriff Red.

Thousands of thoughts raced through Santos' mind.   He hated the corruption that he saw. He felt like a dirty cop all of the time. He knew what his co-workers and Sheriff Red were doing was unethical and probably illegal, but he just didn't know if he could betray them by crossing that thin blue line.

'But Jewels is my soul mate', he told himself

Santos didn't doubt for a minute that they were destined to be together. He hadn't told her yet, but he was in love with her. He wanted to marry her someday when he was financially secure, but if what she was telling him was true, then as Assistant Deputy Sheriff he would be much better off financially. He could then propose to Jewels, and they would have each other forever. It was a perfect plan in Santos' mind, except for the fact that he would have to betray all of his buddies in the process.

His brain wrestled with his heart.

"Okay," Santos told Jewels. *"I will do it for us."*

Jewels knew that he would. Her night of dominance and obedience had worked perfectly. Santos was a sexy and satisfying play toy, but he was also her puppy; so eager to please.

So she in turn gave her little doggy his treat.

"Do you remember what I told you tonight's game was called?" she asked seductively as she cupped him.

"Oh yes," said Santos gulping in excitement. *"It's called, Toe Job or Blow Job!"*

"That's right, my sweet lover." He remembered how she moistly licked his nipple and kissed his belly softly with her amazingly sexy red lips until she swallowed his excitement completely.

"What the hell are you doing in here, Deputy Salinas?" boomed the Sheriff.

Santos jumped. He hadn't been be expecting anyone. And he definitely hadn't expected Sheriff 'Red'. He had been daydreaming about Mistress Rojo.

"Oh, Sheriff," said Santos, *"You scared the crap out of me, sir."*

The Sheriff's stature along with his Stetson hat filled the door. His face was grim with a countenance that had a hardness to it that came from years of suspicion.

"What are you doing here so late and in the old records room?" repeated the Sheriff.

Santos could feel his heart thumping in his chest. His knees had gone numb. He was eight years old again.

"Uh?" Santos' mind scrambled. *"I am just getting a report for a court appearance that I have tomorrow in Judge Wood's court."*

The Sheriff gave him one last suspicious look.

"Well, let me help you." offered the Sheriff.

"Oh, you don't have to do that sheriff. It's filthy down here and you don't want to get all dirty." Said Santos sweating pools under arms. *"Besides, I got it already. I just have to put a few boxes back up,"*

The Sheriff stood silent for a moment reading his deputy. He was young, and he has just got popped up on by the big boss. Kids always acted squirrelly, Deputies weren't any different.

"That's okay, son" said the Sheriff as he released his gaze. "I don't mind helping one of my boy's out."

The big sheriff hoisted a box and handed it to Santos.

"Great." replied Santos with feigned gratitude.

*****

The camo SUV sat hidden in the shadows.

The deputy sitting in it hated doing surveillance. It wasn't at all like they made it out to be on TV. It was hot and boring. Really boring. However, he was a professional and he would sit here until he spotted his prey. He didn't know why he had been targeted, but he would find him.

The deputy was no longer in his uniform; and what he was there to do wasn't part of his official duties, but it was part of his sworn duty to his brothers.   This assignment had come from the top. So as the chief enforcer of the fraternity, he decided to do this job himself.

Surveillance gave a man time to think, and the deputy couldn't help but think about how that little punk had gotten away from him at the auction. He had the truck dead to rights when the little shit slammed on his brakes and sent the deputy flying by him; ripping his side mirror clean off.   The deputy had been furious and wanted to turn around and finish the kid off, but that gang of motorcyclists had appeared out of nowhere to help him.

They even began to chase him, but those big heavy hogs weren't any match for his high suspension SUV with its off road mud tires and four-wheel drive. They had caught up to him on the blacktop road, but when he turned onto the bumpy and hilly dirt roads, their pursuit fell off at the first sign of big mud.   He saw the lead motorcycle bury its front wheel into the muck and flip it's rider over the handle bars.   The deputy whooped out loud to himself as he watched the motorcycle rider do a face plant into the sticky east Texas mud.

'That'll teach them damn motorcycle gangs not to mess with us good ol' redneck boys.'   Thought the deputy as he disappeared into the backwoods.

As he sat in the hot SUV on surveillance, he wondered if that could have been the same gang that kidnapped and tortured his buddy, Ernie Sinclair.   If it was, he had been lucky to get away or else he might have ended up being tortured in some back woods shack naked with a sack over his head.

The deputy bit into another patty melt sandwich from the Hot Biscuit. That Darlene sure was a good cook. She wasn't bad on the eyes either. He liked to stop in late at night to get a little coffee and conversation.

And with Darlene, both were always hot.

The deputy was slurping his Mountain Dew when the suspect emerged leaving the house.

The young hippie looking stoner got into a beat up old car and drove off with black smoke belching out of the tail pipe. The deputy threw his half-eaten patty melt into the grimy passenger seat and slammed his drink into the cup holder as he cranked the camo SUV's engine.

The old car with its black smoke was easy to follow. The deputy stayed a couple of car lengths behind in order not to attract attention, but judging from the look of the stoner, he couldn't notice much.

They continued to meander through the town until the stoner pulled into the student parking lot of the local college. The stoner parked the piece of crap car far away from the others as if it were a priceless Ferrari. 'And who knows,' thought the deputy, 'it might just be to this little creep.'

The stoner jumped out with a grungy backpack on his shoulder and slammed the door. The deputy pulled out the printed copy of the driver's license and compared the picture to the kid now walking.

"Gotcha!" said the deputy talking to himself. *"You little fuckin' punk."*

*****

Santos' was sweating buckets as he exited the old courthouse and made his way down the big stone steps. After five o'clock the old town square became deserted as all the city and county workers left work and went home. The one thing you could count on was that no government worker would work one minute longer than he had to, so it always amazed Santos how it went from county seat to ghost town in literally a matter of minutes, which was why he was so surprised when the Sheriff had discovered him in the dungeon.

His heart was racing as fast as his legs as he sprinted to his truck and yanked the door open.

"Boo!" hollered a voice from inside the truck.

Santos jumped back two feet and wrestled to pull his gun out of its holster. He leveled it at the intruder inside his truck.

"Don't shoot!" screamed the voice.

Santos noticed the curly red hair and immediately dropped his pistol.

"What the hell are you doing?" Santos screamed back before he could catch himself.

He looked around and was grateful that the square was deserted. He holstered his weapon and jumped in behind the wheel.

Jewels started to come up from her crouched position in the floor board when Santos put his manly hand on top of her head and roughly shoved her back down.

"Stay down." He commanded.

Jewels didn't argue because she could tell that something was wrong. Santos was really spooked. It wasn't like him to be afraid of anything, and he was really scared now. They drove several minutes in silence with Santos constantly looking around and checking his rear view mirrors.

Finally, he pulled over and stopped the truck. *"I am so sorry, baby, but I think we may be in big trouble."*

Jewels rose up and sat on the seat beside Santos. She could see that he was visibly upset as she placed her hand on top of his. She couldn't let him escape her or her mission now. She had to keep him focused. She needed to calm him down and reassure him that everything was going to be okay, but first she needed to find out what the hell happened to make him so upset.

"Darling," she said calmly, *"tell me what happened."*

Santos felt reassured at her touch and he began to calm himself in order to tell her how he had gotten caught by the Sheriff himself.

"You mean he knows that you were there to get the reports on Dr. Braxton's arrest?" Now it was her turn to get panicky.

"No, I mean I don't so, but I just don't know." said Santos as he now looked into Jewels eyes and saw how worried she was. *"I told him that I*

was there looking for one of my arrest records in order to testify in court tomorrow. It was the first thing that popped into my mind."

The relief in Jewel's mind and body was immediate. *"Well, that's great, baby."*

"No, it's not. I don't know if he bought my story or not. I haven't been on the force but for a year, and all the records down there are over two years old. What if he realizes that and questions me about it?" asked Santos.

"I am sure that he has more important things on his mind and has already forgotten the whole thing." said Jewels reassuringly.

Jewels was acutely aware of exactly how bad it could get if the Sheriff got suspicious, but the most important thing at this moment was to calm Santos down. He was becoming unraveled by the stress.

"Baby, look at me." Said Jewels. *"I am not going to let anything happen to you. Let me see what you got. This could be everything we need to take him down and you will never have to worry about anything again."*

This was it. This was her ticket to the White House. If this file contained what she hoped that it did, then Boyce Braxton couldn't refuse her. He would do whatever she wanted. This was hard ball now and the stakes didn't get any higher. She perused the reports, but until she had Guy's information from Dr. Braxton to compare it to, she didn't have anything. She hated waiting, but she had come this far and she could wait just a little bit longer. She could taste the power within her reach.

What a rush.

They were right. Power was the best aphrodisiac.

She leaned over and grabbed Santo's mouth with one hand and his crotch with the other.

Santos put his head down dejectedly.

"I didn't get it." he said not wanting to face her.

He knew that he failed her and he felt the grip on his manhood noticeably loosen.

Chapter 42

Doc was wheeled back to his cell and dropped off unceremoniously by the Medical Trustee. Doc couldn't believe that this kid just dropped into his lap. He couldn't wait to tell Farmer. In the meantime he pulled down all of his legal papers and rifled through them until he found what he was looking for.

He sat down decidedly on the small round desk stool that was attached to the wall by a large piece of gray steel I-beam. He sat slumped shouldered with the sheets of flimsy paper loosely held in his hands.

He mentally recounted the past two years of his life and all that happened to him. What he saw in his mind's eye wasn't good at all. How had his life of privilege and affluence become such mess?

He reminisced about the decisions that he had made in his life and the consequences he had reaped because of them. This wasn't how life for someone like him was supposed to turn out.

A crocodile tear dropped from his cheek splashing down between his feet on the painted concrete floor.

He started to cry. Then he began to grieve. He was ashamed of himself. The legal papers dropped from his hands and floated down to the ground as he sobbed uncontrollably into his hands.

The system had beaten him.

No one ever wanted to admit total defeat, but Doc could no longer lie to himself. He had nothing left. No real family. No real friends. No real future.

But the most humiliating thing he had to admit to himself was that he no longer possessed any dignity. He had nothing he could be proud of anymore. He had frittered it all away on pompous and superficial pleasures of the moment to buy the affection of people who didn't really love him and never would.

For the past two years he might as well have been dead. No one came to see him. No one put money on his books for food to eat. No one had written him to inquire about how he was doing. No one had lifted a finger to try and help him.

That was, until today, when some kid had showed up out of the blue.

He didn't know this kid from Adam. In prison you didn't ever trust someone you didn't know. Doc knew what prison life was and what it had to offer him for the next eight years. He wanted out of here more than anything in the world. He wanted to go home and apologize to Boyce, tell him how much he really loved him, and show him how very sorry he was.

Long streams of clear mucus dangled precariously to the floor from his runny nose and hot tears streaked his face as he finally realized what and who was really important in life. Doc was not a complete man. He was a broken man, and he was missing the most important thing in life.

Family.

Family, along with a few real friends were what made a person complete. Tangible things like cars, houses and jewelry were nice to have, but when it is all gone or taken from you, what's left?

Only family and friends.

The only thing that you could ever leave behind with someone else was a memory. It was up to you to decide whether you were going to leave them with a good one or a bad one. All he had given Boyce and others were bad times and bad trouble.

As he looked around he admitted to himself that he, and he alone, had put himself into this pit of hell. He now struggled like an animal just to survive. Like any other animal trying to survive, sometimes you get desperate.

Doc was desperate.

Doc was going to jump at this kid's offer of help. He put the sheets of paper into the envelope. It was the only copy in existence, and without it he would never get out of prison. Just sitting in prison with it wasn't helping him either. He needed this kid. He needed him badly, but he didn't know this kid nor if he could trust him. This might just be another elaborate scam to get the evidence sheets from him and to destroy them. If they could be destroyed, all evidence against them would be gone.

Doc wrestled in his mind for another few seconds before he wrote down the woman's name and address that the kid, Guytana, had given him to send it to. The kid had told him to also use his celly's name as the return address since that was how the prison censors checked to see whose mail it was. Prisoner's letters had to be left open so that the prison censors could, if they wanted to, check and read them before being send and, especially, if they were monitoring the mail of someone specific.

Doc wasn't taking any chances and gave it to the trustee to drop in the mail box.

Doc had just gotten his legal papers put up on his shelve and was lying in his bunk.

"Out of your cell." Yelled the wing guard.

"What's going on?" Doc asked as he jumped down from the desk stool and crawled down to the floor.

"Random cell search." said the guard. *"Strip down to you boxers and socks and then step out."*

Doc complied and was frisked while another guard felt all through his clothes.

276

"Stand against the wall." Said the guard

Doc saw the two man shakedown squad enter his cell. He recognized one as the officer who had been at the Law Library. He was the one that never came back to let them out.

The hairs on Doc's neck stood on end. This was peculiar. There was something strange going on here. Guards didn't do random searches on Saturdays. Now the same guard appears to shake down his cell. Something was fishy.

Doc felt strange vibes and he was looking around.

The first guard went to Farmers bunk and lifted up the mattress to look under it and just fingered around Farmer's toiletries; however, the other portly guard went straight to Doc's bunk and pulled the mattress off and was throwing Doc's things onto the floor without even looking at them. When he got to Doc's legal papers he started going through them meticulously and methodically. It was as if the guard was looking for something specific. Doc knew that guards weren't allowed to even look at prisoner's legal work; but if he said something, he would just be told they looking for contraband. That was always their ace in the hole phrase, which allowed them to pretty much do whatever they wanted. Just then one of the prisoners watching from the dayroom yelled out what Doc had been too timid to do.

"Hey! You can't be doing that." screamed the old black man. *"I see what you are doing and I am going to file a grievance on your ass. Courts say, you can't even touch a man's legal work and you sure can't look at it."*

The wing guard told the old man. *"Pipe down."*

"Oh, hell no." the old black man yelled back. *"I want some rank down here right now."* Rank was prison vernacular for an officer of Lieutenant or above. If one of them had to come down, they would have to write up the incident in order to document the facts of the case and why they were called. There would be a paper trail.

"It ain't your cell, old man. You ain't got no standing in this search. You can't get anyone down here." said the wing guard.

Doc had overheard the old man and the guard's bantering and realized that the old black man was right. The only person who could do anything was Doc.

"Excuse me, wing boss." Doc said politely. *"I would like to have some rank come down. I believe that my rights are being violated by that officer. He isn't allowed to go through my legal papers."*

The portly officer was alerted by his partner that the prisoner was requesting rank. The guard took Doc's legal file and turned it upside down completely emptying all of its contents all over the floor. It would take hours and hours to put it all back together properly. That was his final gig at Doc before he left.

"Can I still get some rank down here?" asked Doc to the wing boss.

"What for? Ain't nothing going on now. Maybe if you would have said something earlier." Said the guard. *"Now there ain't reason for me to call anyone."*

He put Doc back into the cell and locked the door behind him.

"Oh my goodness!" said the wing boss mockingly and with feigned surprise. *"Your cell is out of compliance. If you don't have all the stuff off of the floor in five minutes, then I am going to have to write you a case."*

Doc was fuming mad. They just fucked with people because they could. Guards like the wing boss were just the typical sadistic petty bastards who didn't ever progress past high school football and had usually knocked up some cheap girl after prom. Guards like him soon realized they were now the uncool ones left behind with a screaming baby, a fat wife and no future.

They were the bitter ones, and they always landed in Texas prisons, either on one side or the other.

Doc knew the portly guard had not come just to fuck with him for having a free world pen or an extra sheet. He had a purpose and the surprise search was just his cover. Since all of his papers had been unceremoniously dumped into the floor Doc couldn't be sure exactly what he was looking for.

But he sure had a good idea.

*****

Officer Sinclair marched doggedly to his car. His shift was over, and he was pissed. At this rate of progress, he was never going to get out of this south Texas hell hole.

Chapter 43

The stoner was half-baked from the 'chronic' that he had fired up with some gnarly dudes out on the commons. Now he had a raging case of the munchies and couldn't wait to graze on the dollar menu at the first fast food burger joint on his way home. Everything sounded great to him right now.

"Excuse me, man," said the guy working on a truck tire. *"Can you help me out here for a sec?"*

"Righteous ride, dude." said the Stoner looking at the big SUV *"I love the camo paint job."*

"Thanks, man, I did it myself." said the old guy with pride.

"What do you need?" asked the Stoner.

"Can you just hold the wheel steady while I loosen the lug nuts?" asked the old helpless looking guy. *"I just don't have the strength that I used to have in these old hands."*

"No problem, pops." said the stoner as he put his bag on the ground and grabbed the big mud tire; not noticing that the enormous tire wasn't even

279

off the ground.

"Thanks," said the man, *"my name is Jonesy. What's yours?"*

"Pete" said the stoner.

"Really? You're 'the' Pete Parris?" asked the old man.

"Yeah, dude, how did you know?" asked the surprised stoner, but the old guy's response came in the form of an electric shock to his rib cage. Everything in Pete Parris' head went haywire. His eyes crossed as his vision disappeared and he lay writhing on the pavement.

He never felt the two strong hands of the old man grab him and toss him into the back seat of the camo SUV.

*****

Pete Parris woke up in hazy fog, which wasn't an unusual thing for him. He realized immediately that he was naked and tied to a bed.

'Certainly not the first time', he thought.

However, the duct tape was something new and it was making it difficult to breathe.

'Damn that 'chronic' must have been some good shit.'

He shook his head to clear the cobwebs. The room slowly came into view. He didn't remember a thing about how he got here or who he had come home with. Whoever it was had a pretty crappy place, even by his low standards.

He had been going pretty heavy on the hydroponic chronic ever since his roommate had dropped him two hundred dollars in order to use his I.D, but for the life of him, he couldn't remember anything about how he got here. He looked around the place as much as his neck would let him. It looked like a hunting cabin. A really run down hunting cabin, a hunting cabin that no one had bothered to clean for a decade.

'What the hell am I doing here?' he asked himself.

As he surveyed the ramshackle hovel more closely, he didn't see anything that looked feminine. No clothes. No drapes.

Nothing.

His mind was racing now.

'Oh fuck!' he thought as he suddenly remembered the strange old man with the flat tire.

He knew he had been high, but he hadn't ever been so high that he had turned gay. He had woken up with some pretty ugly chicks in the day but never a dude, especially, some old fat dude with stubble. Even if he were as sausage smoker, he knew he could do a lot better than some decrepit old geezer with a pot belly beer gut.

'I have to get the fuck out of here.' Pete told himself.

He clinched his butt cheeks to check to see if anything disgusting had been done to his anus while he was unconscious.

Everything felt normal.

He didn't have much experience to go on in that area. The only reference that he had was when some gothic chick had managed to surprise him with a sudden finger up there one time during sex. That had been quite a bit more than he was comfortable with.

He felt immensely relieved because he knew that anything the size of a baby's arm shoved up inside of him repeatedly would have left him stretched out and in agony. He felt alright and everything seemed to be normal except for the fact that he was strapped to an old chair frame with duct tape over his mouth. There wasn't any padding or fabric. He was lying on top of crisscrossed metal straps. The cold hard metal cut into his back and buttocks.

'Who in the world would buy something this uncomfortable to sit or to sleep on, especially in a shack like this?' He thought. 'This was the most uncomfortable chair that he had ever sat in.'

It was awful.

"I trust you are comfortable" came the male voice from somewhere behind him.

"Ha! Ha! Dude." said Pete feeling more than a little embarrassed at being naked in front of some other dude. *"Who the fuck are you?"*

"Don't you remember?" said deputy Jones as he came into Pete's view.

"Dude, I don't know what's going on or what happened, but I'm not gay and this isn't cool at all." Said Pete. He couldn't help notice how diminutive his manhood was as it lay exposed and limp.

Not his most manly moment in life.

Jonesy started cackling. *"I ain't gay either boy, but if I was, I would have definitely already popped the cherry of that sweet little ass of yours. It looks as pretty as a little girl's."*

Pete was beginning to get more than a little nervous. If this guy wasn't some fag, then why the hell was he tied naked to the metal chair?

The cabin door flew open. Darkness filled the open space and Pete knew he was about to find out why he was here.......a few minutes later, warm piss began to run down his leg and he passed out.

Chapter 44

Voice mail. Voice mail. Voice mail.

Guy tried calling Lola, Jewels and finally his roommate, Pete, but no one was answering their phones. Guy couldn't ever understand why people had cell phones but then couldn't seem to answer them. It didn't make any sense.

'What was the purpose of having a cell phone then?' he asked himself in frustration.

He was a bit cranky this morning. He had paid thirty dollars for a motel room and ended up having to sleep in the tub. Dion still didn't have a place to stay after her performance, so she slept in the bed that Guy paid for. She had told him that he could sleep there too, but there was no way he could ever explain that.

Plus he was scared to death of Dion. She was one big dude.

He had started out on the floor, but it was stained, filthy dirty; and there were things crawling around on it in the dark, so he had ended up in the tub with a wet leg from the dripping faucet and a crick in his neck from lying in it wrong.

It was almost check out time and Guy needed to get on the road. He needed to get home and tell Jewels everything he had found out. He missed Lola. He just wished he could talk to her at least. He realized he needed the solitary time on the road to figure out what he was going to tell her.

Dion was finally up, and no one who saw him now would ever believe that the creature peeing in the bathroom could ever be the stunning diva from the club last night. She was the Beauty and the Beast both rolled up into one.

Guy stuffed his phone into his pocket and found a card in it with Blake's telephone number on it. Blake had been really nice. And normal, however, his boyfriend who had been in the amateur drag show, was a little too friendly in Guy's opinion.   He had introduced himself as Jacky Orgasm.

"Or you can just call me Jacky O! Oh! Oh!" he said while mimicking an orgasm in his best Marilyn Monroe imitation.

Guy was more than a little taken aback by the aggressively forward Jackie O because he had flaming red hair that was tightly curled and kinked just like Jewels'. It was scary how Jacky looked so much like Jewels.   He even wore the same color of nail polish and lip stick. Guy couldn't take his eyes off of Jacky. And Jacky couldn't seem to keep his hands off of Guy.

The more Jacky drank, the more handsy she got with Guy's thigh. Guy had to remind Jacky more than once that he was straight and had a girlfriend. Guy looked over to Blake for help, but Dion had him out on the dance floor gyrating to trash disco from the 1970s.

Jacky O ended up winning the drag contest with her torchy rendition of Little Red Riding Hood by Sam the Sham, which distracted her long enough for Guy to escape the groping grip of her red painted nails. Dion had broken her heel and was ready to leave right after she awarded Jacky O. with the traditional tacky tiara emblazoned with a blue poodle created out of rhinestones.   One would have thought by the tears running down her cheeks that Jacky O. had received one of the crown jewels of England.

Guy would not forget this night for as long as he lived.

Nor would he ever be able to forget the grizzly creature coming out of his bathroom.

"I don't mean to rush, but I have got to get on the road." said Guy. *"Check out is in an hour, so you can take your time and just turn the key in when you leave."*

"Darling," said Dion in his silky but husky voice, *"you have been a perfect gentleman. Your little girl is one lucky lady."*

Guy stood in the open doorway. He couldn't believe it, but he had grown kind of fond of Dion and was a little sad that he was leaving. The past twenty four hours had certainly been some of the most entertaining of his life. That was for sure.

"Thanks for everything" said Guy.

And he actually meant it.

Dion clutched his hand to his chest and Guy could see that he was tearing up. He may have been big, but he was sensitive. Dion walked over and picked up Guy's bag and walked him to the truck. Guy opened the door, but, before he could get in, he was twirled around and was suddenly thrust into Dion's chest and held there by the drag queen's enormous arms. Guy was about to pass out from lack of oxygen when he was suddenly released.

"Thank you for treating me like a lady by being such a gentleman." Dion said with tears in his eyes. *"It's been a long time since I have been treated so well. Thank you!"*

Guy was at a loss for words and stood there in awkward silence.

"Well, I gotta get going." he said. *"But who knows, maybe we will run into each other again someday."*

As he drove out of the motel parking lot, the door to room 9 and the curtain in room 15 closed at the same time.

*****

"What are you looking at?" asked Blake as he came out of the bathroom towel drying his hair.

Caught by surprise Jackson spun around.

"Nothing." he said.

"Really?" said Blake sarcastically. *"Then why do have that guilty look on your face? Could it have something to do with why you closed the curtain so fast?"*

285

Blake walked over and peaked out. There was nothing going on in the motel courtyard. He was about to close the plastic lined floral curtain and walk away when the flash of brake lights from a truck caught his attention as it pulled out and turned onto the street. Before Blake could get a look at the driver, the blue Chevy had disappeared behind some buildings and was gone.

Blake turned around. *"Who was in ..."* but Jackson was no longer there. From behind the closed bathroom door, he heard the sound of running water as Jackson started the shower.

*****

The Pitt was a small diner that served big plates of greasy food for only a small amount of money. The place was packed as Blake and Jackson finally got a couple of stools at the counter.

"Oh my God!" yelled Jackson, as he snatched up the local paper that had been left on the counter by the previous patron.

Blake looked over to what Jackson was looking at. The headline read in large bold letters, 'Twilight Rapist Strikes Again'.

"It can't be the same one." said Blake dismissively. Jackson had been obsessed with the Twilight Rapist back home. Every day he would go on and on about what he read in the paper and what his theory was about who the rapist was and why he only chose elderly victims. Every day he had a new theory, and every day it was wilder than the last. Blake let it all go in one ear and out the other.

"Oh yeah?" snorted Jackson derisively. *"It says here that he started a month ago here."*

"So?" said Blake as he sipped the fresh squeezed orange juice the waitress had delivered. *"That doesn't mean anything."*

"Well, Mr. Smarty Pants," Jackson said as he took a piece of bacon from Blake's plate, *"if you had ever bothered to listen to what I had tell to you, you would realize that it was exactly a month ago that the rapes suddenly stopped in Prickley Springs."*

"That doesn't prove that it was the same guy." said Blake as he stuffed a fork full of chicken fried steak and eggs into his mouth.

"Oh, and I guess it is just a coincidence he only rapes elderly women and is described as a pudgy or doughy fellow. That is the same description they gave in Prickley Springs. It has to be the same guy!" Exclaimed Jackson excitedly.

Blake had to admit that the timing of the rapes, the age of the victims and the description of the guy were a little too coincidental. Maybe Jackson was right.

Blake looked over at the paper and saw the photo of an old Jamboree motor home. *"Wait a minute."* Blake said as he pulled the paper away from Jackson. *"I know this RV. It was at the prison yesterday. Nice old couple. I parked next to them. Their daughter and I went in at the same time."*

Jackson was about to jump out of his seat. *"What! You know the victim?"*

"Yeah. After we got finished with our visitation, the daughter offered me a cold drink and introduced me to her folks."

"What were they like?" asked Jackson.

"My grandparents." Stated Blake. *"They were a sweet old couple that were still in love. She even gave me a homemade cookie. Oatmeal raisin."* Blake shook his head. *"The poor sweet lady."*

"It says here that he ordered her around like some drill sergeant as he did disgusting things to her in the camp shower." said Jackson as he read from the paper. He dropped the paper and looked over for more bacon on Blake's plate. *"You know, wouldn't it be weird if it turned out to be a prison guard or somebody like that?"* Jackson threw a half piece of bacon into his mouth and went back to the paper.

Blake stopped mid chew.

Until this moment, he thought Jackson was just a little batty over the whole Twilight Rapist thing, but when he mentioned a prison guard it made his veins run ice cold. In an instant, everything intersected and came together in his head. The perfect storm of knowledge.

'It was crazy.' He told himself. 'But it all fit perfectly.'

"Are you listening to me?" Asked Jackson. *"You haven't heard a word I said, have you?"*

Blake turned his head and looked Jackson right in the eyes.

Jackson saw the strange look on Blake's face. *"Are you alright, baby? Are you sick?"*

"No." said Blake. *"But you are absolutely right about it being the same person."*

"Oh, I don't know for sure, and no one can possibly know until they catch this creep." Said Jackson. It was so nice of Blake to be supportive of him.

"Oh, I know it for sure." said Blake. *"But, most of all,"*

Blake emphasized the importance of the moment by putting his hand on Jackson's arm.

"We know who the rapist is."

Chapter 45

The door to the little cabin flew open with a crash.

Pete would have jumped completely out of the chair if he hadn't been tied to it.

"Blind fold him now," came the authoritative voice from the door. Pete's eyes were covered. His world became complete and utter

darkness. With his sight momentarily removed, his hearing became more acute in order to make up for the loss of his other sense.

He heard footsteps as they entered the door and shuffled their way across the old wooden floor. Only it wasn't just one set of footsteps. There were lots of them. They seemed to be going in several directions. He tried to keep up with each set, but there were too many for him to follow. He tried to move his head to no avail. He was strapped down tight. He tried to count them all. One, two, three, four----or was that last set the same as number two? Some of the footsteps were heavy, like someone wearing big boots. Another was so light that it was barely detectable at all unless he strained to hear them.

The silver duct tape that had covered his mouth was suddenly ripped away without any warning.

"AAAAAHHHHHHHHH!" screamed Pete Parris. Even though he was completely blind folded, the darkness now filled with shooting stars of light from the sudden pain.

"Well, Mr. Parris, it seems that you have been a very busy man." Said the deep voice with its slow southern drawl.

"What do you want, man?" hollered Pete. *"Whatever it is, I will do it."*

"Now that's the kind of attitude I like, son." said the voice. *"And as long as you tell me everything I want to know, I think we are going to get along swimmingly."*

Pete relaxed. *"Sure, I will tell you anything you want to know."*

"Very good" said the voice. *"What I want to know is why you went to see Dr. Braxton yesterday?"*

"What?" said Pete *"I didn't see no doctor yesterday."*

Pete felt someone grab his right foot and place something under it. It felt like a large brick. It was cool and rough.

"That's too bad, Pete. I thought we were going to get along so well."

said the voice. What he couldn't see was a twenty ounce auto-body hammer with its flat head as it came slicing through the air. It landed with such force that his pinkie toe popped like a grape. The hammer was still ringing from its impact against the concrete, and Pete's toe was completely smashed on the cement brick under the brute force of the unforgiving hammer. Blood sprayed in every direction as Pete let out a curdling scream that echoed for a mile.

"I am just going to let you think about your answer for a minute." Said the voice. *"Jonesy, why don't you prepare our friend for the next question."*

Pete was still sobbing as Jonesy pulled at his left hand. Pete could feel his thumb being put into some sort of metal contraption that encircled it above the knuckle.

Hot tears soaked his face as a cold chill ran down his spine. Why were they doing this to him? His foot had ballooned up and the pressure was excruciating. If he could have seen it, he would have screamed even more since the hammer had broken and crushed more than a dozen bones in his foot causing it to turn purple and black as it swelled to the size of an extremely large egg plant. He would never walk normally again. Each throb made the pain even more and more unbearable. He was sobbing uncontrollably now.

Fear finally overwhelmed his body and released his bladder.

Warm piss ran down his leg, and he passed out.

*****

Guy made it home by evening. He had desperately tried to get hold of Lola on the phone, but all he got was her voice mail. He had hoped she wasn't still mad at him for leaving her behind.

Jewels was his second call.

"How did it go?" asked Jewels without even a perfunctory greeting. *"Did you get it?"*

"Yes." said Guy. He could hear Jewels squeal with delight. *"Sort of."*

"Sort of? What the fuck do you mean 'sort of'?" Jewel squeals of delight had quickly transformed to four letter expletives. *"Either you got it or you fucking failed. Which is it, Canova?"*

"It's on its way." Chirped Guy. *"We will have it in a couple of days, but we may have another problem."*

"Oh great! Another problem?" exclaimed Jewels. *"That's just great because I don't have enough of those. What is my new fucking problem, kid?"*

She was really exasperated, and Guy hated dealing with her when she was in this kind of mood; so Guy just decided to spit it out.

"Someone tried to kill Dr. Braxton."

Jewels didn't miss a beat. She was an instant decision maker. *"Then just have him request to be put on Safe-Keeping."*

"I don't think that is going to solve the problem, boss." said Guy.

"Why not?" asked Jewels.

"Because the person trying to kill him may be one of the guards." He proceeded to tell her about everything he had learned and how he thought that Sheriff Red had someone on the inside of the prison doing his dirty work.

There was silence on the other end of the phone.

Jewels ran it all through her mind. The kid was good. He had accomplished a lot more than she had sent him down to do. She was going to have to think about keeping him around in the future, but right now, she needed to figure out how she was going to keep the good doctor around for a while longer. She couldn't have anyone killing off her golden goose before she got her golden opportunity.

"Good work, Canova." Jewels said. *"Don't worry about it. I will handle it from here. Just get me that report the second you get it.*

Understand?"

"Yes, boss." said Guy. *"I will. I promise."*

*****

Jewels hung up the phone.

It was game time. She was so close. She could not let it all slip through her fingers now. This was why she was the most successful campaign manager in Texas. She was the best. She didn't ever lose.

In fact, it was time to double down. As her daddy always said, "Go big or go home."

It was time to put on some big girl panties and kick some ass.

That's how Texas girls did it.

She picked up her phone and dialed it.

"Yes, this is Jewels Sapphire. I would like to speak to the Senator please."

*****

"Are you alright?" came a soft voice. *"Wake up."*

Pete could feel himself regaining consciousness. The man's voice was so soft and soothing. He tried to open his eyes, but all he saw was darkness. He must still be dreaming. He was having a terrible nightmare about being tortured. Why couldn't he wake up? Why couldn't he open his eyes?

"There you go." said the soft voice. *"He's coming around now."*

"Good" said the deep voice with a slow drawl. *"Mr. Parris you nodded off on me."*

Pete realized it hadn't been a nightmare. He felt the throbbing pain from his right foot. He started to cry.

"Now there is no need for water works here." said the deep voice. *"It time that you start acting like a man."*

Pete tried to still himself and regain his composure. *"Please, I don't know anything."*

"Well, that's what I am going to find out." said the voice. *"Now, I know that your foot must hurt, but I need you to concentrate for a moment. I am sure you can feel the pressure that the good doctor here is applying to you left thumb."* Just then Pete felt something clamp around his left thumb with pressure.

"Pleeeeease" Pete begged.

"As I was saying, I am going to ask you another question and if you do not answer me correctly this time, then the good doctor here will remove your thumb." said the voice matter-of-factly and without any emotion. *"So please think carefully before you answer because I hear that losing a thumb is quite painful."*

"I don't know anything." Pete blubbered. *"You have the wrong guy."*

Pete could hear the man move over near him. *"Mr. Parris, who sent you to Huntsville to see Dr. Braxton?"*

"I have never been to Huntsville. I don't know what you're talking about or anybody named Braxton." whimpered Pete.

"Go ahead, doctor." said the deep voice. *"Slowly."*

"NO!" Pete felt the pressure of something cutting into and completely around the thick flesh of his thumb. *"OH MY GOD! Please. NOOOOO!"*

The cutter was efficient, but it wasn't surgically sharp. Pete's screams for help could not drown out the crushing and crunching of the bone of his own finger as the device moved in to do its job. The pressure it exerted cut through Pete's flesh and began snapping the bone of his largest digit. Pete screamed louder than he had ever heard himself scream before, but it was as if each splintering of the bone was right in his ears. It was as if every nerve in his body was located in his thumb. The pain was intolerable and blinding. Pete screamed on and on. Tears streamed down his cheeks as he begged for mercy and prayed for death, if it would just make the pain end. Then, with a sudden pop, Pete felt his thumb fly off the end of his hand as the amputator finally severed it completely.

With each beat of his racing heart, Pete could feel hot sticky liquid pumping out of where his thumb used to be. Pete felt himself getting dizzy and light headed. He felt himself going into shock.

Then he felt nothing, except the warm comfortable blackness as he lost consciousness once again.

*****

The screams had gone on and on for what seemed like an eternity. She had never heard anything so awful in her life. Someone was screaming for his life. Normally, she would have called the police; but she had seen who had entered the cabin, and she knew the police were already there. She felt sorry for the poor soul, but she was more afraid of what would happen to her if she were discovered. It wouldn't do anyone any good if they both ended up dead. She knew she shouldn't be here, but she wanted to help her man. She wanted to prove to him that she was more than just arm candy. She was ambitious and tough. Only right now, she was scared out of her wits.

What was going on in that cabin?

Guy hadn't let her go with him because it was too dangerous, but she was in this as much as he was. After all, they had tried to kill her too. She knew that Dr. Shaddix was up to something. She had heard whispers about how he was called 'Shady Shaddix' behind his back. He was a slime ball, and she hated working for him. She had plans of her own. If she could get something on him and help Guy too, well that would be great.

Guy treated her like gold. They had both talked about how they wanted to get out of Lloyd County and live real lives in some place glamorous like Dallas or Austin.   Any place but Prickly Springs.

She had heard Dr. Shaddix on the phone talking to someone in hushed tones. He always did that when he was up to something. She thought it might have something to do with what Guy was working on but wouldn't tell her. She decided to do her own detective work. She would show Guy that she was more than just a pretty face.

She had followed Shaddix using the techniques she had learned from her brother, Santos.   When he was going through the academy, he would use her to practice his following and surveillance techniques. She got to where she was just as good, if not better he was. Nobody suspected a young girl. It was like she was invisible.

Now she really did need to be invisible. The East Texas backwoods was the kind of place where you really had to know how to blend in or even disappear when necessary. She had been hunting out here for years with her uncles and brother. She knew how to step through the tender brush and to use the woods as her camouflage.

Lola crouched into the underbrush and used the natural curves of the terrain to stealthily approach the old cabin.   She had even managed to put together a makeshift gilley sack to help her maintain her anonymity as she slithered and crawled her way towards the cabin.

By the time she got close enough, Shaddix was already inside. There were several vehicles parked outside, including Shaddix's yellow Porsche. She was shocked to see that one of the cars was the personal patrol vehicle of none other than the self-righteous sheriff of Lloyd County, Hardon 'Red' Johnson. There was no mistaking his brand new Cadillac Escalade.   He was the only one who drove such a pimped out patrol vehicle. It was as expensive and ostentatious as any drug dealer's car. It was tricked out with all of the latest lights and decals. There was absolutely no mistaking who vehicle it was.

Lola took out her iPhone and snapped photos of all of the vehicles including a camo SUV that she recognized. It was the same one that tried to run her and Guy off the road after the auction. It even had a new mirror on the driver's side.

The second set of screams had started up, and Lola was really getting scared now. She didn't know what they were doing to the man, but he was screaming for his life. Much more than he had the first time. Lola didn't know how much longer she could endure hearing the man's screams. She was just about to leave when they suddenly stopped.

"Oh Shit!" came a voice from inside the cabin that she recognized. It was Shaddix. *"The son-of-a-bitch just crapped all over the place. Oh, Jesus! I got to get out of here and get some air."*

The cabin door flew open and three figures emerged. Shaddix came out first, gulping the fresh air. The sheriff and a portly man followed. All three stood around and lit up cigarettes. The surgeon general's warning about smoking didn't mean a thing to them.

Lola thought to herself, 'Cigarettes actually seem like the least deadly thing around here tonight.'

After their short break, the sheriff gave instructions to Shaddix and the other man to bring the man outside. The pair disappeared into the cabin and re-emerged with a naked man tied to chair. They laid the man on his side still tied to the chair.

"Jonesy, hit him with the hose." Ordered the sheriff. *"I don't have all night to mess with this piece of shit."*

The one called Jonesy turned the water hose on and began to spray down the man's posterior, which was covered in his own feces. Then he turned the hose on the man's face until he woke up sputtering and coughing up water.

"Please. Please. I don't know anything." cried the man.

"Mr. Parris." said the sheriff *"It is late, and I am tired of your stonewalling. I am going to give you one last chance."*

Lola watched as Dr. Shaddix put on a pair of blue latex gloves. She had seen him do it a thousand times at the office, but she had no idea what he was going to do tonight. Surely he wasn't going to do any dentistry.

Dr. Shaddix pulled an instrument from his pocket that Lola had never seen before.

"*Remove the blind fold.*" said the sheriff.

As Jonesy removed Pete's blind fold, the sheriff proceeded to talk to him. "*Mr. Parris, you may feel the good doctor here diddling with you. I assure you that he is not just diddling you for fun. I don't know how much you know about farm life or calf season, so let me tell you about what you are fixin' to experience. I assure you that it will be a totally unique experience unlike many men have ever known.*"

"*Are you comfortable? Because the next part might be a wee bit discomforting. You see the doctor is about to use what is called an elastor tool.*"

"*Please, I am begging you!*" screamed Pete.

"*What is that, you ask?*" asked the sheriff, not even acknowledging Pete's plea. "*It is an instrument that we use to stretch a tiny rubber band around the balls of a calf so that he doesn't bleed to death when we cut his balls off.*"

The sheriff gave a nod and Dr. Shaddix place the shiny instrument around Pete's balls as he pulled and stretch them through the metal slats of the chair that he was tied to. Pete was lying on his side, and when Dr. Shaddix released the rubber band, Pete began to bang his head on the ground.

"*Now, now, Mr. Parris.*" said the sheriff. "*I know that it is an unusually tight fit, but you will thank me later.*"

Pete was muttering to the ground over and over as he was sobbing "*I don't know anything. I don't know anything. I don't know anything.*"

"*Mr. Parris, I am not a patient man, so I am going to ask you one last time before I cut your balls off. Who sent you to see Dr. Braxton and what did he tell you on Saturday?*"

Pete began screaming as he had never screamed before. If they hadn't been twenty mile out in the boonies someone might have heard him.

"I don't know any Dr. Braxton and I have never been to Huntsville. I swear. I swear. I swear." Screamed Pete.

The sheriff walked over and calmly picked up the rustiest and dullest looking pair of hedge clippers that Lola had ever seen. He walked back over and stuck them in the ground in front of Pete's eyes.

Pete's saw them and closed his eyes as he began to sob into the dirt.

"I'm going to ask you one more time, son, and then I am going to chop off your balls with these hedge trimmers and feed them to the hogs. Now who sent you to Huntsville?"

Pete just lay there and cried. He didn't even try to answer.

The sheriff was so angry that he stood up and began to kick Pete in the ribs repeatedly. Lola heard them crack all the way over to where she lay hidden.

"Answer me, you little prick." yelled the sheriff, who now had spittle coming out of his mouth. Then without warning, he grabbed hedge clippers from the ground. He walked slowly around to the exposed under side of the chair that was laid on its side and placed the rusty clippers just below the rubber band that was around the man's ball sac. With a firm hand gripping each wooden handle, he brought them together with viciously ferocious force.

Lola had thought the man's screams had been loud before, but she was totally unprepared for the horrific sounds that came out from him as the long blades of the rusty hedge clipper came together with an almost melodic scraping sound as they sliced the man's balls completely away from his body. They dropped to the ground with a thud into the mud puddle of wet feces.

She couldn't believe what she just witnessed. How could someone do something so barbaric to another human being? But the sheriff wasn't finished yet. He picked up the man's severed and bloodied ball sac out of the fecal mud with his bare right hand. In his blue cowboy boots, he calmly walked around as the man continued to scream unrelentingly.

Leaning down, the sheriff opened the young man's jaw with his left hand and shoved the fecal covered balls into the man's mouth to shut him up. However, the sounds of the man's agony didn't completely cease until the sheriff reared back and delivered the coup d' grace with a vicious kick under the jaw with his cowboy boot. The man's jaw snapped shut as his head was violently thrown back, leaving the young victim completely unconscious with his own gonads and feces oozing out of his mouth.

Lola was on the verge of hysterical shock. She had never witnessed anything so graphic and brutal. She lay motionless in her hiding spot; too scared to even cry for the poor bastard.

She knew that it could just as easily be her lying over there.

'Oh my God' she thought. 'We are truly in danger.' She knew that she had to get back to Guy and warn him. But how? She was stuck in this shallow depression in the backwoods with no way to escape.

Shaddix and Jonesy were both visibly disgusted with their hands covering their mouths. They looked as if they were about to hurl. And then Shaddix did.

"Don't just stand there, you two." Said the sheriff as he wiped off his custom made boots. *"It's time to feed the hogs."*

Chapter 46

Lola's mouth was filled with mud.

She lay in the natural depression of the land. The black Texas dirt was all that she had to muffle the sounds of her emotions. She lay there almost all night replaying in her head the violence she had witnessed over and over again.

The sheriff had departed and left his minions to dispose of the young man's body. Shaddix was almost useless to the one they called Jonesy. Jonesy ordered Shaddix around like a peon. It was extremely gratifying to Lola to see her boss treated like a piece of shit. In Lola's eyes that was exactly what he was.

"Untie the body from the chair" demanded Jonesy.

Shaddix timidly moved to the limp corpse and began to do as he was told. Jonesy disappeared around the cabin, and Lola heard the startup of an engine. A large green tractor appeared with Jonesy driving it. He was pulling a very large yellow contraption behind it that said Vermeer on the side. Jonesy maneuvered the machine next to the hog pen. The big animals were stirring with excitement now.

Jonesy dismounted the tractor. He walked around to the side of the yellow contraption and swung around what resembled a bent metal chimney so that it was aimed towards the hog enclosure. The hogs could be heard in the darkness as they rooted and stomped around the pen. The commotion was growing quite clamorous.

"Hurry up, Shaddix." yelled Jonesy as he opened a side panel and pushed a button. The yellow machine started up, and black smoke could be seen in the silver moonlight as it belched and coughed its thick diesel carbon into the silhouette of spindly trees. The racket it made was deafening.

This was Lola's chance to run. To get away undetected. There was no way that they could hear her over so much noise. Lola was frozen. She wanted to move. She knew it was the smart thing to do.

'Get up and run, damn it!' She told herself.

Her common sense was screaming in her head, 'get out of there and save yourself', but her curiosity wouldn't let her move a muscle.

'What were they going to do to that poor guy?' She had to know.

Jonesy stomped over to where Shaddix was struggling to get Pete untied from the chair. *"Move, Shaddix. Let me do it."* Jonesy ordered. Jonesy flipped open his pocket knife with the minutest flick of his wrist. The razor sharp blade sheered right through the wet cotton rope, Pete Parris' naked lump of a body fell to the muddy dirt in a beaten and crumpled heap.

"Grab a leg" ordered Jonesy.

Shaddix silently complied. The two accomplices showed no respect nor compassion for the young man as they dragged him face down through the dirt to the loud and rowdy machine.

Lola looked on in absolute shock as she realized what the machine was and what they were going to do with the boy's body.

Jonesy wrested the body up into the feeder tray and began to push it forward.

"Shaddix, push his feet together." hollered Jonesy.

Even in the silver light of the moon, Lola could see that Shaddix was almost green in the face. He looked as if he was about to vomit at any moment. Shaddix swallowed hard and shoved the boy's smashed and darkened foot into the feeder.

Lola could see that the feeder resembled a tank track. Once it grabbed the foot it began to pull the body into the machine.

Suddenly, the boy began to scream.

'Oh, dear Lord!' thought Lola. 'He isn't dead.'

At the boy's sudden resurrection, Shaddix jumped back several feet and landed on his ass, yelling and screaming in fright. Jonesy, however, barely flinched as he shoved the boy's left foot into the feeder, too.

The boy began to scream even louder as the wood chipper began to literally eat away at him. Lola began to see chunks of bloody meat and bone fly out of the spreader nozzle. To Lola it was as if time was moving in slow motion. She noticed every little detail as if it was under a microscope.

As the fresh carnage of meat rained down over them, the hogs erupted into a feeding frenzy. A moist red spray began to fill the night air as it too was ejected from the spout. Pete Parris could feel the blades sawing and ripping away at his body as the feeder pulled him all the way into the chipper. It had only lasted four seconds, but to Pete Parris it was the rest of his life.

The last thing he saw was Jonesy waving good-bye to him as he was churned and chopped into savory slop for Big Bertha and her babies. The hogs feasted and fought over the fresh flesh. Everything down wind was covered with a light coat of red mist as tiny droplets were carried by the night air.

Jonesy turned to leave, but stopped. He stooped down to pick something up from the ground. He looked at it for a second. Lola knew instantly what it was.

"Here, you forgot something." chuckled Jonesy as he tossed the boy's severed ball sac and gonads into the chipper.

Tiny chunks flew out the back instantly.

*****

"What time is it?" asked the voice on the phone.

"Son, when I call you, it doesn't matter what time it is." said the sheriff.

Ernie perked up. *"Yes, sir."*

"Did you find it?" asked the sheriff. There was no small talk or pleasantries.

"No, sir." said Officer Ernie Sinclair *"It wasn't there. He had already sent it out. But I intercepted it. He gave it to one of my trustees to put in the mail for him. All it cost me to get it was an extra chow tray and a cup of ice."*

Ernie Sinclair snickered at his own clever victory.

"Good! Said the sheriff. "Then you need to finish what I sent you down

there to do and you need to do it quick. I don't care if you have to do it yourself. Just make sure he is dead. Do you understand?"

"Yes, sir." replied Ernie.

*****

It was four thirty a.m., when the doorbell rang.

Guy jumped up off of the sofa and ran to the door.

"Lola, where have you been." yelled a concerned Guytana Canova. *"I have been trying to call you all night."*

Lola was standing there sobbing. She ran into his arms. Guy held her tightly and immediately felt deep remorse for yelling at her. *"I am so sorry, baby, I didn't mean to yell at you, but I was so worried about you."*

He pulled her in the house and closed the door. For the first time he noticed that she was filthy dirty.

"Are you alright? Why are you crying." he asked.

She just continued to sob into his chest. He had never seen her like this, but holding her felt right. It felt like the most natural thing in the world. He loved her with all of his heart and soul. He wanted to hold her forever, but he needed to find out why she showed up at his place in the middle of the night covered in dirt and filth.

"Honey, what happened? Why are you so dirty?" he asked as he wiped her face. *"And what is all this red stuff on you?"*

Lola jerked away from him and ran to the bathroom to look in the mirror. She began to tear off her clothes as she jumped in the shower. The water ran off of her body carrying all of the dirt and blood down the drain. Guy finally wrapped a towel around her and carried her to his bed.

He slipped her under the sheets; but before he could cover her, she reached up and pulled him into her.

It had been the most intense and passionate love making that Guy had ever experienced. The love they shared was pure and raw.

After they both had given everything they had to the other, they fell asleep without saying a word.

'Explanations could wait until later.' Guy told himself.

Chapter 47

Jewels entered.

Yes, she entered like a tornado.

The office was already ablaze with activity.

Jackson was sitting at his desk as she passed. *"Tea. Please."* she said.

Moments later Jackson entered with a hot cup of sweet tea. Jewels put the Limoges cup to her mouth. No one made hot tea as well as Jackson. It was heaven in a cup.

"Battle dress? On a Monday?" Snarked Jackson. *"What's his name?"*

"I don't know what you are talking about?" said Jewels coyly.

"Oh, really?" Jackson retorted sarcastically. *"Let's see. We will start with a pair of Valentino four inch yellow patent leather pumps. Plain enough for office, but just high enough to be a little slutty. Price, six hundred and ninety five dollars."*

Jackson smugly looked Jewels up and down with his eyes. *"Next, a small Va-Va Voom embellished glam lock shoulder bag. Also in yellow and made by Valentino. Price, three thousand forty five dollars."*

Jackson was on a roll as he circled Jewels standing stoically with her fine French porcelain cup of tea. He slid his finger up to her jacket lapel and continued his couture fashion parlor trick.

"Then we have a seductive little number here in the form of a vintage Coco Chanel black and white hounds tooth wool suit jacket, complete with a classic matching pencil skirt. Price, over six grand, if you could find one, since they are no longer made."

Now Jackson really threw in some theatrics as he whirled around Jewels' back and popped up at her right hip. *"But, me thinks the lady has altered her fair outfit by raising the hem line just a tad, in order to fit her personality. The suit ensemble says, I am ready for business, but the raised hem clearly announces that you must be at least this tall to ride this ride."*

Jewels gave Jackson a smoldering glare. He was a savant when it came to women's designer fashion. She was more than a little impressed by his exact knowledge of her outfit, but she would rather step on her own lip than give him the satisfaction of seeing how dazzled she was with his encyclopedic knowledge.

"And last, but not least, one magenta colored ruffled silk blouse that, alas, must pull double duty as it titillates and teases the intended male victim with flashes of fair and freckled cleavage while simultaneously concealing the blackened heart of its master." Jackson derived great joy at badgering Jewels about her cold lust of the opposite sex.

"What?" Jewel spat out sardonically. *"No designer or cost? You are losing your touch, Mary."*

Jackson inhaled loudly at the affront. He couldn't believe that she would challenge him so mockingly. He removed his faux glasses with a flourish and looked her dead in her eyes. *"Neiman-Marcus. Private label. From the second floor of their flagship store in downtown Dallas. Three hundred and eighty nine dollars."* And then because she called him Mary, Jackson derisively threw out, *"Cruella."*

"Ha! Wrong." Jewels spouted. *"It was two sixty at Last Call, bitch."* And with that she stuck her tongue out at him and sat down in her chair.

"So you still haven't said, who the spider is that you are trying to catch in this little designer web of deception that you have wrapped yourself in

today." Jackson said as he sat down crossing his legs in the chair opposite her.

"Well, if you must know, it's Nunya." said Jewels. She looked up to see Jackson's face as he was trying to place the person.

"Nunya who?" asked Jackson earnestly. He couldn't place anyone named Nunya.

"Nunya god damn business who it is, that's who." cackled Jewels.

"Ha, Ha!" said Jackson. *"Well, if you won't tell me, then at least let me fix your hair. You have that FFL"*

"What is FFL?" asked Jewels.

"Fresh fucked look." answered Jackson. *"You can't go out looking for a new fuck, if your hair looks like you just rolled out of bed with the old fuck."*

Jewels' slightly blushed because Jackson was right. She had just rolled out of the sack with Santos.

"Let me get my combs" said Jackson as he skipped out of the office.

Jewels almost spit up tea through her nose when Jackson ran back into the office sporting an enormous embroidered Blue Poodle sash and matching blue rhinestone tiara. As he fixed Jewels' hair he wore the tacky blue regalia and entertained her with stories of how he was now the reigning Miss Gay Blue Poodle.

"I met a mutual friend of ours this weekend" Jackson dished as he worked the comb.

"Oh really, who would that be?" asked Jewels nonchalantly.

"None other than our own Mr. Guytana Canova."

Jewels nearly fell out of the seat. Jackson grabbed her tea cup to keep it from spilling.

"That's just crazy." said Jewels. *"You have to be mistaken."*

"Nope, I had my hand on his thigh half of the night." reported Jackson proudly.

"WHAT!" screamed Jewels. Guy hadn't mention anything about seeing Jackson down there.

"Yep, only he didn't know it was me because I was dressed up as Jackie Orgasm." Jackson struck a starlet pose with his hand near his face as he glanced upward. *"He introduced himself as Pete, but it was Guy."*

"That can't be true. It has to be someone else" said Jewels. *"Guy is straight. I think he even has a girlfriend."*

"Well, he might have a little girlfriend up here." said Jackson as he poked his head around to look Jewels in the eyes, *"but he has a big DARK secret down there in Huntsville."*

"It has got to be someone else." said Jewels. *"Someone else named Pete, who just looks like him."*

"Pictures don't lie." Jackson whipped out his camera phone to show her the photos that he took. *"Our room was right above his and his boyfriend's room".*

Jewels looked at the pictures of Guy with his hand on Dion's hip escorting her into his room and then what looked like a tear filled good-bye complete with very amorous hug at Guy's truck.

"I just can't believe my eyes." said Jewels as she sat stunned. *"She is so big. And black."*

"Honey, ain't that the loving truth." Snapped Jackson. *"You ought to see her up close. He is one big ass girl. Who would have thought that our shy little Guy would have a big black drag queen girlfriend?"*

'Not me.' thought Jewels as she sat there in silence. What was she going to do? It didn't really change anything, except that she would never be able to look at Guy the same way again.

Who would have ever believed that her sweet little Guy would have so many secrets? The old adage was true. Still waters run deep. And silent too, apparently.

"Well, your little Guy has another secret also, which is what I really want to tell you about." Said Jackson.

Jewels saw that Jackson looked serious. *"What is it, Jackson?"*

Jackson took a big breath. *"He was visiting his uncle in prison. They call him Doc."*

"What?" asked Jewels. *"How do you know that?*

Jewels had told Guy that he wasn't to be noticed by anyone, and now she is finding out that he was seen by her assistant; and that he had a black drag queen girlfriend that he partied with all week end. Jewels was about to blow a gasket.

"My boyfriend, Blake, saw him visiting his uncle while he was visiting his brother at the same time" Jackson was telling everything now. *"I don't know how to tell him that his uncle is in a lot of danger without letting him know that I saw him in Huntsville. That would open up a big can of worms. You know I don't believe in outing people if they don't want to be out of the closet. That is his business and not the rest of the world's, but his uncle is in serious danger."*

"Why do you think that?" asked Jewels. She now had Jackson sitting directly in front of her while they held hands. She needed to know everything that he knew.

Jackson told her everything that Guillermo had told Blake about the new guard that tried to kill Doc and how Blake had recognized him from the Lloyd County courthouse as a former deputy.

Jewels was horrified at what she was hearing. Guy had been right. Dr. Braxton was in great jeopardy. She now knew who Sheriff Red Johnson sent down there to do his dirty work. It was real, and she needed to act fast before the new guard succeeded. That made her meeting today all the more important.

"But that's not all." Jackson said. *"The guard that is trying to kill Guy's uncle is also the Twilight Rapist."*

"Oh, c'mon." snorted Jewels. *"Not that nonsense again."*

Jackson knew that she would say that, so he had spent the night pulling every newspaper story there was about the rapes. He showed her all the dates and descriptions and compared them to Deputy/Officer Ernie Sinclair.

Jewels had to admit that Jackson had done his homework, but more than that, he had convinced her that he was right.

Jewels' mind was processing everything she just learned. This was a game changer. If she could keep this under wraps, she would be in the proverbial cat bird's seat at her meeting today. The Gods were smiling on her, but timing was everything. She couldn't have any of it exposed until she could make sure it would benefit her.

This was a chess game, and she needed to put every piece in the right spot for the big check mate.

"Who else knows this?" asked Jewels intensely.

"No one." said Jackson. *"Except Blake."*

"Good" said Jewels. *"Don't breathe a word of this to anyone yet. We don't want to get Guy upset by outing, him and we don't want his uncle to get hurt. I will handle everything."*

"Thank you, Jewels." sighed Jackson. *"That is such a weight off of my shoulders."*

"Don't mention it." said Jewels sweetly as she patted his shoulder. *"It's my pleasure. I am glad to help you anyway that I can."*

Chapter 48

Half a dozen tall and very muscular men in custom made suits exited the trio of black SUV's as they rolled to a stop.   All six men had bulges under their coats and little coils of wire behind their ears. Upon exiting the vehicles, the men spread out and each took in everything around him. Two broke off from the group and entered the building where Jewels was waiting.   They walked right past her as if they were ignoring her but she knew they had examined and evaluated her in the first split second they entered the building. The security sweep was finished in under a minute. They were complete professionals.

"All clear." said the Secret Service Agent into his wrist mic.

Upon his signal Jewels could see the four agents surrounding the middle SUV open the rear passenger door and move into a diamond formation around their protectee.   As he entered the campaign headquarters, the Secret Service men opened up and fanned out to reveal Boyce Braxton, Texas' newest senator. Jewels couldn't help but get a tingle up her spine and between her thighs at the display of such important power.   This was the world she craved to be in. She wanted the power, and she wanted the pomp that went with it.

She wanted the armor plated limos with armed drivers and chase vehicles filled with security men. She dreamed of standing in a big odd shaped government office making life changing decisions. She had dreamed about that kind of life since she was a little girl. She knew in her heart that she was meant for greater things than just getting local yokels elected to office.   She was meant to change the world.   The man standing in front of her could make it all possible, if she played it right today.

"My God, Jewels, you haven't change one bit." boomed Senator Boyce Braxton as he opened up his arms and hugged Jewels. *"You are still the most beautiful woman I have ever laid eyes on."*

Jewels was more than a little taken aback. She hadn't expected him to be so friendly. He was good. He was using all of his seductive charm to disarm her.   And she had to admit it was working. She hadn't expected him to still be so damn good looking.   The man had somehow managed to become even more handsome at forty than he had been at twenty. She had seen photos of him in the papers, but they didn't begin to convey how gorgeous he was in person.

He was still the same sexy Boyce Braxton that exuded charm and confidence.

"Oh, you men lie so easily and quickly." retorted Jewels. *"But I appreciate the compliment."* Jewels knew that she looked stunning, but she wanted Boyce to know that she was a force to be reckoned with. She appreciated his flattery, but she wasn't going to be defeated by it. Today he was going to have to pay her a lot more than just compliments. If he wanted his brother out of prison, he was going to have to give her a seat at the big table.

It was Jewels' turn to use her charms on the sexy senator as she leaned in and pressed her ruby red lips softly against his cheek and her firm breast against his arm. She felt Boyce Braxton stiffen for the slightest moment, but the senator countered with a quick arm around Jewels' lower back and pulled her in even deeper until she felt the pressure of his groin against her hip. She regaled at his touch as she inhaled his intoxicating cologne, L'eau D'issy. They held each other for an extra second, but not long enough to let anyone else know what had just happened between them.

As they pulled apart, they held each other's eyes.

"I see that you still use sex as a tool." Said Boyce as he looked Jewels up and down.

"And I see that you finally learned to use sex as a tool, Senator Braxton. It's about time." retorted Jewels as she took hold of his arm and led him to her office. *"If you had learned how to do that twenty years ago you might have beaten me at the Law Review."*

They shared a laugh. The kind of laugh that only old friends with a common past can have with one another. Rivalries from so long ago seemed trivial now as they sat together as two very accomplished and successful people. The ice had broken between them, and Jewels honestly just wanted to help him out now. She couldn't explain how seeing an old friend could make her feel the way it did. He had made her feel different inside. She felt connected for a change. Even though their past had been tumultuous, it had still been shared. It was a part of both of them. No one else in the world would ever feel the things that she and Boyce did from that time in their lives. She had a commonality with someone for change.

She felt something odd in her heart. She wanted to help him with no strings attached. 'What the hell is going on?' screamed her brain. This was her magic moment. This was what she had worked so hard for. It was within her grasp. Just tell him that if he will make her his Chief of Staff, she will get his brother out of prison.

'Do it you silly bitch!' yelled her brain, but her heart wasn't hearing any of it.

She looked at his face. It was a beautiful face. The kind of face she could look at every day for the rest of her life.

"Jewels, it is great to see you, but you called me last night saying that something was a matter of life and death. I get here today and everything looks great." Said the senator. *"Including you, by the way."*

She took his hand and held it tightly. *"It's your brother."*

"What do you know about my brother?" Boyce's jovial mood was completely erased.

Bentley was Boyce Braxton's Achilles heel. His little brother had been a source of trouble and disappointment with his wild lifestyle and his frequent trips to re-hab. Boyce loved the kid, but he had been forced to distance himself over the past several years in order to avoid being tarnished by his sibling's nefarious exploits. Politics was a game of perception, and Boyce couldn't be tainted by drugs in any form or fashion. He had tried and tried to get Bentley help, but it never stuck. Bentley repeatedly went back to the same old friends and bad habits. It broke Boyce's heart, but he couldn't let the kid's troubles taint his political aspirations and future.

"What is it you want, Jewels?" asked Boyce. *"You are blackmailing me, aren't you?"*

Jewels' heart sank knowing that he thought the worst of her, but she couldn't really blame him, could she? After all that had been her original plan.

"No" said Jewels.

"I haven't spoken to him in over two years. Is he alright?" asked Boyce earnestly. *"I have sent him letters numerous times, but he has never responded. I don't think he wants anything to do with me."*

Jewels saw the hurt in his eyes. *"I think you may be wrong about that."*

"What do you mean?" asked Boyce hopefully.

"His life is in danger." she said plainly. *"As we speak, I believe someone is trying to kill him."*

"What?" Boyce was stunned, but like any big brother, he was ready to come to his little brother's rescue.

Jewels began to tell him everything that she knew. After she was done, Boyce Braxton sat quietly for a moment. Then he pulled his phone out of his pocket.

"Who are you calling?" asked Jewels.

"An old friend." said Boyce.

"A very old friend."

Chapter 49

Doc was sick of smelling sweaty ass.

The Monkey Trap

"Next" hollered the guard as he motioned for Doc to approach.

He took Doc's gym boots from his hand and turned them upside down; banging them together like old chalk board erasers to dislodge any contraband that might be hidden or stuffed inside.

Nothing.

The fat guard threw the black lace up boots onto the floor and grabbed all of Doc's clothes from his other hand. Doc just stood there naked as the obese officer squeezed and search his clothes. The officer smirked at Doc. It was obvious that the guard enjoyed making the inmates stand before him naked and humiliated, but this officer seemed to be enjoying it a little too much.

The officer threw Doc's clothes on the ground and hollered, *"Next."*

Doc bent over and scrambled to pick them all up as fast as he could, but it wasn't nearly fast enough as he fumbled with his boots and clothes. The pervert behind him used the opportunity to brush is cock up against Doc's ass as he moved forward to give the guard his shoes.

Doc hated the constant perversion that permeated every aspect of prison life. Everything was about sex. Doc was constantly bombarded with people overtly, and covertly, trying to use him for their own twisted sexual gratification. They were constantly grabbing his cock or his ass.

A new prisoner moved into the cell next to Doc yesterday. Hammer, as he called himself, had been a real friendly and nice guy. He and Doc had talked through the bars for over an hour getting to know one another.

"Dude, try some of this spread that I just made. It's the bomb." said Hammer.

Doc was always grateful for a new friend, especially one that would share food with him because he didn't ever get to go to commissary. The taste of food that didn't come out of the chow hall was always a treat to him. Doc reached around through the bars and put out his hand.

"Here you go, buddy. Try this." said Hammer with excitement.

The Monkey Trap

But all Doc got was a hand full of Hammer's slimy wet cock. Apparently, Hammer had been in the next cell jacking off during the entire hour of conversation. Doc was disgusted and drew his hand back as if it had been jabbed with a red hot poker. It was covered with Hammer's white gizz. Doc was disgusted. Inadvertent globs of thick and sticky sex yogurt dripped from the bars and slid slowly down the wall.

Now Doc had another pervy getting his jollies by rubbing up against him as he was trying to go to the gym. The onslaught was never ending.

With his new physique Doc could have turned around and beat the crap out of the guy, but discretion was the difference that kept him out of lock up. So Doc shot through the gym door and redressed next to the abandoned ping pong table with his back to the wall.

"About time you got here." said Joey Flowers as he walked up. *"Why are you over here?"*

"Just protecting my ass from the damn perverts." said Doc.

Doc looked forward to his workouts with Joey. They were his mental escape from prison. Joey wasn't like the other inmates. On the outside he was big and tough. He looked mean as hell and had huge muscles; but when it was just he and Doc, Joey was silly and extremely funny. Doc liked him because he treated him like a real friend. It sounded funny, but he wanted Doc for his mind and not his body.

"Well, come on. We'll work on upper body today" said Joey. *"Maybe we can get them to start looking at your chest instead of your ass."*

"Ha. Ha." retorted Doc as he hopped on one leg to put his boot on. *"You really think it's funny, don't you?"*

"Yep, I kinda do." snickered Joey. *"Just as long as it is happening to you and not to me. Besides, if some guy was hitting on me or grabbing my ass, Casino would lose his fucking mind."*

"Is someone touching my celly's tushy again?" said Farmer as he walked up and slapped Doc on the ass as hard as he could.

The Monkey Trap

"Yeee-owwww!" screamed Doc as the slap reverberated through the gym.

Joey and Farmer laughed until their sides hurt.

"You could have warned me that a crazy person was sneaking up on me." said Doc to Joey as he rubbed his butt.

"Are you kidding," snorted Joey through his laughing *"I wouldn't have missed that for the world."*

"I am heading out to shoot some hoops." said Farmer *"Y'all wanna join me?"*

"I gotta spot our boy here on the weights first," said Joey *"but I might be out there in a little bit after I make him work up a sweat."*

"Sounds good. I will be practicing my three pointers, so bring your 'A' game." Said Farmer as he headed out the door.

Joey was true to his word. Doc was sweating like a pig. His dingy white t-shirt was soaked with perspiration and his hair was wet against his head.

Most everyone had finished their workouts and headed outside to enjoy a little sunshine before the steam whistle blew that would signal the end of rec. Joey and Doc were the last two inmates left in the weight room cage. The weight room cage had been constructed so that inmates passing through the gym at other times of the day couldn't steal the weights. Guys would do anything to have weights to work out with in their cells. The most popular thing was to fill plastic garbage bags with water and then tie them inside a modified t-shirt. It was simple and crude, but it could be assembled and disassembled easily to escape detection by the guards.

"Well, it looks like you might have done a little bit of good today." said Joey as he punched Doc's left pectoral muscle. *"How about we go shoot some hoops with your celly in the sunshine?"*

Doc thought about it for a moment. *"I think I will just stay here and do a few more reps."*

"Okay, suit yourself," said Joey. *"But you are going to miss you celly crying like a little bitch when I put the whoop ass on him on the basketball court."*

"I think I can live without seeing that." said Doc as he walked back to the bench press.

"Don't hurt yourself." said Joey as he went out the door. Doc laid down on the old torn bench. It had been covered repeatedly with old towels and duct tape in order to make it usable. The weight bar sat in its cradle with sixty pounds on each end. It was plenty of weight for Doc to cool down with.

Doc grabbed the bar and took a big breathe before he lifted it up and out of the cradle.

"Eight.....Nine.....Ten." Doc counted as he finished his first rep.

Doc allowed his muscles rest to for one minute just like Joey had taught him before he lifted the bar and began another repetition.

"Eight....Nine..." this time Doc was feeling the burning in his biceps as he struggled to lift the weights up into the cradle arms. *"and.....ten."*

Doc dropped the bar into the iron cradles and let his arms lie completely out to his sides. He looked as if he was ready to be crucified.

A minute later Doc was back at it, except that this time the burning in his muscles came quicker. *"Five...Six...."* Doc closed his eyes and gritted his teeth as he struggled to push the weight straight up.

"Seven....Eight....." Doc was pushing as hard as he could. His eyes were closed, his jaw was clinched, and he was pushing against the ground with his toes in order to arch his back. The weight was fighting back against his arms when suddenly the weight came crashing down against him with a powerful push.

In an instant Doc felt the weight of the barbell slam down against his chest with so much force that it immediately sent all the air out of his lungs. Doc's eyes opened wide with fright, because what he saw caused him to panic.

Standing over his head looking down on him was the pygmy. His eyes were yellow and filled with hatred. The pygmy was holding the bar bell with both hands and pushing it against Doc's wind pipe. Doc flailed as he tried to breathe, but pressure against his wind pipe was too much for him to get any air through it.

Doc began to thrash about with his feet trying to bring them up to push the squat bodied pygmy off of him.

"Hold his legs." yelled the pigmy.

Doc felt someone grab his knees and pin them down. Doc fought to free them, but the person only leaned on them harder and with more weight. Doc was stretched out so that he could no longer put his feet up on the bench nor use his legs as leverage to pry himself loose. Now it was almost impossible for Doc to keep the bar from crushing his larynx. Doc's neck muscles were completely stiffened and the rigid cartilage on both sides of his windpipe was all that was keeping his life from being crushed out of him.

Doc's strained and tired arms were burning like someone was holding a blow torch to his biceps. Doc's vision started to blacken around the edges and stars were shooting from the back of his eyes.

Suddenly Doc felt the pygmy ease up a miniscule amount and Doc gulped as much oxygen as he could in that split second.

"No. I don't want you to die yet, mutha fucka!" hissed the pygmy. *"You is got some major payback coming for what you did to all my brothers."*

"We ain't got time for this bullshit" said the voice from the other end. *"Just kill him and let's get the fuck out of here."*

Doc recognized that voice. It belonged to a white man. And not just any white man. It belonged to the guard that ransacked his cell. It belonged to the guard that left him in the law library. It belonged to the guard that shook him down coming into the gym today. It belonged to the person that was holding down his legs right now.

"You gonna die, bitch," said the pygmy, *"and the last thing that you are ever going to see and taste are my hairy black nuts."*

The pigmy raised his left leg and propped his foot on the cradle's crossbar. Doc was now looking straight up the open leg of the pygmy's oversized and baggy gym shorts. The smell of rancid crotch sweat nauseated Doc and made breathing even more difficult than it already was with the bar bearing down on his throat. The pigmy swayed his hips from side to side. The fleshy pendulum of Pigmy's dark and wrinkled sac swung menacingly back and forth. With each pass of the offensive black sac, Doc felt the light brush of short and curly pubic hair on his lips. If he wasn't already choking to death, the putrid aroma of the pygmy's black stinky unwashed nuts would have made Doc gag and vomit.

Pigmy was enjoying every moment of Doc's torment. *"Lick my nuts, bitch!"* Pigmy commanded. Doc tried to turn away, but pigmy pushed down on the barbell causing Doc's mouth to open wider as he was being choked harder. Pigmy dropped the smelly sac of his sweaty scrotum into Doc's open orifice.

The taste of salty sweat covered Doc's tongue and he began to squirm violently to escape the hellish torture, but the more Doc fought the more the pigmy freak seemed to like it. The pigmy was now sitting on Doc's face and Doc's nose was now lodged into the pigmy's dirty rectum.

The barbell was choking him and now he was being suffocated, too. It was unlike anything that Doc had ever experienced in his life. Doc momentarily thought that he should just let go of the bar and let it crush his life away in order to end the terror, but the pigmy felt Doc release the pressure on the weight bar. He countered immediately by reversing his grip. He wasn't going to let Doc deny him his revenge. He had waited too long for this day. He was going to relish every moment that he could and make the torture last as long as possible before he killed Doc.

The pigmy began to bounce up and down in Doc's face. Doc was helpless to fight back. The pigmy was now maniacal in his abhorrent torture. With each bounce Doc's nose was engorged into the pigmy's sweaty and dirty anus. Doc felt fecal dingle berries inside of his nostrils. The bouncing continued unabated, and Doc could now feel pigmy's penis banging on his chin with every bounce.

Doc was in agony. His throat was ulcerated and sore. He was gagging on a sweaty black ball sac and being simultaneously asphyxiated by nasty man-ass.

Doc's will to live was gone. He no longer wanted to survive.

Doc prayed to die.

*****

"And.....swish!" boasted Farmer as the basketball sailed through the rusty rim. *"Nothing but net, bitch!"*

Joey was soaking wet with sweat and heaving in the blazing sun. Joey had more muscle than Farmer, but anyone could see that Farmer had more wind. Farmer could run up and down the court all day in the heat and still never get tired.

Farmer was sinking the basketball into the net before Joey could even get past the half court line. Joey was getting a proverbial beat down on the old asphalt court.

"Joey!" screamed a voice.

"Casino?" Joey was surprised because Casino rarely came to rec yard. *"What are you doing here?"*

"Come quick. Your friend Doc is in trouble." Said Casino as he turned around and began running back to the gym. *"They are trying to kill him."*

Joey and Farmer began to sprint as fast as they could. With his head start, Casino reached the door first and held it open as Farmer darted through it followed immediately by Joey.

The Monkey Trap

Farmer saw Doc pinned down on the bench press, but what was more shocking was that one of Doc's attackers was wearing gray. He wasn't prepared for that. He had assumed that the attackers would all be other inmates. Fighting with a guard was a serious offense. In most instances, a fight between an inmate and a guard ended with the inmate either dead or in the infirmary after the guard's buddies showed up.

While Farmer was slowed by a moment of slight hesitation. Joey was not. Joey showed no such compunction as both of his feet left the air and he dived into the pigmy. Joey's fist struck the pigmy's face causing his head to snap back in a grotesque and unnatural position. A loud pop of dislocating cartilage could be heard as Joey's hardened fist connected with the over-sized and protruding mandible that was the pigmy's jaw. Joey's momentum carried the pigmy completely off of Doc's face and into the rusted steel mesh that was the wall of the work out cage.

The pigmy began screaming in agony as he crumpled to the floor and felt the sagging looseness that used to be his jaw. Any words he tried to say just came out as unintelligible gibberish. As it swung around loosely below his face, his enormous jaw looked even more grotesque than usual.

Joey's adrenaline was raging, but he was in control enough to realize that he couldn't kill this pint sized pervert that was sitting on the floor in front of him. The punishment would be that he would never get out of prison; but short of killing that little freak, he could do anything he wanted.

"Here you go." screamed Joey *"let's see how you like it?"*

Joey grabbed onto the steel mesh wall of the cage with his finger tips for stability as he thrust his hips forward banging the black mangled dwarf directly in the face with his cock. The pygmy's head violently thrust back into the steel mesh with a hard thud, only to be rebounded back again into Joey's thrusting cock. Joey continued to cock drive the short thug's nappy head into the mesh wall despite the pigmy's pitiful pleas for him to stop.

"What? I can't understand you?" said Joey sarcastically as he placed his hand to his ear *"But what I think you are telling me, baby boy, is that*

321

you like it rough and raw."

Joey pulled his white elastic prison pants down easily with only a pull of his thumb. Farmer's eyes widened almost as much as the pigmy's at the enormous uncut porn sized penis that had flopped out of Joey Flower's pants.

"Yeah, my little nigga," said Joey *"I am gonna give you what you are looking for."*

Joey grabbed the pigmy's nappy curls in his right hand and the shaft of his huge manhood in his left. Tears of fear cascaded down the pygmy's puffy black cheeks.

"Open wide." said Joey as he rammed his cinematic manhood into the pigmy's broken mouth. All that could be heard was the pigmy's pathetic gurgling for air as he gagged on Joey's junk.

"Karma's a bitch, ain't it?" said Joey. To emphasize his point, he crammed his cock into the pigmy's mouth. *"Choke on it, nigga!"*

Farmer was conflicted. Years of institutionalization in Texas prisons had made him fearful of laying hands on a guard. It didn't matter if they were crooked, wrong or even straight up sadistic, it never turned out well for the inmate; and it damn sure never came out fair in the prison's kangaroo courts. Farmer knew that if he hit this officer that he would never leave prison again for the rest of his life. It was a fair assumption that he probably wouldn't make it out of the gym alive after a goon squad of his buddies showed up, which would be at any instant by his calculations.

"You are going to die today, one way or another." hissed the guard to Doc as he pulled a pepper spray off of his belt and aimed it at everyone. *"Because I am tired of trying to get incompetent fucks like that pigmy and his idiot friends to do it for me."*

"What about us?" said Farmer stalling for time. *"We are all witnesses. You won't get away with it."*

Officer Sinclair laughed. *"Are you fucking kidding me, spook?*

Witnesses?" Sinclair laughed again and looked directly at Farmer. *"There ain't gonna be no witnesses."*

"You can't kill all of us and get away with it." said Farmer.

Officer Sinclair giggled maniacally like a hyena. *"Are you fucking kidding me? I done killed seventeen of those fucking low life Muslims in the law library, and the investigators never asked me a single question."* snorted the guard with confidence. *"All of you are going to die today in a terrible prison fight and I am going to start with your prissy ass first"* he said while staring cold death at Doc.

Officer Sinclair released his grip on Doc's legs and pulled out a homemade shiv. It looked like a million others that were made by prisoners every day to protect themselves.

Farmer needed to delay him for a little longer until the goon squad arrived. Sure they would get beaten, but as long as they didn't touch the guard they wouldn't be killed.

If he could just hold the officer at bay for a few more moments, then they, Doc and Flowers, might get out of here alive today; but that was a big 'If', and it disappeared completely when Doc slammed his knee, suddenly and without warning, straight up into the fat guard's crotch.

Doc was still lying on the bench press as the fat guard doubled over him in agonizing and retching pain. Doc tried to squirm loose, but the guard grabbed Doc by the hair and pulled his head straight back. The shiv was still in his other hand and he aimed it Doc's throat when an explosive concussion filled the gym; causing everyone to grab their ears.

The main door to the prison gym flew open and guards came through it by the dozens clad head to toe in riot shields and sparking electric cattle prods.

"Everyone get down on the ground" came a scream *"NOW!"*

Farmer and Joey hit the ground with ringing still in their ears from the flash bang grenade. They knew the type of beating that they were about to receive. They had seen it done a hundred times, and there was no defense against half a dozen baton wielding goons beating the crap out of you as you lay helplessly on the floor. All you could do was take it and hope that they got tired of swinging before they killed you.

The goon squad came in charging at full speed, but they didn't start hitting Joey nor Farmer. The first goons inside the cage grabbed the officer and dragged him out protesting and screaming. The pigmy was next but all that could be heard were garbled and unintelligible gibberish that sputtered from his broken jaw.

Farmer and Joey laid on the ground untouched.

Farmer looked at Joey and mouthed silently to him. *"Those aren't prison guards."*

Joey just shrugged his shoulders and lay motionless. He too was confused as he watched the men in riot gear drag out the prison guard and the pigmy. The men in riot gear were extremely professional and amazingly efficient. They were physically fit and moved with military precision. They definitely were not prison employees.

A man and a woman emerged through the gym door. Both wore civilian clothes, but the woman wore a stiff pale colored cowboy hat on her head and a very large pistol on her hip.

Officer Sinclair started screaming. *"Thank God, you showed up when you did."*

"Yes, it was." said the man without the cowboy hat.

"They were about kill to me with this" Sinclair said holding up the home made shiv, *"but I held them off with my pepper spray."*

"Really? Well, you must be the bravest son-of-a-bitch that I have ever met then." said the man as he took the pepper spray from Officer Sinclair *"because there doesn't seem to be any pepper spray in here."* He put it up to Sinclair's eyes and pulled the trigger. Sinclair flinched; but when nothing happened, he opened his eyes.

The man in civilian clothes unscrewed the pepper spray container.

"Hmmm," said the man. *"Well, here is your problem right here. Your pepper spray seems to have been replaced by my miniature video camera and microphone."*

"But , but ......" babbled Sinclair.

"Can't think of anything to say, Mr. Sinclair?" asked the civilian. *"That's okay because I am U.S. Marshal Kent McCaslin, and this distinguished young lady in the snappy cowboy chapeau who is handcuffing you right now and who is about to read you your rights is Texas Ranger Sandy Smith."*

Doc had been lying on the floor exhausted and almost comatose from his adrenaline comedown and the flash bang explosion, but despite the fog of war that was in his head, he heard the name that he had dreamed about since he was a teenager.

"Sandy?" Doc said as he raised his head.

"Get your head back down." commanded the riot officer nearest him.

"Sandy is that you?" hollered Doc louder. They would have to kill him before he would let her get away again. *"Sandy!!!!"*

Ranger Smith heard the commotion in the cage before she heard someone calling her name. She didn't know anyone in prison, so who was calling her name? The voice called her name again, but it wasn't just any voice.

It was his voice.

The voice that proposed to her so many years ago.

The voice of the only boy she ever loved

'But it couldn't be.' she thought to herself.

It would impossible. 'Why would he be in a place like this?'

She walked over to the cage. Three men were laid out on the floor, but one had his head up calling her name with tears in his eyes and a cattle prod at his neck.

It was him. It was her man. It was Bentley.

*****

Ranger Sandy Smith had not been briefed on the entire operation. She had been called by her commander in the middle of the night and told to report to the US Marshal's office to assist them in a high priority and sensitive arrest.

"But, Commander, I am deep undercover right now with a biker gang trying to apprehend the Twilight Rapist. Can't you get someone else?"

"No I can't because that is exactly who I want you to arrest." said her Commander.

Sandy was stunned.

He took only a few moments to brief her on the phone but informed her that a well-placed tip from a very important source had come across some with information about the Twilight Rapist in another completely separate investigation. He couldn't give her the details because it involved high political connections and police corruption. She was to keep this completely to herself. He knew that he could trust her. She was his best undercover agent and one of his favorite Rangers.

US Marshal McCaslin had told her she was there because the Governor himself had requested that this be a joint operation. Normally, dirty cops and such are solely the domain of the Texas Rangers, but he had been informed that this particular case had political implications because dirty politicians fell within his purview as the enforcement arm of the federal government.

"Our target is a dirty deputy from Lloyd County posing as a guard. Our information is that he is down here on the orders of Sheriff Hardon Johnson to kill an inmate that might be able expose the "good Sheriff's" corrupt department."

"If it is just a dirty sheriff, then why is the US Marshal's office

involved?" Asked Sandy *"This sounds like it is in the jurisdiction of the Texas Rangers."*

"Yes, it sounds like it, but Sheriffs are a special breed because they are elected officials first and peace officers second." said Marshal McCaslin. *"We think that the official corruption may go even higher, but we don't know who that is yet, which is the reason that you, your commander and the governor are the only ones who know about this. So don't be upset if I can't give you every little detail of the operation."*

"I understand." said Sandy *"Now tell me who you think the Twilight Rapist is and why?"*

McCaslin had told her all of the information that he had obtained from Jackson after he had been called by his boss and the Governor himself.

"The kid did some impressive deductions." Said McCaslin. *"But like half of all cases, it really came down to sheer luck. According to his boyfriend and his boss, he was obsessed with the case, and they just happened to be in the right place at the right time."*

Sandy reviewed all of Jackson and Blake's statements and deductions. McCaslin was right. They were smart and lucky. Most of all, Sandy believed that they were right.

She and McCaslin had developed a plan to switch out Sinclair's pepper spray with one that contained a hidden video camera and microphone in hopes of catching Sinclair in the act of trying to kill an inmate witness for the sheriff. They then planned to use their evidence of his rapes to get him to roll over on the good sheriff and his corrupt cronies in Lloyd County in exchange for not being put into the prison's general population as a rapist and an ex-cop. A man will tell you almost anything in order to stay alive and a virgin. Especially in prison.

At no point was Sandy ever told, nor had she ever asked, who Sinclair was supposed to kill. It didn't seem germane to her side of the operation. After all, she was only there for the Twilight Rapist.

When she saw the man that the Twilight Rapist was trying to kill was her

Bentley, she rushed over to the man that she loved and took him in her arms.

Tears rolled out of her eyes, and Doc sobbed with grief as his soul released all the disappointments and losses he had held on to for all of the years since he had lost her. It had been so long that he was utterly overwhelmed by the site of her beautiful face in this horrible place. She was here, and he knew deep down in his essence that everything was finally going to be okay.

Doc had his Sandy back and love in his heart. All his prayers had been answered.

Hot tears of joy ran down Sandy's face as she clung to Bentley. Her arms and her heart ached while she held the man that she loved on the dirty and smelly prison floor.

Why was he here? And what was she going to do now?

She had more questions than ever, and she didn't seem to have many answers yet.

She did know one thing for sure.

All of their lives were about change in a big way.

Chapter 50

US Marshal Kent McCaslin wasted no time in flipping the fat deputy turned prison guard. Time and secrecy was crucial. Marshal McCaslin didn't know how many stooges the crooked sheriff might have down here. The old goat had been in office for over forty years, so it was a good bet that he had connections and friends all over the state and specifically this prison.

Marshal McCaslin had to act fast before the news of the raid and the arrest got out. There was no way he could take Deputy Sinclair to the

Walker county jail to interrogate him. Sheriff Johnson would be tipped off immediately that his hit man had been captured and arrested. Sinclair would be dead from a suspicious "suicide" by morning, and McCaslin's case would be only a memory.

McCaslin had no other choice but to use this moment in the prison while it was locked down and controlled by his men to interrogate his new prisoner.

"This place is now on lock-down. Nobody moves anyplace. No prisoner, no guard and no civilians are to move anywhere. No calls or anything. In or out. This is a full scale isolation quarantine." yelled US Marshal Kent McCaslin. *"Does everyone understand?"*

Nods and yeses were affirmed by everyone.

"Good. Then let's get started." commanded McCaslin. *"Bring our new prisoners to the cage."*

Farmer, Joey and Doc were brought out and seated on the floor outside the cage. The pigmy, who was still groaning in pain, was taken to the other end of the gym as far away from ear shot, and Joey, as possible.

Former Deputy Sinclair was now handcuffed and seated inside of the cage on the very bench where he had attempted to kill Doc.

McCaslin walked up to Sandy. *"I am sure that there is a lot that you want to tell me, Ranger, about you and that inmate; but right now I have more important things on my mind. I know that you are only interested in the Twilight Rapist. If you can just wait until after my interrogation, I will be glad to turn him over to you; however, you might want to step away so that you won't have to lie about what I am going to do, in case you are ever asked to testify."*

Sandy looked down at the white Stetson in her hand and then to the star on her chest. There are times in a person's life when they are presented with a choice of what is easy and what is right. The easy thing would be to walk away from all of this mess. It was fraught with headache and heartache. She had a good life. She had someone special in it already.

She had put the past behind her. She was a shooting star with Texas Rangers. She was happy. Why would she possibly want to screw up all of that up?

Sandy stood still and stared at McCaslin for a moment. McCaslin stayed silent.

Sandy knew of only one reason.

Sandy Smith put her Stetson on her head and raised her chin. *"I don't think so, Marshal McCaslin. You see, Rangers never take the easy way out. We always do what is right. We can figure out what to tell people later."*

McCaslin smiled. *"Well, then I suggest we go get what we came for."*

*****

Jonesy ran all the way from the new criminal justice center to the old courthouse two blocks away. On his uniform, big 'V's of wet sweat cascaded down from his neck and armpits. His breathing was so labored that he was near collapse as he reached the door of the sheriff's office.

Jonesy wheezed with as much urgency as he could muster. *"Where is the sheriff?"*

"Lord, have mercy, Jonesy. What is the matter with you?" asked Evelyn, the sheriff's secretary, as she jumped up out of her chair. *"Are you alright?"*

Jonesy waved away her motherly concern. *"I have to find the sheriff. Right now!"* exclaimed Jonesy as he slowly began to get his breath back.

"Well, he is over at Clara's Cafe having lunch with Judge Wood" said Evelyn *"but if you are going over there, I suggest you straighten yourself up. You know how the sheriff likes his deputies to look professional."*

Before she could finish admonishing him, Jonesy was gone.

Jonesy ran across the town square and into Clara's. As usual, it was filled with working class ranchers, farmers and county government workers. Clara always had a daily special, but Chicken Fried Steak with cream gravy reigned supreme on most plates. After all, it was Texas.

Jonesy had spotted the sheriff and the judge sitting with two other fellows, but they were all engaged and seemed to be talking to every other table and person around them. They were both elected officials and this was an election year, so schmoozing and glad-handing was done anywhere and everywhere they went.

"Sheriff!" Jonesy wheezed and huffed. *"I gotta talk to you, sir."*

"Lord, son," the sheriff laughed politely to all the people around him. *"Can't it wait? I'm eating lunch."*

"No sir!" said Jonesy *"It's urgent."*

The judge stood up and pushed his chair back. *"If you boys will excuse me for a minute? I think I better go see what the matter is before my deputy here has a stroke."*

All the good old boys laughed at the sheriff's joke and waved him on as they went back to half a dozen different conversations to each other.

"My Lord, Jonesy, what the Sam hell is wrong with you?" asked the sheriff as they stepped outside.

"Sheriff, we got a big problem." exclaimed Jonesy. *"Estelle Unit in Huntsville just went dark."*

"So, that happens all the time down there." Said the sheriff. *"It's probably just a fight."*

"That's what I thought too, so I called my cousin who works down there." said Jonesy. *"He didn't answer and his wife said that she was cut off while talking to him. He was telling her that the Feds raided the place but before he could tell her why they were cut off, and now there is some sort of quarantine lock down by the feds. No calls in or out. They have even jammed all cell phone signals. The few guards that were in the barracks sleeping said that since that time they haven't even been able to get inside nor communicate with anyone on the inside. They also report*

that there are hundreds of inmates stuck outside on the rec yard."

Sheriff Johnson didn't like how this sounded. This was too coincidental. And Sheriff "Red" didn't believe in coincidences. He also didn't believe in taking any chances.

"I don't like this, Sheriff." said Jonesy. *"They are getting too close. If they figure this out, it's only a matter of time before they figure it all out. We have to protect the other thing at all cost."*

Jonesy was loyal and he was right. The other thing was more important, and they couldn't take the chance that anyone might discover it. The sheriff made his decision.

"Alert the others and implement the safe guard plan on my instructions." said the sheriff to Jonesy. *"Call our friends down south, and tell them to expect us."*

"What about Sinclair and Braxton?" asked Jonesy.

"Don't worry about them." said the sheriff. *"Someone owes me a favor."*

"Well, it had better be a big favor if they are going to get inside that prison." Said Jonesy.

"Oh, it is." said the Sheriff 'Red'. *"It most definitely is."*

*****

Former deputy, turned prison guard, Ernie Sinclair, turned out to be tougher than US Marshal McCaslin had expected. Sinclair just sat there in silence. He refused to even answer a single question or admit to anything about Lloyd County or Sheriff 'Red'. He had seen firsthand some of the old sheriff's handiwork when he was double-crossed. It was vicious and messy.

No, this US Marshal couldn't do anything to him that would even compare to what the sheriff would do to him if he blabbed. Sheriff 'Red' had friends everywhere. All Ernie had to do was to hold out until the

Calvary arrived and keep his mouth shut.

He didn't know how they knew about the rapes; but as long as he didn't say anything, all they had was circumstantial evidence. They didn't have any DNA, witnesses nor proof of anything. They had grilled him for hours telling him what happens to ex-cops and rapists in prison. They must have thought he had just fell of the turnip truck because he had been working in a prison for months. He knew that ex-cops and sex offenders were housed separately to insure that nothing happened to them. They thought he was some kind of idiot or pushover.

Shit. All he had to do was sit here and wait them out. He wasn't some fucking punk that they could just threaten into a confession.

'Keep your mouth shut' Ernie told himself. 'They can't do shit to you. Just wait for Sheriff 'Red'. He will take care of everything. He always takes care of everything. They don't know who they were messing with.'

*****

Farmer, Joey and Doc had been sitting outside of the cage listening to it all. Inmates hated sexual predators in prison. Especially ones that preyed on old people or kids. Their life expectancy wasn't very long once the general population found out what they were in for. The State of Texas had instituted a program called Safe Keeping that separated and segregated them away from the general population. Ironically, they put them with the homosexuals and transvestites.

Farmer and Joey were fuming as they heard about what the fat guard had done repeatedly to the little old ladies.

"You sorry piece of shit." Yelled Farmer from his place outside of the cage. *"If I ever get my hands on a slimy pervert like you, I will fuck you up, bitch."*

Every time that Farmer or Joey started yelling out threats, McCaslin had to send Ranger Smith out to quiet them down; but the more they heard, the angrier and more vocally threatening they got. They began to yell out the graphic sexual things they were going to do to him.

Sandy had agreed to stand back and observe while McCaslin did the interrogation. After four hours, she finally noticed that McCaslin's threats weren't having any effect on Sinclair; but Farmer's and Flowers' threats were disturbing him greatly.

Sandy had been sent out several times to quiet them down, but a few minutes later they would start up again with the threats of how they would hurt him.

Every time he heard their voices, his feet would begin to bounce and shake.

"Excuse me, Marshal." said Sandy *"May I have a word with you?"*

Sandy walked Marshal McCaslin out of the cage and across the gym.

Sinclair could see the Ranger and the Marshal in a heated discussion. There was lots of head shaking back and forth. The Marshal was clearly unhappy, but the lady Ranger had prevailed in the argument.

Another man in a suit approached Marshal McCaslin and handed him a weird looking phone. McCaslin listened for a few moments and handed it back to the suit.

"Okay, listen up everyone." commanded McCaslin out loud. *"Let's take a break; and we will let the prison personnel change shifts, but that will be the only movement. Prisoners are to remain where they are. We are still locked down. Is that understood? The only people coming in or going out will be the prison personnel only."*

McCaslin walked back to the cage where Sinclair sat stoically silent.

"Mr. Sinclair, that was the Governor. I have been informed that you are no longer under the federal protection or under my jurisdiction. You will now be in the custody of Ranger Smith."

"Thank you, Marshal." said Sandy curtly and dismissively. *"I will take over now."*

McCaslin turned and walked away dejectedly.

Once McCaslin was gone, Sandy wheeled around to face Ernie Sinclair. Only now Ernie noticed that she had a completely different and more irreverent demeanor.

"Well, well, well." said Sandy as she paced slowly over to Ernie Sinclair. *"It's been a long time since we have seen each other."*

Sandy could see that Sinclair was baffled by the expression of confusion on his face.

"What?" cooed Sandy, as she placed her foot on the bench. *"You don't remember me, Porky."*

With that she shoved the bench over on its side with her boot sending Sinclair crashing to the floor.

Sinclair instantly recognized Sandy now.

"You're that biker bitch!" he exclaimed.

"That's right, Porky" said Sandy as she put her foot on his neck. *"This time I'm not going to be so nice."*

"Fuck you, Bitch!" screamed Sinclair.

Sandy smirked at Sinclair. *"Ohhhh, I was hoping you would say that, Porky."*

Sandy turned and walked to the cage door.

"I have to go make arrangements to transport you and to use the little girls' room. I will be gone for a bit, but don't worry. I am going to leave you some company, so that you don't get lonely." said Sandy. *"Mr. Farmer. Mr. Flowers. Would you two mind waiting in here for a while with Mr. Sinclair?"*

"Oh, it would be our pleasure." Said Farmer as he and Flowers entered the cage.

Sinclair watched as Joey closed the door and both men began to pull their pants down.

Sinclair began to scream. *"You can't do this!"*

Sandy continued to walk away never even looking back as she heard Sinclair's cries.

"HELP! HELP! HELP!" Sinclair screamed repeatedly until a mighty slap silenced him.

"Turn that snow bunny over." said Farmer in his deepest and most menacing ghetto voice. *"I am gonna tear that fat ass up with this big black cock."*

"NOOOOOO!" Screamed Sinclair at the top of his voice.

Joey had Sinclair by both wrists holding him face down over the workout bench while Farmer pulled the fat guard's pants down to his ankles. Farmer spread Sinclair's legs open with his foot and stepped up between them so Sinclair would know the vulnerable feeling of having a violent stranger up so close to him.

"Yeah, snow bunny, you are going like my kind of lovin" said Farmer as he let go of a big stream of saliva that landed on Sinclair's lower back and slid down into his porcine crack.

Sinclair jerked and pulled with all of his might as he screamed in terror for what was about to happen to him.

'Where was Sheriff Red, and why hadn't he been rescued yet?' Sinclair screamed to himself. 'This can't be happening to me.'

"Ummm..." moaned Farmer *"I am gonna enjoy this so much"*

He used his meat shaft like a paint brush to smear the warm spit all over Sinclair's round mounds. Farmer was really dragging it out and torturing the fat prick as much as he could.

Farmer hated sexual predators like this maggot. He wanted to hurt him and hurt him bad. *"Get ready, slime ball."* grunted Farmer as he stoked and stiffened his black shaft. He grabbed it and pushed his purple head through Ernie Sinclair's fluffy butt cheeks.

"I am going to bust that hole wide open." Said Farmer a creepy giggle.

"I am going to rip your ass up so bad that you are going to bleed to death by the time I finish." said Farmer sadistically. *"And if your sick ass does live, then you will never be able to hold your shit in ever again. You will be shitting all over yourself in a diaper for the rest of your pathetic life.*

Then Farmer leaned over Sinclair's back, so that he could whisper chillingly into his ear. *"And every time you do, I want you to remember how you feel right now, you sick fuck, because that is exactly how those grannies felt when your fat ass was on them."*

Ernie felt the pressure of Farmers penis as it touch the pucker of his rectum. *"Oh God! Please no!"* But Farmer pushed on anyway until he felt that special give. He knew that he wasn't supposed to go that far, but this guy and all the others like him deserved it. They deserved to know how Farmer's grandmother and all the others had felt.

"This one is for my granny, bitch!" said Farmer. As he pushed in he felt the rip of Sinclair's ass as it began to split open.

"Okay! Okay! Okay! Please.......Marshal. I will tell you whatever you want to know." screamed Sinclair as he cried like a baby. *"I will tell you everything I know."*

*****

Joey and Farmer were pulled out. Ernie Sinclair lay in the corner crying.

"You weren't supposed to go that far." said Sandy. *"I didn't want there to be any evidence, marks or scars."*

"Not my fault." Said Farmer. *"He did it himself."*

"Yep. That is exactly how it happened." chimed Joey. *"He pulled away from me and backed right up on Farmer's old hog leg. Farmer didn't do*

anything. I was a witness. He did it to himself."

Sandy looked at the two of them with a smirk on her face. She couldn't condone it, but she was glad they had done it. She had seen too many women hurt and scarred for life by shits like Ernie Sinclair. This was the kind of justice she envisioned Texas Rangers serving up in the good old days when Texas was a wild frontier and the only law was the Ranger with badge, a horse and a rope. This kind of justice was fast and fair. It was also very satisfying. Sandy actually felt a little intoxicated over it all.

Sandy had used the time during McCaslin's interrogation to read Ernie Sinclair's body language. He had never been afraid of McCaslin or what McCaslin could do to him, but, ironically, he was afraid of being raped.

Imagine that, she thought, a rapist who was scared of being raped.

During her many trips to supposedly silence the guys, she had secretly hatched a plan to have them scream and threaten him more and more. Then the plan was to put them into the cage with him to let them scare him even more. She had no idea that they would do what they did, but she couldn't argue with the results. It had worked perfectly.

Ernie Sinclair was now singing like a bird to Marshal McCaslin and his little recorder.

"You men did a good job and I won't forget it." said Sandy.

"Just don't forget our parole dates." Said Joey. *"That's all we ask, Ranger Smith."*

"I promise I won't. I will be there myself to stand up for you." said Sandy shaking both of their hands and giving them a hug. *"I won't ever forget either of you."*

Farmer turned to Doc who was standing out of the way. *"I have said it before and I will say it again, you are one lucky ass white boy, celly. I can see why you have never gotten over her. She is special. Don't let her get away this time."*

Sandy watched as Farmer and Joey walked away, then she turned to Doc.

"You still talk about me?" asked Sandy.

Sandy felt a lump in her throat and tears in her eyes.

"I have never stopped talking about you, Sandy." said Bentley as he took her hand. *"And I have never stopped loving you for a single minute."*

*****

Marshal McCaslin had learned from former deputy Sinclair that Sheriff Red and the other deputies in his department were in the protection business for the county's main drug supplier. They regularly escorted shipments of cocaine and marijuana that was brought up by the MS-13 drug cartel to their distributor in Hopkin's county. He told how they also arrest anyone else that sold or brought drugs into Hopkin's county, so that the MS-13 wouldn't have any competition. He told how they would confiscate the drugs and everything else that the person owned. That was what they had done to Dr. Braxton. Then they would tell the court that the person was still a threat to society and a part of an on-going investigation. The court would then secretly order that the inmate's mail be confiscated and sent to the Sheriff's department first on the pretext of the department gaining information on further drug activity, but what the Sheriff was really doing was guaranteeing that the person was isolated and never got any outside help from family or friends. It had been the perfect set up until Doc figured out how to get the county records department to send him the original arrest report. Since it had come from Lloyd County, it was assumed to be okay, and thus it had inadvertently made it through to Dr. Braxton.

Doc and Sandy listened as Sinclair spilled his guts.

"But I was just passing through. How did you know about me?" asked Doc.

Former Deputy Sinclair chortled and then answered. *"Because the big guy wanted you. You were set up, dude. We knew you were coming through."*

"How did the Sheriff know I would be coming through?" implored Doc.

"It wasn't the Sheriff that knew. It was Shaddix." said Sinclair. *"Shaddix is the cartel's distributor. The sheriff was just his muscle. His protection."*

"But that's impossible." said Doc.

Sinclair laughed again. *"Dude, you were tracked all the way from Florida by a GPS tracker that had been put on that pretty yellow sports car of yours. We even knew that you would be carrying half a kilo instead of a third."*

"But nobody could have known that. The third guy only pulled out of the deal at the last minute." said Doc.

But as the words came out of his mouth, the reality began to flood into his brain. Shaddix had always been shady in school. He had been an outcast and the butt of many jokes. The one that humiliated him the most was when Bentley and Malcolm had stuffed a pair of cadaver gonads into his lab coat pocket. It had been at lunch, and he had pulled them out onto his lunch tray in front of half of the coed class. From that day on he had been scorned by every girl in school. He had graduated miserable and angry at the world, but especially at Drs. Bentley and Malcolm.

"Shaddix had a hard on for you, Dr. Braxton." Said Sinclair. *"He had been planning your arrest for years. All of your contacts, friends and supplier's in Florida and Dallas were people he knew, controlled or bought off with drugs. The guy who backed out of your last deal was going to be paid a kilo to set you up until he opened his mouth at the wrong moment and ended up as shark bait. Your old buddy, Dr. Malcolm, owed Carlito and the MS-13 cartel, two hundred and eighty thousand dollars because he had gotten himself in too deep by living the high life in Miami. He was told that if he helped set you up, his debt would be paid, but if he didn't, he would be wearing a Colombian necktie."*

Doc felt completely betrayed as he heard how his old buddy, Malcolm, had gone to his practice in Dallas with Dr. Shaddix to tell all of his employees that Doc was staying in Miami to work with him. Since Malcolm was Doc's best and oldest friend they didn't doubt him at all. They were all give a generous severance check and no one ever questioned anything. Everything had been planned down to the last detail.

Doc listened and absorbed every word and realized what it meant. The only real friends he had were the ones right here in this prison. Farmer and Flowers were the only two friends that had ever protected him. And Sandy was the only one who had come to rescue him.

Bentley turned to Sandy with a lump in his throat and quiver in his voice.

"I love you, Sandy, with all of my heart. You are the only one I have ever loved."

Tears streamed down Sandy's face just as a shot rang out.

Doc saw the right side of Sinclair's head explode outward in red splatter and gore. Marshal McCaslin was thrown backwards as the large caliber bullet exited Sinclair's brain and plunged deeply into his shoulder.

Doc felt himself being propelled to the floor. Sandy shoved him with her right hand as she drew her pistol with her left. The concussion of air was deafening as she squeezed off four rapid shots in succession that passed within inches of his ear. The pistol had been so close he felt the heat from the muzzle blasts as she fired them past his head.

Panic had erupted in the gym as prisoners scattered and ducked for cover. Sandy's shots had all hit their mark. An MS-13 gang member lay on the gym floor outside of the weight cage with a pistol still clutched in his dead hand.

The gang member had executed Sinclair, and his next target had been Doc. Sheriff Red wasn't taking any chances. He was tying up all loose ends. Sandy had seen the gang banger fire the first shot and reacted with lightning speed by shoving Doc out of the way and killing the assassin with deadly accuracy.

What she hadn't been able to do was stop the assassin's second shot that was aimed at Doc. It had hit her square in the chest as she shoved him aside.

Doc realized Sandy had just saved his life with her own.

Lt. Sharp, whom had come on duty with the change of shift, had been escorting prisoners from the rec yard through the gym when the shots rang out. Doc had crawled over to Sandy's motionless body to cradle her in his arms as tears streamed down his face.

'How could she be taken from me again?'

"Nooooo!" he screamed at God.

"Get up inmate." hollered Lt. Sharp in his usual nasty voice. *"Let her go and come with me."*

"No." Doc answered through his tears. *"I am not leaving her."*

"Oh, don't worry." said Lt. Sharp as he put a pistol to Doc's head. *"You will be joining her in just a few seconds. I will find another spick to finish you off since that idiot couldn't do what we told him to do."*

Lt. Sharp grabbed Doc by the hair and lifted him off of Sandy, but as he did, he felt a strange sensation. It was the feel of a gun muzzle sliding roughly between his legs with the steel site pressed firmly against his rectum.

Farmer and Flowers had also heard the first shot that killed Sinclair and rushed back to help their friend during the commotion. They had seen Lt. Sharp put the pistol to Doc's head. Flowers grabbed the gun out of the dead gang-banger's hand and dived on the gym floor sliding up in between Lt. Sharp's legs.

Lieutenant Sharp's finger began to pull the trigger of the pistol. If he was going to die, so was the Doc. He would at least fulfill his mission.

However, before Lt. Sharp could react, Flowers pulled the trigger and sent a 45 caliber bullet straight up through the lieutenant's torso piercing his heart and brain. The big bore bullet finally exited through the top of the lieutenant's skull obliterating the entire top of his head. Bloody brain matter rained down over them all.

The wetness on her face caused Sandy's eyes to pop open.

"What the hell happened?" yelled Sandy as she looked around at all of the gore on the floor.

"That asshole got the Smith & Wesson enema that he deserved." said Flowers.

Doc grabbed Sandy. *"You're alive!"*

"Yeah, thanks to my Kevlar vest." Sandy said. *"But the important thing is that you're alive too."* Sandy threw off her Stetson and pulled Bentley to her bosom and kissed him deeply.

Chapter 51

News of the prison killings had spread like wildfire in the Texas papers and had even made CNN and Fox News. There was no covering things up this time for Sheriff Red.

Stick a fork in him. He was done in law enforcement, and now he was a fugitive from the Texas Rangers too. The biggest manhunt in Texas history had failed to find the old sheriff or Dr. Shaddix. They had simply vanished into thin air.

One minute they were there, and the next morning, when Texas Troopers raided their homes, they were gone. Their clothes, cell phones, wallets and cars were all still there, including Dr. Braxton's yellow Porsche. It was still parked in Shaddix's driveway.

Sandy had received cards and visits from all one hundred and two Texas Rangers. She was a state and national hero. The Texas Rangers had arrested almost all of the Lloyd County sheriff's department. One of the few deputies not arrested was Deputy Santos Salinas.

Jewels had told Senator Boyce Braxton about how Deputy Salinas had risked his life trying to get evidence to expose the crooked sheriff. The Governor by executive order, and on the recommendation of Senator Braxton, had appointed Deputy Salinas as acting Sheriff until a special election could be held as soon as possible.

"I guess this means that we aren't going to be able to see each other for a while." said Santos.

"Why not?" asked Jewels.

"Well, I just figured that since I am the new sheriff and since you are Joe Don Lilly's campaign manager, it would be a conflict of interest." said Santos.

Jewels rolled off of Santos and looked him straight in his beautiful brown eyes. *"You are only the acting sheriff until the special election. There is no conflict of interest if you aren't running too."*

Santos was quiet.

Then he raised his right eyebrow and shrugged his shoulders.

"Really?" exclaimed Jewels. She had asked Boyce to have the governor appoint Santos as acting sheriff as a favor for freeing his brother. She never knew that Santos had those kinds of ambitions. It had been a test. He had tasted power now, and he wanted to keep it. She had big plans. This revelation put their relationship into a whole new perspective. He was no longer just her boy toy.

This was a game changer for her. Their professional relationship would never be the same.

"Well, I guess that only leaves me with two choices, doesn't it?" Jewels said.

"Two choices?" asked Santo quizzically.

"Yeah," said Jewels sadly. *"I can either unlock your handcuffs and*

throw you out of my bed right now or...."

Silence hung in the air.

"Or what?" he asked.

"Or...." She said flipping her flaming red hair in his face and climbing on top of him. *"I can leave you like you are and make love to my new boss and the next Sheriff of Lloyd County one more time."*

Santos started to object, but was silenced with a single finger to his lips.

"Relax, baby." cooed Jewels. *"Leave it all to me. I have plan."*

Then she smothered him with red lipstick kisses.

*****

After their night of love making Lola had shown Guy the video from the woods. Guy felt responsible for Pete's death. If he hadn't used his roommate's identification, he wouldn't have died such a gruesome and horrible death. Lola had insisted that they give the evidence sheet and the video of Pete's death to the Lady Ranger. He also gave her the video of Deputy Sinclair's roadside and midnight confession.

It had been Sinclair's taped confession to agent McCaslin and the video evidence that Lola had recorded in the woods that convinced the appeals court to overturn Dr. Bentley Braxton's conviction. Hundreds of cases were now being considered before the court, but Doc's was the first to be overturned. While it was clear to the judges that the confession was less than completely voluntary, they ruled it admissible since the coercion had not been done by law enforcement. A technicality for sure, but the defendants, Sheriff 'Red', Dr. Shaddix and Chief Deputy Jones, were all missing and no one was challenging the court's ruling.

Sheriff Red had disappeared, in the middle of night just ahead of his imminent arrest. Everyone assumed that ol' Lilly White would be the next sheriff of Lloyd County. However, to everyone's surprise three days before the election, ol' Lilly White was discovered in the company of a very large black drag queen at a local no-tell motel. The newspapers had a field day with the story. Little local Texas newspapers just didn't get big juicy headline stories like this happening in their own backyard every day. The story spread like wildfire.   Even TV stations from big cities like Dallas and Houston had sent their news trucks to Lloyd County to get in on the action. For three days they talked to every person in town who had ever met or even seen Joe Don Lilly.   Slick haired reporters reported every salacious tidbit over the air live with their microwave dishes and satellite trucks.   The day after the scandal hit the front page of the Lloyd County Gazette and the Prickley Springs Press half of the volunteers and employees quit or just didn't come in. By the second day it was all over the TV and no one except one person showed up for work at the campaign headquarters. His name was Guytana Canova.   Santos had won by a landslide on Election Day and Joe Don had disappeared never to be seen again in Lloyd County.

His campaign manager Jewels Sapphire conceded the election early at the vacant Piggly Wiggly that had been Joe Don's campaign headquarters with Guytana standing in the back of the room next to a very large black man on one side and Lola on the other.

In the following months Lola testified about everything that she witnessed at Dr. Shaddix's dental offices.

She had told how her boss, Dr. Shaddix, had lots of strange shipments arrive at the dental office and about how lots of strange motorcycle biker people, called Banditos, made appointments to see Dr. Shaddix.

"They would come in every week for appointments, but they didn't really get much, if any, dental work done." testified Lola. *"Dr. Shaddix would always see them alone for a consultation and he would always give them a dental bag to take with them."*

"What kind of dental bag?" asked the prosecutor.

"The kind we gave out to patients usually that contained a new tooth brush, floss and tooth paste." said Lola to the bespectacled lawyer. *"Except they weren't clear like our normal ones. You couldn't see what was inside of these. Dr. Shaddix told us that they were for his special patients."*

"And you didn't think that was strange, Miss Salinas?"   Asked the

prosecutor.

"Yes, I did." said Lola guiltily. *"But Dr. Shaddix could be very mean when you asked him too many questions and I needed that job desperately."* Lola was in tears now. *"I was too scared to ask."*

The prosecutor marched over to the exhibit table and picked up a dental bag. *"Is this one of the bags that Dr. Shaddix gave to his special clients?"* asked the prosecutor.

"Yes!" said a sobbing Lola.

"Let the record show that the witness has identified the bag that the FBI discovered in Dr. Shaddix's office" boomed the prosecutor for everyone to hear.

Later in the trial it was a wounded FBI Agent Kent McCaslin with his arm in a sling that testified the dental bags for special patients had been discovered locked in a hidden safe in Dr. Shaddix's office.

"Now let me ask you, Agent McCaslin" the prosecutor was now holding a special dental bag in high over his head. *"What make these dental bags so damn special?"*

"Well, for starters," stated Agent McCaslin *"each one contained one pound of pure uncut Peruvian Flake cocaine."*

Upon that revelation the federal prosecutor unzipped the small dental bag with a flourish to show the jury that it was indeed filled with a sparkling white powder. A collective and audible gasp was heard from the courtroom.

"And how many of these special dental bags did you find at Dr. Shaddix's office, Agent McCaslin?

"One hundred and fifty five." stated the wounded agent. Murmurs of amazement could be heard all over the crowded courtroom as people added it up in their heads. *"Which came to almost seventy five kilos."* At this point reporters jumped out of their seats and ran for the doors so that they could be the first to broadcast or print the news.

The trial ended with Dr. Shaddix, Sheriff Hardon "Red" Johnson and

Chief Deputy Scott Jones, AKA 'Jonesy', all being convicted in absentia.

On that day, Lola was only allowed ten minutes in a private secured room inside the old courthouse to say good-bye to her family and loved ones before she entered the witness protection program for the rest of her life. Agent McCaslin had entered her into the witness protection program since Shaddix and Sheriff Red are still at large.

The room was mournful and filled with tearful good byes. Maybe it was the moment, but Santos saw his sister in an entirely different way. She was no longer that little pain in the ass that he had grown up with. She was no longer the pest that bothered him and took too long in the bathroom. She was no longer a little girl. She was a very grown up young woman. It pained him deeply to realize that it took him this long to recognize that fact. Because this would be the last time that he ever laid eyes on her. There would be no more Christmas'. No more Thanksgivings. No more Cinco de Mayo's. All that would be left of her would be photographs and memories at the holidays.

This was it. This would be the last time that ever saw his little sister.

It had been like a living funeral; everyone saying their good-byes and his mother weeping and grieving in the floor as her little Lola, her little nina, was escorted away never to be seen again.

However, it was his sister's last good-bye that stuck in Santo's head. She had saved her last and most tearful good-bye for Guy. They embraced lovingly. It wasn't until the US Marshall pulled her away that she let go of the man that she had come to love so much and so deeply.

As the elevator doors closed, Sheriff Santos Salinas had two major epiphanies. The first was that his little sister had grown up in to a fine young lady. And the other was that Guytana Canova wasn't such a bad guy after all.

*****

Ranger Smith took Guy by the arm to bolster him as the elevator doors shut. She knew what it was like to be torn away from the first love of your life.

They walked quietly down the hall.

"You know," said Sandy *"I couldn't help but notice that the video of Deputy Sinclair seemed a little shorter than I remember."*

"Yeah, well, I guess I forgot to hit the record button when the biker girl slapped Deputy Sinclair like a little bitch and kicked his car into the ditch." said Guy to Ranger Smith with a sly smirk and tears still in his eyes.

"Yeah," repeated Ranger Smith as she winked at him. *"You must have forgot to hit the record button."*

Sandy liked the kid. He was smart and he was ambitious. *"You know, we are always looking for good people with skills and smarts. You seem to have both."*

"Thanks, I appreciate the offer, Ranger Smith. I really do, but I think I am going to stick around Lloyd County for a while."

"Well, you be sure and let me know if you ever need anything, kid" said Sandy as she patted Guy on the shoulder.

Epilogue

"Here he comes!" yelled Jewels.

They were all there at the Walls Unit in Huntsville to see Doc released. He walked out of the front door and not the side one. When a man walked out the front doors, it indicated that he was a free man. No paper. No parole.

He was free. Totally free.

Sandy and Boyce both ran to Bentley and hugged him.

Doc was unable to speak. The air felt so different outside the prison walls. He had imagined this day a million times, but he couldn't believe it now that it was happening to him for real.   In the dark recesses of his mind, he was still scared that it was a cruel joke and that they were going to come drag him back inside.

Boyce was the first to speak.

"It's going to be okay, little brother. No one is ever going to take you away again." It was as if Bentley was a little boy again and Boyce was reading his mind. As they walked to the Senator's limousine, Bentley saw lots of people that he didn't know, except for Guy.

"All of these people helped get you out." said Boyce.

Doc met and thanked each one with tears of gratitude in his eyes.

When he was all done, Sandy took him by the hand and pulled him to the side under a big shade tree.

"You know that I love you, Bentley, and I always have. The last seventeen years, since I last saw you, I have had another man in my life." Sandy was being as gentle as she could be. Bentley could see that she was torn and emotional in telling him about another man.

His heart was broken.

In prison you just always imagine everything turning out perfect when you get out. You never think about people moving on with their lives and without you, but he should have realized that Sandy would have moved on and created a new life. It would have been unnatural if she hadn't. He just hadn't wanted to think about that possibility.

"I want you to meet him." said Sandy as she opened the limo door.

From the limo emerged a tall good looking young man. He wasn't at all what Doc had imagined. In fact, he looked a little young for Sandy.

Bentley put his hand out. *"Hi there, I am Bentley Braxton."*

The young man reached out and took Doc's hand in a firm grip. *"My name is Bentley, also. Bentley Braxton IV. My friend's call me Quatro."*

******

The next exciting novel of the series.

Coming Soon......

The Monkey Deception

By

S.Hark Phillips